W9-BCD-508

SONG
IN
THE
DARK

— The Vampire Files —

SONG
IN THE DARK

P. N. ELROD

ACE BOOKS, NEW YORK

THE BERKLEY PUBLISHING GROUP
Published by the Penguin Group
Penguin Group (USA) Inc.
375 Hudson Street, New York, New York 10014, USA
Penguin Group (Canada), 90 Eglinton Avenue East, Suite 700, Toronto, Ontario M4P 2Y3, Canada
(a division of Pearson Penguin Canada Inc.)
Penguin Books Ltd., 80 Strand, London WC2R 0RL, England
Penguin Group Ireland, 25 St. Stephen's Green, Dublin 2, Ireland (a division of Penguin Books Ltd.)
Penguin Group (Australia), 250 Camberwell Road, Camberwell, Victoria 3124, Australia
(a division of Pearson Australia Group Pty. Ltd.)
Penguin Books India Pvt. Ltd., 11 Community Centre, Panchsheel Park, New Delhi—110 017, India
Penguin Group (NZ), Cnr. Airborne and Rosedale Roads, Albany, Auckland 1310, New Zealand
(a division of Pearson New Zealand Ltd.)
Penguin Books (South Africa) (Pty.) Ltd., 24 Sturdee Avenue, Rosebank, Johannesburg 2196,
South Africa

Penguin Books Ltd., Registered Offices: 80 Strand, London WC2R 0RL, England

This book is an original publication of The Berkley Publishing Group.

This is a work of fiction. Names, characters, places, and incidents either are the product of the author's imagination or are used fictitiously, and any resemblance to actual persons, living or dead, business establishments, events, or locales is entirely coincidental. The publisher does not have any control over and does not assume any responsibility for author or third-party websites or their content.

First edition: September 2005

Library of Congress Cataloging-in-Publication Data

Elrod, P. N. (Patricia Nead)
    Song in the dark / P. N. Elrod.— 1st ed.
        p. cm. — (The vampire files)
    ISBN 0-441-01323-6
    1. Fleming, Jack (Fictitious character)—Fiction.   2. Private investigators—Illinois—Chicago—
Fiction.   3. Chicago (Ill.)—Fiction.   4. Vampires—Fiction.   I. Title.

PS3555.L68S66 2005
813'.54—dc22

                                                                                        200504322

PRINTED IN THE UNITED STATES OF AMERICA

10   9   8   7   6   5   4   3   2   1

To my good friends
Ian Hamill
Roxanne Longstreet
Roxanne Longstreet Conrad
Roxanne Conrad
Rachel Caine
AND ESPECIALLY
Julie Fortune!

Stand-up buds, all!

1

Chicago, January 1938

I SLOUCHED in the backseat of Gordy's Cadillac, the one that had just slightly less armor than a German tank, keeping clear of the rearview mirror out of habit, not because I cared one way or the other. The driver, a stone-faced guy named Strome, probably wouldn't have said anything about my lack of reflection even if he'd noticed. He almost certainly had other things on his mind, like whether or not he would be the one delegated to kill me tonight.

It was really too bad for him, because I got the idea that he'd begun to like me. I already had his respect.

A scant few nights ago Strome had seen me apparently dead, an ugly kind of dead, then had to contend with my quick and mystifying return to good health. I gave no explanations to him or any of the others who were aware of my experience, and soon he'd accepted that I'd somehow survived. So far as he knew now I was still healing from that bloody damage, yet able to walk around and carry on with what passed for normal life, which in his eyes made me without a doubt the toughest SOB in Chicago. Strome couldn't have known about my supernatural edge; anything to do with vampires was well outside his view of the world, which was fine with me. Like others of his ilk, even if specifics about the Undead escaped him, he was aware that I was dangerously different. He knew which questions *not* to ask, and that made him a valuable asset to the mob. And me.

Most of the time he and his partner, Lowrey, were bodyguards to their gangland boss and my friend, Gordy Weems. We all tripped and fell down on the job a few nights ago, leaving Gordy with a couple of bullets in him. He'd survived, too, barely.

While he'd been out for the count, his lieutenants decided that someone had to step into his shoes to deal with the running of their mob during the crisis and elected me to take his place. I thought it to be a singularly bad idea, but took on the burden for Gordy's sake. I wouldn't have been any kind of a stand-up guy to have ducked out when he needed the help. I'd been too cocky assuming the mantle, though. Because of my edge, I'd come to believe in my own indestructibility. I thought I could handle anything.

Circumstances and a drunken sadist named Hog Bristow taught me different.

I got my payback on him. Bristow was dead. Ugly dead. I'd killed him, and now I had to give payback to someone else about my actions. Even Gordy couldn't get me out of this one. It was serious gang business, the resolution of which would take place in his soundproofed upstairs office at his nightclub.

Or the basement. I'd been there once or twice. Not on the receiving end.

"Turn on the radio," I told Strome.

He obliged. Dance music flowed from the speaker grille. "You want this or something else?" he asked.

"That's fine." Music helped to distract me, to seal over the fissures inside. I had lots of those going deep down into blackness full of sharp, cutting horrors along the way. If I focused on the radio noise, then I didn't have to think about certain things, like what Bristow had done to me after hanging me upside down from a hook in a meat locker.

That's what this ride was about: the repercussion over what I'd done to him once I'd gotten free.

It wasn't fair that I was being called on the carpet for that bastard's death, but the mobs had their own rules and ways of doing things. Bristow had powerful friends back in New York; they'd give me a few minutes to give my side of the story—Gordy had wrangled that much for me—then I'd die.

Strome drove to the back-alley entrance of Gordy's club, the Nightcrawler, which was the normal ingress for bosses. The front was for the swells come to see the shows and try the gambling in a strictly private section of the club. The gaming was the main difference between my own nightclub and this one. If the stage shows were a bust, then Gordy was still guaranteed to make a ton of money from tables and slots. He thought I was nuts not having some as well as a backup, but I chose early on not to take that road. Sure, I had an accountant who could cook the books to a turn and, with Gordy's influence, could manage bribes and all the rest, but I wouldn't risk it even for that kind of money. All it'd take was one raid, one arrest, one daylight court appearance with me not there, and that would be the end of it.

Maybe I did some sweating when profits were thin or non-existent, but that was better than losing the whole works.

Not that any of it mattered much to me now.

Strome parked. I quit the car, sliding across the seat to get out on the driver's side, slamming the door harder than was necessary. It drew attention. Despite the cold there were a number of guys hanging around the Nightcrawler's back door. Two of them were Ruzzo, brothers in Gordy's outfit, strong arms, bad tempers, and not much brain. Being too hard to tell apart, they went interchangeably by the one name.

A few nights back, in order to assert my authority as temporary boss, I'd had to punch them both out to make a point. Now they lurked close enough to force me to notice them. Both looked like they'd shared the same bad lemon. Ruzzo the Elder had a split lip; his brother had a black eye. Two ways to tell them apart. They must have thought my number was up and were already figuring how to get me alone for some payback of their own before the boom lowered.

Ruzzo the Younger showed an exceptionally hard glare. It effectively distracted me from his brother.

Who threw a punch toward my ribs as I walked past.

Bad move.

I took it solid, but didn't collapse the way I was supposed to; instead, I sliced out sideways with my forearm and slammed him broad across the middle. I'd seen something like it on a tennis court, only you're supposed to use a racket.

The Elder staggered backward halfway across the alley, folding with an *oof* noise onto the cold pavement. The Younger blazed in to kill, pulling out a gun.

Which I plucked away from him almost as an afterthought.

He stared at his empty hand.

Strome finished up. He had a blackjack ready and swiped it viciously behind the man's left ear. The Younger dropped.

I held the gun out to Strome, addressing him loud enough for the others to hear. "These dopes shoulda kept in school. They could have found out how rough the big boys in first grade played. Maybe learned something."

His turn to stare. "You okay? He caught you a good one."

I pretended to shift uncomfortably. "Yeah, he did. Let's go."

We climbed the loading-dock stairs to the club's kitchen, but instead of turning toward the stairs up to Gordy's office, Strome led the way to the main room of the club. Band music, live, played there, though the place was still an hour or so from opening. A last-minute rehearsal for their big star seemed to be going on.

"Have to wait here," said Strome, gesturing at a ringside table. It was the one usually reserved for special guests of the boss. It was also the farthest from any exit, and my being placed here was no coincidence. A glance around confirmed I was expected to stay put. All the doors were covered by at least two mugs, armed, of course. Strome sat with me, keeping his hat and coat on. I did likewise.

"How long?" I asked.

He gave a small shrug. "Donno."

No need to inquire whether word had been sent up about my arrival. That would have happened the instant we parked. I was supposed to sit there and stew about my fate.

Instead, I watched the rehearsal. Nothing else to do. As with the radio, the music kept me from thinking too much.

Things seemed to be running late and going badly. This week's big star was Alan Caine. I'd heard him on the radio, and he was a popular name in Broadway revues. He'd done speciality numbers in short-subject films I'd never seen. He had a stadium-filling voice and was presently using it to hammer at the red-faced bandleader.

"Three in a row—you going for some kind of record? Read the damn music, if you can, and give me the right damn cue!" Caine wore his tuxedo pants and suspenders, an undershirt and dress shoes. He was so handsome that even men looked twice at him, and with women it was a foregone conclusion they'd faint if he gave them a half second's glance. The line of dancing girls behind confirmed it. Instead of being put off by his tone, they all looked to be in a giggly, flirty mood, eyes bright.

He eased into a gap between two of them, pasted on a huge, absolutely sincere smile and froze, waiting.

The band, for the fourth time, swung into the prologue for his number, and must have gotten it right. Caine and his leggy troupe stepped and strutted smarter than smart for eight counts, then the girls retreated, leaving him out front to sing the rest of his song. I didn't like him on sight, but he had a hell of a voice.

"Wanna drink?" Strome asked.

He got a blank look from me. Taking requests from the condemned man? Or was he in need of fuel for what was to come? So far as I knew he would be the executioner. He was like Bristow, a killer. Unlike Bristow, Strome didn't make a big thing of it, and if he enjoyed the work, kept it to himself.

"No thanks."

Strome signed to someone I didn't bother to look at and got a draft beer, the glass opaque with frost. They knew how to serve things up right at the Nightcrawler: song, dance, drinks, girls, gambling, and death.

Alan Caine broke off in midnote. The dancers continued their routine for a few steps; the band continued as well until the leader caught on that he'd committed another sin. I'd been listening and hadn't heard anything wrong. Caine heard different and laid into him on the brass being too loud.

"They're paying money to hear *me*, not you," he stated, his sincere smile on the shelf for the moment. "What the hell do you think you're doing trying to drown me out? That's *my* name on the marquee, not yours. Get your people in line or get another job."

I waited for the leader to lay into him right back, but he just nodded and began the play again, starting a few bars before the interruption. This time the horns were softer, and Caine's voice went right to the corners of the room.

"Is he always like that?" I asked Strome.

"Since he got here."

"Why does Derner put up with it?" Derner was another of Gordy's lieutenants and also the general manager for the club.

"The guy packs in the crowds."

"No one's worth that kind of crap."

"This one is. He gets every seat filled and has a standing-room line at the bar. Even on the weeknights we can charge a two-fifty cover, and they come in herds."

"Two-fifty?" That was unheard of, some clubs in New York got away with charging so much for their cover, but less so in Chicago. You only did that on weekends and only when it was a real Ziegfeld-style spectacular. Nothing so elaborate was going on here with just Caine, the band, and eight dancers. There was no stage decoration, either, just the usual long curtains backing the musicians and someone to man the lights and keep the spot on the star. "He's worth it?"

"Depends who you talk to. The bookkeepers say yes, the performers say no. Bookkeepers win."

"He must be blackmailing someone."

"Hey!" Caine stopped the show again, this time his attention squarely on our table. He broke away from the dancers, striding over to glare at us. He was teeming with sculpted cheekbones, graceful jaw, and a perfect nose. Anger on him didn't look at all threatening. Maybe a little with his baby blues steaming up. He narrowed them, arching a too-perfectly shaped eyebrow. "I'm trying to *work* here. If you two can't put a lid on it, take your romance to the men's room."

A week back I might have reacted to him; tonight I had no reaction at all, just stared. I chanced to take a breath and caught a powerful whiff of booze from him, as though he'd just gargled with it. "Just do your song and dance, Caine," I said, hardly raising my voice above a whisper.

"Do I know you, punk?"

He was in his late thirties; I looked to be in my twenties. I was well used to the penalty of perpetual youth. "Be glad you don't."

"A tough guy, eh?" He could belt a song, but delivering dialogue didn't quite work for him, especially when it came out of the wrong kind of films. He should have stuck to showbiz stories and not tried imitating movie gangsters.

"That's right. Go back to work."

"Where's Derner?" he demanded, switching focus to Strome. "I want this punk tossed out on his ear. Go get him."

"Sorry, can't do that, Mr. Caine. I'm working, too."

Caine saw the beer at his elbow. "Nice job." He swung around, eyes searching. "You there! Go find Derner and bring him here."

The mug he addressed registered puzzlement at being ordered around by the stage talent.

Strome craned his head. "Never mind, Joe. Mr. Caine was just joking."

"Joking? We'll see who's laughing before the night's out."

Caine didn't appear to be drunk, but my instant-hypnosis act likely wouldn't work on him; besides, he wasn't worth the headache. I looked past him, hoping to spot the stage manager, but no such luck. However, a fierce-faced woman in a poisonous green dress and black fur-trimmed coat came barreling toward us from the front entrance. It was still too early to open. I wondered how she'd gotten in.

So, it seemed, did Caine. Genuine surprise flashed over him. "Jewel, what the hell are you doing here?"

Her lip color was so dark a red that it looked black, matching her hair. Two lines framing her mouth cut themselves into a deep, hard frown of contempt. Her eyes were wild, the pupils down to pinpoints. She braked to an unsteady stop. "The alimony is three weeks overdue, why do you *think* I'm here?"

He recovered composure, shifting to pure smarm. "You'll just have to wait till I'm paid."

She went scarlet, her whole body seemed to swell from outrage. "That's what you said three paychecks ago, you bastard!" She hit him with a green purse the same shade as her dress. He got an arm up to block any blows to his face and unexpectedly started laughing like a lunatic, which just made her madder. She cursed, he giggled. Funny on a movie screen, not so much ten feet away when all parties are dead set on inflicting damage, each in their own way.

It went downhill from there.

Not inclined to interfere, I watched the domestic drama with an equally unmoved Strome, content to let other guys rush in to bust things up. Several of the bouncers who'd been on the exits moved remarkably fast for their size. That would have been the ideal time for me to make an escape, just dart to the front lobby, duck around the corner phone booth, and vanish. It was one of my specialties. Instead, I kept my seat and wished I could still drink beer. A cold one would have gone down good about now.

It took three bouncers to remove Jewel Caine: two on her left side for her shoulders and feet, one on her right for her middle. She didn't make it easy for them, bucking and cursing the whole way as they carried her bodily from the room like a log, green purse and all. So far Lady Crymsyn, which was my nightclub, had suffered no drunken rows on this level, only comparatively mild, easily dealt with skirmishes. I could count myself lucky.

Alan Caine, grinning wide, called after her: "Why don't you get a job?"

She heard. "I'll *kill* you, you son of a bitch! I'll cut your throat if you don't pay what you owe me!" The rest was incoherent and, from the tone, likely obscene. Closing doors spared us from more opinions and threats.

One of the chorus dancers trotted up. "Alan, that was awful. Are you okay?"

"Yeah-yeah, Evie." He waved her off. "Back on your mark, let's get this over with."

She seemed disappointed he wasn't making more of a fuss over the disruption and visibly swallowed back the load of comfort and sympathy she must have had ready to pour out. Evie was just about the cutest little doll I'd seen in many a week and affected a tiny Betty Boop voice. I thought she could do much better than Caine. "Well . . . if you're *sure* . . ."

"I'm sure. C'mon, bub." He turned her around and gave her a light swat on her nicely rounded rump. This cheered her up, and she went trotting back to her envious and/or amused sisters. They formed their line again. Caine called a cue to the band, and they began in midstanza, this time making it to the end. He cut an exaggerated bow to them. *"Finally!"*

"About damn time," muttered Strome. He wasn't one for offering much in the way of comments. His beer, which he'd drained off, must have loosened him up.

"How's that?" I asked.

"He's been at it all day. If he was a dame, he'd be one of those primer dons. He better pray he don't ever lose his voice. That's all that's keeping him alive. Derner's been busy just holding off people from busting him one."

"Yet he packs the club?"

"He keeps that mean side away from the audience. With his looks they think he's an angel. People in the business know he's a jerk off but they put up with it. He's got enough push from bringing in cash to get them fired."

"Or tossed out."

Strome spared me a look. He must have thought I was referring to myself, not Caine's ex-wife. "Derner woulda talked him out of it. Caine don't know who's who in this town yet."

"In my case it doesn't matter."

His stony face had almost become animated, but shut down at the reminder of why we were here. "It's just the business," Strome said. This was the closest he would ever get to making an apology to me for whatever was to come.

"Yeah."

A business where a guy like Strome could come up to me, his former temporary boss, and tender an invitation to take a ride that I had to accept. He'd been so sure of the end result that he'd left the motor running in the car when he walked into Lady Crymsyn to deliver the summons. We eyed each other in the yet-to-open lobby, as though either of us had options. He had to bring me in, and the gun he carried under his arm was the last word on the subject. I glanced around at my people, who were getting things ready for the evening, oblivious of any threat. Strome shook his head, letting me know they weren't on his list.

He wouldn't use them against me. I liked that.

I got my hat and coat and went along, turning the opening of Crymsyn over to one of the bartenders. There was no point putting things off. This way I had some control over the situation. If the bad guys insisted on killing me for killing Hog Bristow, it would be at a safe distance from friends who could get in the cross fire.

The men who took away the acrimonious Jewel Caine returned, two of them resuming their posts, the third pausing to glare at the empty dance floor. Caine and the chorus line were backstage, getting ready for the night's performance. The third guy shifted his glare toward me, but whatever bothered him was none of my doing, and he got a blank look in return. I was getting good at those.

His name was Hoyle, and like the brothers Ruzzo, I was not anyone he liked. He'd resented my taking over for Gordy. Hoyle thought he should have been the one to pinch-hit, but his name never once cropped up. If I'd turned down the job, then Derner would have taken in the slack. Hoyle didn't see it that way, and I heard he'd started blaming me for everything up to and including the Depression itself.

Some people have too much time and not enough to do.

After a minute Hoyle got tired of trying to intimidate me and moved on to the bar, snapping his fingers for a drink.

Strome's partner, Lowrey, emerged from a door with a PRIVATE sign on it and came down to us. He was shorter and wider, with a cast to one eye and few enemies. Live ones, that is.

"Boss wants to see you, Mr. Fleming," he said.

I was surprised. "Gordy's here?" He was supposed to be anyplace else, resting, healing from his gunshot wounds.

"In the casino." He jerked a thumb over his shoulder.

The two of them followed as I hurried though the door into the Nightcrawler's illegal but extremely profitable gaming room. The lights were low, the place gloomy and strangely quiet, like an empty church. I spotted Gordy at the far end by the back exit, seated in one of the semiprivate alcoves favored by the cardplayers. He was fully dressed, and his girlfriend—nurse for the time being—was nowhere in sight.

My escorts hung back as I went forward and slipped into a chair on the other side of his table and nearly echoed Alan Caine's question. "What the hell are you doing here?" I kept my voice low, swallowing anger. Shouting didn't work on Gordy.

His skin was sallow, sagging, but his eyes were clear. I didn't like that. His doctor had him on pain pills, and they tended to dull everything about him. Clear eyes meant he was hurting. "It's business," he said.

"You can deal with things on the phone, and Derner and I do the rest. You're still supposed to be in bed. Where's Adelle?" She'd been looking after Gordy since the shooting.

"She went to the stores to get some stuff, so me an' Lowrey scrammed to here. I had to give her the slip for a couple hours. Makes me crazy, lying around and her playing nursemaid like I was sick."

Adelle Taylor, actress on stage, screen, and radio, and sometimes a headliner singing at my club and his, would throw a fit when she found out. I said as much to Gordy, who gave only the smallest of shrugs. He was a big man and didn't have to move much to make a point. "I left her a note."

"She'll come straight down here. Loaded for bear."

"I'll be done by then."

"With what, exactly?"

"You. Maybe."

"If you wanted to see me, I'd have come over, there's no need to—"

"Wasn't my doing bringing you here. I've been stalling them. They wouldn't stall no more."

"What? Who?"

"New York. Bristow's friends."

"You been running interference for me? In your condition?"

"I'm better off than you were, kid." Gordy knew my real age, which was about the same as his, but sometimes he seemed a lot older. When it came to mob business, he was decades my senior.

"What do you mean?"

"I got from the boys what happened to you. What Bristow did."

I felt my face go red. Mortification does that to me. "I told them to keep shut about it."

"They did, until I woke up enough to ask."

"Gordy, you don't need to be bothering with this. Just go back to bed and get better. I'll take care of things and no problem, okay?"

He just looked at me, eyes sleepy-seeming, but still not dull. "You up to it?"

"Of course I am. I appreciate what you've done, but—"

He raised one hand, shutting me down. "Fleming, I know Bristow put you through something worse than hell. A man don't get over that in a couple days, not even you."

"I'm *fine,* everything's healed up. Really."

Another long look and a twitch of his lips. He was usually as poker-faced as they come.

"What's wrong?" I asked.

"There's a hammer about to fall on you. It should have happened days ago, but I put them off."

"New York?" Gordy's bosses.

"I got my orders. I'm supposed to kill you."

"Yeah? So?" I'd been half-expecting that for days. If Gordy thought I'd get upset at the idea of him having to kill me, he'd have a long wait to see it. Besides, he knew what I was. Maybe he would have to do his job. It could be arranged. Wouldn't be the first time I'd died.

"I put 'em off, did some talking, bought some time, but stalled them too much. Another guy's doing the job. I gotta stand aside while he deals with you or get rubbed out, too."

If my heart had been working, it would have stopped. "Another like Bristow?"

"No. Smarter."

It wouldn't take much. Bristow had been dumb as an empty box. Maybe this guy would be sober for longer than five minutes, and I could evil-eye whammy him into changing his mind.

"He's the one who sent Bristow in the first place. One of the big shots. Name's Whitey Kroun."

The big boss himself. One of them, anyway. "Why should he come here? He couldn't phone?"

"He had enough of you over the phone."

I supposed he had. Our conversations during the turmoil following the murder attempt on Gordy had been brief and curdling, and I'd not made any friends. Kroun didn't know me from Adam and was already allergic. He'd been one of the brains who, in a fit of idiocy, sent Hog Bristow to shake things up in their holdings here. The idea was to make Gordy turn over the Chicago operation to Bristow, only that didn't happen. Of course, it was clearly all my fault.

"Kroun . . . he doesn't much like me."

Gordy almost smiled. "You should try harder to make more friends."

"Not with my smart-ass mouth. Listen, I'll face the music, get the heat off you, off us both, but you *gotta* get home and let Adelle spoil you for a couple more weeks." Gordy was doing a decent job of hiding it, but was visibly weak to my eyes. And ears. His heartbeat was up, and a sheen of sweat was on his forehead. He'd gotten out of bed too soon, pushed himself too much, and there was no need. "When's Kroun due in?"

"He's here now. Waiting upstairs. My office."

Oh, great, fine, wonderful. "Got any advice?"

"Don't get killed."

Huh. Easy for him to say. "What's he like?"

"Scary."

He got a double take from me. Gordy using a word like that? "In what way?"

He shook his head. "Just tell him the truth. Play straight with him."

Strome came forward. "Boss?"

Gordy and I looked his way at the same time. I'd gotten used to answering to the title at Crymsyn and again from being in charge of Gordy's mob. The first time Strome had addressed me as such I nearly told him to stop, but held back. It was a show of respect, for the office if not also for me, and however much I hated to think of how I'd won both, I accepted the dubious honor. Once I completely stepped down he could go back to calling me "Mr. Fleming," or "Fleming" or, like a few others in the organization, "that creep son of a bitch."

None of them called me "Jack," and I was glad of it.

I was conscious of my face shutting down, slamming into the deadpan frown Gordy's kind of job demanded, and replied for both of us. "Yeah?"

"Mitchell's here." He jerked his chin at the back exit, where a man stood in the doorway.

Who the hell was Mitchell? He seemed almost familiar, but wasn't local. I knew most of the boys here by sight, and he matched their type. He stood motionless, hands in his coat pockets, giving me the hard eye, shifting his hostile gaze for a long moment to Gordy—no love lost there, I thought—then back to me. Not the genial sort, but few of them are.

Gordy motioned him over, moving just his fingers. Saving his strength, I hoped.

Mitchell came close. Hands still in his pockets. If he'd had a gun in each one, I would not have been surprised. He would be from New York and represented the big guys, the serious hoods who gave Gordy his orders.

Strome did the honors. "Mitchell . . . Mr. Fleming."

"You kiddin'?" Mitchell asked no one in particular. My apparent youth must have been working against me again. On the other hand, it was often a good thing to be underestimated. He stared like I was a bizarre zoo specimen.

Strome, stony-faced, reiterated. "This is Jack Fleming—the guy who took care of Hog Bristow."

"New York?" I asked. Just to be sure.

Mitchell's gaze flicked in Gordy's direction. "It's time." He said it like an executioner might. One who enjoyed his work.

Gordy started to get up, but I stopped him. "It's okay, I'll see to this on my own."

"You sure?"

"Go home. Look after yourself, would ya? I gotta see a man about a hog."

Easing from the table, I followed Strome to the back hallway, with Mitchell right behind us. Strome looked over his shoulder at me as though trying to figure out a tough problem. I was unafraid when I should have been puking my guts out. It seemed to bother him. I could still feel fear, but not just now. For the last few nights I'd been working at not feeling much of anything if I could help it. That's why pretty-boy Caine had been so unsuccessful at trying to embarrass me. After what I'd been through, his guff was less than a kiddie game.

We had to pass close to the backstage area to get to the stairs leading to Gordy's office. There was some kind of ruckus going on. The bulk of the gathered crowd of chorus girls, kitchen help, stagehands, and tough guys blocked the view, but I did hear a thump and grunt. The sounds of a basic beating going on, nothing I'd not heard before.

"Now what?" asked Strome. He pushed his way through. At the sight of one of Gordy's lieutenants, looking pissed, most of the people melted off, finding better things to do. A few mugs hung around, including Ruzzo. Both of them. Recovered from the alley dusting, they hadn't noticed me yet.

The hall was more spacious than normal since it served the stage. Dressing rooms opened to it, their doors wide, including the one for the star, Alan Caine. He was pressed against the wall next to it, held in place by Hoyle. His forearm was braced on Caine's chest; his other arm was free and swinging. He landed what was apparently another punch into Caine's breadbasket. Caine *oofed* as all his breath left him, but couldn't double over.

"Hey—what gives?" Strome demanded.

Hoyle barely noticed him. "He owes money."

"So collect after the show, we need him tonight."

"This is just a warm-up, so he knows it's serious." Hoyle started to back off, but I heard a quick march of little trotting steps, and, tricked out in her brief dance costume, Evie the chorus girl burst out of nowhere and jumped onto his back.

"Leave him alone—oh!"

That's as much as she got out before he threw her off. She landed on her perfectly padded duff, stockinged legs all over, and still full of fight. She rolled and grabbed one of his ankles and pulled, throwing off Hoyle's balance. He staggered, threw a hand on the wall to recover, then hauled back his other foot to kick her.

I don't know how I got into it so fast. I wasn't aware of moving. No decision to take action went through my brain, suddenly I was just there and throwing the punch that took him down. Almost as part of the same movement I bent and lifted Evie, quickly passing her to a startled Strome. Only then did I stop to look around and wonder what the hell . . . ?

Hoyle was quicker on the uptake, realizing a new player had crashed his game. He got up and shook his head like a boxer, fixing his gaze on me. "You—? This ain't your business."

"We don't hit ladies around here," I said.

"Lady? You calling that piece of—"

He didn't finish. My fist derailed his train of thought, knocking him sideways and down like hammering a nail the wrong way. I was holding back, and it was hard going. Something thick and black and vile in me was just short of exploding, and I didn't know where it'd come from. Instinct told me it would be a very bad idea to let it get out.

I flinched when Strome dropped a hand on my shoulder.

He flinched in turn when he caught my look, but didn't back off. "Is the show over?" he asked.

Hoyle was on the floor with a bloody nose and likely to stay there for a while. Ruzzo (the elder) bent over him, checking for permanent damage; Ruzzo (the younger) gave me the eye, hand in his pocket where he kept some heavy and no doubt lethal object in place of the gun I'd taken away. Alan Caine had wisely removed himself from the field of combat and stood next to Mitchell, who almost looked curious about the proceedings. Evie, white of face, stared at me. Feeling perverse, I winked at her.

"Yeah, show's over," I said.

Caine stepped forward. "Then someone remove *him.*" He indicated Hoyle. "If that fool has damaged my throat, I'll see him in jail. And then I'm suing this place for every penny it's got. To hell with that, I'm suing anyway."

Strome said, "You. Put a lid on it."

"How dare you talk to me that way—I'm the one who pays you."

"Caine"—this from Mitchell, who apparently knew him—"shuddup and go to work before you get a spanking."

Caine's attention shifted quickly, and he grinned. "You'd like that wouldn't you?" He stole the idea from me and winked, too.

Mitchell's eyes sparked murder, but before he could respond, Evie rushed in and took Caine's arm, pulling strongly.

"Come *on,* Alan. Don't waste your time on them. The show's gonna start soon . . ."

He laughed like a jackass, but she was insistent and succeeded in getting him into his dressing room where she could fuss to her heart's content.

She glanced once at me before going in. "Thanks, Mister."

What the hell did she see in that guy besides the pretty face?

Then I caught a whiff of something that froze me out of distracting speculations. Bloodsmell. It was all over my knuckles, Hoyle's blood. Now that there was time to notice, the living scent of it flared through me, abrupt and too harsh to tolerate. I wasn't hungry; it was the memory of a different place strewn with bodies and awash with their blood and mine that made such a strong reaction.

It took a moment, and in that time I was oblivious to everything else, which was damned careless.

It took only a moment, and these were the wrong circumstances to let my mind wander.

Blinking hard, I wrenched back to the present, hoping no one had noticed.

There was a washroom on the left. I pushed my way in and shut the door. Cold, cold water straight from the cold, cold lake. Sluice that over the stained skin, scrub and scrub with the harsh green soap and hope its chemical stink would win out over the bloodsmell.

I suppressed a groan, feeling my corner teeth emerging. I wasn't hungry, dammit. *Not* hungry.

A shudder went through my whole body, and for a second I felt falling-down sick, but kept to my feet by hanging on to the washbasin. Something was *wrong* inside me, and I didn't know what.

I stared at the empty mirror, trying to hold steady. This had happened before. The last time I'd been in the throes of shock and quite insane. Another me had been there then, a me who had been visible in the mirror. He'd been ironically amused by the whole business.

He wasn't here tonight. I had to deal with this alone.

Another tremor started, turning my skin to ice, but I

fought it off, panting, though I had no need to breathe. When I got control again I slapped cold water on my face, hardly feeling it for the inner chill. The runoff in the basin was pink.

I was sweating blood. Bad. Very bad.

Knock on the door. Strome's voice. "Mr. Fleming?"

"Yeah, yeah, gimme a minute."

Teeth receding. Good. Water running clear. Better. The fit passing off, leaving me shaken and trying not to shake. I dried and swallowed back the fear, trying and for the most part succeeding in shutting down the emotions. For me more than for anyone else, I couldn't let them see me scared.

The hall was clear, the lights down, and the band out front playing to the now-open club. How long had I been in there? Just Strome and Mitchell were left, the latter looking impatient.

"Trying to put it off?" he asked.

That didn't warrant a reply.

Strome went ahead of us. Mitchell kept close to my heels. We marched through the kitchen, stopping work for a moment as awareness of our presence rippled through the place. The noise picked up again as we reached the back hall, and I trudged upstairs, taking it slow. They seemed steeper than I remembered.

More mugs lounged about the upper floor. I walked the gauntlet. Did everyone in Chicago know about this? I nodded to a few, gathering dark looks or grim curiosity in return. Some respected me, others were like Hoyle and resented the punk kid clumping around in Gordy's big shoes.

Oddly enough, the attention revived a strange kind of confidence inside that I'd not felt in a long, long time. I speculated on whether this surge was what happened at the last moment for some prisoners as they took those final steps to the guillotine.

Probably not.

2

GORDY'S office was several times larger than mine and filled with lush furnishings in black leather and chrome. He liked lots of cushioning on stuff sturdy enough to hold his big frame. In contrast to the streamliner-inspired couch and chairs were several wall paintings of soothing landscapes. The vivid greens, blues, and browns were like suddenly discovering a park in the middle of a concrete sea.

There were more guys here, but they moved, clearing my view to Gordy's massive desk. Behind it, sitting easily in the huge chair, was the man I assumed to be Whitey Kroun. He was lean and long-boned and even at a distance I felt a powerful presence about him. I tried not to let Gordy's summing up of "scary" influence me, but it was hard going. What I picked up the strongest came from the men around him. These were some of the toughest guys in the mob, and they were giving Kroun plenty of space.

He focused wholly on me as I crossed the room to stop

before the desk. There was a radio on it playing dance music. It was out of place, and I questioned why it was there now, then remembered it was a way of foiling eavesdropping microphones. Some of the smarter guys in the gangs knew that the FBI tapped phones. It was illegal as hell, but still went on. If the phones had wires, then so might the walls. That made Kroun smart or paranoid or both.

I couldn't tell what kind of impression I made. His eyes were warm brown, a solid opposition to the cold cast of his craggy face. He couldn't have been much into his midforties, his brown hair going iron gray except for a surprise streak of silver-white that cut oddly across the left side of his skull, obviously the source of his nickname. He spent a long slow time scrutinizing me, which I imagined was supposed to be unnerving, but I'd long grown immune to that kind of thing.

Certain protocols were to be observed, though. He was the big boss. So as not to let down Gordy in his own place I had to show respect.

"Mr. Kroun." I took off my hat, holding it straight at my side. Humble.

"Fleming," he said. No "mister" in front, but that was all right. I knew his voice, which was deeper for being undistorted by the long-distance wires.

"Glad to meetcha."

"We'll see."

Opening courtesies—such as they were—finished, the guys standing nearest made more space around me. There was one chair square in front of the desk that was evidently to be my very own hot seat. It put about seven feet between me and Kroun, hardly suitable distance for a private conversation. Maybe he was going to go for a public dressing-down. It didn't seem to suit the situation unless he wanted plenty of witnesses to see me killed as an object lesson.

Hoyle and Ruzzo were nowhere in sight for the show, but I spotted Derner, who was the club's general manager and also in charge of the day-to-day running of this mob's business. Since the run-in with Bristow, Derner and I had had discussions over what to say about it. Derner would stick to the script we'd agreed on; it was in his own best interest to let me take the fall for him, too. He'd probably already been questioned thoroughly while I'd been down in the main room. He was projecting total neutrality. Smart guy.

Strome stood off to my left, hands clasped in front of him. Mitchell was behind me.

"Sit," said Kroun. To me.

I unbuttoned my overcoat, put my hat next to the radio, and took the chair. The immensity of the desk was before me, and looking across that dark ocean of wood, I realized that Kroun was not overwhelmed by it; he had a surfeit of authority packed into his lean frame. It wasn't anything physical, but you could feel it coming from him like the low hum a radio gives when the sound is down.

More staring. He was good at it. No one moved. It was disturbing, like being in a zoo cage with a lot of meat-eating animals who'd figured out I was on the menu.

"You're just a kid," Kroun finally said. To someone with his no-doubt colorful past giving him more than enough experience at life and hard times, I would be young—ridiculously young—to have been placed in charge of Gordy's organization.

I lifted one hand a little, palm up. "I've proved myself. Ask them."

Some of the men stirred, possibly reluctant to admit anything in my favor.

Strome jerked his chin. " 'S true, Mr. Kroun." That was a

surprise. He'd been told to keep shut, the same as Derner. I'd not expected any volunteered support. "He's stand-up."

"Oh, yeah? How so?" Kroun continued to study me, his dark eyes almost hypnotic.

"He took the worst Hog Bristow could dish and came back swinging."

"So I heard. Swung so hard he killed him. The other guys, too."

"Hog went buckwheats on him. I saw. Fleming—"

"Buckwheats," Kroun repeated.

"Yeah. Ugly."

This was news to a few of the men and sparked a whispered reaction among them. Giving a guy the buckwheats treatment was to kill him slow and painful. It was an object lesson, not so much to the victim, but to others who might dare to cross the mob. But sometimes it was for the satisfaction of the killer.

Bristow had thoroughly enjoyed trying to turn me into a permanent corpse. My changed nature had worked against me, keeping me screaming and aware long after a normal man would have found merciful release in death.

I could almost smell my own blood again. I flexed my hands, but they were quite clean and whole, not the skeletal claws I'd used to drag myself across the slick concrete floor to . . .

Bracing inside, I waited for the wave of nausea, for the shakes to return. Now would be the worst, the absolute worst time, for them to hit, so of course they would. There'd be no sympathy from this bunch. They'd see my real face, learn firsthand what Bristow's knife work had done to me. . . .

"What's the matter?" Kroun gave me a narrow look. "You sick?"

"Not much."

I breathed in warm air that smelled of booze, stale smoke, sweating bodies, bay rum aftershave . . . and blood. Not a ghost scent from my imaginings, nor the fresh stuff of a flowing wound, but the muted kind that lurked beneath the skin. It was always present, but I wasn't always aware, like the way you ignore traffic noise. For a few deep and profound seconds it struck me that every one of the tough guys crowding this room, the muscle, the sharps, the thieves, the killers, from Strome to the boss in charge, were all little more than walking bags of blood. I could feed myself sick on any of them. They had no way to expect it, no way to stop me if I made up my mind to do it.

Even the biggest, deadliest, meat-eating predator was my *food.*

So it had proved at the end when I'd killed Bristow.

I held on to that most interesting thought, sat a little straighter, and slowly breathed out again.

Well. How about that? Not one hint of tremor in my whole body. Skating so close to the memory should have had me doubled over and whimpering again, but it was like a switch had been flipped, and I was in control.

For how long I couldn't say.

Kroun still watched me, hardly blinking. "He doesn't look like he's got so much as a stubbed toe."

"He was hurt bad, Mr. Kroun," Strome continued. "Derner saw, too."

"I'm a fast healer," I said.

"Convenient," said Kroun. "What'd you do to get Hog Bristow pissed enough to go buckwheats?"

"Being stand-up for Gordy. Hog jumped things when he shot him out of hand like he did. I stepped in. Hog didn't like it much."

"What'd you think to get out of it by helping Gordy?"

"I wasn't thinking to get anything. I stepped in because that's what you do for friends."

"You had a two-grand hit out on Hog."

"Not a hit. That was a reward for *finding* him, nothing more. If you'll recall, I told you several times over the phone I wanted to keep Hog alive. I knew what kind of trouble it would make if he got killed. But at the end he didn't give me any choice."

Kroun's brown eyes were odd in this light, hard to look at, with strangely dilated pupils like holes into hell. He must have known their effect and used it plenty. "And that may just be something you came up with to cover yourself with me."

"You talked to Derner? Then you know it's what happened."

"Doesn't matter. Someone has to pay for killing Bristow. You're it."

Still behind me, Mitchell shifted, and I felt something pressing cold against my skull. I turned only enough to confirm it was a gun muzzle. One trigger pull and my brains would be all over Gordy's rug.

I nodded. "No problem."

"What?" Must have been a disappointment to Mitchell, me not being terrified. I just didn't give a damn. After surviving Hog Bristow there was little that could scare me these nights. Just myself.

My reply was to Kroun, not the hired help. "I know the rules."

Kroun watched me closely. I still had that strange serenity gripping me. He was food. Walking, talking food.

I smiled at him.

"You think I won't?" asked Kroun.

"You'll do what you have to do. But one question: after I'm gone is Gordy still running things? I'd hate to think I went through all that shit with Bristow, then got scragged by you and it be for nothing."

No one spoke, but another murmur ran through the room about that fine point. I could feel all of them looking at me. Impossible to tell what they might be thinking.

The simple response for Kroun would be something smart-sounding and harsh, but he didn't do it. "You're ready to die?"

I shrugged. "During my time with Bristow I kinda got used to the idea. If you need to kill me, there's nothing I can do to stop you. I just want to make sure Gordy gets something out of it."

His dark eyes flickered once. "You sound like you got an angle to bargain with."

"Maybe."

"What would that be?"

"Nothing you'll want to share with so many ears flapping." Even with the radio to mask most of our talk, there were plenty of listeners at hand. Too many for a paranoid man.

He thought it over. They'd seen Jack Fleming the wiseacre, not the wiseguy, called on the carpet and giving respect to the boss. Kroun had made his point. He shot a look to Strome and signed to Mitchell. The muzzle went away. Strome told the boys to leave.

There were protests from those who knew the best part of the show was about to take place. Others flatly refused, standing firm, arms crossed.

Kroun stood up. There was nothing threatening to his posture, and the lines of his natty brown suit were undistorted by hidden firearms of any size. Many of the guys here were taller or wider or both, but to a man, they fell silent. He didn't make a sound either, just looked at them while the radio blared. He was quite still, just his head moving enough so he could rake them with those intense dark eyes.

Damned if it didn't work. Some grumbled as they left, but they filed out. Derner, Strome, and Kroun's man Mitchell remained.

"Private enough?" Kroun asked. He turned those eyes on me.

"If you trust your guy like I trust Gordy's."

He gave a short grunt. Couldn't tell if it was a laugh. He came around the desk to look down at me. "What's your angle, kid?"

"You. You being smarter than you let on to me over the phone."

"Oh, yeah?" He hitched one hip onto the desk.

"For which I want to apologize. I got a mouth on me, nothing personal. Whenever you called things were running tense on this side, so I was talking short without much time to think things through. But that's changed, and since then I've seen what was going on more clearly."

"Which was . . . ?"

"For starters: why your boy was sent here in the first place. Gordy told me Bristow had powerful friends he'd convinced that he could do a better job of running the Chicago operation. Gordy was expected to hand it over. If he didn't, he'd be killed or in the middle of a gang war. That, Mr. Kroun, was . . . extremely brainless."

"Uh-huh." He wasn't agreeing, only encouraging me to continue.

"You guys had to know Gordy would never roll over for the likes of Bristow. Now it was either New York being stu-

pid and for the hell of it putting him and Gordy in the same
pen like a couple of fighting dogs just to see what happens
or . . . you had something else going."

"Which was?"

"Playing Hog Bristow to the limit. You sent him out
here, apparently to give him what he wants, then Gordy
does what he's best at: listening, collecting information. He
got plenty out of Hog every night until the guy was too
drunk to talk. And all that time Hog is feeling sure of himself because he has New York to back him up and thinks
Gordy's got no choice about handing over the operation.
But I'm betting that every night Gordy called you up afterward to give you an earful."

"This is what Gordy told you?"

"All I heard from him was the first part, that Bristow
takes over or Gordy dies, which struck me as fishy. I went
along with it since Gordy's a friend, and the talks were taking place at my club. He probably thought that was all I
needed to know. The rest of it . . . well, Hog Bristow was a
loudmouthed drunk and dangerously dumb, certainly the
worst kind of man to put in charge of anything. Guys like
him are a liability and never last long. You either let them
go—one way or another—or send 'em someplace where
they can't do any harm. But for some reason you couldn't do
that with Hog. You had to find a less direct means to bury
him. My guess is he's got important relatives protecting
him, or he had to know a lot of stuff, damaging, dangerous
stuff. The only man you could trust to shake it out of him
was Gordy."

"Maybe." There was a subtle change in Kroun. He gave
no clue on whether I was hitting home or not, but was listening hard.

"Gordy did his job, but Hog got impatient and frustrated. He set deadlines, forgot them, then set more, but eventually he had enough and made his hit. He wasn't supposed to, but someone back home knew him well enough to gamble he'd sooner or later go over the edge. Gordy must have known that would happen, but not when. The night of the shooting we thought Bristow was too drunk to know which end of a gun to point. Maybe he had one of his boys do it for him, but the result was the same. He'd overstepped the rules and could be considered a legit target in turn."

"Gordy put himself in front of a bullet so as to do all that?"

"He didn't *intend* to get shot; he'd have some alternative planned out, only Hog threw a wrench into the works, surprising everyone. Then I got into the middle of things—"

"Yeah-yeah, and he went buckwheats on you. Except you don't look hurt."

"I'll be glad to show you my scars when the bandages come off. In the meantime, I get a cigar for hitting the bull's-eye."

"Ya think?"

"I know."

"It's a sweet story, kid, but that's not enough of an angle to get you off the hook. We wouldn't like any of it generally known, but blabbing it around won't help you."

" 'S nothing I wanna do. Your boy came out to take over this town, and him being stupid got himself and the others killed. Someone's supposed to pay for it. Gordy's in the clear, which is fine with me, so I'm the one who's elected. I get that."

"What if Gordy was the one who set you up from the first to take the fall?"

I laughed out loud. I laughed long and heartily, right in his face. And damn, it felt *good*. "Oh, no. That was my *own* doing. Before I ever got involved, Bristow didn't like my looks, and things went bad from then on with us. If I'd been more on the ball, I might have sidestepped him, but it didn't work out that way, which was my own bad luck. Well, I took it on the chin good and hard, and what I am thinking is that I've *paid* for killing him and his boys. I've paid several times over. What he put me through has to count for something. I survived it; I've earned the right to live."

"If he went buckwheats on you even halfway," said Mitchell, bending close, "you wouldn't be sitting here. And you sure as hell wouldn't have done what you did downstairs." I'd forgotten he was behind me. As if that mattered.

"What happened downstairs?" Kroun asked him.

"He punched out a guy who was getting rough with one of the chorus girls. Never saw anything move so quick."

"*That* was adrenaline," I said. "I paid for it afterward, which is why I was in the john for so long, or did you forget that part?"

Mitchell wasn't buying. "From what we heard Bristow skinned you alive. Even if you got through it, you should still be laid up in a hospital."

"What d'ya want from me? I said I healed fast."

"Prove it."

"Okay. Seeing's believing." I stood and shrugged carefully out of my overcoat as though I were in discomfort and stiff. "Mr. Kroun? In the washroom, if you don't mind. These mugs don't need to gape at the freak show." Without waiting for a yea or nay, I moved slowly toward a door that led to the toilet. I went in, swatted the light on, and stood well out of their view. It was a big room, bright, black-and-white tile, a hefty tub. Gordy occasionally stayed over when work demanded, and he liked his comforts.

In the office the radio volume went up. Loud. Good. We'd have privacy from the boys listening in. Hopefully, they would stay out. All my worst scars were on the inside, but that wouldn't count with this bunch.

After a minute, Kroun came to the door and stepped through. He'd produced or borrowed a gun from someone and held it ready in one hand. Talk about being cautious. He waited, head tilted slightly, and holding very, very still. He didn't need a gun to fill the place with himself.

"Well?"

"No tricks," I said wearily. "Just the truth."

"Which is . . . ?"

"That Bristow chained me upside down from a meat hook and . . ." I stopped there, the words clogged in my throat. Weakness showing. Not something I intended. "Oh, jeez."

"Just show."

I had my suit coat open, but my hands hung straight at my sides as I looked steadily into his eyes. "I want you to *listen* to me, Mr. Kroun. Listen hard . . ."

He wasn't the only one with an effective stare.

It didn't work immediately. He might have had a drink earlier. He stared in puzzled annoyance for a moment as I focused hard on him and kept up the soothing drone that would put him under. Then he gave a small headshake and blinked once, twice, before his eyelids sagged to half-mast. I had him hooked, landed, gutted, cooked, and on the plate. His gun was pointed in the wrong direction, at me. I calmly told him to please put it away, and without fuss he shoved it into a pocket. His eyes were flat and dull. Perfect.

But inside my skull things began to thump badly, a building thunderstorm. I had to make this quick. Very fast and intense, I whispered some choice and vivid word pictures about what damage my torso was supposed to have. Kroun's face went the same color as that white streak in his hair. For a moment I thought he might be sick, which meant I'd overdone it.

"Take it easy," I murmured. "Nice and easy. We're friends now. You remember that. Remember that you look after your friends and help them. Watch out for me, I'll watch out for you. I just want out of this alive and no problems for Gordy, okay? None at all. He's been loyal."

Though positive I could have ordinarily talked him out of killing me, this would speed the process. I was fed up having a death sentence hanging overhead. But the thunder in my brain was starting to boom. Insistent, distracting. I licked my lips and tried to concentrate.

Kroun nodded agreement to my suggestions, his eyes still empty.

I had plenty more to say to him, only it never came out. A pain like nothing I had ever known before blasted through my skull. For the briefest instant I thought I'd been shot, but no one else was with us. Kroun stood motionless and staring. That was the last glimpse I got before the agony doubled me down. I clutched my head with both hands, biting off a cry. They couldn't see me like this. God, what was *wrong?*

The pain rose, tripled, tripled again. My head would explode from the pressure if I didn't—

Then peace, sudden as flicking a switch, plunging me into sweet gray nothingness.

I'd vanished.

Sometimes that happened to me involuntarily when I got too badly hurt to control the reflex. How I'd wished for it when Bristow had been skinning me, but a piece of ice pick buried deep in my back prevented that escape.

This was like heaven after hell. The pain went away, but not the memory or the fear that it might be waiting to fall on me again when I went solid.

I'd have to risk it, though. If the others got too curious and came for a look-see . . . I told myself it would be all right. Vanishing always healed me, bullets, paper cuts, even headaches went away. So it was now.

Melted back slowly. If Kroun was aware he didn't show it, continuing with the empty-eyed gaze into the distance. That was good. Hypnotizing people had always made my head hurt, but the pain had gone way out of hand now. *Why, though?*

Solid again, I moved away and sat on the edge of the tub, biting off the groans because I couldn't afford to give in. But for an awful second I actually felt on the edge of tears. My face twisted, and I rocked back and forth, arms wrapped tight around myself, resisting the urge.

My *body* was just fine. Healing had taken place. The head agony was gone, but inside I was a train wreck.

"God, I'm so tired." I was unaware of speaking until the words were out. I hoped the overly loud radio covered it.

There would be no more evil-eye work for me tonight. Maybe I was too nerved up for it. Kroun would come out of the trance on his own in a few minutes. I'd better use what was left of them.

"Okay, Mr. Kroun. You know Bristow hurt me. I just want to go back to my job and forget any of this ever happened. Keep Gordy in charge and go on your way home and no harm done, okay?" I did not look too-directly at him.

He mouthed the word "okay." That's all I needed. The suggestion would last for a few weeks—months, even—after that, if I was lucky, he'd have other things to concern him, shoving out any second thoughts over tonight's "decision."

By the time he surfaced I was pretending to settle my coat and tie back into place. I walked past him into the office and slowly resumed my chair.

Kroun emerged from the washroom after a few moments, face still pretty pale. "He got the buckwheats treatment all right," he announced.

Strome and Derner gave me bleak looks, the closest they could come to sympathy. Mitchell was clearly mystified and stepped in front of me.

"Lemme see."

He got a glare instead. I was careful not to put any power into it.

"Come on."

"No." Absolutely, categorically.

"Boss." He appealed to Kroun.

Kroun waved Mitchell down and sat behind the desk. "Lay off him. That's Hog's work for sure. You don't wanna see, trust me. Fleming, how the hell are you able to walk around like that?"

I eased carefully onto the chair. "I got a good doctor. Jabbed me full of some *great* medicine. It blunts things. It's no circus, but I can do my job. I'm about ready to go for another shot, so if you don't mind, let's wind this up."

"How?"

"Like I said—I've paid for Hog Bristow's death. You can convince New York of that. Go back home, tell 'em I'll finish out my turn at watch nice and quiet. When Gordy's fully on his feet again I'll fade away and just pretend none of this happened. You guys forget about me; everything goes back to normal. Upheavals are bad for business. It's time this one blew itself out."

He thought it over. The new attitude that I'd forced on him would hold firm, but he still had to work out how to square it with whatever orders he'd have from his pals back home. "I should be able to do that."

I hoped so. I didn't want to have to hypnotize every mobster in New York into leaving me alone. It'd kill me. "I would be very appreciative."

"You'll get it. But there's other things I gotta straighten out."

"Name 'em. I'll help if I can."

"Where's Bristow? I need to know."

I glanced at Strome.

"He and the rest are in the lake," he answered.

"The lake." Kroun frowned, and I got the idea he hated watery graves as much as I did. "That's not good. Bodies always float to the surface no matter how much weight you use."

"Not these guys. We know how to do it here so that don't happen."

"And how do you do it here?"

"You get a really big oil drum, bigger than you think you need. Put the guy in it and pour in cement good and tight, no air pockets. The trick is to make sure the cement weighs more than twice what the guy does. You punch a hole in the lid to let the gas escape, then take 'em way far outta sight of land and dump 'em."

"That's the trick?"

"Yeah."

"Huh."

"It helps if you cut the body up and use two drums, three is even better . . ."

"Strome," I said, correctly reading the look on Kroun's face. He'd had enough.

Strome shut it off.

I'd been told in only the most general terms of what he

and a couple of other carefully picked cleanup men had done to get rid of Bristow, and wanted to keep it that way. The bodies had been in a meat storage locker, and there must have been butchers' cutting equipment conveniently at hand . . . I gave a headshake to try to jostle that picture out of my mind, with indifferent success.

"Anything else?" I asked Kroun.

"I wanna know about this Dugan bird that you got it in for."

He'd taken his time getting to that one. Hurley Gilbert Dugan, society swan, blackmailer, murderer, kidnapper, and all-round useless bag of poisonous air, held a unique place in my life. He was the one man on the whole planet I wanted dead. I wanted to kill him the way Bristow wanted to kill me. I'd put a bounty on him, and had every gangster in Chicago and beyond looking for him.

"No one's told you?" I would have thought Derner might have filled Kroun in.

"Only that you want him alive, and you'll pay ten grand to anyone bringing him in. That's as much as Hoover put up for Pretty Boy Floyd."

"I didn't know that. The reward on Dugan could be a lot less than ten by now. He took off with that much cash on him. I let the boys know whoever brings him in alive gets to keep what's left, and I'll make up the difference out of my own pocket."

"Why you want him?"

"Personal matter."

"Details. Give."

I pretended a sigh. "Maybe you didn't get word of the society kidnapping case we had here. Gilbert Dugan was the big mastermind, killed some innocent people that didn't need it. He's garbage. I tripped him, made an enemy. It was because of him Hog Bristow was able to get me, so I owe him for that. When Bristow and the others died, Dugan was there. A witness. Neither of us needs him running loose. The cops are looking for him for the kidnap and murders. If they get him first, he could and would try making a deal that puts us all in the clink."

"Dugan saw you kill Bristow?"

"And what they did to me before that. Everything. If you thought Bristow was a liability, then don't meet this guy. He's a thinker. He can talk his way out of just about anything given the chance. He's full of more shit than a goose, but smart. People *trust* him. Even ones who should know better."

"You want him bad."

"Just looking after the company's best interests."

"Why you want him alive?"

"To prevent mistaken identity."

"What do you mean?"

"If the boys found someone who only happened to look like Dugan and killed him . . . not good. I don't want accidents on my watch, so I'm making it worth their while to be careful."

"How long's he been gone?"

"About a week. He could be anyplace." Each night right after waking, my first phone call was to Derner for a report on whether Dugan had been found. So far, no good luck.

"You'll never catch him now."

"I'm hopeful." But I thought Kroun might be right. With his head start, Dugan could be nearly anywhere. If he was ever found, it'd be by accident. "He's got smarts, but not for practical stuff. I heard that Einstein guy wears loafers because he can't figure out how to tie shoes. The same goes for Dugan. All he has to do is hide out in the wrong flop, and one of the boys spots him."

"What'll you do if you get him?"

"Depends on the situation, but . . . I'll maybe need a couple of oil drums."

That amused him. Kroun's frown lines eased a bit. "I'm seeing why you got put in charge."

"It's also because I don't want to keep the job. Gordy knows I won't get attached to it. It won't be for long. He's getting better every day." If he took care of himself. I hoped Adelle had tracked him down and hauled him off to sensibly rest.

"I can offer you another job when this one's done."

This guy was full of surprises. Maybe I'd laid it on too thick about us being friends. "No thanks. I don't belong. That's why some of the guys kicked such a fuss. They know I'm not one of them."

"Oh, yeah, you are." Kroun actually smiled. On him it was damned unnerving. "You just don't know it yet."

Word of my reprieve spread fast.

By the time I'd wound things up with Kroun, put on my hat and overcoat, shook hands like we were dear old pals, and left, the guys waiting in the hall had either magically vanished or were lying in wait to congratulate me. How they learned was a mystery unless they were the ones with a microphone hidden in the office. Not that it would have worked with the radio on in there and Alan Caine's show playing downstairs.

Or they'd just pressed ears to the door and, when no shots were fired, figured it out.

One of the hall mugs pumped my hand and made to thump my back, but Strome got in between.

"The boss needs to leave," he said, and ran interference for me through the rest of the gauntlet.

Belatedly, I reminded myself that I was still supposed to be healing from Bristow's torture and should act accordingly. Strome was trying to protect my hide from further damage. He must have thought I had a truly amazing painkiller working away. I considered asking him what he thought was going on, but I'd have to hypnotize him afterward. Not worth it. Let him think what he liked.

We emerged from the kitchen entry into freezing night air. It was heavy with damp from the nearby lake and seemed much colder. The wind was up and on the hunt, knifing through my coat. That I was able to notice the chill told me I was tired, the weariness wholly mental and emotional. The interview with Kroun and reaction to the hypnosis had wrung me out, but I'd not been hung up to dry. Not as bad as it could have turned out.

Of course, there were still guys who thought that had been a cheat. Ruzzo, for two.

They were standing by a fat panel trunk parked behind Gordy's car, and their mad must have been pretty serious to keep them out in this wind. Moving like one man, they straightened to face me as I descended the loading dock steps. Strome started to move past, but I stopped him.

"No. It's got to be from me, or they won't learn."

He grunted displeasure toward them and hung back. I could be reasonably certain that he had a hand closed around the gun he kept in his overcoat pocket.

I decided to steal from Kroun's bag of tricks by going up to Ruzzo and stand in place and not say anything. It would get a rise of one kind or another.

"You lettin' him get away with it?" Ruzzo the Younger demanded of me.

The problem with some guys is that they will chew over whatever's bothering them, be extremely familiar with every tiny part, and fully expect you to know exactly what the hell they're talking about when they finally blurt it at you. This was out of the blue. I thought they'd be challenging my right to be their boss.

"Let who get away with what?" I asked patiently.

"That singer you're soft for. He owes."

"Yeah, owes," echoed the Elder. "You make bets and lose, you pay the markers."

Cripes, I should send them off to Tierra del Fuego to breed wombats. "Not my business," I said.

"You stopped Hoyle from doin' his job."

I'd have to use small words with these two. "Hoyle can collect from him *off* the premises—after Caine's done his act. If Caine can't sing, he can't pay."

"That's bullshit."

Dangerous words in this gathering, meant as a challenge; I couldn't let them go by. "You're calling me a liar," I carefully informed him. Them. I hoped theirs was a very small family.

"The singer *owes.* You talk to Hoyle. He'll tell you. You don't know everything."

"Neither does Hoyle."

"*He's* the boss on this."

"Sez him. I'm running things, not Hoyle."

"Sez you." Ruzzo grinned. Both of them.

Then they stopped being there. Both of them.

I couldn't understand it. Had the night swallowed them up? Were they like me and had disappeared into thin air? What the hell . . . ?

I was lying on my face on cold metal, which was moving under me. Rumbling through my body was the throaty noise of a truck motor going at a good clip.

Ow. Head pain. Not right.

What the hell . . . ?

Ow. Bad now, very bad.

What the hell? Again.

I repeated that several times, eventually working out that I'd been bushwhacked. While Ruzzo kept me distracted someone must have come up behind and . . . ow . . . yes, the back of my head. A familiar tenderness, bruising, and a knot. That's where he'd got me. With wood. *Had* to be wood. It was the only thing that could put me out without causing me to vanish. So . . . was it dumb luck or had someone known what would work?

Strome? Sure, he was a killer, but he had no reason to lay me flat. Unless he had special orders from Kroun. But I'd neutralized the threat.

Hoyle. Much more likely. He wasn't the forgiving type, not that I'd have apologized to him for busting him one over the dancer. He and Ruzzo were shoulder-to-shoulder apparently. Against me. Despite Gordy. Despite Kroun.

Oh, hell. This crap I didn't need.

3

I BLINKED against blackness. Very little light filtered through the painted-over rear door window, just enough for me to ascertain I was alone in the back of the panel truck that had shared the alley with Gordy's Cadillac. No one had bothered tying me up. Chances were, after clobbering me they noticed I wasn't breathing and assumed I'd been killed. Which would leave them with a body on their hands. Better to get rid of me and delay the news of my death than have someone from the Nightcrawler's kitchen staff stumbling over the corpse a few minutes later.

Feeling queasy, I thought of how Strome had sunk Bristow and his boys in the water to lose them. Nope. That wasn't going to happen to me. I'd had too much of that damned lake already.

When I felt steady enough to get up I damn near cracked my head on the low ceiling. Not much space in here for a tall guy. On hands and knees I worked over to the windows, finding my hat along the way. My head wasn't to the point of supporting that much weight yet. Hell, even my hair was too heavy. I folded the thing and stuffed it in a pocket, glad it wasn't one of my fancier fedoras. Lately I'd taken to wearing only my second- and even third-best clothes, fearing (rightly) that something like this situation might drop itself on me like a net. If I didn't take things in hand with these mugs, I'd end up with a pawnshop wardrobe.

I pulled out my keys, using one to scrape away paint from a corner of the window. When I had a peephole I looked through.

Not a lot to see. Flat, snow-crusted fields. Farm country. How long had I been out? I held my watch up to the feeble light. An hour? The way I felt it had to be more than that. The watch still ticked, though, the time correct. No one at my club would miss me until closing, which was in the wee hours. It was still well on the right side of midnight, though to me it felt much later.

The rumbling changed in tone as the driver made a sharp turn. The truck shook like an earthquake, indicating unpaved road. I braced, holding on to a length of wood bolted to the metal side. Damned wood. Why couldn't they have just shot me? It'd have ruined a suit, but I could have taken care of them back in town. Idiots. Both of them. And Hoyle.

I deliberated about vanishing and sieving through to the front compartment to surprise the driver.

Not at this speed. The peephole showed an undistinguished country lane of frozen churned mud that made the truck bounce and skid erratically. This kind of road at this time of year tolerated sturdy vehicles going no more than ten miles an hour, if that much. We were moving considerably faster. I didn't care to be in a crash and have to walk home.

And if we were an hour's drive from Chicago, meaning a *long* walk, then I wouldn't be seeping my way out the back to escape, either. If my luck ran bad—and lately I had no reason to expect different—I'd have to improvise shelter from the sun. That meant spending the day away from my home earth, which meant I'd be a prisoner of whatever nightmares my brain threw out. After Bristow's work on me, it'd have plenty of horrors to draw upon. No, I wouldn't put myself through that. Better to wait until we stopped, then hijack the truck, leaving *them* stranded.

And roughed up. A lot. Yeah, I liked that idea.

We slowed somewhat. I took another look out the back. Lots of snowy acreage, twin furrows of tire tracks leading back the way we'd come and . . . headlights in the distance. Someone following? Maybe it was Hoyle in his own car, taking it easy to keep from breaking an axle. I'd break his head given the chance.

A shift in the gears and the truck's voice. Slowing even more, then finally coasting to a stop.

We were in an open yard by a low metal barn. A single electric light burned bluely against the dark. It was on a tall, lonely pole under a shade shaped like a Chinese hat. The cone of light from the oversized bulb covered a wide area before the barn. A car was already there, and four men emerged from it. One of them opened the trunk and handed out . . . what? . . . baseball bats? . . . to the others.

The truck doors in front slammed shut almost in unison, and Ruzzo joined their friends getting something swingable. They must have thought I was still alive, then, or they'd have been hauling me out instead.

I'd heard about this kind of send-off. Find a deserted spot for some batting practice on some poor son of a bitch, then either leave what's left in the cornfield for Farmer Jones to find come harvest, or make a shallow grave in the stalks. It was too late in the season for that; harvest was long over and the ground frozen, but they might not care. Just leaving me under a drift of snow would be enough until spring. Scavenging animals would do what they were best at and . . .

Shut the hell up, it's not going to happen.

The star-filled gray sky layered the surrounding landscape in a silvery sheen, turning it to day for me. In that soft dream-glow the electric light sparked brighter than a diamond. So, just how would I take out half a dozen guys armed with something that could actually stop me? One at a time? Sounded good.

A car horn blared in the distance. The six men all looked back the way we'd come, their attention on the approaching headlights I'd seen. Just how big a party was this?

Well, since they were distracted . . .

I vanished and slipped out under the door. A smooth, invisible tearing over open ground to the count of five, then I slowed to wash gently against the very solid side of the tin barn. Jeez, this was perfect. I glided on, keeping the flat surface of the barn's wall on my left, reaching an opening, and going in. An instant later I was solid again, standing upright in brisk freezing air I barely felt. I was in time to take in the show.

Hoyle, Ruzzo, and four other guys I knew by sight were less than twenty feet away. The start of a nice little gang.

The second car was Gordy's Cadillac. It braked majestically; the motor cut. Strome got out. He didn't look too good, seemed to carry himself gingerly. Though he wasn't obviously showing it, I got the impression he was pissed off.

"Hoyle," he said, by way of greeting.

Along with a baseball bat, Hoyle had a gun ready in his other hand. "What the hell are you doin' here?"

Strome would be armed, but made no move for his shoulder holster and the semiauto .45 he kept there. He looked around the yard, probably for me. My broken body was not lying out in the snow. Was *he* in on this? When Gordy got shot Strome had been more than ready to leave for greener pastures, but I couldn't think why he'd throw in with Hoyle.

Hoyle repeated the question. He tossed the bat to one of his men, who caught it neatly and held it ready to use.

Strome was able to summon some cold-eyed threat to pass around, enough so four of the mugs backed off a few steps. He was still one of Gordy's lieutenants, after all. "Whatever you're doing here, you stop."

"Not doing nothing, Strome. Just a little batting practice." Hoyle's smile was ugly. There was nothing specifically wrong with it, and that's why it made my back hairs rise.

"You boys pack it up and go back, and I won't say nothing to the boss."

"Which boss? Gordy or Fleming?"

"The boss what's in charge. The boss who will see you here next if you cross him." He nodded toward the group in general.

Hoyle and some others snorted. "Fleming, then. We don't take orders from that punk bastard."

Strome went patient, reverting to ingrained habit. "Gordy put him in charge. Every one of you knows that. Ain't for us to argue with Gordy."

"Yeah-yeah. *If* we can believe that it was Gordy who said so. All we know is what you and Derner let drop, and you guys got plenty reason not to rock the boat."

"So do you. You mess up on this—"

"Aw, screw it. You wanna run errands for that punk creep, fine, but we got regular business to do, an' it's gonna get done. Gordy'll agree with me on this, and the hell with Fleming."

They'd formed a rough half circle around Strome, but it was ragged, with four of the guys having drifted outward. Their collective attention was on him. I hoped he was dead-pan enough to not react as I stepped clear of the barn.

If he did, I got too busy to notice, swiftly coming up be-hind the nearest man holding a baseball bat. I pulled it ca-sually from his hand, slammed a left into his jaw as he turned, then swung the bat smartly into the next guy's gut. Both men dropped just that fast, and I rounded on another, giving him a low and mean bunt just under his rib cage. Half the opposition now lay on the snow, either unconscious or gasping for air. Hoyle had been alert for trouble, though, and spun with his gun raised. A joyous sneer lit up his nar-row mug as he recognized me. I had a perfect view directly up the short barrel of his gun. At ten feet it was a cannon.

He immediately fired, point-blank. Three shots as quick as he could pull the trigger.

He had good aim, holding the muzzle steady on my un-moving form, the sound sharp yet toylike under the wide sky. The smoke was swept away by the icy wind, and for a few crucial seconds I had to fight its force to keep from be-ing carried off as well. I'd surrendered just enough solidity so the bullets passed right through my near-ghostly body, spanging hollow into the barn's tin walls behind. Being just outside the nimbus of the light, I gambled that I could get away with such a risky stunt in front of witnesses.

Strome belatedly grabbed Hoyle's arm, and they wres-tled and danced, cursing. The remaining two guys, Ruzzo, stared at me, probably because I should have been falling down and wasn't. Instead, I charged them, yelling and swinging the bat and moving a hell of a lot faster than anything they'd ever remotely experienced. Then they were also on the ground with their friends, not being any further problem.

I stepped into Strome and Hoyle's rumba and plucked the gun clear before Hoyle could shoot either of them. That didn't stop his fighting. My cracking one of his legs with the bat did. He broke off fast with a high scream, clutching his shin. It wasn't broken, but the bone would be bruised. I'd felt the impact through the length of the bat and judged he'd be limping for a week. Good payback for the knock he must have landed on me earlier.

"You summabitch, you busted—ah, Jesus God!"

He went on like that for a while, loudly expressing pain and outrage. Strome, huffing to get his breath back, kept an eye on him while I made the rounds of the others. One of them was recovered enough to fumble for his gun, but I whacked his wrist with the bat, then tapped him lightly on the forehead. Lightly for me, anyway. He hit the snow and stayed there. It was obvious they were in no condition for a counterattack.

I shoved Hoyle's gun into my belt. The barrel was hot. It struck me then just how quick he'd been to shoot. There'd been no hesitation, no thought of the consequences to hold him back from killing me. He either had a grudge on that was beyond restraint or must have done his thinking beforehand and made up his mind then what to do if we ever crossed. I barely knew the guy, so it was disturbing to have inspired such a reaction in a stranger, but not unexpected given this kind of work.

Hoyle sat flat in the snow, clutching his leg, still cursing, but in a lower, more dangerous voice. Having passed through the initial agony, his invective was for me, not his pain. His threats were basic and brutal and nothing I'd not heard before from other guys. He was a rangy, long-boned specimen whose loose-jointed manner of walking might be mistaken for clumsiness, but he was one of the rare ones who could instantly pull himself in quick and tight to surprise an overconfident opponent. I'd heard from Gordy that Hoyle had been in the ring about ten years back, but got thrown out because of a betting scandal. It left him soured on boxing, but he'd never forgotten his training and still looked fit and granite-solid. Strome had taken a hell of a chance mixing with him.

I looked down at Hoyle. He shot pure hatred right back. I grabbed hunks of his overcoat and hauled him up. He piled an iron fist into me. It was a short swing; he didn't have enough room to really get behind it, but sheer muscle made the blow sufficiently powerful to send anyone else reeling. I took the impact like a heavy workout bag, swaying a little, but not really moved. Before he could go for a second punch I lifted him right off his feet and thumped him bodily against the truck. Several times. I'm tall, but on the lean side. I don't look to have the kind of muscle to deal so easily with a 200-pound man. It stole the fight out of him and, once he shook his head clear, had obviously surprised him. Apparently Hoyle wasn't used to being thrown around.

He smothered his shock with glowering resentment but didn't attempt any more punches.

"You," I said, holding him upright, "are annoying me. Which means you are annoying Gordy."

"Go ahead and tell 'em, I ain't afraid of Gordy."

"Then you damn well better be afraid of me." I emphasized my words by smacking the side of his head with the flat of my hand. It must have made his ears ring, for his eyes went dull for a few seconds. I waited until he was able to pay attention again. "Gordy put me in charge for a reason. He knew I'd be able to squash bugs like you with no problem if there's a good enough excuse. You've given me a hell of an excuse with this stunt."

"You are screwing up business! That singer shit owes me money!"

"So beating him to death will get it for you?"

"It's to learn others!"

I cracked him again. "School's out. Gordy put me in charge to hold things, and I am holding things until he's back full-time. Everyone else is clear on that except you and these gutter bums. Your second mistake was going after me. You got one chance to stay alive. Get clear of town by morning."

"Or what?"

"Or I take you and all your apes apart like a Sunday chicken, only slower, and they'll be finding your bones over these fields from now until next year's harvest."

He held to a snarling expression, but his eyes flickered. He must have picked up from my voice that I was being literal.

"You got lucky, Hoyle. You didn't kill anyone, so I don't have to kill you. But I *am* annoyed. If I get even a hint that you're only just *thinking* about being stupid again, you will be walking on stumps. Now pick these saps off the mat and stay outta my way."

"Or what, you tell Gordy?" He'd reduced serious business down to schoolyard-level snitching.

Logic would never work on him, only pain. I knew a lot about pain. I hit him again, plowing tough into the hard shell of his middle. A strike from a bare fist is different from the boxing gloves he'd been used to; the force is more concentrated. Some men hold back to spare their hands. That wasn't anything I needed to worry about. I stopped short of rupturing his insides, but only just.

"Or," I said, talking quietly right into his ear, "*I will kill you, Hoyle.*"

He was doubled down, and when he managed to suck in air, it came out again as profanity. Weak-sounding, though. No breath for it.

Couldn't let him get away with even that much. I dragged him up again and pulled his gun from my belt. He favored a revolver. I clapped it against the side of his skull to get his attention, then shoved the muzzle into his nose.

"I will kill you, Hoyle. Same as you just tried on me—only I won't miss."

To drive the point home, I threw him on the ground and quick-fired close to his head, using up the remaining three bullets. The gun didn't seem to make any sound at all, but for Hoyle it must have been a hell of a roar. Arms up, he convulsed away from where the lead struck snow inches from his face, then held still, staring at the gun, not me. He must have known it was empty, but a jolt like that is not easily shrugged off.

"What will I do, Hoyle?"

Trembling, he looked up blankly.

"*What will I do?*"

"Y-you'll kill me," he whispered.

"You're gonna remember that every time you think of me, every time you say my name, every time you *hear* my name, that's what you will remember. I will kill you."

I broke the gun open, tipping the cylinder clear. Shell casings rained out. Grasping it in one hand and the frame in the other I gave them each an opposing twist that hurt even my hands, but it was worth it. The metal held for a second, then abruptly snapped. I dropped both pieces on either side of the astonished Hoyle.

"*Every* time."

I slouched across the Caddy's backseat for the return trip to Chicago, a strange reprise of how the evening had started, just a different mood. Playing tough was getting easier the more I did it, but afterward the reaction would set in, leaving me surly and almost as torn up inside as the people I'd leaned on. Of course, I couldn't show any of that to Strome. My breaking the gun in two had breached even his expressionless reserve, and I didn't want to lose what awed respect had been gained. Not that I didn't already have it in spades.

I wanted Gordy on his feet again real soon. Some number of the boys in the gang were like Hoyle, resenting an outsider giving them orders, but they'd behaved themselves out of respect for Gordy. That Hoyle had a grudge against me for taking the big chair wasn't news, but he'd given no hint till now about making an open challenge. It wasn't only against me but Gordy as well, which was a few miles past stupid, but brains were in short supply for some of them. Hoyle had thrown down the glove, mob style, and I'd beaten him silly with it. Would that and my promise of death be enough to hold him in place?

"Is Hoyle going to be smart?" I asked Strome, interrupting the long silence of the drive.

Strome didn't answer right off, which boded ill. He thought it over a while. "He might."

"But . . . ?"

"He might not." He gave a minimal shrug, which reminded me a lot of Gordy. "He could get over his scare and try something else. You shoulda scragged him. Or at least sent him onna vacation like you done others."

I had a reputation for persuading stubborn people to do very unlikely things, like suddenly running off to Havana. None was aware they'd been forcibly hypnotized. It was part of my edge. I used it to get out of troublesome situations, like earlier tonight with Kroun. But after that head-busting agony I wasn't about to try anything fancy so soon. Hoyle wasn't worth the pain. I'd broken the gun to keep from breaking him. Which I could have done all too easily. It's a frightening thing to find out what one is capable of when the restraints are gone. Hog Bristow taught me that.

"Keep an eye on Hoyle," I said. "See to it he leaves town and have someone keep tabs where he goes and what he does when he arrives. If you think he'll step out of line, I wanna know before he does. The same for his goons. You tell me, and we'll take it from there. If I'm not available, use your best judgment and take care of 'em yourself."

"Right, Boss."

"And don't get caught."

"Right, Boss."

It was just that easy to put a death sentence on people. God, what had they twisted me into? I wasn't supposed to be like this. I was a normal guy with parents in Cincinnati, friends, a girlfriend, my own business. I liked flashy clothes, reading dime magazines, and was trying to turn myself into a writer one of these nights. So what that I was also a vampire? Killing people wasn't part and parcel with the condition. Hell, I didn't even have to kill to eat, just drain a little blood from cattle that could spare it . . .

Bad line of thought, that. Head it off. Quick.

"Strome. What happened back at the club? How'd you know where to go?"

"One of 'em clobbered me from behind, only he didn't make a good job of it. Knocked me down but not out. I saw them toss you in the back of the truck, then some piled into a car with Hoyle and took off. Good thing it was Ruzzo driving the truck, too."

"Why's that?"

"They got into a fight over who'd drive. By the time they figured it out I was able to get up and into Gordy's car. Then I just followed."

"You did good, Strome. Thanks."

"No problem."

"Your head bad?"

"I'll live. How'd you get outta the truck?"

I stole the idea from him. "With Ruzzo driving? I just let myself out when we stopped. I kept low. They didn't see a thing."

Thankfully, he accepted it. He nodded. "Before all that, I was gonna say something to ya about Mitchell. That you should look out for him."

"Oh, yeah?"

"He didn't like what Kroun did. Letting you off."

Mitchell had been poker-faced and then some through the whole session. The only time he showed anything was when I refused to display my war wounds. Such as they weren't. "How could you tell?"

"Used to see him around. Here. Back when Slick Morelli ran the business."

I did my damnedest not to react. Morelli had been one of the bastards who helped murder me. "How far back was that?"

"Couple years. When Gordy took over, Mitchell left for New York. He didn't mind being third fiddle when Slick was in charge, but he wouldn't stand for being second fiddle to Gordy."

Strome was revealing new depths. I never thought the man was so musically inclined. "He was that high up? Third in line?"

"He was in there, but mostly in his own head."

"Was Mitchell ever up for Slick's job?"

"Not that I heard. There was a hell of a mess with Slick and Lebredo suddenly both gone, but Gordy stepped in and kept things smooth, and that's what the big bosses wanted. No waves. Mitch didn't like how it turned out, so he moved to greener pastures."

So there was a very good possibility that Mitchell remembered me from then, which might better explain his initial reaction. It wasn't my looking young, but that I was the same Fleming who'd been around when Slick Morelli and Lucky Lebredo killed each other.

That's how we made it *look*, anyway.

I didn't specifically remember Mitchell from my encounter with Morelli's gang. Aside from Gordy, who was too big to ignore, I hadn't paid much attention to the muscle. The most I could say now was that Mitchell probably hadn't been one of the guys who actually crowded me at the time, though he might have been on the fringes looking on.

"Gordy can tell you plenty on him," said Strome. "More than me. He knows the real dirt."

Gordy could have mentioned something when we'd been talking in the casino. On the other hand he hadn't been feeling so well. He couldn't think of everything, and when Mitchell arrived it'd been too late to give me a heads up. Then again, Gordy might have held back so my attention would be on Kroun, not his lieutenant and bad memories about my own murder.

"So I should keep an eye on Mitchell?"

"I was just sayin' he didn't like what happened up there. Don't see what diff it should make to him. It's just something to know."

"You talk like Gordy."

He took it as a big compliment, nodding. "Thanks. You worked it okay with Kroun. I didn't think you'd get out alive."

"Neither did I."

"Sure you did. You knew before going in you'd walk clear. I could tell. I thought you was wrong, but you knew."

"The power of positive thinking."

"Maybe. But you got Kroun on your side pretty fast. He's seen men hurt before. Looking at what Bristow did to you ain't gonna bring a guy like him out in hearts and flowers. How'd you do it?"

I gave a minimal shrug like I'd seen Gordy do a hundred times. "There was stuff going on under the talk. I could see Kroun didn't want me killed. That would create more problems he didn't want to bother with. He just needed a reasonable way out and took the one I offered."

"Who'da thought it?"

Me. Just now.

"Radio," I said, not wanting more questions. "Put it on."

"Got it."

Strome turned the knob and fiddled the tuning until I said stop when he found a comedy. We listened to the remaining ten minutes of Jack Benny. The stuff was funny enough that Strome actually smiled once. I thought his skin would buckle and crack under the strain.

I lay back, well out of range of the rearview mirror, and

shut my eyes against the growing brightness of Chicago. The jokes and puns and sound effects washed over me, and I didn't have to think about anything.

I couldn't sleep, of course, not until sunrise, and then it's a different kind of sleep, a shutdown of everything, dreamless, silent, too peaceful to last. I longed to be able to voluntarily conk myself out like that whenever I wanted, but the night wouldn't let me go.

The next program was longhair music, so I had Strome find a station with another comedy going. It was good to hear familiar tinny voices talking about ridiculous situations that had nothing to do with my own personal disasters. I was too isolated inside myself to be able to appreciate the humor just yet, but maybe in a couple weeks . . .

Or months. A couple years. Maybe never. But could I live with never?

My girlfriend, Bobbi, one of the reasons I was still more or less sane after Bristow's damage, would have something unsympathetic to say about that kind of thinking. She had plenty of caring for me, but no patience for self-pity. It was sometimes hard to know the difference between it and honest pain. I used Bobbi's probable response to my unspoken thoughts as a way of keeping the balance. Angst or honesty? Hell, she'd just tell me to flip a coin about it, then walk away from the result without looking.

Sensible gal, my Bobbi.

We were well into Chicago when the comedy ran out, replaced by a weather report. The announcer mentioned sleet, which roused me enough to look outside. Yeah, nice and wet and miserable, cold, but not to the point that the frozen rain glazed the streets yet. The stuff was smaller than rice grains, ticking gently against the windows, clinging for a moment, melting, sliding down, gone. This was a night to be inside next to a fire. I could arrange it, but couldn't trust that the thoughts keeping me company would be the warm and cozy kind.

I asked Strome to find another radio show. A broadcast of *The Shadow* was on, so we listened to it. I liked that guy. Life was simple for him. All his troubles could be solved by clouding a man's mind or shooting him—the kind of stuff I'd fallen into—but Lamont Cranston always made a fresh start with each episode. He didn't have to think about consequences to himself or others in between or carry them along all the time with him like a lead suitcase full of bricks.

We headed north a few blocks until I directed Strome to go east.

"You wanting Escott's place?" he asked.

My occasional partner's office was in the right area. Close enough. It didn't surprise me that Strome knew the location of the business. "Yeah, there."

The Caddy had special modifications to support the extra weight of the bulletproof windows and armor, but you could tell from the ride there was something different about the car, especially the heavy way it had of taking corners. That gave a nice feeling of security. Escott's Nash was similarly smartened up, but not to this degree. I'd have to take him for a ride in this one while the opportunity was available and watch his reaction.

Despite the fact the car was half tank, Strome took short cuts, moving quick enough for the evening traffic because of the powerful engine. It swilled gas and oil like a drunk guzzling cheap hooch, but daily stops at a filling station seemed an even trade for the smooth running and safety.

There seemed to be a lot of stop signals, and they were all against us. Being a man of careful, attention-avoiding habits

Strome didn't miss any of them or go over the speed limit. He braked in midblock before the stairs leading up to the Escott Agency.

This was where my friend ran a business that was a close cousin to private investigation, though Charles W. Escott insisted he was not a detective but a private agent. He sometimes referred to himself as a glorified errand runner, doing odd jobs for people who would rather not touch the chore themselves. The private-agent angle earned him a living, and I helped him out on cases when he needed it.

I got out, walking around to the driver's side. The sleet dotted my back.

"I'll be a while," I told Strome. "Doctor's appointment." Whether he believed that excuse or not didn't matter. The abuse I'd taken tonight certainly justified my going in for treatment.

"You want I should circle the block?"

All the parking spaces were filled by local residents. "Yeah. Do that. Take your time."

"Right, Boss."

"Just a sec—find a phone and call Lowrey. Gordy will want to know how things went with Kroun."

"He'll already know."

"Oh, yeah?"

"One of the boys will have told him by now. Maybe Kroun himself."

"That's fine, then."

"What about telling him about what Hoyle tried with you?"

"It's not important enough. Derner should know, then maybe tomorrow for Gordy. Let the man rest."

"Right, Boss."

Strome took himself away, bits of paper and stray leaves

kicking around in the departing Caddy's exhaust. Midnight was still in the future, but the street was wee-hours empty. The neighborhood was mostly small businesses, marginal manufacturing, and cheap flats. Few of the shops were open much past eight, except for an all-night drugstore in the next block and the nearby Stockyards.

Once the Caddy made its turn at the corner to head north again, I walked south, cutting over a couple streets until the lowing of cattle added a somber note to the night wind. Their accompanying stink made for a whole nasal symphony, though the freezing weather mitigated the worst of that. Breathing wasn't a habit for me, but I could still take in a potent whiff of concentrated wet barnyard when the motion of walking caused my lungs to pump all on their own.

I went invisible some distance from the first fence, floating purposefully forward and sieving through, holding on to the sweet and easy grayness until I was well inside. My corner teeth were out when I went solid again. After an anxious, dry-mouthed moment to find a likely animal, I ghosted into the holding pen. A last quick look to make sure I was unobserved, then I literally tore into my meal.

I couldn't feel much of the cold, but I was totally aware of the living heat swarming into me. The cow made a protesting sound but held still. Its blood pulsed fast and strong. Maybe I'd bitten too deeply; it could bleed to death afterward. That hardly mattered since it was headed shortly for slaughter anyway. I was just one more confusing, frightening incident in its horrific trip from pasture to plate.

Feeding doesn't take me long, even when I'm hungry, but I stretched it out. There seemed a boundless supply in that open vein, so I took more than I needed, filling up forgotten corners until it hurt.

Then I fed some more. Far more. Gulping it down.

Fed. Until it was an agony.

Fed. Until it was *past* agony.

And then beyond that.

When I finally broke off and reeled away I had to grab the fence to keep my feet. I held on like a drunk, head sagging, brain spinning, as the red stuff billowed through my guts at hurricane force. For a second I teetered close to vomiting, but the urge passed, and my belly gradually settled into sluggish acceptance of the awful glut.

I heard someone groaning nearby and snapped my head around to find him before realizing I was the guilty party. What a terrible sound it was, of pleasure and pain chasing each other in a tightening circle, neither one winning, neither one stopping, both leaving me exhausted and nerved up at the same time.

This, I told myself for the umpteenth time, was not good.

Down in a dark little cavity within, in a sad, chilly place I didn't like looking into but could never forget about, clanged the weary and terrifying alarm of what was happening.

The blood kept me alive.

And the blood was *killing* me.

4

NEON lights, streetlights, warm lights from house windows, cold lights hovering meekly in doorways, and no lights at all in some patches, Strome drove us past a myriad of such beacons of city life until we reached the fiery red diamond-shaped windows of Lady Crymsyn, my nightclub. As soon as we paused in front a man was there opening the car door for me. I stepped out, protected from a thin sleet by the entry's arched red canopy. I greeted the doorman, then bent for a last word to Strome.

"See how things are going with Hoyle and phone me. If I'm not in my office, ring the booth downstairs. I'll be here the rest of the night."

"You sure?"

"What d'you mean?"

"You don't look so good."

I didn't expect that. Not from him. "I'm fine."

Pushing away from the Caddy, I barely gave the doorman

time to do the other half of his job. He moved quick, though, ushering me inside, then came in after. Some places insisted on having a guy stand his whole shift out in the cold, but I didn't see the point. Just as many customers would go out as came in, and so long as he did his job he could decide for himself where he wanted to be.

Wilton was busy at the lobby bar setting drinks before a newly arrived foursome, and nodded a greeting my way. There was a concerned look on his face, too. He'd been getting ready to open when Strome came to take me away.

I tossed the greeting back and asked how things were going so Wilton would know I was none the worse.

"Slow, but a good crowd for the weather," he replied.

"Any sign of Myrna?" Myrna used to be a bartender here long before I bought the place. Now she was a ghost. I didn't have anything to do with causing that.

"Not yet." Wilton was the only guy here who didn't mind working the front by himself. He liked Myrna even if she did switch the bottles around. "Whoops—spoke too soon."

"What d'ya mean?"

He pulled out a bowl of book matches and put it on the bar. Instead of being in orderly rows, neatly folded to show red covers with the club's name in silver letters, they were all opened wide and tossed every which way.

"Guess she got bored," he said, looking bemused.

"Ask her if she won't put 'em back right again."

"If she likes 'em that way, who am I to argue?"

The hatcheck girl came to take my things, but I waved her off, heading for the stairs and my office. I'd left a stack of work there a few ice ages ago.

From the short, curving passage that led into the main room came Bobbi's clear strong voice. She was doing a better job with "The Touch of Your Lips" than Bing Crosby could ever hope for. I paused next to the easel display for her. It held a large black velvet rectangle where her name glittered from silver cutout letters, surrounded by four stunning pictures of her, none of them doing her justice.

A second, similar display proclaimed the dancing talents of Faustine Petrova and Roland Lambert with an art poster of two stylized dancers locked together. It was surrounded by a half dozen stark black-and-white photos of them frozen in action. Classy stuff.

The third easel had a single dramatic portrait of Teddy Parris, a young guy Bobbi had discovered when he delivered a singing telegram to her. His long face and soft eyes were better suited to comedy, but he'd gone for a serious expression and gotten away with it. Silver stars fanned out around his picture, filling up the blank space since he could only afford to have the one photo done. Along with his name was an additional description identifying him as "Chicago's greatest new singing sensation!"

Well, most advertising exaggerated one way or another. He was good, though, or Bobbi wouldn't have given him a break.

Bobbi finished her set for the moment. She would wait backstage while Teddy came out to earn his keep, then join him in a duet they'd worked up.

I wasn't sure how much to tell her about why I'd missed the first show. Certainly I would let her know what had happened with Kroun, the question was just how detailed to get and if I should mention Hoyle and Ruzzo. Lately I'd been doing too much that I wasn't proud of; she understood that the rough stuff was often a necessary evil, but she didn't need to hear about everything.

She would know, though. If even Strome noticed how bad I looked, then Bobbi would see red flags and hear sirens.

I plodded upstairs.

The office lights were on, as they usually were, since they didn't always stay switched off. Myrna liked to play with them. She used to make me uneasy, but no longer. I had other spooks to wrestle with, truly scary ones. Like what I'd done to myself at the Stockyards. My body still hurt from the excess.

For all the vanishing activity in dealing with Hoyle I had not grown hungry, having fed only the night before. But I'd given in to I didn't know what demon and gorged myself to the point of sickness. In the hurried walk from Escott's street to the Stockyards I'd not thought to stop, turn aside, or even consider that feeding like that might be a really bad idea. I did it without thinking, the same as Hoyle when he shot at me. At some past point he must have known that killing me would bring down Gordy's full wrath, and yet he'd done it anyway.

So what horror would drop on me if I didn't shape up and get control of myself?

What if it dropped on someone else instead of me? If I . . .

Inside, the excess blood seemed to churn, thick and heavy.

The radio would help. I wanted other voices besides the nagging ones in my head. Turning the set on, I shed my overcoat, tossing it and the crumpled hat on the long sofa.

Then I paced, impatient for the tubes to warm up, for distraction to intervene. My skin felt like it was on inside out.

An unfortunate picture to conjure, the kind that bunched my shoulders up around my ears. I tried forcing them down. But the thought of blood and pain and screaming and a sadist's laughter—

Don't start. No more of this . . . no more . . .

I told myself not to listen to the echoes, to ignore, to hold on a little longer, and above all, not to scream. There was no actual pain, but the memory of the agony was enough to shred reason and sheet my eyes with blinding tears. Then I doubled over, hugging myself tight against a wave of uncontrolled shivering. It clamped around me like a giant's fist, shaking, shaking.

This time I was not cold. Far from it. The blood in me was fever-hot, and there was too much of it. My body seemed bloated to the point of bursting. Crashing just short of the sofa, I lay helpless and praying for the fit to pass, unable to control my limbs twitching and thumping against the floor. As before in the Stockyards I heard an alien noise; this time it was the sad keening whimper of a suffering animal.

And as before it was me, myself, and I.

Gulping air I didn't need, I wheezed and puffed like a living man and labored through the worst as it slowly passed. At least I'd not given in to the urge to scream. Knowing that there were people downstairs who could hear and come running might have tipped things. I must not be too crazy then, not wanting them to see me like this. Crazy enough, though.

Scared, too. Scared sick.

The radio had warmed up, and dance music filled the room. I didn't know the name of the song, but seized on it, listening closely to the melody, following the rise and fall of the notes. The knots in my muscles eased, and eventually I was able to pull together enough to stand up again as though nothing had happened.

Then I swiped at my damp eyes and came away bloody. *Damn.*

In the washroom across the hall I scrubbed off the red evidence of my latest fit, convulsion, seizure—I didn't know what to call it. Once it had a name it might gain more power. The one I'd had earlier at the Nightcrawler had been far more mild, but this kind of bloodshed . . .

There was too much in me. My eyes might still be flushed from feeding; maybe that's what Strome had noticed. Too much, and it had simply seeped out under the strain.

I took care not to look at the empty mirror over the sink. Since my big change well over a year ago, I had grown mostly used to not reflecting. This avoidance was in case I did see something. Me. Like when I'd really been out of my mind that night when everything changed. I'd seen me smiling ruefully and shaking my head over myself. Not anything I wanted to repeat. Too creepy.

Back in the office I ran a damp hand through my hair, grimacing to take the starch out of my too-tight jaw.

"So . . . when's this gonna stop?" I'd asked the general air, which never offered an answer.

But the lamp on my big desk abruptly dimmed out and came on again. It flared brighter than it should have for the wattage, then settled into normal.

I untensed from my initial startlement. "Hello, Myrna."

Of course, someone downstairs might have been working the light panel for the stage, and the load on the circuits could account for what had just occurred, but I knew better. The club's ghost was here somewhere, as invisible to me as I was to others after going incorporeal. Maybe she'd seen the whole sorry show.

I read that ghosts tend to haunt the places where they died. Myrna's regular stamping ground was behind the lobby bar. About five years back when the place was under different, much wilder, management the poor girl caught some grenade shrapnel in the throat and bled to death. The floor tiles there had a dark stain marking the spot. It was pointless trying to replace them, the new ones stained up just the same. Even in death, Myrna still seemed to like tending bar, frequently shifting bottles around for a joke. She also liked Wilton, but lately she preferred hanging around me. Maybe she knew what I'd been through and was worried, like my other friends. But I didn't feel as though I had to put up a front for Myrna.

The lamp flickered, almost too fast and subtle to notice.

"I really look that bad, honey?"

Steady burning.

"Yeah. It stinks, don't it—doesn't it? Aw, hell. Look what they're doing to me. I'm talking like 'em even on my own time."

She was on the ball tonight for responding. Usually she wasn't so overtly active. I took a breath to say something more, then forgot what it was. A strong scent of roses was suddenly in the air. Instant distraction.

For a second I thought it might be Bobbi's favorite perfume; she favored something like it, but this was different in a way I couldn't pin down. It also made gooseflesh flare over me like I'd not felt since I was a kid listening to ghost stories by a campfire. There was a reason for that feeling, and she was right here with me.

Roses. A message from the dead. I'd said things stank; she fixed it.

I rubbed my arms, working out the tightness. Who could be afraid of roses?

"Trying to tell me something, sweetheart?"

Silence, steady lights, the smell of roses in a room with no flowers.

Silence . . . ? But I'd turned the radio on, had been listening to the music. The volume was all the way down now. When had that happened? I turned it up again, just enough to hear the chatter of a sales pitch for something I'd never buy.

Myrna was branching out. How far would that go? Hopefully she'd remain harmless. She'd always been a good egg, even helped me and Escott out of a jam once. I had nothing to worry about from Myrna. Myself was someone else again.

I stared without interest at the paper mess on the desk, the mechanical pencil for ledger entries right where I'd dropped it the night before. That stuff used to be important; Lady Crymsyn was my own business, a source of pleasure and pride. Now it all seemed so damned *futile*.

Pacing around once, I inspected the walls, then peered through the window blinds at the dark street below. Because of the thickness of the bulletproof glass, the world without had a sick green tint to it and was slightly warped. I had the feeling it would look like that to me no matter what window I might use, maybe with no windows at all.

Enough of that crap. I needed a change quick before I swamped myself in more of the same and brought on another paralyzing bout of bad memory. The radio wasn't enough.

Vanishing, I sank right into the floor. Not a particularly pleasant feeling; but it doesn't last, and I'd known worse. In a second or three I sensed myself clear of solid construction, flowing forward to and then through a wall. Though muffled, there was a change in the level of sound. Teddy Parris was singing. From the direction of his voice I was above him in the lighting grid over the stage. I went back to the wall again, following it until bumping into another wall, then eased straight down. It was just like swimming underwater with your eyes closed, and this pond was very familiar. I knew exactly how to get to my corner booth on the topmost tier of the main room.

But it was occupied, dammit. This seat was my usual spot to watch over things, and the staff always kept it reserved unless there was a really big crowd. No chance of that in midweek, so what was going on?

I brushed close to count how many. Just the one, but he was a paying customer and entitled. I guess. Nose out of joint, I'd just have to settle for the next booth over.

Then Charles Escott said, "Hello, Jack. Won't you sit down?"

The voice and precise British accent were unmistakable. If I'd had solidity, I might have snorted.

I lowered into the booth on the opposite side of the round table and slowly took on form. From the grayness emerged the soft light from the table's tiny lamp. Its glow fell on the lean features of my sometime partner in business, strife, and well-intentioned crime. Shadows lent a sardonic cast to his expression, but they didn't have to work too hard to bring it out. Escott's bony face and big beak of a nose were the kind that could easily shape themselves into a villainous look. Years back when he'd been on the stage in a Canadian repertory company, young as he'd been, he was always given the lead in *Richard III*. I'd have paid money to see that.

"How'd you know it was me and not Myrna?" I asked, once I could draw air again. It was fragrant from his pipe smoke. Cigarettes were his habit when on the move. Pipes were for his office or at home—unless he had a problem that needed to be thought through. Instead of the usual gin and tonic, there was a brandy in front of him. Must be one a hell of a problem.

"I didn't, but the odds favored you." Escott had developed a wary respect for Myrna. He'd annoyed her once, and she'd plunged the whole club into darkness, then the room got arctic cold, but only for him. After that he was always careful to be extra polite to her.

"She's in my office. Made my lamp flicker."

"I'd wondered where she'd gotten to," he said. "It's been quiet, no lights playing up. How are you?"

Of course I was ready to attach all kinds of meanings to the innocuous social inquiry. But if anyone had a right to be irrational . . . "I'm fine."

"Why the unseen arrival?"

"I didn't want to distract from Teddy's number." Nor did I want the whole room see me going up to my table. Some of the regular customers might follow and want to chat with the friendly owner, and I'd have to pretend to be cheerful. Not in the mood for that just now.

The place was much less than half-full, not bad for the middle of the week slump with sleet coming down, but il logically discouraging. It was the same as for any other club in town, and by Thursday things would pick up again. Come the weekend we'd be packed. Business wasn't on its last legs just because I'd not been at the front door as usual to greet people. Until a week ago I was always there, shaking hands, fixing my gaze on customers, and *telling* them they would have a good time, and so they did. But I couldn't trust myself yet to look happy and sincere, nor could I trust the hypnosis to so casual a use if it meant an instant killer migraine. Safer to keep a lid on it until I was in better shape.

A spotlight pinning him to the stage, Teddy sang smoothly through his number in good voice. I contrasted him with Alan Caine. Teddy didn't have Caine's onstage experience, but he sure beat him for offstage personality. Caine might draw in the patrons, but he wasn't worth the trouble. Gordy's outfit, being much larger and grander in scale than mine, could handle that kind of problem child.

"What happened earlier?" asked Escott. Though not on staff, he liked to come over and help out. Maybe it reminded him of his theater days. He'd been here since before opening tonight and must have seen my exit with Strome. "You've had adventures."

"What is it? My tie give it away?" I could feel it was on crooked.

"That and a few dozen other clues. Mr. Strome walking in and you two going missing for several hours led me to think that Dugan might have been found."

"No such luck."

While Teddy sang, I told Escott almost all of it, from the talk with Kroun to Hoyle's murder attempt, leaving out the falling-down nightmare of a headache, the Stockyard gorging, and its sequel in my office. He made no comment afterward, for by then Bobbi came shimmering onstage for the duet, and we watched her instead. She wore a glittery silver gown that clung tight till it reached her hips, then flared wide. She said it was perfect for dancing. Teddy took her hand, and they made a couple fast turns, enough to raise the hem daringly to her knees. Dandy view.

Seeing her, even at a distance, warmed me in a deep and gentle and basic way, like a flame on a cold night. She could make me forget, for a time, what it was like to be alone in the dark inside my head.

The band swung into the introduction for "The Way You

Look Tonight," getting a smattering of anticipatory applause that faded when the singing started. She and Teddy
sparked off each other in such a way that it seemed as
though they'd fallen in love for real and hadn't quite figured
it out yet. I knew better, but the audience ate it up. The applause came not only from the customers, but the waiters as
well. They adored her.

Instead of taking their bows, she and Teddy remained
onstage. For a second I wondered if anything had gone wrong
with Roland and Faustine's exhibition dancing. Bobbi leaned
toward the microphone and made an announcement, nam-
ing some couple celebrating their anniversary, so I eased
back in my seat. One of the stage crew swooped the spotlight around until it rested on the right party, and everyone
clapped. Bobbi and Teddy began a second duet, this time of
"The Anniversary Song." During an instrumental part
Teddy squired her around the stage in a very staid waltz,
looking so serious that it bordered on parody. The cele-
brants in the audience got teased from their chairs by
friends and took to the dance floor. Before the end, it was
filled with other sentimentally minded couples. In all, a
very successful moment.

Bobbi left the stage, and Teddy continued with another
of his love songs, which wasn't part of the regular program.

"Where's Roland and Faustine?" I asked. They'd arrived
at their usual time. I'd unlocked the door for them myself
before heading toward my office to work on the books. Then
Strome came in and . . .

"Backstage, I believe," said Escott. "There's nothing
amiss. They'll be waiting for the dancers to clear so they can
start."

Teddy and the band gave out another three minutes of
crooning, then ended with a big flourish, the lights coming

up. Everyone looked pleased as they wandered to their tables and put the waiters to work. The musicians changed their sheet music during the pause. Waiters circulated, snagging empty glasses, replacing them with fresh drinks. All normal. I eased back again. For someone who seemed to think his business was damned futile I was showing too much nervous concern. Escott certainly must have picked up on it, but made no remark. He finished his pipe and tapped the bowl into the thick glass ashtray between us.

"Well. About Hoyle," he said. "That's a remarkably nasty business. Very sudden."

"Nah, he's been building up to it. I just wasn't paying attention. You ever deal with him?"

"Rather less than you. Strome will be your best source of information on him, should you need it. Or Gordy."

Who was on the bench for the moment. "I won't bother him with this. My job is to hold the fort and try not to break anything. God, I can't believe he turned up there tonight. He looked like hell."

"He must have been worried for you."

"He's worrying *me*. If he'd just rest up like he's told he'd be back in a week."

"I think you should inform him of tonight's near calamity."

"It's covered."

"Hoyle and five others made a sincere effort to kill you. You may well be nearly bulletproof, but it would be unwise to so lightly shrug off such an assault."

"I'm not. Hoyle's been seriously discouraged. He'll be too busy licking his wounds tonight to do anything else. If he's stupid and hangs around town, I'll have him brought in for a more severe talk to keep him out of trouble. I'll send him on a long vacation, maybe his whole crew."

"Havana again?"

"I don't feel that kindly." I quirked my mouth, remembering some of the words to "Minnie the Moocher." "What do you think of Sweden? Some place really cold so he can cool off."

"There's always the lake," he said casually. "Very cold down there."

Every once in a while Escott scared me. It wasn't a joke. He had a dark streak in him and definite opinions on what to do with troublemakers. But maybe there was more going on here. Maybe he wanted to see how I'd react. "I just want the guy away. When Gordy's back he can deal with this kind of bother. He's good at it. I'll turn the whole mess over to him and forget about it."

"One may hope for as much."

"What do you mean by that?"

"It's come to my attention through Bobbi that Gordy's lady friend is urging him to find another type of business."

If Gordy left, my temporary position could become permanent. My still very full belly tensed at that horror. I made myself ease down. Adelle Taylor had a lot of influence over Gordy, but not in certain areas. "Gordy won't leave. This kind of work is what he's all about."

Escott made a noncommittal grunt and sipped his brandy. "I wish you good luck then. None of this can be too terribly easy for you."

"Actually, it is. Derner does all the day-to-day stuff and keeps the Nightcrawler running smooth, Strome sees to the rest. Mostly I'm a convenient figurehead—or target—and now I've got Kroun's approval. Sort of. It would have been fine if Hoyle hadn't put his foot in. There won't be a repeat with him, but others might want to try."

"Hm." He managed to put a lot of meaning into that.

"You think I should have killed him to discourage future challenges."

"It's the way their world spins 'round. Do you see Gordy as some sort of gangland Robin Hood? That he never killed anyone to keep his position secure?"

"Of course not. I know the score with him. But there's guys out there lots worse than Gordy. You and I've both met 'em."

And I let it hang in the air. That was one Escott couldn't dispute.

The lights faded, and the general conversation noise died down. The band started in on a low, dramatic fanfare, growing louder as the darkness increased. The drums and horns came in strong like a thunderstorm. For a few seconds the whole place went pitch-black, then *wham*, a spotlight picked out Roland and Faustine magically on the dance floor, still as statues, poised for their first step. Their timing was perfect as the music launched into a sultry tango, carrying them along. At first it seemed too dated, until the rhythm shifted to swing, but they went on with the South-American-style dancing, holding eye to eye, body to body and generally steaming up the place.

It shouldn't have worked, but it did. More than half the heat came from their own kind of electricity. They were recently married, and passions were high, but they'd already crashed into some rocks, one of them right here at the club. Roland loved Faustine, but had a hard time keeping his pants buttoned around other women, like Adelle Taylor. She was his ex-wife from a decade back. From what I'd heard through the walls of their impromptu backstage reunion, the renewed attraction was very mutual. But since Adelle was with Gordy, it was just a bad idea from every angle for her ever to be alone with Roland again.

Not wanting a future problem—like him ending up with broken legs—I'd had a talk with him, so he was behaving himself, and apparently Faustine was slowly and cautiously forgiving him. As long as they kept the fights away from the customers and did their act without any hitch, I was satisfied.

Then the music shifted to a darker, more intense mood, and the white spot flared red. Faustine's white gown took on that color, her skin, too; she looked like a diabolic temptress. Roland's black tuxedo blended with the background shadows and his white shirtfront, cuffs, and gloves also went blood red. It was a new addition in their routine, and the effect raised a collective gasp from the audience.

Faustine broke away from her partner and did graceful ballet-style spins, then he stepped in to support her through other classically inspired moves, finally lifting her high. Stretching her arms, she arched her back so much it looked close to breaking, but held firm as he carried her around, making it seem effortless before bringing her to earth again. The crowd was enthusiastically approving with their applause.

"So that's what they've been rehearsing," Escott muttered. "Bobbi said it would be a showstopper."

"Yeah, it's great." My voice didn't sound right to me. Too tight. Too fast.

Not again. Please . . .

"What's—" He turned.

Ham-fisted, I tried to switch off the little lamp and succeeded in knocking it over. The bulb shattered with a hollow pop, like a very small gun going off. It made me flinch.

"Jack . . . ?"

"Minute." I'd not wanted him or anyone else to see me doubling over. I resisted the urge to hug myself, holding tight to the edge of the table, fighting a flash of nausea and an involuntary shudder. Escott's eyes must have been used to the thick shadows. He watched with apprehensive concern as the fit peaked and finally passed. Thank God he was being sensible and not going agitated on me. I had enough of that on my own.

This seizure wasn't as bad as the last, but bad enough. I wanted to shrink away into a small hole.

"All right now?" he asked after a moment.

"No, goddammit." If I was alive in the normal sense, I'd have been panting like a dog. As it was, I barely drew in enough air for speech, so my reply came out a lot milder than I felt.

The lights on the dance floor rose a little, and Roland and Faustine enjoyed their extended bows, then broke apart to do the other half of their job. He picked out a lady from one of the closer tables and invited her to a fox-trot. Faustine simply stood in place and a couple of guys nearly broke their necks trying to be the first to get to her for a turn. The shorter and more nimble of the pair won, and she granted him the honor of her company. Within a minute the floor was half-full of other dancers.

Everything for everyone else was as normal as could be. I hung on by my fingernails and managed not to slip, convulsing, under the damn table.

Escott found the small switch for the broken lamp and made sure the juice was off. "I suppose this is an improvement over your pacing and the jumping up to stare out windows and not talking for hours on end. Any more left to go?"

"Donno. Just that red light caught me by surprise. It looked like . . . reminded me . . . you know."

"No need to go into it. Has this happened before?"

"No. Yes." Now why in hell had I said that aloud?

"Indeed?" He expected more information. Waited me out.

"W-when my guard's down. Or if I think too much. I don't dare relax."

"Understandable."

"Any blood around my eyes?"

He hesitated, probably working out why I'd asked, then said, "I can't really tell."

Just in case, I pulled out my handkerchief. It came away clean. Small favors. My hand trembled, though. Aftershocks from the earthquake. I stuffed the square of white silk back in my pocket.

"I knew a guy in the army," I said, staring at the dead lamp. "Shell shock. He just couldn't stop shaking. Any sudden noise would set him off even worse. It was hell during a thunderstorm. They had to dope him to the eyeballs with morphine to stop his screaming, and he'd lie there tied to his bed twitching like a fish."

"Well, you're not as badly off as that poor devil."

"Maybe. Guess this will take a while."

"More than just a couple of days, but you'll get through it. A bit more rest on your home earth—"

Had done me squat. "I should be through it now, Charles. It's finished. The bastard who worked me over is gone, he can't come at me again, it's never going to happen again . . ." But I got a flash in my mind of Hog Bristow's grinning face and his knife blade flashing, catching the light, and what came next, and another freezing wave churned my insides around so much I had to grip the table again, head bowed. "Oh, damn."

Almost as a physical effort I pushed the shuddering away, then dropped weakly back in the shadowed plush of the booth.

"Intellectually," Escott said, "you know the ordeal is over.

But your body and, certainly, your subconscious mind do not understand that yet. Your reactions are to do with survival instinct, the overwhelming need to escape. It tends to hang about long after the threat is gone. The symptoms *will* subside, given time."

"I want it to stop now. I'll be fine, then right outta the blue it hammers me flat. Am I really nuts or just being self-indulgent and looking for sympathy?"

"The latter? Certainly not. You're nuts." He said the so-American colloquialism with such matter-of-fact conviction I came that close to taking him seriously. Then I wanted to sock him one. Then I wanted to laugh.

"Maybe I'm just half-nuts. Should I see a head doctor about this?"

"The best thing for you would be a vacation. That's nearly the same as escape and might fool your internal watchdog. Go off someplace where it's quiet."

"Then I think too much."

"Don't we all." He made it a statement, not a question, giving me a sideways look. He'd been through his own version of hell and survived. "That's why they invented this marvelous stuff." He lifted his brandy snifter. "Have you tried mixing alcohol with your preferred beverage? You might begin with a really good vodka. It will likely not alter the taste, only thin things a bit, and there's the added advantage of no telltale smell on your breath—when you bother to breathe, that is."

I'd already tried that ploy. It hadn't worked. "You wanna turn me into a drunkard?"

"If it will help, yes, of course, certainly."

What threatened to be another shudder turned into a half-assed chuckle. Not much of it, but better than screaming.

He lounged in his end of the half-circle booth, failing to

keep a smug look in check. It was the first time in days he'd seen me give out with a smile. His pipe apparently finished, he tapped it empty in the ashtray and laid it aside to cool.

"I used to be a drunk," I said.

His smile faded. He'd been down that road, too, knew how rough it could be. I'd never before mentioned my own irregular trips. The new ground must have surprised him. "Indeed?"

"Back in New York, after Maureen disappeared. I could only manage to do it part-time. The newspaper job didn't pay enough to buy a lot of drinks, so I'd have to wait for my day off to get in one good binge a week. Now look at me: I got a bar full of booze, and it isn't doing me a damn bit of good."

"Quite ironic, that," he agreed. "But perhaps just as well. The consequences of too much of a good thing are not pleasant, and one tends to offend one's friends while under the influence. I had Shoe Coldfield around to bludgeon sense into me once he was sufficiently annoyed by my being a drunken fool. I doubt there's anyone about who could do the same favor for you."

"There's Barrett."

"True, but he's far off in his Long Island fastness, happy with his dear lady. You'd have to delve yourself into an incredibly deep crevasse to warrant my asking him to come all the way out here to bash you between the ears for the salvation of your soul and restoration of sanity."

"Donno. He'd probably enjoy it."

Jonathan Barrett and his reclusive girlfriend Emily were the only others like me that I knew of; we're a rare breed. He'd been the one who'd made Maureen, who, some decades later, made me before vanishing out of our lives forever. We'd both loved her. She was a sore spot between us, though that was gradually healing. Barrett had been around since before the Revolutionary War, giving him a longer perspective on life, and he wasn't above rubbing that in when he thought I needed reminding. Though our case with him was long over, I knew Escott kept in touch. Sometimes the mail would have an embossed envelope with Barrett's distinctive old-fashioned handwriting on it. The fancy calligraphy was always made by a modern fountain pen, though, not a quill. He wasn't the type to stand fixed in the past.

I should take a lesson from him on that. An idea glimmered in the back of my mind about running off and visiting him and Emily for a week or so. It faded pretty quick. Until Gordy was on his feet I was stuck in Chicago; besides, I couldn't leave Bobbi in the lurch to run Crymsyn by herself.

Escott righted the little lamp; shards of bulb glass dropped from its miniature shade. He used a napkin to sweep the pieces into the ashtray. "You will recover, Jack. Just not tonight."

"Tomorrow for sure, huh?"

"Of course."

It was one hell of a lie, but heartening. I wanted to get through the rest of the evening without any more shakes. Laughing *had* helped. The back alleys in my head knew that, which was why I had Strome tuning the car radio to comedies. Even when I couldn't summon the energy to laugh at the jokes, the desire was there. I wanted more. Unless I could pick up a second broadcast for the West Coast, it was past time to try finding other shows. The best stuff was usually on too early, since I was dead to the world until sunset. I wished there was a way of getting recordings of favorites so I could hear them later. Recording machines were pretty large and cost a fortune, but I did have space upstairs and money in the bank. It would be a legit business expense. Certainly Bobbi could find a use for it, maybe doing up sample records to send around to the local stations so they'd remember her name. The radio shows I wanted would use up a lot of record blanks, though, with only fifteen minutes for each side.

"And that's a lot of bucks to invest just so I can listen to *Fibber McGee and Molly.*"

Escott stared. "I beg your pardon?"

I realized he'd not been aboard my train of thought. "Nothing. I think I'm getting better."

"If you say so."

"You want another brandy? There should have been a waiter up here by now. We shorthanded?" I leaned forward for a look, but all the boys seemed to be at work.

"No, thank you. I told the fellow who tends this section that I did not want to be disturbed for the remainder of the evening unless I specifically signaled him. I had the idea that you might prefer some privacy once back from your errand with Strome. He was rather grim of visage when you two left."

"I didn't know that you'd seen us."

"Yes, I was just coming into the lobby as you went out front door, and it took a great deal of restraint on my part not to dash after to find out what was afoot."

"Why didn't you?"

"You actually appeared to be concerned about something. I wasn't about to step into the middle of that. It was time you showed signs of life. Whatever the crisis, I thought it could only do you good to get out and deal with it. Perhaps slamming a few heads together would wake you up a bit."

"You knew it'd be like that?"

"Given Strome's place in the organization, he would only

engage you in something really important, and given the nature of the organization itself, most crises tend to be of a violent nature. However, I would never have suspected Mr. Kroun's direct involvement. I understand he's rather high up in the ranks."

"You know anything about him? Just in case he's not sensible and tries to surprise me with a bullet."

Escott looked at his pipe as though considering another smoke. "But you hypnotized him."

"If he was really set on rubbing me out, he could start having second thoughts after a good sleep."

"Then you're the best judge of the chances. Weigh that against your perceptions of the man."

"Go with the gut, huh?"

"Yes."

I usually did, only lately I wasn't that trusting of my instincts. "I'm safe enough. I'm not too worried, just paranoid."

"Which is an excellent means for maintaining good health. As for Mr. Kroun, I am familiar with the name, which has occasionally appeared in the press. Even allowing for exaggeration, he is not a fellow one wishes to cross. There have been a number of New York mob deaths connected to him, but the links were so tenuous as to make prosecution impossible. By that we can infer he is clever at avoiding legal action and entirely capable of either ordering a murder or committing it himself."

"I can believe it. He knows how to get people to move without putting out much effort. To the right types he can be pretty intimidating. Had the damnedest eyes. Nightmare eyes."

"Didn't care for him?"

I shrugged. "Even Gordy said he was scary. I might think so, too, if I was still on that side of breathing, but I got him under control, and he agreed with me on the important stuff."

"You pique my interest. A man defined by such a word by a man like Gordy must be a rarity."

"I should hope so. We don't need more of 'em wandering around."

Down on the dance floor a new song started up, and this time a woman cut in to dance with Faustine, which startled her at first. She was gracious about it, though, and did her job. I wondered who would lead. Roland, with another lady, seemed amused. Would he have that grin if a man cut in on him for a turn? Show business was wonderfully educational.

"How'd you know I'd be here?" I asked, meaning this, my favorite booth.

"You may be in the throes of a difficult mending, but you are a man of habit. Sooner or later you'd show yourself in this haunted gallery. It struck me as the best place to waylay you for an account of your impromptu jaunt."

"Not my office?"

"No. You would logically go there first, but might not be in a receptive mood for talk. When you were ready to deal with people you'd emerge."

"Optimist. You hung around here all evening instead of going to see Vivian?"

"She's busy. A bridge gathering for one of her charity organizations. In between play they plot out fund-raising strategies."

"She's finally going out again?"

"It's at her home. She's not up to venturing forth just yet."

Vivian Gladwell had been his most recent client. During the two weeks when he helped her get through the kidnapping and recovery of her daughter they'd grown very close indeed. A rich society widow and a gumshoe calling himself a private agent—I'd seen worse mismatches going up the aisle and thriving. Besides, it was about time he settled down. Maybe he could sell me his house. I roomed in his basement and was kind of used to the place.

"A hen party," he said, staring down at the dancers, perhaps watching Faustine and her partner.

"Huh?"

"Vivian's bridge night. Ladies only. Otherwise, I might be there. It's important to her, her first social occasion since the notoriety of the kidnapping. She's been a bit nervous about it, hoping her friends will have ignored the yellow press headlines and turn up as usual."

"What's this? You feeling left out?"

"There's no room for me in what promises to be a gossipy gaggle of hats, gowns, cucumber sandwiches, and tea."

This didn't sound good. If I read him right, Escott was actually moping. "Tell you what. Ask Vivian out this Saturday. Bring her here. We'll give her a red-carpet good time. Find out her favorite songs, and I'll ask Bobbi and Teddy to sing 'em all."

"I could never persuade her to leave Sarah home alone. The poor child's still not over her ordeal."

I could fully sympathize and then some. Sarah was the daughter who'd been kidnapped. Sweet sixteen in body, only around nine or ten in mind and would remain that way for life. She'd survived the wringer, though, which made her a tough cookie in my book.

"Bring Sarah," I said. "After all they've been through I bet they could do with a night out."

"But the reporters . . ."

"Haven't come by as much, have they?" The kidnap case

had been pretty sensational, but now it was the day before yesterday's news.

"Only a few of the more stubborn ones."

"I can shoo them else-place and no problem. What d'ya say? It'd help me, too. Get my mind off myself."

"Very well. But . . . I'll put it to Vivian as being your own special invitation."

"Why? Is she cooling off with you?"

"If I've interpreted that correctly, then I don't think so, but a nightclub like this is well outside their routine. The idea wants getting used to for them."

"You worry too much. They'll have a good time. I'll even have a birthday cake for Sarah."

"It won't be her birthday."

"What kid's gonna turn down a surprise party where she can make a wish and blow out candles? We'll have funny hats and horns and give her a rhinestone crown."

"Let's not overdo things." He looked alarmed.

"Okay, but at least cake and ice cream and a few balloons. We deserve a little celebration."

"Well . . . all right. Thank you." Under the reticence he seemed pleased.

I actually felt normal, even cheerful, for having a purpose in life again. One that didn't involve mayhem and killing. It lasted nearly a whole minute.

The layout of the club's main room was such that from most any point in the horseshoe-shaped tiers of tables, you could see the entry and thus anyone coming in. That's how I spotted Evie, the little dancer who was so inexplicably sweet on Alan Caine. One of the waiters came up to guide her to a table, but she started talking to him, looking upset even at this distance. She still wore her overcoat, gloves, and hat, and carried a big purse. Under all that I glimpsed spangles on her stockings and the flashy shoes she wore for her dance routine with Alan Caine.

"Now what?" I asked.

Escott followed my look. "Trouble?"

"I hope not. She's the chorus girl I told you about. The one that Hoyle was going to use for a football."

"Hm. Then it's likely trouble, else she'd be at the Nightcrawler doing her show. Let's hope he didn't return to finish what you interrupted."

"She seems to be okay."

The waiter gave in to whatever Evie wanted, leading her up the long, carpeted stairs. He couldn't have known I was here and must have decided to turn the problem over to Escott.

Who must have got that, too. "For what we are about to receive . . ." Escott muttered out the side of his mouth.

"May we be truly thankful," I also muttered, completing the blasphemous old battle prayer.

5

THE waiter reached the booth. "Uh, Mr. Escott, this lady wants to see—oh." He spotted me. "Didn't know you were here, Mr. Fleming."

Escott and I stood as the little lady trotted up the last steps.

Her big-eyed gaze fell on me. "Jack Fleming?"

"Yeah. Something wrong?" I signed for the waiter to retreat.

She waited until he was out of earshot, then nodded vigorously.

"What?"

"They're going to kill Alan Caine," she blurted in her Betty Boop voice. Apparently it wasn't an affectation after all.

"Who?"

"Those men."

"What, they're back?"

"Not yet, but they will be. His life is in danger!"

"As in later tonight, but not just this minute?"

"Please, this isn't a joke! He needs help!"

Escott cleared his throat, giving me a look, the kind with a raised eyebrow in it.

"Just checking the urgency of the situation," I told him, then turned back to her. "You're Evie . . . ah . . . ?"

"Montana. I'm Evie Montana, just like the state, it's my name."

"Charles Escott," he volunteered, taking her hand and adding in one of his polite little bows.

"Pleased, I'm sure," she said, cute as a Kewpie doll.

"If the emergency is not immediate, perhaps you will sit and tell us all about it," he suggested, motioning her into the booth.

She cocked her head. "You're English, aren't you, just like in England?"

"Once upon a time. Please . . . ?"

She took the hint and slipped in. Released from our gentlemanly duty, we sat opposite her. I leaned back in the middle of the half circle; Escott clasped his hands on the table in his best listening posture. "What is the problem, Miss Montana?"

"Well, Alan Caine is just the greatest singer ever, better than Caruso even, and he's just really too artistic and innocent and people take advantage of him and he gets into jams and he's in a jam now and these guys are gonna kill him if he doesn't pay what he owes and they really mean business."

"I see," he said. "And who are they exactly?"

"They're muscle for the Nightcrawler Club. They got gambling there and these cardsharps took advantage of Alan and he ran up a marker and they're gonna kill him if he doesn't pay off."

"The cardsharps?"

"No, the *muscle*. They want him to pay the club."

"So the money he owes is to the Nightcrawler, not Hoyle?" I asked.

"Who's Hoyle?" She turned her big eyes on me, blinking.

"That guy you jumped on earlier tonight."

"He's the *muscle* trying to collect the *marker*," she said, as though I should know already. "They got dozens of guys just like him, and they're all gonna kill Alan tonight if he doesn't pay off."

"I get that. You're sure he doesn't owe personally to Hoyle?"

"He owes the *club* and that goon is their *muscle* and—"

"Okay-okay. I get that, too. So why'd you come to me?"

"Because you helped us earlier and because some of the other girls said you were all right because you dated one of the singers there once and they said you were all right because she was all right."

"Not because you think I'm running things?"

"You're running things? What things? They said *this* was your club. If you're running things at the Nightcrawler . . ." She started to get up, but Escott caught her hand.

"It's all right," he assured. "I'm sure Mr. Fleming can sort this out for you."

I said, "Shouldn't be a problem. If he owes money, he has to pay the marker, but no one's going to kill him for it."

"But that big goon was *hitting* him!"

"The big goon won't be back. I'll make a call and put in the fix for you. If Caine's dead, he can't pay off his marker, so he's safe enough."

"It's not just them, it's that witch of an ex-wife, too. She keeps calling him and threatening him and it gets him all upset and then he goes into the casino to try to win what he owes her and then they take advantage of him and then—" Her voice rose shrill, threatening to compete with the band.

I put my hand up like a traffic cop. "Slow down, Evie."

She stopped altogether, looking like I'd just slapped her. She made a peculiar *sup-sup* noise, then her face suddenly screwed up. She plowed blindly in her handbag and pulled out a handkerchief just in time for the waterworks.

Escott was better at holding hands and saying "there-there" than I was, so I gritted my teeth and sat out the next few minutes until he got her calmed. Sympathy came easier to him; he'd never met Alan Caine.

"Don't you believe me?" she asked. "He's in real *danger*. I thought you might help. I thought you could make them leave him alone."

"I said I'd fix it."

"But I *heard* them and they were saying awful things about him and they got no right to do that. They're all just so *mean*."

Likely they were blowing off steam about Caine and his singular lack of personal charm. "I'll make a call and take care of it. Caine will be fine, just keep him sober and—"

"Oh, but he *never* drinks! He just gargles with a little brandy and hot water to keep his vocal cords loose."

From what he'd been breathing on me earlier tonight he kept them loose enough to flap on a windless day.

"It prevents colds, too," she brightly added.

"Aren't you supposed to be dancing in the show?"

"This was more *important*, because he doesn't know just how much danger he's in, and I could lose my job, but I thought you could help him because . . ."

After repeating everything in full she eventually ran down. No wonder Caine drank.

"I'll take care of it," I said. "You can go back to the club and don't worry about anything."

"You will? You really, really *will?*"

Escott stood so I could get out. "Baby-sit?" I muttered.

He gave a good-sport smile and nodded.

I made my way down, going to my office in the usual manner, no vanishing. A few regulars noticed and waved, inviting me over to their various tables. I smiled automatically, mimed a mock-helpless shrug to show I was busy, and moved on. Given a choice I would rather go with Strome to face Kroun down again than pretend to be jovial to the customers.

A quick call to the Nightcrawler's office soon put me in touch with Derner.

"Back at the desk again?" I asked him.

"Pretty much. Anything wrong?" Derner was a man who expected phone calls to have trouble on the other end of the line.

I ascertained that Evie Montana had the basic facts correct and got how much Alan Caine owed the club. It was a lot, but nothing he couldn't afford on what they had to be paying him. I found out how much that was, too.

"Okay, ban him from the casino and let him know what he owes is coming out of his wages."

Derner laughed once. "He ain't gonna like that much."

"Tell him it's pay up this way or get another working-over."

"He won't like that much, either, but I'll make him listen."

"Who booked him in, anyway?"

"His agency. They never mentioned he was walking sandpaper, though. He's outta New York like Kroun."

"They hooked up in some way?"

"You kiddin'? Kroun wouldn't stand for that kinda crap. By the way, congrats on getting out alive."

"Thanks. Where's Kroun now?"

"He left not long back, with Strome driving. Gordy said treat him good, so he gets the fancy car till he goes home."

Having Strome playing chauffeur was also a good way to keep tabs on Kroun. "When will that be?"

There was a shrug in Derner's tone. "Who knows. He's the big boss. Comes and goes, it's his business an' no one else's. He can't stay away from New York for too long, though. Has to be busy like the rest of us."

"Did Strome tell you about our run-in with Hoyle?"

"Yeah. Congrats on that, too. None of those guys has showed here."

"If they do, they're on the outs. Especially Hoyle and Ruzzo."

"No loss with that bunch."

"Did Gordy go home, I hope?"

"Yeah. He left after he got word you were still walking. Lowrey took him home."

"Great. If he calls tomorrow, fill him in on Hoyle, but don't bother him tonight."

"No problem."

If it would only continue to be so, I thought, hanging up. The mob's idea of no problems and mine were usually two different animals.

And it looked like a new one just strolled in my front door. As I came down the stairs a threesome in dark overcoats entered the lobby. One of the men removed his hat and ran a hand through iron gray hair with a distinctive streak of silver-white on the left side.

Ah, shit. Now what?

Whitey Kroun spotted me almost in the same instant and sketched a wave and smile. Mitchell and Strome were with him but in an odd way were almost invisible. Kroun seemed to fill the room as though he was the only one with a right to be there and telegraphed it clear to the corners. Some of the people lingering at the bar for the next show glanced up from conversations as if he'd called them by name.

I wiped off what must have been a "Hell, what are they doing here?" look and assumed my friendly host face, coming the rest of the way down the stairs.

"Good evening again, Mr. Kroun." I managed to sound sincerely welcoming, but there was something about the man that set the skin to rippling on the back of my neck.

Kroun took in the chrome-trimmed, black-and-white marble lobby, impressed. "Fleming," he said as a greeting. "You look like hell. How's the damage?"

"My doc says I'm still healing."

"And after just a couple hours. That's pretty good."

Had he heard about my fun and games with Hoyle? I couldn't tell from Strome's expression whether or not he'd mentioned the incident. Not that any of it mattered, but Kroun's curiosity reminded me that I was supposed to be walking wounded. I'd better act accordingly.

"Quite a place you got here," Kroun said, very approving.

"Thank you." It could be a mixed blessing when a guy in the mobs liked something of yours. They were in a position to take it from you. "May I offer you a table?"

"Sure."

The hatcheck girl hovered within view, but none of them handed over their coats. Maybe they wouldn't stay long, then. So far the lights held steady, indication that Myrna— if she was around—didn't see trouble ahead. She messed with them when she got upset about something.

Mitchell did a double take on the display easel for Bobbi, fairly gaping.

It hit me smack between the eyes that he'd remember her from when he worked for Morelli. I felt a cold twisting inside again. Bobbi did not need to stroll down memory lane to the bad old days without first getting a fair warning, but I didn't know how to tip her off without broadcasting it to these guys. Play it by ear and hope for the best, then.

I led the way through the short, curving passage to the main room and a second-tier table looked after by the most experienced waiter. He appeared out of nowhere, took orders, vanished, and returned with a trayful almost before my guests were settled in. He'd correctly read the discreet signal I'd given. There would be no check for this party.

Glancing up, I noticed Escott watching us with interest. He knew Strome and would identify Kroun easily enough. That white streak was hard to miss. But beyond that, Escott had a hell of a memory for names and faces, especially the ones in the mobs. I suspected there was more in his head about the Chicago wiseguys than the FBI files.

"Gentlemen," I said, "Excuse me a sec—club business." I withdrew as the waiter handed out glasses, and went up to the third tier, remembering to move slow and stiff.

"Anything afoot?" Escott asked.

"I don't think so. Kroun probably just wants to check me out some more. We're friends now, after all." I was starting to regret that suggestion.

"Did ya put in the fix for Alan?" asked Evie, anxious. "Did ya?"

"All done. So long as Caine pays his marker, no one gets hurt."

She let out a little squeal and jumped up to hug me, planting a kiss on my jawline, which was as high as she could reach without a footstool and me helping. "Thank you! Thank you!"

Well, this was nice, but attracting attention. I was supposed to be feeling tender around the middle and with difficulty gradually unpeeled her. "Glad to help, but maybe you should get back to the Nightcrawler while you still have a job there."

"I won't make it in time for the second show. The El doesn't run—"

"You certainly will," said Escott. "I'll give you a lift."

I almost raised an eyebrow, but didn't quite have the trick of it the way he did.

He still caught it, though. "Just being polite, old man," he said dryly.

That was good to hear. After Vivian, Evie didn't seem to be his type, though she was cute. He guided her downstairs, and I went back to take a seat at Kroun's table, him on my left, Strome on my right, Mitchell opposite. The band went on break just then, marking the end of the first show. Some of the patrons got up to leave, a few new ones trickled in to replace them, and the rest stayed put, which was good.

I looked around for Bobbi, but when performing she tended to stay backstage even when on break, seeing to God-knows-what details and her own costume changes. I wanted her busy with that tonight.

Kroun had finished his small whiskey, Mitchell was still working on his, and Strome sipped a short beer.

"*Quite* a place," repeated Kroun. "What's she pull for you?"

There is a certain level of business where such inquiries are not considered offensive. "Last night, sixty-three dollars."

That got me a stony look, then comprehension as he realized I was talking net, not gross. "I mean outside of the booze sales."

"That's it."

"He don't have tables, Mr. Kroun," Strome explained.

"No tables? What about slots?"

"Nope."

"That's crazy." He turned on me. "You could pull in a hundred times that a night in a back room. You got the space for it."

"I do," I agreed. "But Gordy's better at keeping track of those kind of earnings than me. I thought it'd be best for everyone just not to compete."

Kroun's eyes narrowed with additional understanding. "Smart operator."

I didn't correct his assumption that I wanted to avoid cutting into Gordy's profits. It sounded better than the real reason, a desire to avoid legal trouble. To guys like Kroun the law was only a minor nuisance, not a major threat. He'd think I was chicken, too, but there is also a certain level and kind of business where such an assessment of character can contribute to one's survival. I'd gotten along pretty well in the past when people underestimated me.

Mitchell nodded toward the entry where Escott and Evie had gone. "Wasn't that the little trick you got in a fight over at the Nightcrawler?"

"I just kept her out of harm's way is all." A change of subject would be good about now. I decided to play the card Strome had given me earlier. "You used to work here in town, didn't you, Mitchell?"

His eyes hardly gave a flicker. "A while ago, yeah."

"Why'd you leave?"

"The weather stinks."

"Stinks just as bad in New York."

"Oh, yeah? I never noticed."

Kroun made a snorting noise. "Mitchell likes to work easy and get paid well for it. He found that in New York."

"Why you interested?" Mitchell asked.

I was chancing a fall on my face, but thought the risk would pay off. "Because you remember me from before you left."

He hooked a small smile. "Guess I do."

Bingo.

"What do you remember?" asked Kroun.

Mitchell's smile edged close to contempt. "That Fleming was some kind of half-assed threadbare reporter sniffing around Slick Morelli's operation, looking into stuff he shouldn't. Next thing you know Fred Sanderson's dead, Georgie Reamer's in jail for it, then Morelli's dead, Lebredo's dead, Frank Paco's in the booby hatch, Gordy's in charge—and *this* guy who was in the middle of it comes up smelling like a rose."

Kroun held silent for a moment. "That's pretty interesting. What about it, Fleming?"

I shook my head. "I don't know nothing about any of it. I was looking for a newspaper job here and heard there was some war brewing between those guys. Checked into it, thinking I could land a sweet place with the *Trib* if I wrote a good piece on it. That's how I met Gordy, but he steered me out of the way before it went rough. When things settled down after the ruckus I did a couple of favors to help Gordy, and that's all. We been friends since."

"Must have been some kind of favors to be able to afford this kind of club."

"I earned the club on my own. I got lucky at the track and hauled in a pile of cash. Gordy helped me with finding a good location and getting set up with suppliers, but that's all. He's been a good friend and stand-up. I'm returning the favor by helping him out now."

"And you don't expect anything out of it?"

"I'm getting plenty: a nice quiet town to run my business. We can all use some of that."

Kroun murmured agreement. "Quiet is what we want. Things are always changing, though."

"Oh yeah?"

"You gotta expect change. It's the way things are. Lot of the guys thought it was the end of the world when we had Repeal—Bristow was one of 'em—but it was just temporary. There's still plenty of tax-free booze being delivered. We're keeping an eye open all the time for new stuff to do. As soon as they make a vice illegal, we find a way to get rich by supplying it."

"Yeah, but those government guys are getting smarter at stopping up the chinks."

"It won't last. There's always a way to get around the rules. Like right now. Couple guys I know practically got the FBI in their pocket, or J. Edgar Hoover, anyway. They think they own the world, but it won't last."

"Why, is he onto 'em?"

"Nothing like that. He can't sneeze without they give him the say-so, and they think it's great, but they're going to have problems soon. The guy's forty-two, has ulcers, and is crazy-obsessed about commies. If the Russians don't bump him, he'll do himself in chasing his own tail and trying to nab headlines about it. I don't give him more than another year at the job before he drops stone dead. *Then* I'll start to worry. That damn FDR will put in some stand-up guy who knows what he's doing and can keep his nose clean. When that happens we'll have to start running for cover."

"How do they have Hoover in their pocket?"

Kroun shook his head, amused. "You don't wanna know. The key to owning anyone is knowing what a man wants most and knowing what he most wants to keep hidden. A man with small wants who doesn't give a damn what people think of him is usually free. Of course, that guy is not generally in a position where we need to own him, but there's a few out there. They're the ones to look out for."

And what secrets do you want most hidden? I thought. God knows I didn't want people hearing about mine, especially the current ones that were eating holes in my brain like acid.

"That canary out front in the pictures," said Mitchell, whose mind was clearly on other things, "when does she sing?"

"You mean Miss Smythe?" I asked.

"That's the one. Bobbi."

I didn't like the way he said her name. "Later. The second show."

"We're old friends. I'd like to go back and say hello to her."

He got a long look from me, and I didn't blink.

"What?" he asked, coming up with a puzzled front like he wasn't getting my message. "She don't take visitors?"

"That's right."

"C'mon, she won't mind a friend."

I didn't like the way he said that, either. Oily and unpleasant, yet with the smile. I wanted to knock it from his mug along with his front teeth. On this, I knew I could absolutely trust my instincts. "She'll mind."

"You go ask her, give her my name. She'll tell you different." He waited.

I still wasn't blinking. And had gone corpse-quiet.

He chose to ignore it. "What's *your* problem?"

"Mitch," said Kroun, who watched the exchange. "Lay off. She's just a skirt. There's plenty more back on Broadway you can say hello to instead."

Mitchell seemed to verge on a reply, thought better of it, and subsided. There was a "We'll see about this later" glint in his eye for me, though. I wasn't worried. They'd be on their way back to New York soon, end of problem. Maybe I wouldn't have to burden Bobbi with this ghost from her past.

Strome, who'd been silent all this time, let out a soft sigh that only I heard. I interpreted it as relief. I got the impression he was worried I'd do something stupid. It had been close. My second choice after punching Mitchell's face to pulp would have been hypnosis, but that would have risked another skull-splitter for me. After talking with Escott I'd gotten the firm idea that this suddenly excessive head pain was also connected to Bristow's torture, and it seemed pretty sound. I could hope the symptoms would go away after a while, but for now was stuck without one of my edges.

On the other hand, this was my club with my rules running. I had a right to refuse service to anyone, which included allowing undesirable types to bother my girlfriend.

When I started paying attention again, I noticed Kroun studying me, his own face unreadable. "Another drink, Mr. Kroun?"

He made no reply, just looked around again at the people, the band, even the lights above. "Quite a place." he echoed his comment yet again. "I like the chairs."

"Chairs?" I hoped he wasn't trying to drive a point home, because I was missing it.

"Yes. These are really nice chairs. Some places never get that right, but when it comes down to it, you have to offer people a place to park themselves. Really *nice* chairs. Nice. Chairs."

Maybe he was drunk. Mine might not be the first

whiskey he'd had tonight. "Thanks. Took a lot of hard work to haul together."

Mitchell flashed an interesting expression. Made me think he thought his boss was being an idiot. It only lasted an instant.

"But all these chairs and no gaming tables," Kroun continued, unaware. "Seems like too much effort for no real payoff."

"It's plenty for me. I keep my vices simple."

"Like not drinking yourself?"

For social cover I had a glass of ice water in front of me, my usual, and all the waiters knew it. I'd not sipped any. "Well, you know how it is, the boss has gotta stay awake. You guys enjoy yourselves, though."

Mitchell smirked. "He wants to get us drunk like Gordy did with Bristow. Thinks we'll talk." His tone was meant to bait. Kroun would know what he was up to and be watching my reaction.

Strome shifted in place, anticipating trouble.

I pretended amusement and confided to Kroun, "That's a cute kid you got there. Lemme know when he's outta short pants, and I'll find him a job."

Mitchell didn't take it well. If his boss hadn't laughed, he might have tried a swing at me. He'd get just the one shot.

"Relax, Mitch, we're off the clock," said Kroun. "Let the man run his bar. We'll be going now."

"But we ain't seen the show," said Mitchell.

"So?"

Under Kroun's dark stare, he subsided again, dropping into silence like it was a foxhole.

Doing a good impersonation of civilized gentlemen, we

rose and strolled to the lobby. Kroun thanked me for my hospitality, and I walked them outside. We stood under the canopy while Strome went to get the Caddy. The sleet had stopped, but the streets were still wet, the wind bitter. For a moment it was eerily similar to the night of Gordy's shooting, and I couldn't help but look around, anticipating another hidden gunman.

"What is it?" Kroun asked, picking up on my nerves. His eyes were sharp. No sign of whiskey in them at all.

"Just feeling the cold."

He nodded, removing his hat to brush a hand through his hair. It seemed to be an unconscious gesture, always on the left side where that streak was. "Yeah, you'd think those bandages would keep you warmer."

He got a look from me. Was he playing games or just showing a weird sense of humor?

"Ease off on yourself, kid," he said sotto voce so Mitchell couldn't hear.

"What d'you mean?"

"I mean I know what kind of hell Bristow put you through."

"Oh, he skinned you alive, too?" I was jumpy enough to give him lip. Not smart. He just stared. Nothing hostile in it, but I wasn't about to ascribe anything like sympathy to the man. Guys like him were born without or had it burned from them early by life in general.

He leaned slightly, talking close to my ear. "I know what he was and what he could do."

"And you sent him."

"Yeah. I did that. It was supposed to be between him and Gordy alone, and somehow you got in the middle. But you survived. That makes you the stronger. Then you put Bristow exactly where he belongs."

"Yeah," I echoed. "I did that."

"So . . . ease off on yourself." He straightened and settled his hat firmly against the wind. "He was a bastard, but you beat him."

A pep talk from a killer? Some of it skated close to being almost apologetic. And how did he know about what was in my head?

On the other hand, he thought we were friends. Maybe this was how he was with them. He couldn't have had many the way he put my back hairs on high. I didn't get a chance to find out; Strome drove up, Kroun and Mitchell got in, doors slammed, and off they went.

Lady Crymsyn was officially closed for the night. Except for my Buick, the adjoining parking lot was empty, everyone gone home or off to unwind themselves at places that kept even later hours. The neon sign above the red street canopy was dark, but lights showed within. Of course, that didn't mean anything with Myrna in residence. Sometimes she'd have them blazing, including the neon; other nights she would only leave a small one on behind the lobby bar. She was the most consistent with it, wanting it lit nearly all the time.

I stood under the shadow of the canopy, not quite smoking a cigarette. My lungs refused to tolerate inhaling the stuff, so I puffed for something to do and watched the occasional car drive past. Chicago was too big to ever completely sleep. Someone was always up and around.

Humankind was roughly divided into daytime folk, night people, night owls, and the creeps of the deep night. Most of the latter, unless gainfully employed or with some other reasonable excuse for being out during the truly godforsaken hours, lived down to their name. If not for my job I could be counted as one of them—two jobs, to include the help I gave Escott when he needed it. Three, to include Gordy.

It was coming up on the beginning of the deep night. Lonely time for me since everyone was usually asleep. I was uncomfortable standing out here, not from the cold, but being by myself and out of range of some kind of distraction. No radio, no band playing loud, happy music, just the wind in my ears and the infrequent passing car. This was me testing the demons in my head; I was trying to get better at not thinking, not remembering.

By the time I finished my third smoke, Escott finally drove up, easing his big Nash right next to the front curb. It was a no-parking zone, but the doorman wasn't here to chase him off.

"You're in one piece," I observed brightly as he got out. "Congrats."

"Why should I not be?"

I shrugged. "This town."

"Where's Bobbi?"

"Upstairs counting receipts. You don't wanna disturb her."

"You're curious as to what transpired concerning Evie Montana."

"Well, yeah."

"A gentleman doesn't talk," he said, mock-lofty.

"Come on, you know what I mean."

"Inside, if you please. How can you not be cold?"

My overcoat was in the office. "Has to do with being dead, I guess. Sometimes I just don't feel it."

"I wonder why that is?"

"So we don't feel the chill of the grave after escaping it?"

"Possibly, but there may be some other reason for the peculiarity. After all, not every society buried their dead. The Romans were fond of cremation, and the ancients of my countrymen practiced open-air—well, I supposed you couldn't call it interment. Exterment? If there is such a word; I'll have to look it up. They left corpses in the open air until only bones were left, which would certainly have prevented any of your sort from returning from the dead." He drew breath to go on, but caught me looking at him. Just looking. "Ah. Well. Be that as it may . . ."

I opened the door for us, locked it behind, and felt better for it.

The deep-night world was shut outside and would require no more of my attention for a while. Escort unbuttoned his coat, dropping it and his Homburg hat on the marble-topped lobby bar, the whole time giving me one of his once-overs.

"What?" I asked.

"No holes in your clothing, no damage to the premises, and the lights are functioning. I take it your visit from Kroun ended amicably?"

"Yeah, but he gives me the creeps."

"Must be a novel experience for you."

I ignored that one. "Drink?"

"A very small brandy would be nice, thank you."

The liquor was locked up, but not for long. I couldn't find his favorite kind right away, though there was always a bottle on hand; it was a standing order. It finally turned up behind several similar-shaped bottles, the label facing the wall. Myrna must have been playing again, with him as the target.

The barstools were stacked to one side to be out of the way of the morning cleaners, so we went through to the main room. I forgot how dark it was to Escott until he bumped into a table that was slightly out of place. The insignificant amount of light coming from the small red windows above the third-tier booths was plenty for me. I turned on the little table lamp for him, reaching between a thicket of chair legs. The seats there had also been upended for the convenience of the morning's cleaning crew. I didn't care for the closed-up, dead look it gave to the club. Chairs were supposed to be sanely on the floor waiting for people to use them, not like this. I decisively moved two of them down for us, then the other two so I wouldn't get annoyed if I knocked elbows.

The place was very silent, very empty. A dust cloth was thrown over the piano, turning it into a large blocky ghost shape in the dimness. The stage gaped like an open mouth, needing to be filled with bright lights and people and music.

Listening hard for a moment I did hear music. Thin and distant.

"Something wrong?" asked Escott.

"The radio in my office is on."

"You can hear it?"

"Yeah."

"Your extranormal senses are quite amazing."

"Or I could just be crazy and hearing things."

"What song is playing?"

"Wayne King doing 'Mickey Mouse's Birthday Party.'"

"Ah. Then you are hearing things, and you are crazy. No one listens to that one anymore. It's all your imagination."

"Good, I'd rather be crazy than have it real. So? Evie Montana?"

He swirled brandy, letting it get used to the air. "I took her to the Nightcrawler. Since she chose to fill the drive with detailed and enthusiastic praise of Alan Caine's boundless talent, I was curious to see him and went in to catch the second show."

"And what'd you think?"

"That you met a completely different fellow."

"Huh?" I expected Escott to hate the guy on sight.

"He has an excellent voice, a commanding stage presence, and put across every song with an enlightened earnestness that was on a level with true genius.

"*Huh?*" I didn't want to hear this. "The guy's a jackass!"

"If so, then it's not when he's performing. He really should be singing opera, not wasting himself with popular songs in a club."

"What's with you? You gonna send him flowers next?"

He sipped the brandy, amused by my annoyance. "One can have an admiration for a performer's talent, if not for the performer himself. He's truly gifted."

"And a jackass."

"I'll believe that when I see it."

"Fine with me. Go by tomorrow before the show and watch him rehearsing."

"One only has to know how to deal with artistic temperament."

"Just don't go recommending him to Bobbi for this place. I'd end up strangling him."

"Or you could simply rearrange his mood for the duration."

I'd been known to do that with troublesome talents. Escott was unaware of my going temporarily on the wagon from whammy-work. No need for him to know, either. He'd just give me one of those worried looks I was sick of seeing.

"Mr. Derner came by my table. He had a message for you," he added.

"Oh, yeah?"

"A negative one. Some of the boys thought they'd found Dugan, but it turned out to be a false alarm. Not all of them were convinced, though, and might be coming 'round to claim the remainder of the bounty. Mr. Derner assured me he would take measures to prevent your being bothered by them."

I grunted and wished I could drink real booze again, even the cheap stuff, which was all I could afford back in my reporter days. "The guy they thought was Dugan—he okay?"

"So far as I know. He was dragged to the Nightcrawler, produced sufficient evidence to prove mistaken identity, was given a drink and an apology, and returned to wherever they found him."

"God, I'm gonna have to call it off. Those mugs are too stupid to be let loose."

"You don't think they'll find him, do you?"

"Dugan could be halfway to Hong Kong by now. I know I would be there if I had me after me."

Escott blinked a few times. "It's far too late for that to have made sense, and it did."

I glanced at my watch. The evening was getting into the deep-night hours. "Bobbi should be done with the receipts by now. I oughta get her home."

"Sounds to be an excellent idea for myself. That is, if you don't require me further?"

Escott really did like to help out at the club. "You've done above and beyond. Thanks."

He got up. "No problem."

His time in the States had corrupted him. He sounded just like Gordy.

In the lobby he boomed a loud good night toward the upstairs. Bobbi answered back, asking if I was around.

"Yes, he'll be up directly."

"Okay. Drive careful."

"Thank you, I will."

Theirs was a call and response thing like you hear in some church services. They'd done it several times now at closing, a comfortable form of reassurance. I hadn't been the only one left shaken by Bristow's work on me.

Escott let himself out using his own key. It would be a dark and chill ride home until his Nash warmed up again.

"Drive careful," I muttered, suddenly aware of the emptiness of the building. Were I here on my own, I'd have made like Myrna and turned on all the lights. Certainly I'd have gotten some music going to push back the silence. The stuff seeping thin through the walls from my office radio wasn't enough.

Thank you, Hog Bristow. Thank you so very much, you god-damned son of a bitch, and please, please do be screaming in a really deep, sulphur-stenched pit burning merrily away for the rest of eternity.

"Jack . . . ?" Bobbi's light voice jarred me.

"I'm here."

"Okay." She sounded like she was a few yards from the office door, ready to come down if invited.

"I'll be right up, honey, gotta make a phone call. Private." That was the word we used that meant I was busy with mob business. She knew it was a necessary task and to help Gordy, but preferred to ignore my moonlighting for the time being.

"Okay." Her tone was serene, almost singing, which meant I really should hurry. Her heels clacked down the hall, followed by the office door shutting.

I levered into the lobby phone booth, paid a nickel, and dialed very carefully so as not to wake up an honest citizen cursed with a number similar to Shoe Coldfield's nightclub.

To my growing concern it rang nine times before someone came on halfway through the tenth.

"Coldfield, what is it?" he growled. Since it was his office, not his home, I knew I'd not wakened him, but phones going off at such hours never portend happy news.

"It's Jack. Charles said to say hello." I hoped in this way to tip him that all was well.

Didn't work. "Damn, kid, no one calls this late unless it's an emergency. You okay?" He traded the rough annoyance for rough concern.

A few days ago Escott had informed him about my recent experience; apparently the basic facts had been augmented with a mention of my problems recovering. "I'm fine." I tried to sound normal, whatever that was.

"Charles told me you were, and I quote—'a touch wobbly'—and you know how he understates things."

"Ah, he was just being optimistic."

"Well, you didn't call just to pass on a hello. What's up?"

"One of the New York bosses came to town. The one who arranged Hog Bristow's visit. A guy named Whitey Kroun. Know him?"

"With a name like that? You kidding?"

Coldfield, in addition to running his nightclub, some garages, and a few other businesses, also controlled one of the biggest gangs in the Bronze Belt. Unless it was assigned to him as a joke, any man nicknamed Whitey would not readily blend into the crowd.

"I'll take that to mean no. What about a soldier called Mitchell? He was in Morelli's gang about the time I first came to town."

"Nope, sorry. You know the colored and white mobs don't mix except when they can't help it."

"Yeah, but you generally know who's who."

"Only the local big boys, not the soldiers."

"Okay, one more item. A collector here named Hoyle is on the outs with me along with Ruzzo."

"Those bedbug-crazy brothers?"

"The same. You know Hoyle?"

"By sight. Tough guy, used to box. What happened?"

"He tried to play baseball, with me as the ball. I took his bat away and nearly made him eat it."

He wanted more details, so I gave them. Coldfield liked a good story. As before with Escott, I left out the ugly epilogue in the Stockyards. Even thinking about it threatened to make me queasy.

"You've had a busy night, kid," he said. He knew my real age, but couldn't be blamed for forgetting most of the time. Now and then I would shoot him a reminder, like mentioning something from twenty years back when I was in the War, and he'd throw an odd look my way for a few seconds.

"You don't know the half of it," I said.

"About this Kroun, I can ask around if you want."

"Nah, not that important. Charles can dig. He thinks it's fun."

"Kroun's not giving you any trouble is he?"

"Nothing like that, just me being curious. I figure he'll be going back to New York soon."

"Better hope so. No one likes when the boss drops in to nose around. Just ask my people."

Coldfield did run a tight ship, but I'd not heard of anyone trying to kill him lately. I thanked him; he told me to get some rest and hung up.

I remained in the booth, wanting a moment of quiet. The vast emptiness of the club was easier to handle in here. I liked having a place where I could put my back to a wall.

It couldn't last. I had to boost out and go upstairs, or

Bobbi would come looking, and I'd have to assure her that my sitting shut into a phone booth without phoning was a perfectly reasonable occupation. Before my buckwheats session with Bristow she might have accepted it as absentminded eccentricity. No more.

But I *did* seem to be better. The meeting with Kroun had gone very well. After that inner revelation, seeing those who would kill me as being no more than food, I'd been in control with not one wild, trembling muscle to mar the event. Maybe that's all I'd really needed to restore my confidence. Sure, I was still nervous about some stuff—like now—but there were lots of people didn't like big empty, quiet, dark places.

So perhaps I should get off my duff and see my patient girlfriend. I'd been procrastinating with no good reason other than a vague and ridiculous trepidation that she would see all the stuff I wanted to keep hidden. Bobbi was closer to me and much more perceptive than anyone else I knew. She was the one person I couldn't lie to even when I successfully lied to myself.

Well, maybe she'd take a good look, and if she pronounced me miraculously cured of my waking nightmares, I could believe it.

I pushed the booth's folding doors open in time to hear a click, followed by several more, coming from the main room. A familiar sound, but out of place at this hour. Curious and cautious, I went through the curved passage.

All the little table lights were on. Spaced at regular intervals along the three wide horseshoe tiers, they made a grand sight even with the upside-down chairs, and I said as much out loud to Myrna.

"You're really getting good at that, babe," I added.

I half expected one or any of them to blink in reply, but

they remained steady. There was no point asking her to shut them off. She would or wouldn't at her own whim. Besides, I could likely afford the electric bill; business had been pretty decent this month.

"See you upstairs. Maybe." Actually, I hoped not. Some instinct within told me I was not ready to actually actually *see* Myrna. She was disturbing enough just playing with lights.

Billie Holiday's version of "No Regrets" met me coming up the stairs. Bobbi hummed along to the radio, but stopped as I opened the door. She was busy at my desk, surrounded by empty tills, piles of wrapped cash, rolls of coins, a small stack of checks, the entry books, pencils, and the calculating machine. She'd traded her fancy spangly dancing gown for a dark dress and had a blue sweater around her shoulders. Her blond hair was pinned up out of the way. She punched keys on the machine, pulling the lever like it was a squatty one-armed bandit. When its brief, important, chattering died, she peered at the printed result.

"Hi, stranger," she said, raising her face my way for a hello. She'd gotten a ride in with Escott while the sun was still up, so this was the first chance for us to really be with each other tonight.

I kissed her on the lips, and instantly knew it was right, the way it was supposed to be, the way it had always been for us; everything was going to be fine now.

Which lasted for a few perfect, wonderful seconds.

Then I overthought it, and what began as a warm greeting went subtly and utterly wrong. The demons in my head tore gleefully at me, whispering doubts, magnifying fears, and pointing out the obvious fact that this recovery business was an impossibility, so I pulled back and smiled and tried to pretend everything was great, and the smile was so forced that my jaw hurt, and I turned away so she couldn't see how much it hurt.

Damnation.

Whatever had been repaired and rebuilt in me came apart so fast I wondered if it had been a sham to start with or if the sickness inside was simply overwhelming in its strength.

I didn't want that.

Thankfully, Bobbi did not ask me if I was okay. We'd had that conversation several times already and kept butting into the walls of assurances, protests, and denials I put up, which she would knock down with a word or three, then neither of us felt happy. We'd accepted the fact that this would take a while, and it would not be pleasant. It wasn't her fault that she terrified me. I was ashamed of it. On the other hand, if I avoided her or went on that vacation Escott had suggested, I'd go right off the deep end of the dock. She was my lifeline. I had to keep close to her.

"Ready to go home?" I asked. Her hat, gloves, and fur coat were ready on the couch. I sat next to them.

"Almost." She gave me a long, unreadable look, then peered at the latest printing from the machine, writing a number neatly in the account book with my mechanical pencil. "We had a pretty good night, all things considered."

"Oh, yeah?"

"You made fifty-two bucks and some change."

I looked at the stack of cash before her. "You've got more than that there."

"Subtract your overhead, salaries, and all the rest, and you have fifty-two bucks left over."

"Less than last night's take."

"Cheer up, there's not many guys who make that much in a month, let alone on a single less-than-perfect evening.

It'll be better this weekend if the weather doesn't turn sleety again. What took you away? You were gone for so long."

"I had to talk with a gentleman from New York."

Bobbi understood the implications. "How did it go?"

"Good and bad. I'm still running things for Gordy."

"And what's the bad?"

"I called it right about why they sent Bristow. Kroun's on my side, now, so—"

"Whitey Kroun?"

"Yeah, the guy from the phone. You ever meet him?"

"No. Once in a while I'd hear Gordy mention him, but that's all. Just a name. I'll be glad when you're out of this, Jack."

"Same here." I took a deep breath and exhaled. I thought about asking if she remembered Mitchell, but held back. She didn't care to be reminded of the days when she'd been Slick Morelli's mistress. Gordy would be the best source for my idle curiosity when he was up to it.

Time for a subject change. "That was some nice act you had going with Teddy and the anniversary thing. It went over great."

"I thought it might. We'll make it a regular item if you clear it."

"It's cleared."

"I'll have to look up more wedding-type music or we're going to get really tired of 'The Anniversary Song.' "

"How about something from *The Merry Widow*? For the marriages that aren't going so well."

She rolled her eyes. "Don't be gruesome."

Some of our old comfortable banter had resurrected itself. All I had to do from now on was sit ten feet away from her. "I want to have something special ready for this Saturday, if it's not too short notice."

"Just no street parades, too cold. What is it?"

I told her about helping out Escott's suit with Vivian Gladwell by throwing a "birthday" party for Sarah. Bobbi was all for it.

"But don't go overboard," I cautioned. "You'll scare Charles."

"Don't worry. I've done enough singing at debutant balls to know what's right for that crowd. It'll be fun, but tasteful."

"You can tackle Charles tomorrow for details . . ."

The radio music died away, replaced by static as the station signed off. I reached for the dial.

"Wait a sec," she said, staring at it.

I withdrew my hand and waited, the static buzz making my eyeballs itch. "What?" I asked after a minute.

"Aw, I was hoping . . . I guess she won't do anything when people are watching."

"Myrna?"

"Yeah."

"What'd she do now?"

"I was working and some newsreader came on. I wasn't paying it much mind, and it switched to music right in the middle of a story. Gave me a turn until I realized she'd done it. I looked, and the pointer was on a different station than before. Isn't that something?"

"She didn't scare you?"

"Not really. She just surprised me. It must be boring for her to only play with the lights. Can't blame her for branching out. Maybe she's getting stronger the more we pay attention to her."

That disturbed me, but I kept it to myself, suspecting Myrna might cut the lights entirely in response. I didn't want dark.

Bobbi continued. "I like her company. The place doesn't feel so empty. Kind of friendly, you know? Like she's looking after us. So I talk to her. I think she likes it, must be lonesome, being a ghost."

"What do you talk about?"

She smirked. "You, of course. Women always end up talking to each other about their men sooner or later. Of course with Myrna I have to carry the conversation. Maybe we could get that record-cutting equipment up here and see if we can hear her talk back again."

"Maybe." I'd recently found it necessary to record a conversation and filled the office with hidden microphones. Much to my consternation a third voice, faint and strange, but definitely female, had also been on the wax disk, reacting to what was going on. Even thinking about attempting that once more made my neck hair rise. But . . . perhaps it could get a question or two answered, help us find out more about Myrna. "Wanna go home?"

Bobbi didn't think twice. "Yes. Please."

I put the cleaned-out tills on a table, ready for the next day while she scooped the counted cash into a bank envelope for the night deposit box. I put the change bags in the safe on top of the revolver I kept there, shut and locked, then helped Bobbi on with her coat.

As we started to leave, she swooped to one side and fiddled with the radio tuning until she found music.

"There," she said, as Tommy Dorsey's band came through. "I think this station plays all night. Myrna might end up with farm and weather reports in a couple hours, but it'll be company until then. You don't mind?"

"Nope. Leave the light on, too." I could sympathize all too well.

On the way out I checked the main room. The little table

lamps were dark now. We left the one burning behind the lobby bar alone.

Bobbi shivered and went *brrrrr* during the first ten minutes of our ride until the Buick's heater was warm enough to blow something other than arctic wind. I stopped briefly to drop the money into the bank's night deposit slot, then drove quickly through the near-empty streets to her hotel apartment. Drowsy, she leaned against me for the ride, and things felt normal again. I wanted to put my arm around her but had to have it free to change gears.

She woke up as I braked in the no-parking section in front of her building, got out, and came around to hold her door, leaving the motor running.

"Not coming up?" she asked.

"You're done in, honey, and I had a lot crashing into me tonight."

There must have been a dozen variations of protest hesitating on her lips, everything from "I could get untired in a hurry" to "That's all right, just let me know when you're ready, sweetheart," and she didn't say any of them, including the heartbreaking "Jack, I'm so sorry." It would have been too painful for both of us, so we accepted this nice, safe, not-quite-as-painful illusion.

I walked her through the hotel lobby to the elevator, and like well-rehearsed actors we said the familiar good-bye-until-tomorrow lines. They sounded hollow and sad compared to the cheerful call and response she'd traded with Escott earlier.

She broke, though, and stopped the automatic elevator doors from closing. "You're sure? Just for company?"

"The company is a rare and breathtaking creature of light and music and beauty who would make angels jealous, and I don't know what I did to deserve to be on the same planet with you."

She fairly gaped. I hardly ever talked like that to her.

"But—" I kissed her chastely on the forehead and left it at that.

Her hazel eyes were wide a moment, then she made a little dive at me, wrapping her arms tight around. We held close for a solid minute, and I felt my body responding to hers, felt the rush of warmth, the first build of pressure above my corner teeth, the desire to slowly remove all her clothes and settle in and come up with old and new ways of exhausting her and myself thoroughly before dawn swept my consciousness into its shallow grave.

Resisting while I still could, I gently pulled clear. "Get some sleep," I said softly, backing off. I turned away before seeing whatever look might have been on her face.

The doors knitted shut and took her up and away from me. I hurried to the car, hit the gears rough, and shot clear, taking corners too fast and abusing the gas pedal on the straights. Before I alarmed any cops, I found a space in front of a block of closed shops and pulled in, decisively cutting the motor.

Then I waited.

I'd *wanted* to go up with her, and not just for company. Still wanted. Ached for it. Was sick for it. Wanted to go back even now and surprise her, make love to her. I would hold her close and warm and bring her to the edge of that wonderful, feverish peak and oh-so-gently bite into her throat, and it would just *happen* and she wouldn't fight me, wouldn't even think to, and then it would be too late, and like a mindless, greedy animal I would gorge on her blood as I'd done on that cow, unable to stop . . .

The tremors began their fast rise from within, an icy tide come to drown me. I hugged my ribs and groaned like a dying thing and keeled over across the seat.

6

FULLY clothed, still in my overcoat, I lay flat on the army cot in my pseudotomb in Escott's cellar, waiting for the dawn.

It's really better than it sounds.

I had heat and light—always leaving the lamp on since I hate waking up in the dark—and it was profoundly quiet. My bricked-up alcove wasn't the overwhelming large space of the club, nor so cramped that I'd get claustrophobic, and I could put my back to a wall.

For now my spine was stretched tense on this cot, and between it and the canvas, protected by a layer of oilcloth, was a sufficient supply of my home earth to keep the daymares away. Without that piece of the grave with me I would spend the sunny hours being consumed by an endless pageant of inner horrors.

As though the ones I experienced while awake weren't enough. In the car I managed to cut short my latest bout into hell. I'd felt a scream beginning to rise, and before it went full force I denied it breath and a voice box by vanishing.

The awful cold shuddering melted into soothing grayness, and I let myself float like that for a very long time. To vanish meant to physically heal, and I'd hoped it would work again, with a different kind of healing. One for my soul.

But no such luck. I returned to solidity weak and drained and shivering.

And helpless and terrified, don't forget about those. My body and mind had both turned on me, and there wasn't a damned thing I could do about their betrayal.

I'd been so tired afterward I could not recall driving home, only coming back to myself while parked out front in my usual spot. While other guys could drop into bed and shut off their minds after something like that, there would be no sleep for me. Until the rising sun finally knocked me out I was in for a bout of Undead insomnia.

What I missed about being a normal man was the kind of sleep where you know that you *are* sleeping. When you drift through it, maybe skimming close to the surface of waking, then contentedly turning over to dive back in again. You have a sense of passing time, that you're getting actual *rest*. My daylight drop into death left me very rested, but it's not always satisfying.

Like now. I was still terrified, which would be exhausting to anyone, and the fear would be there when I woke again.

I lay on the cot. Waiting. Sensing the approach of the sun that would take my life away. Some part of me wanted utter oblivion, the kind from which you never awoke.

That would solve a whole lot of problems for me. All of them, in fact.

Out.

And return.

I'd felt it come and shut my eyes in time. They were open now. Another day had rushed over my unheeding head. The only way I could tell for sure was to glance at my watch. Yes, lots of hours were gone for good, with me not in any of them. Winding the watch, I made myself remember that the trembling fits were last night's old news. Hadn't Escott told me time would fix things? Time had passed, so I shut down the internal whining, then vanished and floated, rising through the floor to go solid in the dim, quiet kitchen. My hat was where I'd left it on the table so Escott would know I'd come home.

Damn, but I still felt cold despite the overcoat. "Charles?"

No reply, so he was probably already at the club. He was being a hell of a friend to look after his work and mine. I'd have to find some way to thank him. Bobbi would know what to recommend, besides putting him on the payroll. He was going to have a surprise pay packet come Friday. His own business might be suffering for all the time he'd been putting in helping with mine. He would help for free, but compensation was only being fair.

I went to bring in the mail, but the stack on the hall table told me Escott had been and gone. There was nothing for me, which was fine. I wasn't up to writing chatty correspondence.

Back in the kitchen, I phoned the Nightcrawler office and got Derner. "How'd things go today?"

"Pretty much normal, no problems."

"What about Kroun? He gone home yet?"

"Still in place."

The phrasing gave me the idea Kroun or Mitchell might be in the room with him. "You treating him right?"

"Red carpet all the way."

That was reassuring. "What about Hoyle? Any trouble?"

"Haven't heard from him. If he's gone, I donno where."

"Find out. Keep it low and easy." I wouldn't feel comfortable until I knew where he'd landed. "What about Ruzzo? They behaving?"

"They turned up looking like they had a gas attack to go with their shiners. One of the boys thought they were trying to find Hoyle, but not for sure. They know they're on the outs, but you want I should fire them, too? The hard way?"

That meant something fatal. Execution was the normal mob response for what Hoyle tried to do to me. "That'll be up to Gordy when he's back." He'd probably get rid of them, but I couldn't be bumping off all the guys in his gang who didn't like me. There wouldn't be a lot left.

I hung up and went to my second-floor room for a fast shower-bath and a change of clothes. Usually I preferred to sit and soak in a near-boiling tub, but didn't have the time. Too bad, it might have warmed me up. A hurried soaping with the water slopping past the cellophane curtain would have to do.

Shaving, as always, was a touch-and-nick adventure. I'd switched from a straight to a safety razor in the army, same as all the other guys, and once more blessed that change. If I still used the folding cut-throat device my older brothers had introduced me to, I'd probably have lopped my head off by now. Still, I made mistakes, but a quick vanishing fixed that.

What it did not fix were the long threads of scarring that covered what I could see of my chest and arms and certainly my back. I tried to avoid touching them; the white ridges along already pale skin always felt colder than the rest of my flesh. Those scars collected in my lifetime before my change had gradually gone away, even the one from the bullet that had killed me. But not these, no matter how many times I vanished. And I didn't know why.

Most of my physical healing from the damage had taken place that same night. To replace my lost blood I'd fed from Bristow. He'd been dying; my feast had simply hurried the process. I'd gorged—shameless, mindless, desperate.

And enjoyed it.

It hurt to heal then. I had been unable to vanish, and it hurt a lot. Left me shaking like an epileptic. Maybe that was the origin of my fits, just as my out-of-control draining of Bristow was similar to how I'd fed from that cow last night. Though the ordeal was past, some part of me kept me there, like replaying a record over and over but with the sound down low so you don't consciously notice that it's repeating and driving you crazy. I had to find some way to switch it off.

I'd reluctantly talked to Escott about going to a head doctor, but how in hell could any of them help me with this problem?

Hey, Doc, I get blindsided by these shivering fits and drink blood until I'm sick. You got a pill for that?

I didn't think so.

And another less-than-perfect evening began with the discovery that the two street-side tires of my Buick were flat.

The problem didn't register at first. I walked around my car, unlocked the door, and was about to open it when the impression of what was wrong met up with the memory of what was supposed to be right. The car was lower than it should be. I backed off and stared and couldn't believe and stared and couldn't believe; and then I got pissed and wanted to hit something, only that would have left a dent in my blameless vehicle.

I was certain Hoyle or Ruzzo had done it. A kid's vicious prank.

It wasn't anything that could be proved. Not ordinarily. If I confronted Ruzzo about it, they'd happily lie in my face. I had my own way around that. Our next talk was going to be very unpleasant—for them. They would also be paying for the new tires. Four, so they'd all match.

Then I'd probably beat the hell out of Ruzzo. For some guys logic or threats never work. You have to kick their asses to get your message to sink in.

I called Derner again and explained the situation.

"We got garages, don't we?" I asked.

"Thirty-three, not counting the wrecking yards—"

"That's good. Find one close to my house and send someone over. I want the tires on my Buick changed out to four new ones." As long as the mob boys called me "boss" I might as well benefit from the position. "Have that done before tomorrow evening."

"Right, Boss."

"And I need a car until mine's fixed."

"No problem," said Derner. "You can use Gordy's. Strome'll drive you. He's away now, but can be there in an hour."

"Nah, I'll cab over and wait at the Nightcrawler. In the meantime I want Ruzzo. Both of 'em. Hoyle, too."

"I'll send out the hounds."

"They can cough up cash for replacement tires unless I take it out of their hides."

Derner's "yes" sounded oddly faint, and I wondered why before realizing my own poor choice of words. He'd seen me hanging skinned from that meat hook, after all.

Next I called the lobby phone of Lady Crymsyn. Wilton answered. I told him I'd be late on account of business and to open as usual. He said okay and no problem, unknowingly echoing Derner. At least some pieces of my life were still in place. Then I phoned for a cab.

I was still too mad to let the tire slashing go. Directing my driver to the Nightcrawler, I blew off steam to him. We both heartily agreed that crime was completely out of hand in this town and, united against the world by our mutual righteous outrage, were fast friends by the end of the ride. He got a dollar tip for my two-dollar ride, since by then I felt almost good. Maybe I didn't need a head doctor, just a lot more taxi trips.

The outer bar was open, but the Nightcrawler's main room was still being readied for the evening show. I sent someone up to tell Derner I was here, then settled in at one of the tables, breaking one of the rules for surviving in the mob: sitting with my back to the door. If I'd had vulnerable company along, I wouldn't have made such a slip, but while on my own I really didn't give a damn. The mugs watching the front were on my side. Sort of. They'd spot trouble and deal with it. I kept my coat and hat on. For some reason I just could not shake the cold tonight. All in my head, probably. Everything else was, so why not?

Without being asked, a girl brought a glass of water to me and inquired if I wanted anything stronger. I said no and shooed her off with a neutral smile. More waitresses in short spangly skirts hurried to and fro and traded talk loudly across the breadth of the room. I had waiters for my place. In the early days I hired on a few girls to come in on the busier nights. They had red velvet skirts to match the décor and were cute as bugs. Many of the male customers liked their looks as well, taking them to be part of the after-hours entertainment. Some of the girls followed through on it, and made a hell of a lot more money in the parking lot than they did collecting tips in the club.

On one hand I didn't mind, but out of self-preservation had to cut them loose. If something went wrong, it would reflect on the club and me. Gordy could take that sort of heat from the local vice squad; I just didn't want the grief. Bobbi was still trying to figure out what to do with the left-over costumes.

The Nightcrawler's talent trickled in. They weren't supposed to use the front, but did anyway, leggy dancers heading backstage, musicians setting up, everyone busier than me and consumed by their own concerns. I liked that.

Whitey Kroun walked in. People paused to look up; I felt the draw, which is why I turned to see who'd arrived. Even here he filled the place. Some types were like that: actors, singers, politicians. Bobbi had that electric quality, but she only threw the switch when working because it sometimes left her tired out afterward. Kroun's seemed to be going all the time, and if he was aware of it, he didn't let on.

He took off his hat, brushed a hand through his hair. He used the gesture as a means to look around, spotted me lounging, and sketched a casual wave. I returned it, half-expecting him to come over, but he continued on through the casino door. Only then did I notice Mitchell in his wake like a plain-Jane pilot fish.

He gave me a look.

Make that more of a glare.

It must have been inspired by my stay-away-from-Bobbi message of the night before. He seemed the type to stew about things. On one hand Mitchell was only doing his job. A good lieutenant is supposed to make life miserable for anyone who could potentially annoy his boss. But I was getting bored with this one. If he didn't leave for New York soon, I'd be inclined to inspire a sudden interest in ice fishing so he'd go away for the rest of the winter.

I just looked back, again not blinking, not giving a damn about his obvious dislike of me. He finally got bored and went elsewhere. I returned to watching the club's opening routine. It was much the same as my place, but with more money.

Jewel Caine, the obstreperous ex-wife of this week's star performer unexpectedly appeared, beelined to a booth with a view of the stage, and hunched down in its depths. Under her black coat, which she unbuttoned, she was all in blue from hat to stockings. It suited her better than the previous night's green. One of the casino bouncers passing through finally noticed her while she jerkily plucked off her gloves. It was no business of mine, but I signed for him to lay off.

She pulled out cigarettes and grimly smoked, watching the stage with needle-sharp eyes. A woman with a mission, I thought, trying unsuccessfully to read her mind. Sometimes you can tell what's in a person's head by his or her carriage. Now that she wasn't screaming threats she showed some good looks. Hoping she might be in a reasonable mood, I picked up my glass of water and ambled over. I was still boss. Maybe if I found out what her plan was, I could head off trouble, breakage, and hospital bills.

"Mrs. Caine?"

"Who wants to know?"

"My name's Jack Fleming."

"So how do you know me?"

"I'm associated with this club."

Her chin went up. "You gonna throw me out?"

"I hope not. All right if I sit with you?"

She thought it over, giving me a hard up and down, then nodded. "What do you mean by 'associated'?"

I took my hat off, put it to one side, and slipped in opposite. "I know the owner. I'm helping manage the place for the time being."

She made no reply but stubbed the old cigarette and went on to the next, her fingertips yellow from chain-smoking. There were matches on the table. I had one lighted by the time she needed it. She leaned forward and puffed her smoke to life. "So you manage the place. What do you want from me?"

"Nothing. I just noticed last evening you seemed to have a stack of grievances against your ex-husband—"

"More of a mountain. He owes me a lot of alimony, that's the main one. It's pulling teeth with tweezers to get him to cough up anything, but I really need it, the landlord's leaning on me, and I owe for groceries. It's not like I'm wasting anything . . ." She shut herself down, mouth twisted with disgust. "Christ, but don't I sound pathetic."

"If he's holding out, you've a right to be upset. What about getting him into court?"

"That costs money. I can't feed myself, much less some lawyer." She sucked in a draft from her cigarette and politely vented it to one side. "Look, kid, maybe you want to help, but I've been over all the angles, and unless Alan pays up, I'm on the street in the morning. But then he'd enjoy that, the son of a bitch."

I raised a hand and a waitress came over. They knew about my temporary rise in rank. Fast service for the boss was part of the job. "What will you have, Mrs. Caine?"

Surprisingly, she wanted only water and a twist of lemon. From her behavior last night I took her to be a hard drinker.

The waitress came back quick with a glass and a bowl of peanuts. Jewel attacked them, but one at a time, yellow fingers delicate. I wondered if she'd eaten lately. She didn't look starved, but you didn't have to look it to be hungry. I was acquainted with that a little too well.

"Thanks, kid," she said, lifting her glass.

"Just call me Jack."

"Yeah. I've seen you around. Heard you run that red club with the funny name."

"Lady Crymsyn."

"Any jobs open? Or has Alan gotten to you, too?"

"What do you mean?"

"He's a big draw. Bigger than me, now. He won't sing at any club that's given me work. They always go with the money, and I get bupkis. He sees to it."

"What can you do?"

"Just about anything. I can sing, but I'll wait tables, clean the damn toilets if I have to."

"How good a singer are you?"

"I do all right with wistful throaty stuff, nothing fast." She tapped ash off. "These things spoiled my voice, put a limit on my range, but I can't seem to kick 'em. I've got plenty of songs I can get away with that aren't a strain on the cords, and I'm good with mood pieces, I can make a rock cry."

That told me she knew her stuff. "I'm booked for acts this week, but maybe can give you a short set to do."

Jewel stared, hovering between disbelief and hope. "You sure? For real?"

"That jackass is never gonna sing at my place. It's only a short set. It won't pay much."

"Kid, I'm making nothing now, I'll take it."

"Can you start tomorrow?"

"Yeah, but—"

"I'll notify my booking manager." I got my wallet and gave her a business card for the club. "Go over tomorrow around three with your music and work things out. You'll talk to Bobbi Smythe. You know her?"

"Yeah, but—"

"Your landlord? A loan, then." I had forty bucks and gave it to her. "Interest-free. You need more?"

"Christ, kid, that's two month's rent!"

"It's okay, I'll take it out of Caine's salary. He must owe you more than that, though."

"A few thousand."

"I'll set something up at this end. So long as he sings here, you'll get your alimony. It won't be permanent, all he has to do is leave for someplace else, but maybe you'll have enough to get on your feet?"

"Hell, yes." She seemed very taken aback. "Why you doin' this?"

I shrugged. "It gets my mind off my own troubles."

"Must be some troubles."

I didn't want to talk about what churned my guts. "How'd you two get together?"

She snorted. "Ten years back I was the big star and he was . . . well, you've seen him. He's a knockout. He still is."

"Not to me."

"Men." Jewel puffed, wearing her cig down half an inch in one draw. "He got to me with that big smile and those gorgeous eyes and sweet talk like it was going out of style. I went nuts over him. It's the only reason I can think of, that I was out of my mind. We got married, and it was good, and I got him singing lessons, then jobs. I wanted us to work up a duet routine, but he said he got more work as a single act. Eventually I figured out it meant he got more women that way. He was vile about it. Shoved it in my face like it was my fault."

I listened and nodded as she touched on the low points. She had a long list of bitter grievances, the usual for when life and love goes bad for a couple. Caine had gone out of his way to be a jerk, though. Jewel struck me as being able to give as good as she got, but he'd worn her down, then moved on.

She wore a kind of choker necklace made of blue beads, and when she held still the beads moved in time to her pulsing veins. I took a breath and caught the scent of blood under her sallow skin.

Not good. I shouldn't be noticing those kinds of things. I'd fed myself sick at the Stockyards, wasn't remotely hungry tonight, and human blood was off my menu, anyway. Didn't matter. I was wanting it the way I used to want a drink back when I lived in New York. Except for weekend binges when I could afford it, I had that under control. I did it then, I could do it now. Really.

"If you got any brains, you'll never have Alan perform at your place," Jewel concluded. She'd apparently forgotten what I'd said before. This sounded like something she repeated often to many people.

"I'll hire a special bouncer just to keep him out."

She broke into a smile and looked pretty for it. "You're all right, Jack."

Past her shoulder I caught sight of Mitchell, returned from someplace or other so he could watch me for some reason or other.

Jewel noticed and glanced where I was looking, snorting again. Her eyes sharpened into a glare, an odd look on her face, then she smiled again. This time it took away from her looks. "There's another one to keep clear of. Used to run with the Morelli gang before Gordy took over. You don't want to know why *he* had to leave town." She gave a short, unpleasant laugh.

"Of course I do. You can't do a fanfare like that and leave me hanging."

"No. It's vile, too, and I've had enough for one night. Besides, Alan just came in."

True. Alan Caine, with Evie Montana in close and adoring tow, sauntered in on the other side of the room, not noticing us. He did see Mitchell, though, and made a point of walking right by him. Caine gave him a big, disarming smile, and Mitchell went stony.

"You got a problem, Mitch?" Caine acted puzzled.

Mitchell kept shut, but clearly they had some kind of feud going, probably carried all the way from New York. Easy to understand, given their personalities. What was coming out from behind Mitchell's eyes would have melted steel. Evie noticed and tugged on Caine's arm to move on.

"I feel sorry for her," said Jewel. "There's no point trying to wise up her type about Alan, though. She'll have to learn the hard way."

"He's gonna break her heart?"

"Yeah, but only after he's gambled off all her money and hocked everything she's got, up to and including her step-ins."

Evie seemed to be a girl not too interested in wearing much in the way of underclothes. Her satin skirt was pretty tight, and I couldn't see lines showing through. Bobbi did the same thing herself a lot of the time.

And I didn't need to be thinking about . . . about anything.

Caine resisted Evie's efforts to move him, continuing to smirk. The idiot must have thought his talent made him bulletproof, but there is a certain kind of mug who doesn't worry about consequences. Mitchell might be one of them. If Caine wasn't careful, he could get a broken leg or worse. He could sing sitting down, but wouldn't be happy about it.

Not liking Caine, I wouldn't have minded letting matters take their natural course; but as caretaker for Gordy's investment, it was up to me to keep the peace. A week or so back I'd have involved myself, but didn't trust how I might react if either of them got stupid with me. Instead, I signaled to some of the club's muscle to make themselves visible to Mitchell.

He saw, if Caine didn't, and strolled off, Caine laughing at his back. Even from here I could pick up on the booze tone in his voice. This time Evie Montana succeeded in dragging him away.

"Men." Jewel gave a deep, derisive sigh. "Alan's a damn fool. Never does know when to quit. He's the kind of guy who drinks and pretends he doesn't."

"If he's too drunk, you could have a job here tonight," I said, half-joking.

"He's smart enough to never miss a cue. But I *should* have this job. Instead, I got bills and this." She lifted her glass of water. Sipped.

"That mean something?"

"Yeah. It was easier being married to him if I stayed drunk all the time. Trouble was, after the divorce I kept on being drunk. Thought I should warn you . . . in case you want your money back."

"You're having water now, though?"

"I'm on the wagon. You might as well know I'm going to Alcoholics Anonymous. Someone told me they can really help, and so far so good. I've been sober two weeks. Two weeks and six hours."

"Congratulations."

"Thanks. Though when I look in a mirror and see what the sauce has done to me I think maybe I should go back to it so I don't care anymore."

"You look just fine."

She smiled and patted my hand. "Sweet of you to say so, kid. I used to stop traffic in fog at midnight. Don't mind me. This is how I feel sorry for myself when I'm sober. It's better than when I'm drunk, though."

By this time she'd finished off the bowl of peanuts. "You hungry?" I asked. "The kitchen'll do you up a steak on the house."

She hesitated before giving an answer, but finally nodded and smiled. "Thanks. You're too decent a guy to be in this joint."

"No, I'm not. This is exactly where I'm supposed to be." I flagged a waitress, and she wrote down Jewel's order, then whisked off to the barely opened kitchen.

"You got a girl, don't you?" asked Jewel.

"How's that?"

"A guy as nice as you has a girl somewhere. Hope she's treating you right."

I felt myself going red. "Far better than I deserve."

Strome walked in the front, saving me from having to come up with another change of subject. I waved him over and explained about needing the car until mine was fixed.

"No problem," he said. "Except Kroun wants a ride back to his hotel when he's done here. I can get you another car."

"I'll wait." Strome might pick up things of interest from Kroun and Mitchell he could pass on. They'd likely be too smart to talk openly in front of him, but you never knew. "Why's Kroun still hanging around?"

"More business with Gordy. They're talking now."

What? "Gordy's *here?*"

"In the casino."

"He's supposed to be resting, dammit."

"Try telling him that. When the big boss says jump, you ask how high. That's how it works."

Hell. I got my hat and stood, excusing myself to Jewel, adding an apology.

She took it in stride. "Men," she said, lighting another cigarette.

I went into the not-quite-opened casino, but Gordy wasn't there after all.

Strome only shrugged. "Means they're up in the office. You might wanna steer clear."

"Why?"

"The more people in a room talking business, the longer it takes to finish."

That bordered on the genius. "Yeah, okay. But have someone tell me when they're done. I want a word with Gordy, too."

"Sure."

"Anything new on Hoyle?"

"He ain't left town yet. Donno why."

"Where is he?"

"Donno that, either. Dropped outta my sight, but some of the other boys have seen him."

"Doing what?"

He lifted his hands. "Sayin' good-bye?"

"See if you can find out more. I'm getting so I don't like that guy."

Strome's face almost twitched, and he moved on toward the back exit, presumably heading for the office to watch for the meeting to break up.

I found a phone and called Crymsyn's lobby to check in.

Instead of Wilton, Bobbi answered. "You're not backstage?" I asked.

She sounded a little breathless. "I just came down with the cash tills. Something told me that was your ring. You need to put a phone behind the bar."

The place already had one official phone in my office; I didn't see why we needed more, but this wasn't the time to discuss it. "I should be there to help, but I got sidetracked."

"I know, 'business.' We're fine here, Jack, there's no need to worry. Take a vacation why don't you?"

"At another nightclub?"

"Sure, see different faces for a change. Charles is helping me open, everyone's in on time. We're *fine* here."

"Okay." I tried not to read anything into so much insistence. "Listen, you remember a mug in Gordy's mob named Hoyle? Used to be a boxer."

"I know him by sight. What's going on?"

"Just keep an eye out for him if you can. He's got a grudge on for me, and I don't want you or anyone else getting in the middle."

"How big a grudge?"

"Enough so I'm sending some muscle over to play bouncer in case he shows, but —"

"Jack . . . ?"

"*But*—I think I'm overdoing it. Look, I know I've been edgy lately and this will make me feel better. The muscle is only insurance; if they're there, chances are they won't be needed."

"For this I'll want to know the whole story."

"Right now?" Not something I wanted to talk about over the phone, especially with Nightcrawler staff within hearing. There were enough rumors about me floating around.

"You kidding? I've got a show to get ready for, you'll tell me later."

"Deal. And one more thing, totally different subject: you know a torch singer called Jewel Caine?"

"Sure, she's not been around much, though. Used to be good until the booze got to her. Why?"

"She needs a break. I told her to come by to see you tomorrow at three if that's okay. Can you work a short set for her into the show?"

"I think so, but are you sure?"

"She's trying to sober up and needs rent money."

"Oh, Jack." Her tone wasn't reproach for being a soft touch, quite the opposite. If Bobbi had been here, she'd have kissed me. I wanted that. Almost. Another part was glad she was miles away. I fought off a shiver inside my coat.

"What about a guy named Alan Caine?"

"That's Jewel's ex-husband. I don't like him, but he can sing. You going to hire him, too? He's trouble."

"I know. I met him last night, forgot to tell you."

"How'd you meet him?"

"He's working at Gordy's club." Though Bobbi usually kept up with who was playing where in Chicago, she'd lately not had much time to read papers or talk with others in the business. My fault.

"Poor Gordy," she said. "He's all grabbing hands—Alan Caine, that is. I've done some shows with him way back when. He's one of those jerks who thinks he owns a place, lock, stock, and chorus line. The awful thing is most of them go along with it because he's so handsome."

"Except you."

"Back then I was wi . . . well, never mind." Slick Morelli. I recognized the avoidance. That mention of him still made her uncomfortable after all this time told me I'd done the

right thing not bringing up Mitchell's name. "But even before I wouldn't have gone near Caine. He's a big jackass,
and—did you just laugh?"

I'd not been doing much of it lately. I had to be careful or
my face would break. "Sounded like it. I think you must be
psychic, Miss Smythe. I thought the same about him myself. He won't be playing at Crymsyn. He mouthed off to
the wrong guy. Jewel seems okay, but she's had it rough
from him. She's sober, but kinda fragile." I should talk.

"I'll look after her, don't worry. We're out of dressing
rooms, though."

Huh? Oh. It took me a second to get it. Roland and
Faustine weren't the top billing act—that was Bobbi's spot.
But he'd had some minor leading-man work in Hollywood
and British stage, and Faustine was a full-blown Russian-
trained ballerina. The Depression and life in general had not
been kind, but they were still higher up the status ladder
than Bobbi. As a diplomatic gesture we assigned them side-
by-side dressing rooms one and two. Besides, being a couple, they didn't mind sharing the shower and toilet in
between. For some reason I'd not been able to figure out,
Faustine's wardrobe filled up the whole space.

Bobbi had the number three dressing room; Teddy Parris
had number four. I suggested bumping him out.

"Jewel deserves a higher number than four."

"This is nuts, you know."

"Well, I can't put her in the basement with the musicians."

Additional downstairs dressing areas had been roughed
out months back, but so far there'd been little need to finish things. It resembled a locker room with coat hooks
along one wall, a standing mirror, and a couple of long
benches. I didn't go down there if I could help it. Some
years back someone had died in that basement, and it

would take more than a coat of paint and lights to blot out that horror.

"We can rig a curtain across one of the corners . . ."

"Impossible. I couldn't put her there no matter what."

"Hah?"

"Jack, she used to be a big star around here, it'd be terribly insulting to foist her off in a cellar like some has-been."

Showbiz. I was still getting used to the shifting rules of its pecking order. "Well, just don't use my office."

"Actually, that room next to your office will do for me. If she signs on, I'll move my stuff up there, and she can have my dressing room. There, that's all worked out."

Bobbi did have a flair for problem-solving. Concerning club stuff. Not for me so much. Which was no one's fault but my own.

"You know," she said thoughtfully, "maybe you should think about turning that upstairs washroom into a real bath. You could put in a shower easy enough."

"Hey, I'm still paying for the other ones. Let's turn some more profit first before redecorating."

"All right."

Sounding cheerful, she gave in a little too easy. I knew damn well now that she'd gotten the idea it would be executed into reality sooner or later.

And . . . I suddenly realized we were talking normally again. I even felt normal—until I realized it, and that spoiled the moment.

Damnation. If I could just quit when I was ahead and not overthink, I might have drawn that feeling out for whole minutes instead of just a few seconds.

"Jack?"

"Yeah?"

"I have to go get ready for the show. You okay?"

"I'm fine." God, I hated lying to her, but over the phone she might not be able to pick up on it. "I'll see you when I get there. Break a leg." I didn't know if civilians to the stage were allowed to wish good luck to the talent with that phrase, but what the hell. She thanked me and hung up. I stood very much by myself next to the casino bar and fought off another shiver. All the cold in the city was outside these fancy walls; why was it that *I* had to be picked out to carry a piece of it around in my flayed skin?

Distraction. I called over one of the bouncers and made arrangements with him to send some guys to watch things at Lady Crymsyn. They all had to know Hoyle, which wasn't a problem. The story about Hoyle's interrupted batting practice with me had gotten out and made the rounds. Surprisingly, his reputation was in a hole and mine was on the rise. Just when I was getting used to being unpopular. Everyone's favorite part was my breaking the revolver in his face. I hoped they wouldn't ask for an encore as a party trick.

No sign of Strome yet. Thinking I could fill the waiting time with a few hands of blackjack, I went through to the private area of the club where everyone in Chicago with money to lose was made welcome. I'd played more than a few hands here, picking up extra cash when I wanted. Thinking he might open early for me, I looked around for my favorite dealer, the one who always gave away when he had a good hand. Instead, I saw Adelle Taylor coming decisively toward me, threading between the tables. She showed off her elegant figure in a clingy dark dress with a matching hat and purse that were clearly worth more than a few months' rent in Jewel Caine's neighborhood. Adelle seemed to be a woman on a mission; she moved more quickly than usual, but didn't broadcast any sign that an emergency was on. However, her eyes were strangely fixed.

When Adelle got close enough, I saw how it was for her, figured what to do fast, and led her to one of the semiprivate gaming alcoves, one with a curtain. Soon as we were inside I swept the curtain shut then put my arms around her so she could collapse and soak my overcoat shoulder.

7

CRYING women are not my favorite thing, but sometimes you have to come through for them and weather it out. It's not too bad. Adelle wasn't one to casually lose control of herself, either, so it had to be something important to get her into this state. Most likely to do with Gordy.

She didn't make much noise, but it was a strong and violent crashing down of her protective walls. I'd never seen her like this. Adelle was always cool-headed and even in the face of surprise, quick to land on her feet. Like the night of the shooting. Once she got through the initial shock and terror of seeing Gordy drop, she'd pulled together to help out as though she'd trained on a battlefield.

That restraint was nearly gone; the only remnant was how hard she worked to smother her sobs. I could tell she really wanted to let go completely and howl. That would have drawn attention, maybe prompted the curious to come in and interrupt. She needed release, not talk, but a suppressed breakdown was better than none at all.

Adelle knew nothing about what I'd been through with Hog Bristow, and for some reason that helped me to be stronger for her. I felt better for the giving, like my old self, and it lasted longer than a few seconds. I held her tight and murmured the often useless but frequently comforting, "It's okay, everything's going to be all right" at the top of her head.

Damned if it didn't work. After a while, she pulled away. Makeup running, eyes puffed, her whole face seemed bruised. She sat on one of the cushioned chairs and scrounged in her purse for a handkerchief—no dinky lace thing, but a large practical one—and blew and dabbed and swiped. I sat across from her, waiting to listen. Damn, the things I do for friends.

"Most men," she said, her voice deeper, more husky than normal, "go into a dithering panic when a woman cries. They either want to run for the hills or instantly fix the problem so she stops. Or they try to kiss her or slap her. I'm glad you're the sensible type."

"Nah, I'm a fake. I couldn't make up my mind which would work."

She unexpectedly giggled while trying to blow her nose again and made a real mess of it, requiring another handkerchief.

I sat next to her. "If I ran, the mugs here would shoot me out of reflex. I can't fix the problem, not knowing what it is, so that wasn't the right road. If I tried kissing or hitting, I'd risk a sock in the chops from you, being shot by Gordy when he found out, being shot by Bobbi when she found out, or all three."

Adelle put a hand over her mouth to stifle the laugh. "God, I wish you could stay with us. I need the change."

"Maybe I can swing by later." Gordy had been staying at her place I'd heard.

"It's all right. I know you're busy with . . . the business. There's no one I can talk to. Gordy's men are polite, but they're not . . . well . . ."

"You can't let 'em see you cry."

"No. You're different from them. You've got a heart. To you I'm a friend, not just the boss's piece."

"Hey, you're not—"

She waved it away. "I overhear their talk, but it doesn't matter. They can only define me by the limits of their world."

"You lemme know which ones are being disrespectful, and I'll widen their experience. Now, what's the big problem?"

"Gordy."

"What? He not treating you right?" No way. For all his rough side with the mob, he was always a gentleman with her, emphasis on "gentle."

"It's not that. Oh, Jack, he's ill."

"Ill? Pneumonia? Measles? What?" God, if he caught anything while he was still shaky from the bullets . . .

"Not that kind. He's pushing himself and he's up too soon and he's exhausting everything in him and I can't make him *listen* to reason."

She'd work herself into another bout of tears in another second. I made calming motions. "Take it easy, I was going to talk to him about it anyway. Strome told me he was here tonight, and I couldn't believe he was outta bed again."

"Gordy thinks if he doesn't show a strong face, it'll undermine his authority over his men."

"He's got a point, but if he falls on his duff, it'll undermine worse."

"It's more than that. I'm afraid it's killing him. He's so gray, and he hides it, but I know he's weak. He barely made it from the car into here, then Kroun came in, and he went upstairs like nothing was wrong. It's all a front and—"

"I get the picture."

"You'll talk to him? Make him rest?"

"You bet your sweet . . . ah . . . tonsils I'll do that."

"He looked awful yesterday and worse today. That Kroun's got him all stirred up. Gordy doesn't let on to me, but I hear stuff when he's on the phone or talking with Lowrey."

"What stuff?"

"One of the things I heard . . . the boys here said Kroun was going to kill you." She whispered the last part.

I took her hand and gave it a squeeze. "That's *old* news. We're copacetic now."

"You're sure?"

"Yeah. Guaranteed. Everything's fine there, or I wouldn't be here." Not strictly true. If all the guys in the gang liked me, I wouldn't have had slashed tires. Then I wouldn't have been around to help Jewel and Adelle. Instead I'd have been in my upper-tier booth of my club hiding in its shadows and probably feeling very sorry for myself. Funny how things can turn out.

"I wish you could make that Kroun go back to wherever he came from."

"Same here." Maybe I could, if I felt up to it. "Do you need anything?"

She blew her nose. "A new head on my shoulders?"

"I'm fresh out. What's wrong with this one?"

"Gordy makes me crazy."

That was my second time tonight to hear the same tune from a woman. Adelle made me wonder if I was driving Bobbi crazy in some way. The odds favored it.

"It's the life he's got that's doing this to me," she said. "It forces things like that shooting to happen. I've been able to ignore it until now. At first dating a gangster seemed very thrilling, but suddenly it turned different. He's not some kind of a misunderstood hero with a dark side, he's a man with a lot of insane, vicious enemies who will cut him down at the first chance."

"The hard part for you is that Gordy accepts that."

"*One* of the hard parts. There are a hundred other things."

"More like a couple thousand."

"To him it's just part of the job. You prepare as much as you can, then go on like you think it won't happen. But it does and it did."

"He's still here, Adelle."

"And for how long? Oh—no, I'm sorry, that was a stupid, filthy thing to say."

"You're scared, honey. No one blames you for that. But the fact is, whether he's a gangster or a streetcar conductor, it's all the same. Any one of us can die at any time; we don't get to pick and choose when or where, it's out of our hands."

"I know that. But Gordy's in a business where the chances are higher against him. It's one thing to know you could get accidentally run over by a truck; it's quite another to keep standing in the middle of the road."

"Touché and no arguments. But if he did any other kind of work, he wouldn't be Gordy. Don't kid yourself that you can change him."

She made a "ha" sound. "I gave that illusion up when I was married to Roland."

This was the first time she'd ever referred to him with me.

"I tried and tried, but I could *not* change that man, even when it was to save his life from the booze. Gordy's the same. I'm hoping he'll change for himself and quit the mob, like Roland when he decided to stop drinking. So many never do change, though."

"Almost never." I'd certainly done it, involuntarily, doing things now I'd have never dreamed about two years ago. It was about then that I'd begun thinking about coming out to Chicago and starting my life over. My hope to find Maureen was nearly gone, and it seemed like every corner of New York reminded me of her. I did a lot of thinking and boozing and selling off or hocking stuff to save up the train fare. Hard to do when I kept drinking a substantial part of the gleanings. It took me all the way until August to finally save enough cash to leave New York . . . and find death in Chicago. A slow, hard, and ugly dying.

And if I had stayed in New York, what then? I'd be a thirty-seven-year-old reporter rapidly drinking my way to forty-seven, which was about when I could expect Bright's disease or some liver problem or a car crash to do me in, if not sooner.

Looking at it that way made it almost seem like I'd been a different man whose unfinished biography I had read a long time ago. A man who had indifferently squandered his all-too-finite life by spending it feeling sorry for himself.

"Jack?" Adelle touched my hand.

"Yeah?" I hauled myself back from the might-have-been wreckage.

"What is it?"

"I was thinking that once in a while life makes the change, not the man, but whether it's for good or bad is usually up to the man."

"Or woman."

"You got it. Listen, Angel: Gordy has to do the kind of tough dealings you never want to know about, but where you're concerned he's a good man and always will be."

"I've felt that. But I'm not enough. He's already talking about when he gets back to work, the things he's going to do. . . . They're apart from the business, though. He says he wants to set me up at his club like you have with Bobbi. A regular headliner, the big star, Chicago's favorite. I like the life, but I don't know if I like it as much as I used to."

"What, you planning to move to the country, maybe buy a chicken farm?"

She laughed a little. "That sounds pretty good about now. But it would drive me quite rollicking mad."

"So long as you know."

"But I do wish . . . I just want a world that doesn't have this in it." She made a sideways gesture as though to take in gangland and all its grief.

I could wish the same.

With more waiting to do for the both of us, we left the casino for the outer bar. Adelle looked like she could use something to steady her down. I could watch while she drank it.

Jewel Caine was gone by now. I checked with her waitress. The lady had engulfed her meal and departed backstage. I couldn't imagine why she'd talk to Caine unless she wanted to let him know part of his check would be going to her as alimony. Not smart. He'd raise a stink and could find a different club to sing in, cutting her off. I sent a bouncer to go find Jewel; he came back to say she was backstage visiting girlfriends in the chorus. She was nowhere near Caine, or there might have been a ruckus.

Adelle and I parked at the house's best table and watched the place gradually fill up. The band started earning their keep and couples made forays onto the dance floor. A few people came by to say hello, and a woman asked for Adelle's autograph, which lifted her mood.

Then Whitey Kroun emerged from the back, saw me, and came over. Mitchell was with him, still doing his glaring game. He would seriously bore me in a minute. Strome walked through, heading for the front entry. I wondered if he ever got tired of all the driving.

"You might want to leave," I told Adelle.

"Should I? This is my chance to meet the big boss."

"I thought you had."

"Gordy likes me gone when there's business to conduct."

"Why do you want to meet Kroun?"

"The face of the enemy," she murmured darkly. She was all charm when Kroun stopped at the table.

I stood up and started to introduce them, but Kroun beat me to it, taking her hand and looking deep into her eyes.

"Miss Adelle Taylor," he said, making a pleased announcement of it, as though to confirm it to himself. That personal wattage he had going went up a few thousand volts. Adelle actually blinked from his surprisingly warm smile. "This is an honor and a very great pleasure, Miss Taylor. I knew you were in Chicago, but never expected to meet you. Knock me over with a feather, I'm in heaven."

For a second I thought he'd kiss her hand, but he settled for holding it just long enough to make his first impression on her memorable, then released. Somehow, without being asked, he was sitting at our table. Thankfully, Mitchell remained standing, but on the other side. I wouldn't have wanted him looming over my shoulder.

"Mr. Kroun," Adelle said, in turn, graciously.

"Please, call me Whitey. You can see why." He brushed a

hand through his hair, combining the gesture with an ironic but genial, invitation-to-intimacy smile. Special friends only.

She didn't fall for it, but did ask him about the white streak. "It's very striking."

"Well . . . I can't exactly take credit for it."

"Really? I thought it was natural."

"Anything but. I was shot there." His tone softened what should have been alarming news down to the level of amusing anecdote. "Some guy got too frisky and tried to take my head off, but he just missed. The bullet cut this into my thick skull. When the hair grew back . . . well, you can see what happened."

"How horrible for you."

"I didn't feel a thing."

"What happened to the man?"

"They're still trying to figure that one out," he said, which wasn't really an answer.

Adelle was savvy enough to know when to stop.

Kroun smoothly filled in the gap. "I just want to say I am a *great* admirer of yours. Soon as your movies hit town I'd watch three and four times in a row. Couldn't get enough of 'em. Why don't you make some more? You're terrific."

"Why, thank you!" She instantly warmed up. He'd struck one of her favorite chords. "Tell that to the producers in Hollywood. The casting is quite out of my hands."

"That's just not right. They should have you starring in all kinds of things. I've already said you're terrific, now I have to let you know you're wonderful."

Mitchell stopped glaring at me long enough to spare a look at his boss and did a restrained rolling of eyes. I might have done the same, but for picking up that Kroun's high regard for Adelle was absolutely sincere. He seemed to be utterly smitten, but not pushy about it. He held the personal charm note perfectly, drawing it out.

"I'll be around, Mr. Kroun," Mitchell said, and drifted away without waiting for a reply. Good thing, since he didn't get one.

Adelle agreed with Kroun about Hollywood's lack of judgment in regard to her career. They had plenty of common ground: his veneration for her and her agreeing with him about it. I wasn't going to leave her alone with him, but she turned her big eyes on me. "Jack, would you mind doing that little favor I asked?"

"You sure?" This didn't seem to be the best time, but Gordy would be free. She'd keep Kroun well distracted, too.

"Certainly."

I took that to mean she knew how to deal with him, and she had to like the flattery. Who wouldn't? "I'll be back shortly, then," I said, leaving. My money was on Adelle, that she'd learn more about Kroun in five minutes than I would in a week. I was glad she and I were on the same side.

Upstairs I bumped into Derner in the hall. "Gordy wants to see you," he said.

"Mutual, I'm sure." I went past him, not breaking stride. Evidently this would be a private meeting, since Derner went on to clatter down the stairs. Suited me. I pushed open the office door and found Gordy sitting the same as ever in his big chair at the desk. What was unusual was him apparently being asleep. His eyes were fast shut, his head down on his chest. He didn't look so good.

As I drew closer I chanced to take in a whiff of air. In this place with the familiar chrome furnishings and pastoral paintings I was startled to pick up a very out-of-place hospital taint. Heavy, sweet, but with an odd acidic tang to it. Certain smells will trigger memories. This one stripped away half a lifetime and hauled me back to the casualty wards from when I'd been in the War. I'd lost too many friends there.

My heart sank. Adelle's assessment about Gordy being bad off were all too right.

In addition to the sickroom miasma—it wasn't that strong, just enough that only I could have noticed—I picked up bloodsmell. His wounds must be seeping. If it triggered another damn bout of shaking . . . Gordy wasn't the only one who had to limit the number of people seeing him vulnerable. He didn't need my troubles on top of his own, either.

Going to a window, I eased it open, lifting high. The curtains immediately billowed as icy air swept in. We were high enough off the street for it to be fresh. After a minute the place was freezing, but much of the smell dissipated. Because I'd been chilled through since waking, this cold got to me more than it should. I fought off increasingly violent shivers until it hurt. Enough was too much. I lowered the window, leaving it short a couple inches, and turned toward the desk, trying to rub warmth into my arms. Wasn't working. That was for people with circulating blood, and mine . . . well, mine just didn't work that way.

" 'Lo, Fleming."

If my ears hadn't been so sensitive, I might not have heard him.

Gordy's eyelids cracked, and he took a deep breath. "That's good. I tell 'em to leave a window open, but Derner's afraid of pneumonia." He sounded worse than last night and whatever rest he'd had failed to clear away the circles under his eyes and the weary droop around his mouth. He looked a lot older and more tired than he had any right to be. His large body took up just as much space, but seemed oddly hollow, as though all the strength had been scraped out.

My heart went into my throat, and I hoped Gordy didn't see the fear. I made a thumbs-up sign to him and felt like a complete ass for its inadequacy.

"You need anything?" I asked, taking a chair by him.

"Have it. Forgot what air's like. Adelle keeps me wrapped like a mummy when we go out."

"How you doing?"

Gordy shut his eyes and opened them, slow. He looked steadily at one of the landscapes on the opposite wall. It was a good one and must have been his favorite since it faced his desk. I wondered what he liked best about it. "Doc Clarson says the holes are healing clean. No fever. I'm fine. Getting better every day."

Yeah, sure you are. God, but he looked tired.

"He kept me pretty doped at first. I say I want to lay off except at night so I can sleep. I seen what too much of that stuff does to mugs. I'm better. Something wrong? Kroun givin' you grief?"

"Not really." Gordy was throwing out distractions. I knew all about that angle. "You're the problem. You've got Adelle scared half out of her mind."

"What d'ya mean?"

I tapped my shoulder where Adelle had cried. "This ain't rainwater making a damp spot on my coat. The woman's on the ragged edge because of you not taking care of yourself."

"I can do that after Kroun leaves town."

If you last that long. "Hey, you put me in charge, right? Let me do my job and run interference. You've impressed everyone already. Take some time off. Go home and rest."

"Can't. Kroun." He licked his lips, seemed about to say more, then clammed up again.

It hit me with a nauseating certainty that Gordy was *afraid* of Kroun. Impossible. Gordy was a rock. People were afraid of him, not the other way around. But Kroun had that personal electricity going, maybe it was enough to effect Gordy. "So what? I got him all behaved and put in the word for you while I was at it. This is still your organization when you're better, but first you have to *get* better. Even Kroun will see that."

"There's other things going on you don't know. Only I can deal with 'em."

"You worried about being a target to some up-and-comer if you don't keep showing yourself?" That was the way of the mobs, one sign of weakness, and you got cut down, quick as thought.

"Like Hoyle? Derner told me about your tires."

I made a brief scowl. "The guys are looking for him. Anything else happen?" Being out for the day, I could have missed all kinds of grief.

"Nope. He's no problem."

"All right, then. But for now, you need a quiet spot, away from the yapping dogs. Someplace outside your normal haunts."

"Maybe."

That's all I needed, a "maybe." It would slant things in my and—eventually—his favor. An opening.

Of course, this was smack in the middle of doing something for another guy's own good whether he liked it or not. I didn't have the right to impose this, the ultimate manipulation, on him. On the other hand I wasn't about to go back and look Adelle in the eye and tell her I turned chicken.

"Kroun and me did some talking. About you," he said.

"Oh, yeah?" I must have gone too far in giving Kroun the idea we were friends, should have told him to go back to

New York instead. Kroun had had plenty of opportunity to talk with Gordy about all kinds of interesting details relating to myself and how things were running in Chicago. Not that I could blame him. If Kroun asked, Gordy would have to answer. Given the circumstances and the chance, I'd do the same. Knowledge is power, especially with this bunch.

"He wants to know if you'll be taking over for good."

"Of course not—"

"Lemme finish. Taking over . . . if I don't make it after all."

I couldn't believe he'd said that. Gordy dying was just not in the cards. He was my friend—in a very cockeyed way considering his work—and he *had* to go on breathing. "What the hell?"

"You have to think about these things," he continued. "If you don't want the operation, it goes to Mitchell."

"Screw that."

"It's him or you, kid."

I almost objected again, then shut it down. It would be less upsetting to him if I went along with this line of talk. He had to get it out of his system. I hated that he'd been mulling this stuff over.

"But you don't want it. Derner, then. With you helping him, like with me. Like you're doing now."

"Uh-uh, you got my exclusive. Nobody else. So you have to get better."

Before he could respond, I moved in, going as soft and easy as I'd ever done on anyone before with my evil eye. My head immediately began to hurt from even this minimal effort, but I continued, careful as a brain surgeon, speaking low and with infinite confidence. "You're going to heal up just fine, Gordy. You listen to me, you're going to fight this and get well. There's a pretty gal waiting for you. Can't disappoint her. You hear me?"

A low murmur. It sounded like a yes. Good thing he wasn't doped with painkillers just now. I could use some, though. I'd barely started when the thunderstorm behind my eyes began building at record speed. I pressed through it. In the War I'd seen a lot of guys talk themselves into a recovery while others just sat there and got worse. I had to get Gordy to talk himself into getting well.

"This is something that's just going to happen. You're going to listen to Adelle and listen to your doctor and to me and you *will* rest. That rest will make you stronger and better with each passing hour, with each day. You will get well."

The pain rolled in harsh as a fury; I winced and couldn't maintain eye contact, had to brace against the big desk to keep my balance.

"I-I want you to go stay with Shoe Coldfield. You two get along, and he won't mind doing you a favor. You're going stay with him in some nice, quiet place until you're well again. You understand?"

Couldn't hear any reply. The worst migraine in the world was pounding my brain to mush, which was trying to leak out through my ears. Had to ignore it. Gordy was more important than . . .

"You'll do this. You hear me? You'll *do* this and get well."

Too much. It sliced into my eyes like twin axe blades. For a second I thought someone actually had come up to slam razor edges squarely home into my skull. The rising agony shot to a screaming zenith.

I'd really done it. Overdone it. What was supposed to have been a light touch turned into a hammerblow that bounced back in my face. The cold that had bothered me all evening clawed and grabbed hard as death.

Lurching up, I tried to reach the couch, but banged solidly to the floor, doubling in, knees drawing to my chest, arms around my exploding head, trying to cushion the worst and failing.

So *cold*.

Trembling . . . limbs twitching . . . oh, God, not another one . . .

Before the seizure peaked I went invisible.

The grayness was peace and comfort *and free from pain*. No jittering spasms, no betrayal of mind and body or hidden terrors surfacing to rip me or anyone else apart.

What had set it off? I'd not been thinking of Bristow. Just trying to help Gordy. The hypnosis? Why was *that* hurting? It didn't use to, not this badly—

Stupid questions. I didn't want to think them up, didn't want to find the answers. If I could just *stay* like this. Without a solid body to feed and care for, I had no anchor to what had become an increasingly ugly world. So long as I was chained to flesh, I was stuck with its memories, disappointments, responsibilities, and pain. Lots of pain. I wanted to float in this sweet respite forever.

Floating. Invisible. Almost a ghost. But ghosts were sad, weren't they? Or angry or scared. I didn't want any feelings at all.

On the old home farm we had a big spring-fed stock pond, and one rare summer day I had it to myself. Without a mob of older brothers and sisters to spoil the stillness I'd stretched out in the middle, shut my eyes against the noon sun, spread my arms to embrace it, and let the water buoy me up. Baking heat above, chill water cooling below, I drifted, gently rising and falling, each intake of breath like a small tide, and thought it was the best thing ever. Until then I'd never realized how good it was to have that kind of absolute, yet utterly serene solitude.

Soon enough I grew bored and moved on, and I never got to swim there alone again. I should have stayed longer. When you're a kid you *know* things will always be there for you. Growing up teaches you different.

With twenty-five years between me and that perfect childhood moment I came back to solidity in Gordy's office, standing upright, shaken, but at least not shaking. An improvement. This fit hadn't lasted long; my muscles weren't twitching from exhaustion.

Still cold, though. I wanted to turn up the heat, but it wouldn't help. My usual immunity was gone. Perhaps at long last I was finally feeling the chill of the grave. Why, after this long a stretch since my death, was it trying to catch up with me?

What *had* triggered the fit? A run-of-the-mill suggestion, the kind I'd done hundreds of times before? It didn't seem possible that so ordinary a thing—for me—could be to blame. Maybe my subconscious had been saving this one up, waiting to drop it on me at the first opportunity.

The moment I'd let my guard down? I had to do that to focus on Gordy. And it left me vulnerable . . . to things in my head, buried things . . .

Great. If that was true, then to prevent further attacks I only had to go through the rest of life with my shoulders bunched around my ears and never look anyone in the eye ever again. Why hadn't I thought of that sooner?

I waited to be sure the attack was truly over, pacing the room a few times, and making a point *not* to look out the damn windows. Nothing untoward stirred within, so it seemed safe enough to wake Gordy. No more attempts to influence him or anyone else, at least for now.

Thankfully, I didn't have to try for a second whammy to do that part. Just a hand on his shoulder, an easy-does-it shake.

He must have nodded off for real. He woke with a start, one hand automatically reaching for the inside of his coat where he wore his gun.

"Fleming? Jack?" He never called me Jack. Always Fleming. God, but he sounded tired. About the same as I felt. "What's wrong?"

"Nothing. Ain't it time you took Adelle home?"

He thought it over. "I guess so. But not to her place. After Derner told me what Hoyle and Ruzzo pulled on you I should find some spot they won't look. Keep her clear of this."

"You're worried about them?"

"You should be, too. They might not be the only ones wanting to take over, given a chance. I know Hoyle. He'll spout that he's steady for me, but he'd as soon cut my throat if it could get him in charge. Derner's nervous, too."

This was interesting. "And here I thought I was his least favorite."

"You think Coldfield would mind helping me get scarce so I can rest?"

I smiled. The evil-eye whammy had dangled me head-first in hell, but it had worked. One of its influences on others was making it seem to them that they'd thought up my suggestions on their own.

"I'll call him right now," I said. "Why don't you stretch out on the couch while I arrange it?"

"Good idea. I need the rest."

I stood by ready to help, but he left his chair unassisted and made the journey across the room. It hurt to look at him, because he was trying not to shuffle like an old man.

Shoe Coldfield was a little surprised by being asked to play host to Northside Gordy. He'd helped keep Gordy safe before, and didn't mind doing the favor again. Coldfield gave me an address and said he'd be there in person to look after things. I knew the street. It was one of the borderline areas. One side was Bronze Belt, the other side white. Gordy and Adelle showing up there wouldn't raise as much notice than if Shoe put them in the next block over. And day or night, it would certainly be the last place where mugs like Hoyle and Ruzzo would hang around.

Plans fixed, I made a sedate and slow trip downstairs, cautious about setting off another fit. The internal chill clung to me, not as bad as before, but noticeable.

Music played in the Nightcrawler's main room. That helped take my mind off the constant annoyance. Tonight's show had been going full swing for some while now. Alan Caine's voice rolled rich and strong even through the intervening walls. It was really too bad I'd met him, else I'd have enjoyed the sound. He was singing for free for the time being, since a large piece of his pay was going elsewhere. I'd have to ask Derner how that had gone over when he'd broken the news.

I found Strome just off the backstage area and told him he'd be driving Gordy and where to take him. Strome was evidently familiar with the street, too, since his distaste for the idea was obvious. He didn't like colored people, but happily for everyone he wouldn't have to remain there. His partner Lowrey had no such problems and would stay on to play watchdog as usual.

Adelle was at the same table, still holding her own with Kroun. During a pause in the music, I heard him talking, and almost didn't know his voice. It had gone low and pleasantly seductive. He said, "It's a great place, I can get you top billing and an unlimited run, and you can pick anything you want to do, singing, acting, dancing, radio, the works . . ."

"That's very kind of you, Whitey—"

I walked up just then, delaying her reply. "All done," I said. "Sweetheart, you get a vacation until *you* say different."

She immediately understood what that meant. Visibly relieved and beaming, she stood. I put my arms around her because she looked like she needed it, and just held her a minute. She sagged so mightily, I thought I was holding her whole weight, and for a second she seemed about to cut loose and sob, but being in public must have stopped that. But the holding seemed to help. Felt good to me, as well. At times that's what we need, a simple sharing of body presence, just that and no more, then you let go and move on. I patted her, told her everything was going to be fine, and when she seemed ready, stood her square again. She pulled a handkerchief from somewhere and blew her nose.

I looked her up and down. "Doll face, you're always tricked out better than a million bucks, but you should get some sleep tonight. You don't want to give the doctor a second patient, do you?"

"But I—"

Tapping my ear, I shook my head. "Oops, sorry, I suddenly can't hear anything. Happens at the darnedest times, but comes in handy. It means no one can argue with me and win."

That raised a crooked smile from her. "All right, Jack. I'll get him home and turn in. I feel like a zombie."

"Strange, you felt like all-girl to me."

"So that's why Bobbi keeps you around. Good night and *thank you!*" She pecked my cheek and shot away, perhaps worried that Gordy might change his mind if she didn't hurry. He would let her know where they were headed. I didn't think she'd care where they stayed so long as he got better.

Kroun stared after her, then at me, questions all over his craggy face. "What's the deal? Are you an' she . . . ?"

"We're just friends."

"Friends with a dame? You funny or something?"

I let that one pass, still feeling good about being helpful. That hug made all the pain worth it.

Watching her leave, Kroun sprouted a smile of unabashed pleasure that lingered while she was in sight. "I heard Gordy was dating a looker, but didn't know she was Adelle Taylor. What a woman. She just made this whole trip worth it."

We apparently had some things in common. Maybe I should be worried.

He suddenly snapped his fingers. "Damn! I shoulda got her autograph and had the camera girl here to take a picture. Think you could get her back?"

"She won't be in the mood for it. Another time."

"What a woman," he repeated, like a prayer. He leaned forward, arms crossed on the table. "Lissen, Fleming . . ."

I sat at the table to better to hear. He'd lowered his tone, and Caine and the band were going loud. "Yeah?"

"Seeing's how you're such good friends with her, you think . . . you think she'd go out with me if I asked? Asked nice?"

I pulled back, gaping, and was tempted to poke him one in the eye. Kroun held to an utterly serious face, waiting. Then he blinked, head cocked, eyebrows high and innocent, and I finally realized he was pulling my leg. An unexpected laugh popped out of me, lasting a whole two seconds. It sparked an equally brief one from him in turn.

"You're a pip," I said, thinking a little late that that might be getting too chummy with the big boss, but he didn't seem to mind. Against all sense and good judgment I was starting to like him. That suggestion I'd slapped on him about us being friends was working fine, but had it become a two-way street with me not knowing? With the nervy stuff going on inside my head, I could believe it.

"What was that about, anyway?" he asked. "Something with Gordy?"

"She said you were working him too much. I talked him into some time off."

Kroun shrugged. "I don't twist his arm about needing to do business, but it wouldn't hurt him if he hit the mattress."

There were two ways of taking that statement. When a gang war was on, the mob boys dragged their mattresses onto the floor to be out of the line of fire from through-the-window shooters. The other way meant just getting some sleep. Kroun's relaxed attitude led me to figure he meant the second definition.

Good. Real good. I had enough worries. "She hugged you pretty hard," he said. "Didn't that hurt?"

He was too observant for my own good. "I got a pain shot earlier."

"What kinda shot? Morphine?"

I was far too alert to be on morphine. Best to be vague. "Donno. Stuff works okay."

"It sure must." He held my gaze for a moment, his dark

eyes nearly all pupil in the low light, then nodded at the stage. "You like this singer?"

Alan Caine had a spotlight song going. It made me wonder how Jewel Caine might have done the same number with her dark, husky voice.

"He sings okay. Don't like him much," I said.

"Not a lot of people do, only the ones who haven't met him."

"You met him?"

"I've managed to avoid the honor."

"Probably for the best. He's like sandpaper on a burn. Wouldn't know it to see him."

Caine, flashing perfect teeth, drifted along the edge of the dance floor, stirring up the women as he sang to them. He skillfully kept just out of reach while giving the impression he wanted to move closer. It was all a sham, but they ate it up and grinned for more.

"Quite a gift he's got," Kroun added. "Wish I could get women to fall on me like that. Well, actually they *do,* but only 'cause of who I am. Don't matter to them what a guy looks like if he's got money and power. I mean, look at Capone, for cryin' out loud. Face like a nightmare and built like a whale, but the women were all over him. You think it'd have been the same for him if he worked in a butcher shop like some regular guy? Not for a minute."

From the stories I got from Gordy and others, Capone actually had been something of a butcher, but he also knew how to have a good time. That wasn't an observation I felt like sharing, though. I wondered if Gordy was downstairs yet, on his way to Coldfield's neck of the woods. Coldfield was supposed to phone Crymsyn when his guests were settled. If Strome came right back to drive me over, there was a chance I could catch the call.

But . . . Escott or Bobbi or even Wilton could take care of that; I didn't *have* to be at Crymsyn. It just felt *odd* being someplace else.

"Don't you have a club to run?" Kroun asked, still watching Caine.

Damn, was he psychic or something? "Had to take a detour here. Car trouble. Strome's driving me over later."

A waitress came by. Kroun didn't want anything, still focused on the show. I waved her off and lighted a cigarette for something to do. Kroun glanced over.

"You smoke?" He seemed mildly surprised.

"Yeah. That a problem?" Everybody smoked. The club's air was thick from it. The spotlight on Caine fought through a slowly shifting blue haze.

"No. Just—"

"What?

He shook his head. "Nothing."

Maybe he was one of those fresh-air types. I could have told him that smoking actually exercised and strengthened the lungs. I'd read it in a magazine ad someplace. Of course I couldn't inhale, so none of that applied to me. Jewel Caine must have lungs stronger than Walter Winchell's.

Alan Caine's number ended on a big, heartbreaking, and beautifully clean note. I was no musician, but knew enough about how hard that was to pull off. No wonder Escott was impressed. The spot winked out, and the houselights came up. Caine had delivered; the audience wanted to let him know about it. His voice had filled the room, and in the wash of adulation for that talent he glowed. He graciously smiled and humbly bowed, and whatever magnetism he had going sent them wild. The women called his name over and over, blowing kisses, waving handkerchiefs. It was crazy. I'd seen something like it in a newsreel, but the film had been about Hitler. Just as well Caine wasn't in politics. We didn't need an American version of Germany's most famous house painter.

Caine made a last bow and dashed lightly off to get behind the curtains. They didn't quite close, and I saw him visibly shut down his performance personality the second he ducked backstage. He wouldn't need it until the next show. He had thirty minutes for a costume change, going from a black to an all-white tuxedo for the second set. Plenty of time to swap clothes, have a belt of booze. Or gargle. I glimpsed a flash of spangles beyond the curtain: Evie Montana trotting eagerly past to catch up with him. Yeah, there was time for her, too, if she didn't mind rushing things.

I suddenly shivered in my overcoat. Couldn't help it.

"You cold?" Kroun asked.

"Yeah. I must be in a draft."

"Or it's that medicine you take. I heard some of that stuff can do weird things."

"Or I'm catching cold."

Kroun's deadpan look returned. "A cold?"

I'd not been sick from an ordinary illness since my change. Didn't know if I *could* get sick in the ordinary way. For all I knew this could be the Undead version of the Spanish influenza.

"Maybe you should get more sun."

Most of the guys who worked these nightclub jobs were fish-belly pale. I fit right in. "Nah, I'm allergic to daylight."

"Ya think? Never heard that one before."

The band swung into dance music, and couples moved onto the floor for some fast fox-trotting. That was one way to work off the extra energy Caine had built up in them. The waitress came by again, got waved off again. After a few tune changes I checked my watch. Bobbi's first set was over, and Teddy Parris would be stepping from the wings. I could almost see and hear it in my mind. After his set and their duet, Roland and Faustine's red-washed dance—

Shut it down. Quick. Better to not make pictures of anything in my head. I might go fragile, which could get humiliating. Strome should have returned by now. Maybe he'd gotten sidetracked backstage. Plenty of cute girls there, and this was their break time.

Kroun's attention wandered around the club, then he looked at his watch.

"Expecting someone?" I asked.

"Mitchell. He said he was catching up with some friends here. You?"

"Strome's due. Maybe they're having drinks."

He snorted. "Not likely. Mitchell said friends. Those two are oil and water. They only mix when they have to."

"I can have the boys find him." I had an odd feeling about Mitchell. What if he'd decided to make a quick trip to Lady Crymsyn to see Bobbi? I stood to leave. "I'll check on 'em both."

Kroun flapped one nonchalant hand, apparently content to watch the dancers. The waitress, either determined to earn her keep or responding to his particular magnetism, came back with a glass of ice water for him. He smiled warmly up at her. She smiled back. He wouldn't be short of female attention tonight if I read her look correctly. Alan Caine had nothing on Kroun when it came to acquiring company.

There was a phone at the Nightcrawler's bar—the kind Bobbi wanted me to put in—and I used it to call Crymsyn's lobby booth. Several rings went by until a drunk guy answered. I'd expected Wilton, but he was probably busy.

The drunk guy was remarkably unentertaining, parroting my questions back at me and giggling. A woman's voice cut in, there were sounds of a wrestling match, a slap and a yelp from the guy, followed by more giggling. I wondered if I'd been that boring in the days when I'd been able to get properly drunk. One of them hung up the phone.

Hm. Bobbi's idea was looking better by the minute. Crymsyn was a swank place. Busy. No reason why I couldn't have *two* phones in it. I waited a minute, watching Kroun use his charm effectively on the waitress, then dialed again. This time Wilton answered. He sounded harried and said he'd get Escott.

Clunk, as he dropped the receiver onto the booth's small writing ledge. From the sounds filtering through there was a large, noisy crowd in the lobby. That was reassuring. I should be there to greet the customers as usual. A smile, a firm handshake, the suggestion they'd have a *great* time, hit home with a little eye whammy . . . well, maybe not that. Until the axe-blade migraines stopped I'd have to stay on the wagon from artificially winning friends and influencing people.

The waitress was now sitting with Kroun; but that was okay, everyone knew who he was, and none would nag her to get back to her job. In passing I noticed she was slim and dark-haired, very like Adelle Taylor but shorter. He must have liked that type. The waitress sure seemed to like him.

"Hallo?" Escott. Finally.

"It's Jack."

"You all right?"

"I'm dandy. Just checking on things. Remember Mitchell from last night? The mug who wasn't Strome and didn't have a streak of silver in his hair?"

"The ill-favored Casca of the trio?"

I recognized the theatrical tone and perfect inflection. Escott must have had a good dollop of brandy. It brought out the Shakespeare in him. I'd had to read some of the plays just to get his references at times. Looks like I'd have to put another one on the list. "I guess. He's not shown up there, has he?"

"Not that I've noticed. Is there a problem?"

"So long as he stays away. I sent some extra bouncers over. They doing their job?"

"Of looking formidable and threatening? Yes, they're covering that most excellently well. One of them said they were there to keep Hoyle and his cronies out."

"Yeah. It's probably nothing, but I don't wanna take chances. Tell them I said to add Mitchell to the list. I don't want him bothering Bobbi."

"Why would he do that?"

"He knows her from when she was with Morelli."

A pause. "Indeed. I take it you'd prefer she not be subjected to unpleasant reminders of that chapter of her life."

"Bull's-eye. If Mitchell shows, tell him his boss Kroun wants him back at the Nightcrawler, toot-sweet."

"I shall be pleased to do so."

"You seem to be in a good mood."

"Ah. Yes, well, I am, as it happens. Vivian was *delighted* at the idea of a party. Bobbi's setting it up for Saturday. My appreciation is *boundless,* old man."

"Uh, okay, likewise." Escott in love. What a picture. Color it pink. Lace it with brandy. "I'll be by later. I got business here still."

"Take your time, all's well."

I hung up. Next he'd be skipping in a meadow throwing flower petals around.

No he wouldn't. But still.

Kroun looked like he might not care to be disturbed. I left him to proceed with his conquest and went on to pass the word for the help to be looking for Mitchell. Let *him* interrupt his boss's canoodling.

Another shiver. Damn.

Since Strome was likely to come in by the alley door, I made my way to the rear of the club. The kitchen would be warmer than the rest of the place. I'd wait by a fired up stove and hope to thaw out. If that couldn't shake the chill, then I didn't know what else to do. Maybe retreat to my office and turn up the radiator and sit on it all night with a hot-water bottle. Come the daytime, and the cold wouldn't matter.

I didn't get as far as the kitchen. Strome was in the wide hall of the backstage area with Derner, and their heads were close together. Even at a distance I could see something off in their posture. They weren't the sort to broadcast much in the way of emotion, but I did pick up there was trouble of some kind going.

They spotted my approach at the same time, and each gave his own suppressed version of a guilty start.

"What is it?" I asked, my voice low. The lights were necessarily doused here to keep from showing on the stage area in front. Only thin threads seeped from under the dressing room doors. All but one: Alan Caine's.

"Got a problem, Boss," said Derner.

"We can take care of it," said Strome.

"What is it?" I suspected that Caine and Evie Montana were locked in, most likely involved in some very advanced canoodling. Not unheard of in a dressing room. Hell, Bobbi and I had . . .

The grim mugs in front of me said I was on the wrong track. I waited them out, just looking and frowning.

Derner broke first. "There's been an accident."

Strome winced at the word. That he reacted so strongly

was more than enough to put my back hairs up. "Accident, my ass," he muttered.

He *was* upset. "Spit it out," I said.

Derner rubbed a hand over his face, a show of weariness and frustration in the gesture. Next he checked the wide hall, which was empty, which was not normal. There should have been chorus girls wandering about, the stage manager, stray waiters. All I saw were a couple of the muscle boys at the other end, waiting and watching . . . me. Derner opened Caine's dressing-room door. It creaked inward to silence.

No sounds of an interrupted tryst, no squawk of outrage, no movement at all.

Dark inside. The dim spill from the hall didn't penetrate far, even for me.

"What happened?" I asked. "He leave?"

"Caine's still here, Boss," said Strome.

And without going any farther, without any visible facts, I knew what was wrong.

8

OF course I'd have to *look*. I was the boss. It was my job to deal with this kind of disaster.

Disaster it was. An almighty ugly one.

With me on the threshold and using his body to block the view of anyone passing, Derner reached in and flicked the light switch.

Alan Caine had his back to me, slumped awkwardly over his dressing table. There was a big mirror above it, and I couldn't chance Derner noticing my lack of reflection.

"Gimme a minute," I said from the side of my mouth, then stepped in and shut the door on him before he saw. If only I could hypnotize without hurting myself, then I wouldn't have to be alone in a room with a fresh corpse.

I chanced to take in a whiff and got what I expected: talcum powder, grease paint, and sweat mixed with the stink of urine and crap. Death had been brutal to Caine, and once relaxed, his body had given way with everything. No sweet peace here.

Fists in my pockets, I kept my distance. Had to bend low to check his face. What I expected: bloated and purple, broken blood vessels in his bulging eyes, tongue sticking out as though to offer a final opinion to the world. Something that looked like a blue necktie but wasn't was wound tight around his throat, the middle part almost lost in the folds of violated skin. Whoever had done it hadn't wanted noise and was strong enough to make it quick. No signs of a struggle anywhere else; the only evidence of the violence was the body itself.

"Damn."

The guy had been abusive, obnoxious, and *alive* not too many minutes ago. I hadn't liked him, but to take the life out of another this swiftly and easily was just wrong. Having killed as well as been killed, I understood how little effort was needed to do that which should be unthinkable. We unite to build towers to the sky, make music and art to feed our souls, can sacrifice selflessly to help others, yet cling with a lover's greedy passion to the to the lowest and darkest of our emotions. Most of us don't act upon that hate-driven force. We resist.

But for someone . . . not this time.

That blue thing on Caine's neck. Jewel had worn a blue dress. I didn't want her to be involved. A quick check of the closet turned up nothing of similar color.

Ah. Coatrack by the door. There was a blue satin smoking jacket hanging from a peg. Same color as the tie. Empty loops on the garment. Same material. Good. But Jewel wasn't off the hook entirely.

The killer must have stood *here,* watching Caine, maybe listening, but looking for something to use against him.

Something quiet. A .22 being fired might not be heard, or the sound misinterpreted. Knock a wooden chair over the right way and it makes more noise. But the killer might not have known that or possessed so small a gun. Most of the guys in this outfit never went with anything less that a .38.

Why not a knife, then? Plenty of them in the club's kitchen and simple enough to boost one and walk out. Or bring your own.

They can take time to do the job, though. You have to know what you're doing. Human skin is tougher than one would think, and dragging even a razor-sharp blade through a couple of inches of muscle and cartilage of a throat takes effort. The victim doesn't die instantly. There can be messy thrashing around; the killer can get splashed with telltale blood.

But strangulation, it's very intimate. That's one way to feel the whole progression of things shutting down as the life goes out of the body. There's no doubt about death. If you have the strength and speed and cut off the blood to the brain quick, a few moment's effort will do it. After that, then only forty pounds of pressure to crush what needs to be crushed, and it's over and done, make a quiet exit.

Freeing up one of my hands, I lifted one of Caine's by the shirt cuff and checked his manicured fingernails. Small dark crescents were under those nails, but not dirt—bloodsmell. He'd managed to dig in deep in his last struggle and left marks someplace on his killer's body. The wrists . . .

Looked the rest of the small room over. No cover, no place to hide. Just me and what Caine had left behind of himself.

Bobbi had also used this as a dressing room at one time. And Adelle Taylor. And lots of others I knew by name or in person. Their ghosts seemed to shift uneasily around me, disliking what had happened in their sanctuary. I stood and was dizzy from the shift, staggering a step. Waited, expecting another fit to sneak up from within, but it didn't happen. It was the air here. The presence of death. I didn't have to breathe to be overwhelmed.

I got on the other side of the door, met Derner's and Strome's gazes.

"Yeah," said Derner, apparently agreeing with whatever he saw on my face.

"Any ideas?" I asked.

" 'Bout what?"

"Who did it."

He shrugged. "Try a phone book."

"Not good enough. Show me your hands, both of you. Push your sleeves up."

They were mystified. Good.

"We don't shoot dope, Boss," said Strome, misinterpreting.

Derner was clean. Strome's knuckles were banged up and raw, but that was from the fight last night with Hoyle. His arms were free of nail gouging and scratches. I needed these two to be in the clear. On the other hand, they might have ordered someone else to strangle Caine, though the why of it was a mystery. I could settle such questions easy enough, but at the cost of collapsing in agony at their feet. Bosses weren't supposed to do that in front of the hired help.

Until I knew better, I'd just have to keep shut. "Who knows about this? Who found him?"

"Stage manager, just a few minutes ago," said Strome.

"Did he see anyone else in or out?"

"Nope. I asked him special. He knocked on the door, it opened, and he saw, then locked up and went for me and Derner. He won't say nothing."

"We gotta get Caine out of here," Derner advised, casting a glance up and down the hall. "The next show starts soon, there's no backup act—"

"Where's Jewel Caine?" I asked.

"What? His ex? She's here?"

"She was when we opened. Came back here to talk with friends. See if she's in with the dancers."

He did so, banging once on their dressing room door and barging in. No one screamed a protest, and I heard their negative replies to his question.

"She left just a little bit ago," someone within volunteered. "What's the idea locking us up? Hey—"

He returned. "You think *she* did it?"

Strome nodded. "She was plenty burned with him last night."

"I don't know," I said. "We'll figure that later. Where's the stage manager?"

Derner got him, explained that Alan Caine had come over sick and had to leave. The manager nodded slowly, rightly taking this to be the blanket explanation he would pass to others. After that, we did some fast shuffling to fill out the second show for the evening. An apologetic announcement was to be given to the house. One of the dancers also sang, so she'd have to change to a gown and do some solo numbers to keep things going. The other dancers had a hoofing routine already worked up that would pad the bill. The manager went off to fix things.

"What if the audience wants a refund?" Derner asked me.

"Give 'em their money, we can afford it." We sure as hell wouldn't be paying the star. I turned to Strome. "Hoyle might have tried collecting markers again and got too rough. I want to see him before we call the cops."

They were shocked. "The *cops?*"

"You heard."

"But we can't," said Derner.

I almost demanded to know why not, then bit it off. The Nightcrawler was already a favorite target for easy headlines; a murder under its roof just couldn't happen. Too many of the people here had records, and I wasn't about to draw official attention to myself if I could help it.

The trump card against bringing in the law was Gordy. If I didn't clean up this mess, he could get hauled off by the cops. He was in no shape to deal with even routine questions.

I debated over which course to go with, and not for the first time settled things by thinking, "What would Gordy do?"

"All right," I said. "We take care of it ourselves."

"Take care of what?"

None of us were virgins when it came to dealing with death firsthand, but the three of us gave a collective jump at that mildly put question from an outside party.

Kroun stood rather close to our group, and no one had heard his approach. "Take care of what, Fleming?" he repeated.

Now I knew how Derner and Strome felt when I'd turned up. "We got a problem."

"What problem?" Kroun's tone indicated he would like a full and truthful answer.

I didn't want to say it out loud, so I opened the dressing-room door. The light was still on. Kroun looked in, but did not go in.

"That's a problem," he agreed. "What are you going to do about it?"

Strome said to me, "Boss, I can disappear him like the others and no one's the wiser."

"No," I snapped.

"The others?" asked Kroun.

"Like Bristow," I said, to explain. "We're not dumping

this guy in pieces for fish food. He can't just mysteriously disappear, or we'd never hear the end of it. He's too famous."

Kroun gave me a long look and nodded in thoughtful agreement. "What, then?"

"We smuggle him out after closing. Put him in his own place without anyone seeing. He can't be found in the club. We just say he walked away and stick to that and not know anything else. The cops will come by and ask questions, but it won't be on the same level as it might if they knew he'd died here. Strome, you pick some guys who can keep their yaps shut, and I mean buttoned tight. They do the job, then forget they ever did it."

"Right, Boss."

"He was killed with something off his smoking jacket, make sure the jacket is taken to his place along with anything else he might normally have along with him. Make sure his wallet, keys, and stuff like that is on him. Take his hat and overcoat, and don't touch the tie around his neck. Don't just dump everything, make it look like he went home, and that's where he bought it. Everyone wears gloves."

"Right, Boss." He went inside the dressing room, shut the door, and from the sound of it, was preparing things for departure. He would have to work quick before the body stiffened up.

"Derner, find out where Caine hung his hat and case it. Figure the best time to get him inside. Arrange for a closed truck, something that won't stand out. No speeding, no busted lights, or whoever screws up will take the fall. Anyone too stupid or too nervous is on their own."

"Right, Boss."

"I want to know who was where from the moment Caine walked off the stage—wait—was Evie Montana in the dancers' dressing room?"

"I didn't notice."

"Find out. I saw her follow Caine when his act was over. Where is she now?"

Derner cut away to bang on the chorus dancer's door again and looked inside. He traded words, then withdrew, shaking his head at me. "None of the girls have seen her since the end of the first show. They said Jewel came by to shoot the breeze. She stepped outside to have a smoke. Not allowed to smoke backstage."

"See if she's still outside, then."

He tapped on Caine's door, and Strome emerged. If I expected him to be pale and shaken from his grim work, I was disappointed. This wasn't anything disturbing to him. Derner explained what was wanted, but Strome paused.

"Boss—there's something gone from there." He gestured back toward the room.

"Yeah?"

"I looked, but Caine's overcoat's gone."

I digested this a few seconds. "Maybe the killer took it."

"Ya think?" Kroun put in. "You're sure it's gone?"

Strome nodded. "Not that big a place, and it's a hard-to-miss coat. Tan-colored vicuna. Real flashy, expensive. Someone could get some money hocking or selling it."

"It'd be too hot an item. Why else would they take it?"

" 'Cause it's cold?"

Kroun look at me. I shrugged. "As good a reason as any. It'll make a search easier. Strome, go check the alley for Jewel Caine and see if you spot anyone dumb enough to have that coat."

Strome shot off, moving casual, but not wasting time.

With this kind of distraction I'd forgotten about my internal cold. It flooded its way back, and I had to fight to keep from visibly shivering. Evie Montana and Jewel Caine were gone, and the man between them thoroughly dead. I didn't think either or even both working together would be strong enough to strangle him like that, so quickly. As for motive . . . well, Jewel had none to speak of; Caine alive meant money to her. Unless my loan of forty bucks had taken the pressure off, and she'd come back to have a gloat and one thing had led to another. If so, then why had Caine turned his back on her? He liked baiting people face-to-face to enjoy their reaction. Of course, he could have watched the reflection in the big mirror, but then he might have seen the attack coming and put up more of a fight.

Where had Evie gotten to, anyway? The way she dogged him, she might as well have been on a leash. Had she seen him killed and run? That was my main worry. If either of them saw something she shouldn't, she was dead, too.

Derner went off to arrange details, leaving me and Kroun in the hall.

"You handled that," he said, "like you had it written out on a chalkboard."

I shrugged. "Just trying to anticipate. If I left anything out, I wanna know."

We looked at each other a minute. I knew for sure that Kroun hadn't personally done it since he'd been in my sight all during the break in the show. But Mitchell could have managed, and he'd been missing for a long time.

"Where's your boy?" I asked.

"You think Mitchell pulled this?" Kroun didn't seem angered by the implied accusation, only curious.

"He and Caine had a history, what was it?"

"Damned if I know." The deadpan look moved back in. He should charge it rent.

"How can you not know?"

"Mitchell's job is to watch my back and run errands, I don't need his life story for that."

"He was throwing looks at Caine."

"He does that for everyone. You, too, I noticed."

"Yeah, but I'm not strangled yet."

Kroun pushed the dressing-room door open. "Is that how it happened? He was strangled?"

"Yeah. Quiet."

"Knives are quiet, too."

"No knife, or I'd have sme—seen the blood."

He backed out. "Look, Fleming, you got a half-assed reason against Mitchell, and I'll admit it's a possibility. Who else is on your shit list?"

"A guy named Hoyle. We'll find him before the night's out."

"There must be others. From what you've said there could be a hundred people all wanting Caine dead. You said he owed markers?"

"To this club, maybe others. The money was coming out of his pay. He was more valuable alive."

"Not to one person." From where he stood Kroun took another look at the room, a long one, then shut the door. "That's all it takes."

"Figure the cops are going to go in big on this," I said. "Caine was popular. Catch his killer fast, and they get approving headlines. We gotta hand them someone. Preferably the right someone."

"His ex-wife or girlfriend? There's usually a dame behind these things."

I told him why I didn't think they were likely prospects. He was unimpressed. "Maybe you haven't seen how worked up a woman can get when she's mad enough. I have, and it's damned scary."

Actually I had seen a small woman take on two grown men and nearly win before the handcuffs were safely in place and we could call the cops on her. Escott still had the scars. Mine had healed. "I don't get that feeling here."

"Feeling. Uh-huh." Kroun clearly didn't think much of my instincts, and he was probably right. Just because I liked Jewel and thought Evie was cute was no reason to take them out of the running.

"Okay, they're on the list. Might as well add in the chorus girls and the band."

"The band was performing the whole time. Listen, let's just go find these two dames, have a talk, and settle it."

"Why are you so lathered to find the killer?" I asked.

More of the deadpan stare. "Why not?"

Couldn't think of a reply to that one. I'd rather have Kroun stay out of the way, but he was the big boss, and I still had to listen to him. It rankled not being able to influence him to my way of thinking. I'd gotten too used to the luxury of being able to order people around.

Derner came back to say arrangements were in hand, and he also had addresses for Jewel, Evie, and Hoyle. "I'm sending some of the boys for Hoyle. You want him alive?"

"Yes. Even if he didn't kill Caine, he owes me for those damn tires. What about Ruzzo?"

"They move around a lot. Landlords keep kicking them out."

"Lemme know when you bring 'em in. I need a car, too."

"Gordy's is back, but Strome took off to fix things. I can get another driver."

"I'll drive myself. You check everything on everyone who

was backstage. Make up whatever story you need for cover and make it reasonable; don't leave them room to guess what really happened."

Derner nodded, then reached in again from the hall to shut the light off before locking up. Apparently he didn't like putting himself any closer to the dead man than the rest of us.

Kroun and I left by the club's back door. The outside cold abruptly and painfully meshed with my inside chill. Ganged up on me like that, I didn't stand a chance and nearly doubled over from the shivering that hit like a gut punch.

"You okay? What's the matter?" Kroun paused from opening the passenger side of the Caddy, looking over the roof at me, half-annoyed, half-concerned.

"Freezing my ass off," I muttered, and slammed in behind the wheel. The keys were in their slot. No need to worry about anyone thieving this car. I tried to control the shaking to get it going.

"Stop," Kroun said.

I wasn't used to being ordered, even when I knew it was part of the job. "What?"

He made no reply, just walked around and opened my door. "Move over, I'll drive."

"But—"

"Do it."

I did it.

Kroun gave me an irritated up-and-down. "You got a fever or what? Only time I saw a man in your kind of shape he had the DTs. You sick?"

"I donno. Don't feel sick." I hated that he was picking me apart.

"You don't look sick. Not much." He figured out the starter, put the car in gear, and we glided forward. "Which way?"

"Left at the corner, then right."

He drove as directed, throwing a glance my way now and then. The car was still warmed up from taking Gordy to the Bronze Belt. Kroun fiddled with the heater and opened the vents wide. Hot air breathed on my feet and legs. "Better?"

"A little."

He looked unconvinced but kept it to himself. "So what's really wrong with you?"

"Nothing."

"Fleming, you don't have DTs, St. Vitus Dance, or malaria, and that's the limit of my educated guessing. You know what's wrong."

"It's probably the shot I had."

He threw a hostile glare remarkably similar to Mitchell's. "Shot. There's no medicine makes a man cold like that. If it was the winter getting to you, then your teeth would be chattering, too. This has to do with what Bristow did to you."

I shook my head to mean I didn't want to talk about it.

"Yeah, and it's got you bad. I've seen guys just like you going right off the dock, but because they were in the War. It did that to them. You didn't have the War; you had Bristow. The son of a bitch is *dead*, he can't come at you again."

Which I knew very well. Funny, but Escott had been on this same trail the night before.

"I told you to ease off on yourself, so when's it going to commence?"

No answer to that one, since I sure as hell didn't know. "Let's stick to business, if you don't mind."

"Business. That's what we call it. It's what got you where you are. It's what killed that guy back there, sure as shit. Business." He sounded none too pleased with it.

What was this about? But he shut down.

The heater was a good one. Eventually the hot air blowing against my legs filled up the rest of the car, blunting the edge. The pain from the inner cold eased, whether from the warmth or Kroun trying to talk some sense into me, I couldn't tell.

He turned on the radio. "This okay with you?"

"Go ahead." I was surprised he'd bothered to ask.

We listened to Harry James. The music gave me something else to think about besides myself. I'd interrupt with directions now and then, as needed. Our route more or less followed the El line as we headed to Jewel Caine's home. It was the closest to the Nightcrawler.

The song ended, a grimly serious ad instructing everyone to use Bromo-Seltzer to fight off colds replaced it. Foiling the announcer, Kroun turned the sound down. "This is some car," he said. "Gotta plan ahead to make turns, but it's a smooth ride."

"It has truck shocks to take the extra load," I told him. So long as we kept the topic aimed away from me, I didn't mind socializing.

"That would be the armor plating making the weight?"

"Yeah. Top, bottom, and sides, with bulletproof window glass, special tires. This thing's built like a German tank. Gordy had it done by this guy in Cicero. I think he was the same one who fixed up Capone's car likewise. Did a better job for Gordy, though."

"He fix the motor up, too? She runs easy for this kind of load."

"Some other guy did that. I'm not sure exactly how, but she'll do one-twenty on the flat and not raise her voice."

"Sounds sweet. Real sweet."

I could agree with that.

"This the place?"

"Yeah."

He had to circle the block to find parking. The neighborhood was run-down, but not quite on the skids. Sad old piles of brick made up the better buildings, jaded clapboard was on the rest. Even when new, the area would have been depressing, and I speculated whether the architects had been solitary drinkers.

A three-story brick was our destination. It had once been a hotel, but was converted to flats. Nothing fancy. No doorman, no night man out front to watch things. We walked in unchallenged and went up to the second floor. No elevator.

I heard radios tuned to different shows as we walked down a dim, door-lined hall. Someone with a fussy baby walked the floor in there, a couple traded opening salvos in that one, somebody snoring just here—the usual. Down at the end a radio was turned up loud, but not too loud. It was in Jewel Caine's flat.

Kroun did the honors, banging on the door. "Mrs. Caine?"

I stepped close to call through the thickly painted wood. "Jewel? It's Jack Fleming from the club. Open up, would you?"

We waited and tried again.

"This doesn't look good," said Kroun. "Why turn the radio on and go out?"

Had I been alone, I could have answered that for myself by vanishing and sieving inside. Without hypnosis to make him forget, I was crippled on what I could do.

Kroun reached up, feeling along the trim above the door. "No key. I don't want to bother looking for anybody who has one, either. We'll do it the hard way."

He dropped to one knee and pulled out a small case. Picklocks. A very nice set. He used them. To him it was the hard way, to me it was expertly and quickly done, and I was accustomed to Escott's skills. Even he couldn't work with gloves on.

"Turn it," Kroun said, holding two of the picks in place.

I turned it; the door drifted open. He withdrew the picks and put his kit away.

Lights were on, and a single window overlooking the front of the building on the right had its shade drawn. Jewel had left after dark, then. Or come home and left again. I hoped so. The radio was in a corner, a table model. Kroun started over, a hand reaching to perhaps turn it off, then stopped. He put his hands in his pockets.

"What?" I asked quietly.

He shook his head and seemed to be listening, but I couldn't hear over the radio noise. I took in the rest of the place. Jewel was an indifferent housekeeper. The room was small, a kitchen and parlor in one, with only the barest necessities, cheap stuff. Mail, opened and not, was scattered on what served as a dining table. She had a fine collection of sleeping and some other kind of pills for her nerves which made me uneasy. I knew what too many of those in one dose could do. Most of the containers seemed to have stuff in them. The bad thing would have been finding them empty. I wish I'd not thought of that angle.

Kroun went into her bedroom. I followed.

Unmade bed, clothes piled up. I took a whiff and got

stale cigarette smoke, very heavy, some kind of perfume vainly fighting it, and the scent of desperation. I couldn't explain the last one; the feeling just swelled up in me.

And one other . . . oh, *damn*.

I slumped. We were too late.

The bathroom. Pushed the door open. It wouldn't go all the way. Her body prevented that.

Didn't want to, but I had to look, to make sure.

The bloodsmell overwhelmed even the old cigarette reek. It looked like she'd stood in front of the mirror over the sink, put the gun to her head, and that was it. No doubt about her being dead. The white-painted walls were splattered with blood and . . . and other stuff.

"What?" asked Kroun. He had to pull me out to see for himself.

She still wore her coat. Was that normal? If there was a normal. Didn't suicides prepare themselves? Write notes or something . . . ?

Distraction. It wasn't working. I backed away, going to the small kitchen, stood by the sink there, and waited. I was hot and cold both together, feeling the sweats you get as your body works itself up to vomiting.

That didn't happen, though. The sick weight stayed bunched in my throat, twisting through my belly. I wanted to throw up just to get it over with.

The cold won out. I leaned forward and trembled from it. My knees started to go. Managed to fall onto one of the chairs by the dining table instead of the floor.

Kroun came out. Kept silent a while. I couldn't look at him. Too busy fighting off the shakes. I would *not* let myself give in into another damned fit with Kroun looking on.

"Wasn't anything you could have done," he said, after some moments.

"Gotten here sooner."

"I don't think so. Listen, someone makes up her mind to do that, she'll find a way no matter what."

I shook my head. Didn't quite know why.

"What is it?" he asked.

"She didn't kill herself."

"Looked pretty clear to me."

"Someone made it look that way." I sat up straight and did what I could to shove all the sick darkness within into a box and slam the lid. I needed to be thinking. "See if you can find her purse."

He moved around, turned up three purses. One was the same blue as her dress. I upended it on the table, amid the clutter of makeup, keys, tissues, matches, and crushed cigarettes—the twenty and two tens I'd handed over to help with the back rent.

"That's my loan to her." I gave him a short version of my talk with Jewel earlier. "The woman was cleaned up. There's no booze here, check and see. She was sober and had some hope back, had a job waiting. She wouldn't have shot herself."

"She would if she'd murdered Caine."

True. Jewel *could* have killed her ex, then in a fit of remorse came back here to escape earthly justice. But everything in me said it was wrong. "He meant money to her. She had no motive."

"You don't know that."

"I was with her, she was—"

"Wise up, Fleming. You talk to her for half an hour and think you know what's going on inside her head? You can know a person a lifetime, and he'll still surprise you in ugly ways."

"She was murdered."

"Give me a reason to believe it."

Hell, I had to give myself one, besides the churning in my guts. "That gun, what kind is it?"

He went to look and came back. "Long revolver. A forty-five."

"That's a lot of iron for a woman to carry."

"So she kept it under the bed to scare burglars."

"A woman's more likely to have a smaller gun."

"So she was a tougher girl than most. I've met more than one broad carting a cannon around and not thinking twice about it."

"Me, too, but Jewel—" This was getting nowhere. I'd thought of a new angle for him. "Look at these."

He looked. "Pills. The sleeping kind. Okay. What about 'em?"

I shook one of the bottles. There were enough to do the job. "Lemme put it this way: given a choice, wouldn't you rather just fall quietly asleep to do your dying? Why put a big, noisy gun to your head?"

Kroun unexpectedly went dead white, his skin almost matching the streak in his hair. Maybe I'd dredged up a bad memory for him, of when he'd been bullet-grazed. "She . . . might have been in a hurry."

That wasn't funny. "I think someone else must have been instead." Evie Montana? Hoyle? Mitchell? Why, though?

"Someone made her kill herself? How? Holding another gun on her? 'Shoot yourself before I do it for you?' "

"I donno. She could have been knocked out, he stands her up, puts the gun in her hand, and—"

He shifted. Frowned. He went back to the bathroom again. When he returned his color was no better, but something had changed. "Okay. I'm convinced."

"Where did I go right?"

"The gun. It's in her hand. Her hand's relaxed around it."

"So?"

"When a shooter that size goes off, it's gonna kick like an army mule. It should be lying anywhere else, but not where it is. Somebody set her up all right."

Her hands . . . he'd reminded me. Wearily, I went and looked for myself. I made my gaze skip over the blood and mess and focus only on her hands. Enough of the skin was visible. No finger marks, no crescent-shaped cuts from Caine's nails digging into her flesh. She'd not done it.

"C'mon, let's get going," said Kroun.

I blinked, my mind trying to shift gears to keep level. "What?"

"That other dame you wanted to see. Let's find out if she's still breathing."

"Shit."

He snagged up the money. Shoved it at me.

"Hey, I don't—"

"If you don't, someone else will. Use it to buy her flowers, but don't leave it for the damn vultures when they come."

We'd kept our gloves on, so wiping away prints wasn't a problem. We left, moving quiet, but it seemed a wasted precaution. If the tenants here had been able to ignore a gun noise like that, they wouldn't pay mind to much else, including the radio we'd left on.

Kroun drove, with me muttering directions and trying to feel the heater's warmth again. There might not have been anything I could have done to prevent Jewel's death, but part of me thought otherwise, and was beating me up about it.

"Hey." Kroun broke in on the internal pounding.

"What?"

"She was dead before we could have gotten there."

"How do you know?" And how was it this guy could read me so well? I might as well be wearing a sandwich sign.

"The way the blood was dried. I . . . got some experience about that."

I didn't care to ask for details. I had experience, too, and he was likely right, but her death hurt all the same.

"It's not fair," he said, as though agreeing to something I'd spoken aloud. "Not by one damn bit. We'll get the guy, though. Or girl. We will."

Cold comfort, Escott might have said. I wanted him here, but the less contact between him and my current business associates the better. I'd tell him about it later.

Evie's place was in another not-so-great neighborhood. Her flat was one of two above a street-level shoe store. Other small businesses filled out the block, each apparently with living quarters a mere stair climb away. Convenient. Kroun parked out front, and we hurried up to the tenant's entry. No need for picking the lock, the thing was open.

He banged on the flat's door, and I called Evie's name, a too-eerie reprise of what we'd done at Jewel's.

Thankfully I heard movement on the other side of the door. A groggy-sounding woman wanted to know what we wanted. I said I was Evie's boss and trying to find her.

"What's she done now?" the woman asked. Still through the door.

"She left without her pay."

The door was abruptly opened. A thin brunette, rumpled hair, no makeup, wrapped in a too-large flannel robe, peered out. She gave us the eye, a suspicious one. Kroun stepped diffidently back and looked surprisingly harmless and humble.

"Sorry to come by so late, Miss," he said, his smile

matching his apology. "But we're trying to find Evie. It's important."

She blinked against the onslaught of charm, then shook it off. "What's that about her pay? She owes me back rent."

I pulled out one of the ten-dollar bills. "You know where she is?"

"At work, some club—if you're her boss, why don't you know?" She stared with unabashed fascination at the money.

"Evie left suddenly, before the show was over. We thought she might be ill or have an emergency. Is she here?"

"Of course she's not here, or she'd have answered the door. This is the middle of the night in case you haven't noticed."

"Yeah, sorry about that. Where would she go if she had a problem?"

"What kind of problem? If it's with a man, she moans to me about it. If it's about money, she moans to her boyfriend."

"The singer?"

"What singer? That creep Alan Caine? Not him. Her *other* boyfriend, the sailor."

What a surprise, but Kroun landed on his feet. "Is he that big blond Swede from Minnesota who stutters?"

The woman rolled her eyes. "She's got *another* one? The only guy I know is a bald Polack merchant sailor who talks smooth. He lives somewhere by the river—with his *wife.* Evie's got no more sense about men than—than I don't know what, but she's an idiot about anything in pants."

"So where do we find this Polack sailor?"

"Canada. He shipped out a week ago. He sent her a letter from some place. They were stuck in port because the weather delayed a shipment or something, and he said he'd be late getting back. He should be so considerate to his wife."

Probably wasn't, I thought. "You sure he's out of town?"

"Oh, yeah. Evie was in the dumps for a whole hour over it. I had to listen. Say, why are you so interested?"

"It's really important we find her. What other friends might she go to if she was in a jam?"

"That's it. She comes to me first, then her boyfriends. She's angling to be the next Mrs. Caine, you know. What a dope."

"You don't like him much?"

"He walks all over her and thinks it's funny. She doesn't want to see that, though. I don't care how handsome a fella is, if he doesn't treat you right, throw him back in the water, he's not worth the trouble. Is she in a jam?"

"We just have to find her."

"Then call the cops. If she's not here or with Caine or the Polack, then she's not anywhere. She's used up her favors with everyone else."

I pulled out a business card for Lady Crymsyn, penciled the lobby phone number and Escott's office number on the back, and handed it to her along with the ten-dollar bill. "If she comes home or calls, you ring any of these until you get an answer from someone."

She looked from the money to me like I'd just become her new best friend. "Well, *sure!*"

"And you don't have to say anyone was by looking for her."

"Sure!"

We said good night and started down the hall. When her door shut and the lock clicked in place Kroun signed for me to wait, then cat-footed back to listen, his ear to the keyhole. I should have thought of that. I'd have heard a lot more.

After a moment he returned, shaking his head. "I

thought she might call someone, but no dice. I think she went back to bed. Any other ideas?"

"The Nightcrawler again. See if Derner came up with anything."

"There's another place to check . . ."

"Oh, yeah?"

"Alan Caine's."

Damn. I wish I'd thought of that, too. Evie might have taken refuge there given the chance. Strome and his men wouldn't get over for some hours yet. "I'll call Derner for the address."

9

ALAN Caine's rooms were at a good hotel, which meant Kroun and I had to get around the night man out front. It wasn't hard. From a drugstore phone booth I called the desk, said that I was Caine, gave the room number, and instructed him to let up two of my friends as soon as they came in.

"And show them respect," I imperiously added. "They're important." I was taking a chance the guy on the line knew Caine's voice. On the other hand, if I was bossy enough, he might fall for it. Must have worked; I got a weary "yes, Mr. Caine" in reply.

Kroun drove half a block and parked across the street. We walked into the lobby. "I'll handle it," he said, and veered away. He murmured to the clerk there, who eventually nodded and handed over a key.

"When the cops start investigating, he'll remember your face," I said.

"Yeah, but by then I'll probably be back in New York, won't I? Besides, I got one of those hard-to-remember mugs."

He had to be kidding. The clerk noticed us, noticed Kroun, the moment we came in. There was no dampening of his magnetism at all. On the other hand I was wallpaper by comparison and content to stay that way.

He continued, "Most people only see the white streak in my hair, and I kept my hat on. Let's go."

The elevator was one of those fancy push-button ones that didn't need an operator. Everything these days was going automatic, from gearshifts in cars to toasters. Looked like another job was being shut down in the name of progress.

We stopped on the fourth floor, doors magically heaving open on their own. I noticed the fire exit was close to Caine's room. That would be convenient for Strome when the time came.

Kroun unlocked, let the door swing open, and paused, listening. No radio going. In a place like this a loud radio would be investigated. So would gunshots. He went in, flipping on the light.

Yeah, Caine had done himself swell. His shades were up, the curtains wide. He had a wide slice of view of the street below. Nothing spectacular, but better than Jewel's or Evie's lot.

Evie didn't jump out at us. Neither did anyone else. We went through each room more thoroughly than they deserved.

Maid service had been in that day. The bed was in order, fresh towels in the bath, wastebaskets emptied. His clothes were hung up or in a hamper. In the living room was a studio piano parked against the outside wall, a stack of sheet music, and a well-stocked bar. He'd taken generous samples from all the bottles and had a preference for scotch to judge by the many brands.

The hotel's furnishings were in place but no pictures were on display except his own. Handsome portraits abounded. Caine had been a man thoroughly in love with himself.

"Ain't that cute?" Kroun pointed to a large, beautifully executed nude photo of Caine that had a place of honor hanging above the sofa.

Caine was posed full length, but sideways to the camera so nothing really showed, but there was no doubt he had a body to match his perfectly sculpted face. Every lean muscle showed in the play of shadow and light over his form. I knew a thing or two about photography from my days as a reporter, and understood the kind of work that had gone into making such a picture. You had to be able to get the whites white and the blacks black, yet preserve the countless shades of gray in between.

"That cost him a bundle," I said.

"Must have been stuck on himself real bad. Only guys I know who put up pictures of themselves are funny. I've never seen one go this far, though. Singers."

"Vanity's expensive, all right." I went to a desk and dug in, finding nothing as eye-catching as the portrait. Caine had bills, clothing receipts, old letters, and handwritten IOUs. Lots of those. Nothing for less than a hundred, and several for over a thousand. Trusting souls. They must have fallen for the pretty face and charm, too. The people he owed used nicknames mostly, but perhaps Derner might know some of them. Rather than mess up the investigation for the cops, I pulled out a hotel envelope from the stationery drawer and scribbled down those that were legible. One of them might have gotten fed up waiting to collect and decided to get fatal.

I found an address book and decided to take it along. Plenty of names—and nicknames—and numbers for both Chicago and New York exchanges to tell by the prefix letters. I could mail it to the cops later. Or not.

Kroun saw what I was doing, grunted approval, and went over the rest of the place again, poking in cupboards. He whistled once, having found a respectable cache of beer in the pantry, with an even larger number of empty bottles crated and ready to go back for the deposits. "Nothing," he announced when I was done copying. "No Evie, but some of her clothes are in his bureau. It's sweet stuff."

"Maybe he was going to pawn it," I said. I told him what Jewel had said about Caine hocking step-ins.

"You mean women buy stuff like that at a—" He shook his head. "You're kidding. I've never seen those at a pawn shop."

"Ah, Jewel was kidding. Maybe. My girlfriend doesn't tell me where she gets her scanties, and I don't say where I buy my drawers. I'm glad to leave it at that."

Kroun snorted a laugh. "That it for here?"

"Yeah."

I went down the fire escape to see where it came out, which was an alley. Strome could use it as a means of getting in the flat.

When I returned, Kroun considerately inquired after my health. Damn. I should have tied a string to my finger so I could remember to act feeble.

"I'm fine," I said.

"Just watching out for you. That's what friends do." He smiled. It was ingenuous, almost too much so, like he had a private joke.

Was he remembering what I put in his mind the other night? The words were a close echo to what I'd given him.

There'd be hell to pay if he shook off the suggestions and re-called my vanishing act. The hell would be in my head, since I'd have to put him under again. It could kill me.

We went out the front way, so the night clerk could see us leaving. He didn't ask for the key back, but considering the way Caine treated people, it was not surprising. The staff must have gone out of their way to avoid all unneces-sary contact with their guest, and were willing to extend the policy to anyone associated with him.

Fine with me. We'd need that key for later.

Once outside, the cold returned to my bones. I'd almost been able to put it aside up in Caine's flat. It wasn't as bitter as before, but I would be glad when the night was over so I could lose myself in oblivion again. Even when unaware of the passing hours it was still a time of healing. I wanted it to heal me from this before it drove me crazy.

Crazier.

When we got back to Gordy's office Derner was at the big desk, up to his eyeballs in paperwork, phone calls, and loose cash from the casino. Another guy at a nearby table thun-dered away at a calculation machine, punching in numbers as fast as he could read from a clipboard and pulling the lever. Derner looked on my return with too much relief. I knew I was in for it.

Over on the couch, with two of the tougher lugs stand-ing guard, lay a man, gagged, blindfolded, and hands bound behind him.

"What the *hell* is this?" I demanded, and only my sur-prise kept me from roaring the walls down.

"We found him for ya, Boss," said one of the lugs, grinning.

"Found who?"

Derner slammed the phone receiver and came around the desk. "These two brains ain't listening to me—"

"Found *who?*" The guy didn't look familiar.

"That kidnapper you want so bad, Boss," said the lug.

I stared at the figure on the couch. He wasn't moving much, but from what I could read off his posture he was scared shitless.

"The kidnapper?" said Kroun. Hands in pockets, he cocked his head, highly interested.

"Dugan?" I went closer. Gave what I could see of his face good long look. Pulled the gag off. The mouth was all wrong, and so was the voice that went with it.

"PleaseforGodsakedontkillme! I don't know nothing about anything! I swear! I got a wife and kids an—"

"Shuddup!" I snarled.

He shut up.

"Hey!" I said to Derner.

He approached. Cautiously. "Yeah, Boss?"

"Get rid of adding boy there, he's giving me a headache."

He stopped the man from punching more buttons and told him to take a short hike. The guy went, shutting the door. Except for faint band music that I could hear even through the soundproofed walls, it was very quiet.

"Okay," I said, tiredly. "Let's keep it short. You with the blindfold. What's your name?"

"J-j-john C-c-c-oward, sir. I'm from W-waukegan and—"

"Stop."

He stopped.

I found his wallet. Showed the driving license to the lugs. "Gentlemen, may I introduce you to Mr. John Coward of Waukegan?"

"Naw, *he's* the guy! He's just like the picture in the papers!"

"Yeah-yeah, just like an apple looks like an orange. You got the wrong man."

"But—"

I didn't need the evil eye to freeze him, I was that mad. He rocked back and put up a protesting hand. It cut no ice with me. "Get out of here before I ventilate the both of you. And spread the word that the hunt for Dugan is *over.*"

"But if you ain't caught him yet . . ."

"Doesn't matter," I said through my teeth. "It's over, called off, finished, *finito,* shelved in a box. Anything about that you didn't understand?"

They shook their heads.

"Get out."

They got.

"Derner?"

"Yeah, Boss?"

"Did you have any kind of a conversation with them or Mr. Coward?"

"Yeah, Boss. I *tried* to tell those two, but they wouldn't listen. They said you'd tell it straight, so they parked here. They found this guy in a craps game, made him to be Dugan, and been carting him all over Chicago trying to find you, first at your club, then your house, then that gumshoe's office . . ."

"Oh, my God." I rubbed a hand over my face. "They're dumber than Ruzzo."

"Well, they kept him in the car trunk so no one would see. Ruzzo wouldn't have done that . . ."

I snarled, and he corked it. Glanced at Kroun. He was doing his almighty best to not laugh. John Coward sat very still and trembled, his head high. He must have been able to see a little out the bottom of the blindfold. "Okay, I get the picture. Mr. Coward, I'm going to have someone take you back to wherever you belong."

"N-not gonna kill me?"

"Not going to kill you. They thought you were someone else, and I apologize for that. If you'd like to forget about this mistake, we will, too. I'll have to insist you keep the blindfold on for the time being. In this case what you don't know can't hurt you."

"Anything, whatever you want, anything, please! I won't say a word."

"That's good enough for me. I suggest you stay away from craps games in the future, hm?"

"Yes, whatever you want I'll do it!"

I went to the desk, shuffled together five hundred bucks, folding it into Coward's wallet. I put the wallet into his pocket. "Just remember: *none* of this happened."

"Nothing, not anything."

"If we see your face again, well, you wouldn't be happy. Now we'll get you back to the wife and kids where you belong. You just say where you want to go."

Derner took his arm and stood him up, walking him slowly toward the door like an invalid. I didn't relax until they were well down the hall.

"What a night." I groaned and eased onto the couch.

Kroun finally cut loose. He didn't quite bust a gut, that wasn't his style, but his laughter was catching. I succumbed in a much more moderate way. Oddly, the chill inside lessened. Yeah, I was onto something there in regards to a cure. It didn't last. It couldn't. Not with Caine's body still in the dressing room below and Jewel lying in her own blood and brains halfway across town. The cold came back, but I was able to ignore it better. Just had to stay busy, that's all.

Kroun found a chair, sat, and put his feet up on Gordy's desk. "You know what you should do?"

"Tell me."

"Find yourself a quiet shore on one of these lakes, settle in, and see what you can do about decimating the local fish population."

I'd have never suspected that he knew such big words. "I don't eat fish."

"That's not the *point*." He shook his head. "It's not about *eating* fish. It's about *fishing*. For fish. Just . . . just . . . *fish*."

He had an idea there. It was right up there with Escott thinking I should take a vacation. Kroun angled his hat over his face and clasped his hands over his stomach. I got the impression that was how he did his fishing.

Derner returned. "The guy's on his way home. Sorry about that, Boss."

"Never mind. The other boys know the hunt's canceled?"

"The word's getting spread now. No one's gonna be in a good mood over losing that ten Gs."

As though some of them could resent me even more. "They'll tough it out. You got the lowdown about the backstage people?"

"Yeah. A big fat nothing. They saw plenty of it."

"Good trick," said Kroun, from under his hat. "Seeing nothing."

"Who was backstage?" I asked.

Derner parked his duff on the desk and crossed his arms. "That I know of: the dancers, eight of them, the stage manager, Caine, and Mrs. Caine. Seven of the dancers were having a break while Caine did his solo. They said Evie left to hang around just offstage, waiting for him. She usually did."

"They all stayed in their dressing room?"

"Talking with Jewel Caine. She was happy about getting a job, wouldn't say where, and they was just gabbing. You know. Hen-talk."

"Yeah. I know." My mouth went dry.

"Just before Caine's number finished Jewel went out for a smoke. She said she didn't want to bump into him when he came backstage. With all this talking the girls was running late and stayed in the dressing room to get ready for the next show. Next thing they know the stage manager shoves his snoot in and tells 'em to stay put, then locks the door. They were still plenty mad about that, saying if there was a fire they'd be cooked, but—"

"Where was the stage manager all that time?"

"Well, after he found Caine he stayed in the hall to keep watch, so if there was a fire, he coulda let them out easy enough. He called one of the busboys over and sent him up to get me, then I ran into Strome on the way down. By then the manager got a couple more guys in to watch the other end of the hall. They didn't see anyone."

"What about before he found Caine?"

"He was up in the lighting booth. There was a problem with one of the spots, and he had to find a spare bulb. The lighting guy backed him. The manager didn't leave the booth until after Caine was offstage."

"So he had opportunity."

"But no reason. He's not big, either; you've seen him. Caine was near twice his size. He could have fought him off."

"Ya think?" asked Kroun. "If Caine was taken by surprise . . ."

Derner shrugged. "Yeah, maybe. The manager's been with us for years, and Caine was just another act to him. He cares more about this club's staging than anything else. Even if he had a reason to bump Caine, he'd have done it some other place. He's show people, and they're all crazy that way."

"Okay," I said. "He's off the suspect list until we get desperate. No one saw where Evie went?"

"The girls said she went with Caine into his dressing room. She was usually in there during his breaks. They thought they were being on the sly, but everyone knew."

"So maybe Evie did do it," said Kroun.

"When we find her we'll ask her," I said. "And Hoyle. And Ruzzo. And Mitchell." All I needed was to check hands and arms for scratches. I thought about sharing that detail with Kroun, but held back. Mitchell was still his boy. Under his protection.

"Mitchell?" Derner was surprised and glanced uneasily at Kroun for his reaction, only there was none.

"Just covering the bases," I added. "Mr. Kroun doesn't mind."

"It's business," Kroun put in with a snort. "Biz-iii-nessss."

I got Derner's attention back. "Have you seen Mitchell tonight?"

"Only earlier. I heard he left before the ruckus."

"Find out for sure. See to it the guys are looking for all five of them and it's only to *talk*. I want everyone alive and undamaged. Let the boys know when *I* say talk I mean only talk. No sparring sessions, no turkey shoots."

"What if the ones they're after shoot first?"

He got a look from me.

"Okay-okay!" He left to take care of things. After a minute of thinking about it, I moved to the desk and the phone there. Kroun still had his feet up on the edge.

"Nice shoes," I said.

"Thanks."

I dialed Lady Crymsyn's lobby phone.

Wilton answered pretty fast this time. "Yes, Mr. Fleming?"

"How di—ahh, never mind. Everything going okay there?"

"No problems. We had a good night. Good shows, lotta people. You want I should get Mr. Escott?"

"Nah. Just tell him or Bobbi that I won't be back, so they'll have to close. It's business." They'd both understand. Wilton said he'd pass the message, and I hung up.

"Biz-iii-nessss," Kroun drawled, then snorted again.

I checked the clock. "It's pretty late. If you're tired . . ."

"Just resting my eyes, kid. There's still one more errand to run tonight."

⸱

Kroun had surprised me about overseeing the transport job. I'd have thought he'd want to stay well clear of a potential disaster if anything went wrong. Instead, he sat in the front seat of Gordy's Caddy with me on the passenger side. We were parked just up the street from Caine's hotel. It was so late that only the deep-night creeps were out—which included us and a select few others.

A gray panel truck sat backed into the alley between the hotel and the next building over. I couldn't see what was going on. That was good. None of us wanted the activity there to be visible to passing cars. I was mostly worried about cops. They would be the only others out at this hour. A sharp one might wonder why laundry was being delivered at this time of the morning.

Strome was one of the laundrymen. He'd turned up at the Nightcrawler with a couple of shut-mouthed goons, coverall uniforms, and the truck. An hour after the club was closed and the last straggling worker left, Strome helped the goons load in an exceptionally heavy laundry basket, then they drove off. Kroun and I followed at a distance.

Things went without a hitch. About five minutes after parking in the alley, Strome and his crew were out again and driving away. They must have used the service elevator instead of the fire escape stairs to get up to the right floor. No matter, so long as they weren't caught. Kroun had supplied the key. Wiped clean, it was to be dropped on the desk in the room, just like he told the clerk earlier.

There would be a hell of a stink over this tomorrow. I felt sorry for the poor maid, who'd likely be the one to find the body. I also hoped the night clerk would be unhelpful about descriptions of Kroun and me. When it came down to it, we had a pretty lousy cover. Two mystery men go up to Caine's room. Caine is found dead there the next day, but not seen to come in by the front entrance. Any halfway-good cop would tear into that pretty quick and backtrack to the Nightcrawler. The best I could expect from our interference was to confuse things, buy some time to find the killer. Then—if the hideous head pain would leave me alone for long enough—I could whammy him or her to marching in to the D.A.'s office to dictate a complete confession. We'd all be off the hook.

Of course, that was the ideal way for this to turn out. I focused on thinking about it, rather than the countless ways it could go wrong.

Kroun had cut the motor for those five minutes. He started the car again, and the heater blasted air against my legs. I winced. "You still cold?" he asked.

"Yeah." I'd been fighting off shivering again, vowing to buy a heavier coat.

"Go home then. Get some sleep." He didn't look remotely tired himself.

"I need to see to things."

"What things? We're finished here. Even those guys are

flying back to their roost." He gestured ahead, where the taillights of the panel truck made a turn and vanished. "Where's home?"

"Just take me to my club."

"You live there?"

"I flop in the office sometimes. When it's a late night."

"That's what we have here, ladies and gentlemen. A late night. Which way?"

As before, I gave directions, and he drove. He seemed to enjoy hauling the big car around corners.

Kroun dropped me at the front of Crymsyn, and said he knew how to get back to his hotel from there.

"Why are your lights still on?" he asked. "Someone in inside?"

"We leave 'em on to scare off burglars." That was better than trying to explain about Myrna.

He tossed an easy good night at me and drove off, the well-tuned Caddy barely making a sound. I hurried to unlock Crymsyn's front doors.

Kroun was right about this chill not being related to winter. I shook from it, but my teeth weren't chattering.

Shut the door against the cold, cruel night, turned to check the lobby. The overhead lights glowed, as well as the one behind the bar, almost as though Myrna knew I'd be coming in and would need them.

I'd often been here before on my own, and each time noticed the silence. Of course, with my hearing I could pick up on every damn creak and pop, which was ignorable or twanged at my nerves depending on my mood. I was in a foul and fragile frame of mind for now. Something about

Kroun bothered me. The way he'd been acting at some points was worry-making.

The uncomfortable suspicion rolled through my head that Kroun might be immune to my kind of hypnosis. If he was crazy and able to hide it, then just pretended to be under the other night . . . I didn't want to believe it.

Distracted as I had been with the pain, he'd remained dead-eyed and not reacting the whole time—even when I'd vanished. No one could be that good at faking.

Unless he'd met another like me and knew what to do, what to expect. That might explain it. I was one of a rare breed. If Kroun knew about vampires that would account for his changed manner. He might see me as a possible ally to cultivate. Make me a friend, then I cease to be a threat.

Or I was imagining stuff, and this was all a load of crap.

I could just about hear Escott agreeing with me, too. Whatever I was reading from Kroun was certainly colored by what had I'd been through in the last week. There was no reason to trust any of it. I needed to take the advice I'd given to Gordy and get some rest.

Perhaps Kroun was just . . . I guess *relaxed* would be the word. He sure didn't match up with the ill-tempered man I'd first talked to on the phone or the commanding mob boss who could clear a room with just a look. Gordy said Kroun was scary. I wasn't seeing that anymore. Or feeling it. That must be what set off the doubts in my gut. Gordy wouldn't have used that word without good reason.

Capone was known to be as charming as all get out when he was in the mood for it. He was still a killer.

Maybe that was the scare about Kroun. Lull a person with the charm, then bang-bang-you're-dead.

Too late for me.

* * *

I went up to my office—lights were on there, too. The ledgers with Bobbi's neat entries were with that night's respectable take in the desk safe, meaning a bank run tomorrow. I put the money bag back, along with the .38 Detective Special I kept there. Sure, I was fairly bulletproof, but if I could head off trouble packing heat of my own, then why not?

Heat . . .

I turned up the radiator and hovered over it, hoping to thaw out.

It occurred to me that maybe I should have more blood inside my shuddering body.

Rotten thought.

I was *not* hungry, but the impulse strongly tugged to bring that living heat inside, to glut on it and drive away the death chill. In my mind I knew it would be futile, but the malicious darkness within urged otherwise.

Phone up a taxi, it said. There was time to squeeze in a trip to the Stockyards before dawn. Time to drink myself sick again.

I fought it off by telling myself it was too much trouble, would endanger me if I got caught by an early-morning yard worker. I ran through a few dozen other discouraging excuses of varying degrees of likelihood. All served to delay until the craving passed, and depression firmly took over, finally immobilizing me.

It's a sad thing when self-pity becomes a safe and welcome alternative for heading off self-destructive activities.

Left the office, went down to Bobbi's dressing room. I had some spare clothes shoved into the back of the closet there. No need to move her stuff out now that Jewel was dead.

Damnation.

Stripped and turned on the shower water as hot as possible, risking a scald to just stand with the spray square in my face. With no need to breathe I was there for a long while, the water hammering my eyelids. Lost track of how many times I soaped and scrubbed, soaped and scrubbed. I emptied the club's huge hot-water tank. Finally warm, or at least not cold, my skin was cherry red when I emerged.

Except for the long, thin, white scars.

I decided it was time to look at them. Adelle had said *the face of the enemy.* I should lose my fear of this, lose my hatred of them. On one hand the memory of getting them was as sharp as Bristow's knife, on the other, it was as though it had happened to a different man who had told me about a harrowing, but long-ago experience.

They still didn't seem to be fading. Was their trauma so great that they'd always be with me? How would Bobbi react to them?

If she saw them. If we ever made love again. Certainly never as long as I was unpredictable, out of control. I didn't dare touch her.

And it wasn't a big help standing here in her empty dressing room in front of an empty mirror.

I dressed quickly, went up to the office where the radio I'd not turned on now played. I didn't recognize the band or their song, must have been new, and sprawled on the sofa and stared at the ceiling and tried not to think of anything at all.

And, God, it *hurt.*

Too much.

This time I foiled the seizure by vanishing quick, before it could peak.

The floating helped. No heavy body to twitch and flop, no pathetic groaning. Instead, through my muffled hearing I picked up the radio's music. The song, whatever it was, helped steady me. I hovered over the couch. Its cushions each had a bag of my home earth sewn inside for those sleep-over days. I didn't know if its proximity would help.

I held formless for a long time and thought about how I'd floated in the stock pond as a kid. This was very much like it, except back then I didn't have to shut out bad memories.

One other sense was left to me in this state: touch, and it was more muffled than my hearing. I could feel objects, get a general idea of something's shape, size, and the space around me. And people. I could touch them, leaving behind a profound cold.

I felt someone in the room with me. Couldn't think who it might be, but wasn't unduly alarmed. Escott and Bobbi had keys. Why would either of them come here at this late hour, though?

They wouldn't, not without making more noise. Bobbi usually said hello to Myrna. Escott would have called out to me by now.

So who was here? Kroun? He could have picked the lock to get in. I reached out, thinking whoever it was would soon have to move or complain about the cold, and I could identify the voice. Only that didn't happen. The person stayed put.

So *I* moved. I floated into the hall through the door and re-formed, then stepped back in the office again.

I fully expected to see someone *sitting* on that couch.

Nothing. I was seeing nothing. A lot of it.

But I had *sensed* . . . uh-oh. Mouth dry again. I cleared my throat.

"Myrna?"

No reply. But I *knew.*

In taking a breath to speak I was overwhelmed by the scent of roses.

10

Woke up on the dot of sunset, about one minute later than the previous evening. The year was turning, the days getting longer. Shorter nights. Lucky me. Less time to be in oblivion.

The rose scent was much faded by now. That had been . . . spooky. Okay, it had thrown me, but I could figure that Myrna had again been trying to give comfort, that's why I chose to remain on the office couch rather than retreat to my other bolt-hole under the tiers in the main room. How I'd actually been able to *feel* her as a physical presence was something else again. Maybe it was because I was on her side of the veil half the time. Dead.

I'd have given a shiver, but wasn't cold. Now *that* was good news. The radiator had been chugging away for hours; the place must be jungle-hot by now.

I got up to turn it back to normal and listened to familiar activity going on below. Lady Crymsyn was waking, too. She'd started the process earlier, but for her it took more time. A dame's privilege.

Someone had been and gone. Escott, probably. A stack of newspapers lay on the desk like a no-nonsense message. He'd have made a connection between my uncharacteristically spending all evening at another nightclub that was now violently minus its star act. Certainly he'd want to know the real story. The papers sure didn't have it.

The evening headlines were big and harsh, their theme murder-suicide. Apparently after Caine's body was found the cops went to question his ex-wife and in turn found her. Facts were thin, with no mention of Evie Montana or gambling debts. There was no official verdict yet, but Jewel was getting the blame for Caine's death.

My heart sank. Jewel deserved better than that. How the hell could they be so stupid? If Kroun and I could figure out she'd not killed herself—and how could they screw up so badly about the faked crime scene in Caine's flat? Was this some kind of misdirection to throw off the killer, make him think he was safe?

I phoned the Nightcrawler and got Derner. Mindful that the line could be wired, I was as vague as could be managed. "How did things go today?"

"A little rough, but it turned out all right," he cautiously told me. "Everything's fine here."

"What about our guest and his pal?"

"Haven't seen either of them today."

"What about that party I want found?"

"Nothing yet. They're being scarce."

Damn. "Is my car ready?"

"Not yet, Boss."

"What d'ya mean? It's just changing tires."

"Uhh, well, the tow truck guy didn't understand exactly and took your car to Cicero."

I considered that one a minute before asking, in what I was certain was a very reasonable tone: "Why?"

"Uhh, they're gonna fix it up for you."

"In what way?"

"Like the way the Caddy's fixed up."

"*What?*" I had visions of my humble Buick outfitted with steel armor, thick glass, and a motor that should be driving a battleship, not a car. "Call it off! I just want new tires!"

"They're doin' them, too, Boss."

"Don't give me a 'too,' just get my car ba—*what* are they doing?"

"Well, seein's how your tires were cut up like that, they're puttin' on the solid rubber kind. No more flats. You'll love 'em."

"Derner."

"Yeah, Boss?"

"Get my car *back*. No fancy stuff like the Caddy, nothing special. Just put on some *tires* and get it back to me."

He almost sounded hurt. "Okay . . . I'll talk to 'em."

"Good. If you need me over there tonight, you'll have to send a driver to pick me up."

"You mean you don't have the Caddy?" His voice went up a little.

"Our guest has it. Seems to like it a lot."

"Oh, well, that's okay, then. You still want some extra muscle for your place?"

"Yeah, send 'em over. Just find that other party." As soon as I cradled the receiver the phone rang.

"Fleming!" It was Kroun, sounding cheerful.

Now what? "Yeah?"

"You finally warmed up yet?"

"Mostly. What's going on?"

"Thought I'd come by your club, see if you turned up anything interesting on that business last night."

"Not really, no. Been sleeping all day."

"All day? You lazy bum! Your place open tonight?"

"Yeah, in about half an hour."

"Save me a good table, I'll be coming by sometime later."

"No problem. Have you seen Mitchell?"

"He's been out gallivanting with old friends. Still is."

Mitchell had friends? "Shouldn't he be watching your back?"

"I'm safe enough. Besides, he always turns up." Kroun rang off. Wonderful. Why come and hang around my club? I'd have to stop giving away booze.

As I walked downstairs Wilton was getting bowls of matches, ashtrays, and cocktail napkins ready on the lobby bar.

"Hey, Mr. Fleming. Come in early?"

"Yeah. You seen Bobbi or Charles?"

"They're both here. Main room."

"I'll bring the tills down in a minute."

"Sure, Boss."

Somehow, when he called me that, it was perfectly fine. "Myrna around?"

"Not that I've noticed."

I went into the main room. A few early-arrived waiters were there talking with the bartender. Everyone straightened and found something to do as soon as I showed. I liked that and continued on to the backstage area.

Someone banged loudly on the stage door that opened to the back alley. I unlocked and let in the first band members. Five of them barged past out of the cold, smoking like farm trucks and talking a mile a minute and paying me no mind, I was only the boss. I yelled at them to douse their cigarettes, and most of them heard, dropping the stubs into a sand-filled fire bucket hanging next to one of the many extinguishers.

From the corner of my eye I saw Bobbi flit from the number three dressing room, rushing toward the stage like she forgot something. She wore a long silk dressing gown that flapped alarmingly wide as she moved. I caught up with her at the master lighting box stage right.

"Anything wrong?" I asked.

"Hi, sweetheart! Just checking." She absently went tiptoe and pecked my cheek, as normal as could be. But then she didn't know about the fit I'd had in my car after leaving her the other evening or any of what I'd been into last night. That was good. We both had enough worries.

"I'll do this, you go finish getting ready."

"Okay-thanks." She shot off. Her feet were bare, and she scuffed along in quick little steps back to her dressing-room haven. She would be fully occupied putting herself together for the show, and I knew better than to follow after she slammed the door shut. The door didn't exactly slam so much as make a subdued *whump*; they were all fitted out with special rubber stripping on the inside edges to be less noisy. That had been Bobbi's idea when the place was being built. She maintained there was nothing more distracting for a performance than having unscheduled noises coming from backstage.

I looked over the settings for the light box and all seemed normal and unchanged. With Myrna around checking it was an ongoing chore we'd all learned to do. Of course, sometimes the lights played up while the switches were correctly in place, so we tried not to mind too much when that happened.

Roland and Faustine arrived next through the alley entry and seemed pleased with themselves. Maybe things were smoothing out in their marriage. He called a friendly hello; she gave me a regal nod, and said, "Zo pleeeezed" at me. At first I didn't think her Russian accent was real, but I'd come to change my mind. The way she looked she was a knockout in any language.

As the purposeful bustle seemed under control, I got out of the area so the showbiz juggernaut could continue bowling along without interruption from an outsider. The bartender and waiters were getting the main room ready. Most of the chairs were properly on the floor again, and the table lights on. Chatter was up, everyone anticipating a better night for tips since we were one day closer to the weekend.

I returned to the front lobby, half-expecting to see Kroun walk in early just to be annoying.

"Tills, Boss?" Wilton reminded.

"Getting them."

Everything was so *normal* it gave me the creeps, as though last night's deaths had not happened. The papers with their headlines hadn't changed, though, as I saw when I returned to my office.

Escott was seated at the desk, hunched over the phone. He glanced up, nodded at me, then refocused on listening. He seemed intent, but not in a bad way, so I walked around and swung open the false door front that hid the desk's safe. I had to try to ignore his conversation while spinning the combination, and it was hard. The guy was actually *chuckling* at something, and not the dry, sometimes ironic sound I was used to; this one was warm, sincere amusement. It matched his low tone of voice, which at one point dipped even lower into something like a purr.

He wound his call up as I pulled out the cash bag for making change and relocked the safe. "Well, Vivian's sure got your head turned."

"How did you—oh, never mind."

"Hey, you don't talk like that to our booze supplier. If you did, we might get it for free."

His ears went red. When it came to Vivian, he turned into a schoolboy. "Was your evening out as horrendous as these seem to indicate?" He gestured at the papers.

"Yeah, it was tough."

"You didn't call me?"

"I thought you should stay clear. Kroun was all over this one, and he doesn't need to know what you look like. We had to do stuff; none of it made the papers, though."

"And what is the real story?"

I sighed and sat on the couch. "Someone strangled Alan Caine backstage between shows. We had to hide it, then move him to his hotel to take the heat off the club."

"Was it a murder-suicide, as the papers said?"

"No." I gave Escott got the short version of events, and it still was too much bad news.

"You and Mr. Kroun seem to be getting on, then."

"That or he's just responding extra well to my telling him we're friends. He's coming by here soon. I think he wants to talk about this mess. I don't trust him, though."

"Very wise. He could be protecting his man, Mitchell."

"Thought of that, though why Mitchell would want to bump Caine is anyone's guess. My money's on Hoyle. He's a guy who holds a grudge."

"You put him as being behind the flat tires, too?"

"Him or Ruzzo. It wasn't just about trying to make a

flat; someone did a real Jack the Ripper job front and back.
Rubber ribbons. Lot of anger there."

"Dear me. What about Ruzzo strangling Caine? A possibility?"

"Ruzzo don't have the brains to act on their own, though
they might have been put up to it. They're good at anything
to do with intimidation, have a natural instinct for it, but
need direction and specific simple instructions. They could
have gotten away clean on blind luck."

"And Miss Montana?"

"Have to find her." I shrugged. "Women. Who can figure?"

"Indeed. Well, Shoe called me today and passed on the
news he was looking after Gordy at your instigation."

"Yeah, he'll kill himself if he doesn't get some rest. I figured Shoe was the right man to keep him safe for it. Any
news?"

"Gordy was sleeping a lot. Dr. Clarson is supervising and
seems to think that is quite the best thing."

What a relief. Something was going right.

"Was any undue influence applied to assure Gordy's cooperation?"

"It was only for his own best good, I swear."

"And how are you doing?" It wasn't a casual health
query.

"No shakes tonight. So far."

Escott was giving me a look. One of *those* kind of looks.

"I'm *fine!*" For a while I'd almost felt like my regular self.
I resented the reminder that he still saw me as ailing. It had
the effect of dragging me back into the sickroom.

He made an innocent "hands off" gesture and quit the
chair. "Shall we open, then?"

We divvied money up between the tills, ten bucks and
change for each, more than enough for the night. We carried

them down. Escott took one to the main room, I gave mine to Wilton. "Got what you need?" I asked.

"A little short on lemons. Hard to get this time of year."

"Then we do without. It's time."

The extra bouncers from the Nightcrawler were smoking in the lobby and greeted me with respectful nods. Derner must have handpicked them to avoid sending anyone who was personally hostile toward me. They knew who they were to look out for and would be hanging around front and back, two to a door, inside and out, eyes open for trouble.

My regular staff seemed a little walleyed about the tough newcomers, or so Wilton confided when he motioned me over to the side.

"Ain't the people we got enough?" he asked.

"You read the papers today?" I countered. "That club singer who got bumped?"

"Yeah . . ."

"These guys are to make sure that doesn't happen here."

He gave an exaggerated nod of understanding and flashed a welcoming smile toward the toughs. "Gentlemen! If you need coffee, just ask!"

That's what I liked to see. Cooperation. I ascertained that the doorman had his fancy red coat buttoned and that the hatcheck girl was ready for business, then turned on the OPEN sign and the outside lights of the canopied entrance. No crowds were waiting to flood in just yet, but soon.

Before leaving I said, addressing them all, "There's a guy turning up later tonight, forties, lean, has a white streak of hair on one side—"

"That movie star?" chirped the girl, eyes bright. "He was *cute!*"

Not my word for Kroun, but she'd obviously responded to his brand of charm in a big way. "He's no movie star, but he is important. Give him the royal treatment when he shows and take him up to my table. He gets whatever he wants."

"And how!" she agreed. The men merely nodded, and I went on to the main room.

The band was running late, still more drifting in and tuning up. When the leader spotted me he snapped at the others to put some hustle in it, knowing we were officially open. Just over half came to attention and began playing at his signal. The music was thin at first, then gradually surged and filled out as more of the guys joined in on their usual warm-up number. By the time I was seated at my third tier table they were in full swing.

Opening was always a little sweat-making with them playing to an empty house. The worry was that it would remain empty for the evening, but usually within half an hour we'd have enough of a crowd to justify the endeavor. I sat well back in the shadows of my booth, watching, going over details in my head in case I missed anything.

Once I finally admitted to myself that all was well I started chewing over Jewel Caine's murder. Whatever reason someone had had to kill Alan Caine, I couldn't think why they'd go after Jewel, too.

Unless she'd seen them. She'd been smoking out in the alley. It was very possible. If the killer had left by that route—the fastest exit was the stage door—she could have been right there. She might have said or done something to set him off, or maybe it was enough for her to be in the wrong place just then. He'd have to shut her up as a witness; he lured or kidnapped her away, then staged the fake suicide. And as great good fortune would have it, the cops, or at least the papers, had fallen for the sham.

I wasn't going to leave it like that for her. The right per-

son would take the rap for this. All I needed was five minutes with him.

But was I up to doing hypnosis yet or in for another crippling migraine leading to a seizure? The constant chill that
had plagued me last night was somewhat mitigated. I
wasn't shivering in my overcoat and hat. My day sleep had
accomplished some healing after all, but did it extend that
far? I wouldn't know for sure unless I tried, and I wasn't inclined to try.

Escott had been backstage and now emerged from the
side exit door on the left. He had a word with the bartender,
got a brandy, then began the climb up to my table. Several
couples had come in, and the tables were gradually filling
up. It was early, but looked like we'd have a good crowd.

"May I?" he asked, ever polite, even when there was no
need.

I waved him in on the opposite side, and he took a load
off. "Charles, I know you're curious about Kroun coming in,
but you've been doing two jobs. It's okay if you head home
and rest."

"Rest? My dear fellow, gadding about here *is* rest for me.
I always look forward to abandoning my office to enjoy this
glad escape." He lifted his snifter. "And a free drink."

"Okay, if you're sure." That was my way of being polite.
"But where he's concerned I think you should be invisible."

"That shan't be a problem. I agree with you on the
anonymity point. I'd rather not be anyone he knows."

"Did you look up more on him today?"

"Oh, absolutely."

"And . . . ?"

"There is a remarkable lack of material on him. Now and
then his name popped up in the New York papers in connection to certain acts of violence, but he's avoided any ar-

rest and prosecution. One day he's the focus of someone's official attention, the next they've never heard of him."

"He must bribe or threaten them away, then." Another half dozen customers came in. Good. Kroun wasn't one of them. Better.

"What's odd is that reporters seem to lose interest in him. Walter Winchell had the start of what promised to be a very juicy piece connecting him to a murder, then it simply never happened."

"You think he bribed *Winchell?* He'd have boasted about turning it down."

Escott shook his head. "You'd have to ask Winchell that. You're former colleagues. Write him a letter."

I almost laughed. Sure I'd been a reporter, but so far down the journalistic totem pole as not even to exist when compared to Winchell. "Why don't you write Helen Hayes, and ask if she'll put you in her next play?"

"Because I prefer Chicago over New York," he replied.

"Don't tell me you know . . ."

He bounced one eyebrow, very deadpan.

"Ah, never mind."

The band went into a fanfare, and Teddy Parris launched onto the stage, taking charge of it as easily an experienced trouper twice his years. He introduced himself, welcomed everyone, and promised them all a great evening. It was almost how I glad-handed people in the lobby, but without the whammy-work.

He swung his way into "Christopher Columbus" with enthusiastic help from the band. It was a great song; people responded, clustering on the dance floor. During an instrumental interlude Teddy bounded from the stage, cut in on a couple in a comic way, and took the lady around some fast turns. He deftly handed her back to her date and continued to spin, making like he'd gone dizzy, artfully ending up at a table sitting on a guy's lap. Wide-eyed Teddy tickled the guy's chin, then mimed mortified horror and switched laps to flirt with the girlfriend instead. Fortunately they thought he was funny. I'd seen that gag not work in many a spectacular way.

He dropped to one knee, gave the lady the red carnation from his lapel, then made a fast exit, cartwheeling back to the dance floor, managing not to hit anyone. Up onstage again, he was in perfect time to resume singing, but breathless, so he made a business out of that, mopping his brow and purposely wheezing out the words. He miraculously recovered enough to deliver a strong finish. It went over well, with laughs and applause.

"You'll have to start paying him more if he keeps on like that," Escott observed.

"Don't give him ideas."

Teddy's set continued through several more lively songs, and he used his long, expressive face to play up the humorous delivery, sometimes adding in comments, but he included a plaintive love song to prove he had a voice. The women ate it up.

Escott pulled out his pipe and tobacco pouch and prepared a smoke. He didn't seem to be in a contemplative mood. It was strangely very much like any other evening.

"Thought you preferred cigarettes," I said.

"Used to. Vivian prefers the smell of pipe tobacco."

Ho-ho. "So how's the date for Saturday? You sounded pretty happy about it."

"Yes, Bobbi and I had an additional planning session when I drove her in tonight. All is progressing extremely well." Escott looked kind of odd. Pleased and bemused and nervous at the same time, but it didn't seem like a bad feeling to have. It cheered me up seeing him like that. "Vivian gladly accepted your invitation, and Sarah is looking forward to going out to a grown-ups' event. She doesn't know you're the one who actually rescued her, but has picked up from her mother that you're a cross between the *Lone Ranger* and *Gangbusters*. She may want your autograph."

"Son of a—" I broke off, almost laughing. "What a kid."

"You know she plays the piano?"

That hauled me short. "But I thought she wasn't . . ."

He shrugged. "Well, gifts of talent and intellectual development do not necessarily walk hand in hand. She doesn't read music, but she can play whatever she's heard. She's quite amazing."

"Huh. Who'd a thought it?"

"Actually, Vivian did. She read somewhere that doctors had determined Albert Einstein to be so backward that they recommend institutionalization. His parents got him a violin instead. Vivian encourages Sarah in a similar direction. Seems to give the girl comfort, too."

"Oh, yeah?"

He lifted a hand. "She has nightmares about her kidnapping. Has to have the lights on all the time. Doesn't like to be alone."

That sounded uncomfortably familiar.

"Vivian told her that day or night, whenever she felt frightened or sad, she was to go to the parlor and play the piano and she would feel better. It seems to work."

"You dropping a hint?"

"I believe you already understand the merits of music in healing a damaged spirit. You have the radio on nearly all the time."

"That's just to keep me from thinking too much."

"Exactly."

Teddy made his big finish and took his bows, then began Roland and Faustine's introduction. The tone of the band changed dramatically, the drums coming in strong.

"I can't make music," I said. "Can't carry a tune in a bag, and Ma gave up trying to teach me piano when the rest of the family said my practice would lead to a hanging."

"What do you mean?" His pipe went out. He gave it an irritated look.

"If I kept trying to play, one of them was going to kill me. That last lesson was a relief to everybody, especially myself."

"And here you sit, owner of a nightclub full of song."

The lights went out so Roland and Faustine could take their places. Clearly Bobbi had changed the ordering of the show again, leaving out the anniversary duet with Teddy. Perhaps none of the couples here tonight were celebrating. The music built upon itself, horns and drums filling the space right to the walls, thundering into the tango.

"I don't paint but can appreciate art. You saying I need to hang around here more?"

"Yes, of course. The rest of the time you could indulge in expanding your record collection. I would strongly suggest acquiring some of the pieces from the Baroque period. They have a most soothing effect on the nerves."

I knew that stuff; it all sounded alike to me. "Fats Waller is more my style."

He relit the pipe. "Whatever does the job."

We watched the dancers, though I was sure Escott was keeping at least one eye on me and my reaction to the show. He didn't have to; I was worried enough for both of us.

"Any new problems, past or pending?" He was talking about my fits again. Great timing. Keep me distracted as the music reached its apex and the lights changed for the bloodred finale.

Shutting my eyes, I leaned on the table, head low. Bracing. Just in case. "Not tonight. Knock wood."

"Hm. Sounds hopeful."

Closing my eyes made it work. Not long after, a roaring burst of applause told me it was safe to look again. I held up a nontrembling hand. "Maybe there's something to it."

"Then congratulations. Every step forward is for the better." He'd finished his smoke and tapped the dottle into the ashtray. Only then did I notice a shiny leather pouch that had his initials stamped on it in gold.

"That's new," I said.

He smiled a little self-consciously. "A gift from Vivian."

"Well-well, quite a girl you got there." I was going to razz him some more, but Teddy reappeared to introduce Bobbi. She took center stage and seemed to glow all on her own. It hurt to look at her.

Roland and Faustine melted into another exposition dance to complement her opening song. There was a spotlight on Bobbi and a traveling spot on them. The effect was great. While some club owners might object to Bobbi's constant changing of the bill, I welcomed it. She kept the place out of the doldrums of repetition. The regular customers liked it, and the performers stayed interested.

End of number, lights up, bows, plenty of applause, graceful shift as Roland and Faustine broke away to take new partners. This time an impatient guy, still in his hat and overcoat, got to Faustine first, and he wasn't half-bad squiring her around the floor.

Bobbi sang, others danced, and the rest were caught up in her voice as she did a plaintive but not overly sentimental version of "Pennies from Heaven." The arrangement had one of the trumpets doing something that sounded reminiscent of falling water, which was echoed in places by a clarinet. I'd not heard that part before. They must have come up with it during daytime rehearsal.

Faustine's partner maneuvered them close to the stage until they were just below Bobbi, then he held in place, not doing much of anything but looking up at her. Smiling.

What the hell . . . ?

I abruptly recognized Mitchell.

He was waiting for Bobbi to see him. The lights would be in her eyes; maybe there was still time to head him off. I suddenly vanished and shot right over the heads of everyone between, going solid just as suddenly on the dance floor only steps from Mitchell. I didn't care who saw.

But I was too late. Mitchell sidled close enough so she caught the movement and looked his way. Grinning, he waved up at her. She didn't react, singing on, then did a kind of slow double take and froze in sheer horror. I thought she would dislike a reminder of the bad old days, but didn't expect this. It required a hell of a lot to get Bobbi to miss a line, and she did just that, dropping several words and stumbling through the start of the chorus. She pretended to have a throat problem, pulling away from the microphone, hand to her mouth as though to cough. The band continued. Singers forgetting words were part of the job.

Mitchell just kept grinning.

I clapped a hand on his shoulder from behind, grabbed his right arm so he wouldn't go for his gun, and turned him before he quite knew what happened. His baffled surprise turned into a snarl when he saw my face, but I chivvied him along as quick as any of the bouncers. I'm a lot stronger than I look, and where the hell were they?

"Lay off, pretty boy!" Mitchell started.

I clocked him smartly, rapping his skull with my knuckles as though knocking to get in. As mad as I was the force was the same as if I'd blackjacked him. His legs ceased to hold him so well, and I had to take his weight to keep him moving.

By now we were a spectacle. The joker running the traveling spot picked us out from the crowd on the dance floor and followed, much to everyone's amusement. A few applauded, thinking this was part of the show. So far no one was screaming in reaction to my magical appearance out of thin air.

I veered to the right, going toward the door that led to the backstage area. It had the closest exit. I glanced over my shoulder at the stage.

Bobbi made it to the end of the chorus, but her tone was wrong for the mood she'd set, her face fixed, eyes staring at nothing, like a mannequin. She threw a jerky signal to the band leader, and he muttered a song title to his people. The music shifted and changed key. Out of sequence, Bobbi hastily introduced Teddy Parris, calling him up again. He must have been ready in the wings, for he bounced forward and took over as though this was business as usual. The spotlight shifted to him, so Bobbi's hasty departure went mostly unseen.

Mitchell and I blew through the door. Just within was a wide service area with the alley entry at the end and a smaller hall to the right leading to the dressing rooms. To the left were the basement stairs. I wanted to bounce Mitchell down them, but instead slammed him against the backstage wall, my forearm under his chin, his feet dangling free. He recovered enough to put up some fight, so I rattled him again, taking a lot of satisfaction from the rotten-melon thump his head made on impact. The wall was brick.

Then Escott got between us and pushed me back, shouting my name. It was just enough to keep me from a third try, which would have probably killed Mitchell. He slithered to the floor. Escott shot me a loud "What the devil is going on?"

I wasn't in a mood to explain. "Go check on Bobbi. This creep . . ."

Escott instantly got the idea she'd been threatened in some way, but didn't leave. "Jack . . . ?"

"It'll be all right. I promise not to kill him." Not here, anyway.

"Who is he?"

"I'll tell ya later, go to Bobbi!"

He went.

Where were the damn bouncers? But they were on the lookout for mugs like Hoyle and Ruzzo, not Whitey Kroun's top lieutenant.

Mitchell had a thick skull and had roused himself back to alertness. The first thing he did was reach inside his coat for his gun.

Only I'd taken it off him. It weighed down my coat pocket.

Some guys can't handle being without their heat, but he wasn't one of them. He shot to his feet and went after me, fists flying. Very bad move. I got inside his first punch, taking it on the flank under my arm and gave him two sharp ones in the breadbasket left and right. Mitchell gagged and dropped and spent the next few moments trying to get air back in his lungs.

He was vulnerable as he ever would be. I thought of hypnotizing him, my first choice for solving the problem he'd become. It wouldn't take much to give him both barrels in the face and see to it he forgot Bobbi ever existed. But even thinking about the attempt seemed to make a steel band tighten around my head. In my current state I'd either send him insane, send myself off into another damned fit, or both.

However, my second choice—beating the crap out of him—was entirely acceptable. I impatiently paced side to side, waiting for him to get up so I could knock him over again.

"What's your beef?" he gasped, staying down. "I only wanted to say hello."

"Try again, and you'll do it without teeth. She doesn't want to see you."

"Huh. Ask her, wise guy. Think she rolled and spread 'em just for you? She'll wanna—"

I hauled him up and threw him across the room.

He hit the brick wall on that side hard but didn't quite lose enough balance; he staggered and kept his feet. "You're gonna pay, you stupid—"

I was too fast for him to see the move and too angry to stop. Not knowing quite how, I got hold of one arm and yanked the wrong way. For that I had an earsplitting howl in response, followed by some truly foul cursing.

"Ya busted my arm!" he informed me.

"Dislocated," I said. I sounded calm as a doctor diagnosing a cold. How could I be this furious and speak so softly?

He tried another swing with his undamaged arm. I stepped back out of range plus a few steps. I'd promised Escott there'd be no killing. Mitchell was making it hard to remember.

That's when the alley door swung inward. One of the bouncers, I thought, finally reacting to the commotion inside.

Except he wasn't a bouncer. Rawboned and face red from the cold, Hoyle shouldered past Mitchell, raising the gun in his fist until the muzzle was level with my eyes. Hoyle's gleamed with unholy delight. He had me square.

"Kill 'im!" Mitchell yelled.

Hoyle seemed barely aware of him. "Payback," he said to me, grinning. He still looked worse for wear from the pounding I'd given him. "Outside, Fleming. Now."

Mitchell, apparently figuring to have a front row seat, darted clumsily through the door, holding his arm close. Were they working together, or was it just glad coincidence that put them on the same team tonight?

"Outside!" Hoyle repeated. "Or I'll drill you here, you—"

His gaze abruptly snapped to the side, toward the hall leading to the dressing rooms.

Faustine Petrova stood not ten feet away. She was out of her tango dance costume, wrapped in a blazing scarlet silk kimono, a look of fascination on her exotic face.

"You are hav-ink important beeznuss meet-ink, yesss?" she asked brightly.

My guts swooped. "Faustine! Get out of here!"

But she stood her ground staring intently at Hoyle. He glared back at her, and his gun muzzle wavered in her direction. Then his eyes went wide.

Faustine made a small, elegant shrugging motion, and the kimono suddenly fell from her shoulders. She was completely naked except for her lipstick. *"Daunce wit' me, beeg boy!"* she sang out, spreading her arms.

Holy mackerel.

Hoyle's eyes got even wider, and his jaw sagged. He had to have seen a naked woman before, but Faustine possessed a unique electricity, and it always turned heads.

Including his, for just long enough.

I launched a full-body tackle on him. Being stronger, I could cover more distance in a leap. I slammed into him, and down we went. Hoyle's reflexes were too good, though. His time in the boxing ring made him quick to recover. He fired, and I felt the sear as the bullet grazed my side. It was a scratch, nothing to sweat over . . .

But Faustine dropped, giving a little cry.

11

WHILE I tried to take the gun away before it went off again Hoyle got in some double-quick punches. We rolled and grunted and kicked and suddenly he wasn't there anymore, and I found my feet, but he was outside and racing down the alley where a car waited at the far end. It was Ruzzo at the wheel. Didn't know which one. Hoyle made the running board, and they took off.

No sign of Mitchell.

Faustine.

I turned and choked, for she seemed to be huddled in a vast pool of blood until the mass of brilliant color resolved into being her kimono. Took a whiff. The only bloodsmell was my own.

Went to her quick. She stirred and cautiously opened an eye. "Es over, yesss?"

"You okay, doll?" At a loss to help I plucked at the kimono.

A smile. "Amer-i-kans, zo shy." She gracefully found her

feet, slipping the silk wrap around her lithe body in one move. She was unhurt and beaming. "Es like Jeemmy Cagney seen-e-ma, yesss?"

About two inches from where her head had been was a bullet pock in the brick. "Oh, yeah."

"But Jek, you are heet?" She spotted the bloody graze in my side.

"Faustine!" Roland hurtled toward her from the hall and grabbed her up. "I heard shooting! Jack . . . ! My God, what's going on? Darling, are you all right?"

The last was aimed at his wife, who had a ready explanation, except it was in fast-flowing Russian, which he clearly didn't understand.

I went to the alley door, looking both ways as I emerged into the cold wind. All clear. No Mitchell, and no bouncers, either. I shoved the door shut, took a chair off a stacked column of spares in a corner, and angled it under the doorknob. Randomly, I thought I'd better get a new lock, the kind that only opens from the inside.

Faustine recovered enough English by then to provide Roland with the beginnings of a highly dramatic episode of how she'd saved my life. He seemed to be getting more upset by the second, so I skipped toward the main room. The second I was out of sight I vanished, not inclined to see anyone on my way to the lobby. I materialized in the a blind spot in the curving hall leading to it and kept going.

All four bouncers were gone.

"Where are they?" I roared at Wilton. He looked ready to duck behind the bar, and the hatcheck girl went *"yeep!"* and did duck under her counter.

"The men's room," he said, astonished.

All of them? If they were having a craps game, I'd have their balls on a—

I pushed in, loaded for bear, and found them sprawled or heaped on the floor like so many bodies after a battle. I froze for a second, thinking the worst, but one of them groaned. To a man they'd been coshed. From the way they were lying, they must have been lined up and hit one at a time. Even Ruzzo could have done it with no trouble, one to hold them in place with a gun, the other to swing away like Babe Ruth on a Sunday.

Checked them quick. Alive. Fortunately. The man that groaned opened his eyes and squinted. "Boss? Wha' happened?"

Went to the door and yelled for Wilton. He came in and gaped. "Boss, what happened?"

"Look after them, make sure nobody dies."

As I left, the groaning guy made it to a urinal and began throwing up.

I returned to the backstage hall the same way, but going solid more slowly to make sure no one saw. No need to worry. Waiters clogged the place, all looking in the same direction. Faustine was apparently telling her story again, this time with sound effects and gestures. She pointed with finger and thumb, not needing the pistol Mitchell had left behind. That lay forgotten on the floor where it had dropped in my fight with Hoyle. I quietly pocketed it again.

" 'I vill keel you, you dirdy radt!' Zen *beng-beng-beng* off goes de gun, but Jek *leaps* on de bedt guy like de mad tiger! Ah! My heee-rrro!" Faustine beamed at me, parting their ranks as she flew through them to throw her arms around me. Suddenly she was kissing both my cheeks and planting more all over my face. Roland rushed over, too, and grabbed one of my flailing hands, pumping it.

"Grand work, sport!" he yelled, as though I'd gone deaf.

"That will teach those rowdies! You saved her life! I can't thank you enough!"

Teach who? I wondered. *What* had she been telling them?

"Uh . . . well . . . yeah, okay, glad to have been of help." I managed to get out of Faustine's grip, firmly guiding her toward Roland's protective embrace. "C'mon, guys! Show's over, get back to work!"

"What happened, Boss?"

"Drunk customer. He's gone. Now, back out there while we still have others. If anyone asks, you don't know nuthin'."

"But we *don't* know nuthin'," one of them grumbled as they filed past, disappointed.

I leaned against the wall and rubbed my face. My hands came away red, but it was only Faustine's lip color. The vivid red spooked me for a second.

Roland gallantly gave me a clean handkerchief. "I'd like to talk when you're recovered."

He got a vague nod. Mopping the war paint, I looked past him and saw Escott frowning severely at me. I was everyone's favorite tonight. He waited until Roland and Faustine went by to get to their dressing rooms.

"That man was with Kroun the other night," he stated. "His lieutenant?" He said *lieutenant* like it had an "f" in it.

"Yeah. Mitchell."

"What has he done to upset Bobbi so much?"

"I donno, but he used to run with Slick Morelli's mob. He kept saying he and Bobbi were old friends. I warned him to keep clear, but he—"

"Indeed he did, and you nearly gave me heart failure with that vanishing business."

"It was dark, everyone's drinking, they're welcome to prove it. How's Bobbi?"

He frowned a bit more, which was going some. "She is in a 'state.' Extremely distressed."

I started past him, but he caught my arm. "Jack, make her cry, and I'll murder you."

And he knew how to do it, too.

I shot down the hall to the number three dressing room and very softly knocked. The show was still going on, with Teddy doing his best to fill in. Bobbi didn't reply, so I pushed the door open.

"Bobbi? Honey, you okay?"

From the bathroom came a long exhalation of breath. She emerged, wobbly, clutching a wad of tissue in one hand like a soggy bouquet. "No." Her voice was too high. She stared at the blood on my shirt. "Are you hurt? I heard a shot, but Charles made me stay."

"It's nothing, I'm all better, everything's fine. I took care of the guy. He's gone. He won't be back."

"You know who he is?"

"His name's Mitchell, and he's with a guy named Kroun outta New York. I heard he'd been with Morelli before that and didn't want him bothering you . . . I'm sorry."

She sat at her dressing table, back to the mirror. "You *knew* about Mitch?"

Mitch. She called him Mitch. Why was that? "Only that he left when Gordy took over. Strome told me."

Bobbi didn't exactly cry like Adelle, but expressed similar symptoms, subdued, but intense, right on the edge. "Did Strome tell you why Mitch left?"

"What is it? He hurt you?"

She shook her head. "No." She turned toward the mirror and dabbed her eyes. The damage wasn't too bad. I realized she could no longer look at me straight, though I could see her fine, front and back. Why wasn't she looking at me?

That crap Mitchell said . . . "He told me Mitchell wouldn't play second fiddle under Gordy."

"Nothing more?"

"Listen, if you don't want to talk about it . . ." I wanted to hold her, but something told me not to try. I had the sudden feeling of treading on eggs.

"Oh, it's nothing horrible. He's—I'm acting stupidly about the whole thing. He just surprised me showing up so suddenly like that, and then you . . ." She dumped the wadded tissues in a basket and clawed more from a box on her vanity table. Blew her nose a lot. That seemed the end of it, but tears were leaking out now. She stood and made the limited rounds of the room, fiddling with stuff, trying very, very hard not to lose control. "Anyway, he's long gone, right? You made him leave, so everything's fine. You don't need to be worrying about . . . *oh, don't* LOOK *at me like that!*"

I backed off. I didn't know how I was looking at her. *"What?"*

Bobbi made a strange wailing noise and fled into the bathroom, slamming the door.

I called to her. All I got in return were the big, racking, moaning sobs of a full-blown breakdown. "Honey? What is it? Bobbi? Come on." I'd never seen her like this before, and it was scaring me. Somehow dealing with Adelle had been so simple, and this . . . wasn't.

Well, I'd been assured by Adelle that just holding her had been the right thing to do. This might get worse if I waited.

I vanished, sieved through, and re-formed. Bobbi was on the toilet lid with another bouquet of paper to sop up the outpour. My appearance startled her.

"Not fair!" she yelled. "No! Not fair! You leave! I don't wanna—"

I did what I did with Adelle, arms holding close and tight. Bobbi hiccuped and sobbed, stuttering, and finally broke into a steady shower and, oh, God, didn't I hate every minute of it.

After forever went by, she wound down to a slow finish, and was a dandy mess from the effort. Women never look good crying unless they're on a movie screen. That's how you can tell it's acting.

She blew her nose for the umpteenth time, but still sounded stuffy, and her voice was thick. "I'm sorry."

"Honey . . . whatever it is . . . it's okay." And I meant that. I didn't want her going off the deep end again, or I'd wind up in a booby hatch.

"It's about Mitch."

"I kinda figured that. Bobbi, whatever it is, it won't make me hate him any less."

"What does that mean?"

"I don't know, but please don't cry anymore. Say the word, and I'll make him disappear, but *please* . . ."

Sniff. "Okay, Jack."

"You want him gone?"

"Not the way you're thinking. I just don't *ever* want to see him again. That's all I want. He j-just brought all the bad stuff back, and I don't want to go through—"

"Okay! It's done. He won't get within a mile of you, I promise."

"Oooh, now my head hurts."

"Don't move, I'll get you something."

I backed from the room, watching her as though she might vanish like me. Halfway down the hall was Faustine, still in her kimono. Roland and Escott watched from the far end, hopefully out of earshot. They had worried faces and were smoking. They both knew better than to do that back-stage, but it wasn't the time to play theater cop.

"Jek?" said Faustine, halting me.

"Yeah, not now, I gotta . . ."

She held a glass of water and a bottle of aspirin. "Heerrre. Take eet. Gif her thrree, make her drink whole glessfool."

"Uh . . ."

She arched both eyebrows. "Men! Zo 'fraid ov leetle tears. They are de rain ov lof. Now go beck, feex et. Don't come out until she lofs you again! Go!"

I went.

Bobbi settled down after the dosing. She apologized some more, and I told her it was all right and unnecessarily held my breath, but she didn't bust out afresh, so that was good.

"Can you tell me what's wrong?" I belatedly thought that I should have sent Faustine in to do this. Women were better at it.

"This was a couple years ago," Bobbi began.

I nodded.

"Back then it was like I knew everything, yet nothing at all. You know how that is?"

"Several times a night."

"Remember how it was with me and Slick? When we first started it was great, and then it got so he decided he owned me, and I couldn't get out of it. If I did, he'd mess things up for me in every club in Chicago. In order to sing I had to keep myself available and do what I was told."

I nodded some more. I also felt rotten to have to hear all this, knowing how much it tore her up.

"M-mitch was one of the boys there, and he liked me. A lot. For a while I thought he could help me. He said he could get me clear of Slick, and we'd go to Hollywood. We were so careful and it seemed safe and he was much nicer than Slick."

That side of Mitchell I couldn't begin to imagine.

"We planned out *everything*. I figured what to pack into two suitcases, and it was hard, because I was leaving so much behind, but it was worth it for being with him. Starting over. No mistakes this time . . . then Gordy showed up at my hotel flat.

"He knew Mitch and I were going to run away, when we planned to do it, the works; it was like having your mind turned inside out and read like a book. I denied it all, but he went real patient like he does and told me not to be a sap. Slick was beginning to suspect, and if he told Gordy to find out for sure, Gordy would have to tell him."

"Did Gordy talk to Mitchell?"

"No, not then he didn't. Only me. Gordy was nice about it, but he scared the hell out of me. He didn't threaten or anything like that, he just told the truth, very quietly. If I didn't cool things off with Mitch, I'd disappear. There was another guy there, Sanderson, and he did whatever Slick told him, even killing a woman if that's what Slick wanted."

"I remember him." It would probably be decades before the memory of how Sanderson died faded from my mind. Knowing that suddenly made carrying it a little easier.

"So Gordy broke me, not with threats, but with kindness. He said 'You're a good kid in a bad place, an' I don't wanna see you hurt.' He made me hungry for something I didn't have, and I thought maybe he wanted the same, that that's why he'd come, because he wanted me, too, but Gordy said no. I was cute, but it wouldn't work. Then I begged him to help me get out, and he said that wouldn't work, either. The only way I'd leave was when Slick got bored with me. It would take time, but would happen sooner or later. I'd have to accept that I was Slick Morelli's girl until he decided different."

I'd known some of the story. Didn't make it easier to take, though.

"So I got real busy with my work and rehearsals and couldn't sneak off with Mitch, and Gordy looked out for me and would come up with ways to keep him busy, sending him out of town to do stuff. That's how I finally figured out Mitch was only in it to have the boss's twist and a laugh on him. If he'd *really* loved me, he'd have found a way around all that and . . ." She drew and puffed out a deep breath. "And then . . . then one night *you* showed up."

"Well, we know what happened after that."

"Glory-hallelujah. When the dust settled and Gordy took over he sent Mitch to New York. He might have left anyway, but Gordy said Mitch had been bragging to the guys that with Morelli gone he'd be 'inheriting' me. That was the word he used."

"Nice guy."

"That's why I was thrown so hard when I saw him. The look on his face was so . . . so damned *smug*, and I *knew* what was going through his head. He thinks he can—"

"Not going to happen, lady. You tell me what you want, and it's there on a silver platter or heading east on the next train. Unless you want to tell him yourself." It was a genuine question, not a joke. Bobbi was sometimes touchy about her battles and tended to fight them herself.

She shook her head. "No! I don't want him anywhere *near* me. I wouldn't know what to say and he'd go all nasty and then I'd want to belt him and he'd hit back and . . ."

"Okay! It's solved. He's gone."

Bobbi gave me a look of pure and powerful love and

launched up to hug me. It felt good. "Thank you. For this time, anyway. I got to handle stuff like this better. Something else is bound to crop up—"

"No, it's not. Nothing's left in that barrel of woe. It's empty and dry, and we'll bust it up for kindling and roast hot dogs over the fire."

A strange light came to her face as she pulled back to look at me. "Oh, Jack, I do love you."

I almost froze up at that, but miracle of miracles, did not. No shakes, no chill, only warmth. From her and for her. The other night I'd been terrified about getting close. Tonight . . . not so much. I welcomed the familiar heat of her touch, and soon felt the pressure above my corner teeth that would cause them to descend . . .

And decisively extricated myself before anything bad happened. I didn't have the warning symptoms of an approaching seizure, but did recognize the roiling within that proceeded a bout of gluttony in the Stockyards. No matter how tender my feelings toward her, she was . . . was *food.*

God help me.

"Jack? What's wrong?"

"Nothing. There's stuff going on in the club because of that goon, and-and I gotta go . . . it's business."

I might as well have slapped her. She blinked, startled, then recovered, squared herself. "Okay," she whispered. I left before she started to cry again.

Faustine was still in the hall. "Vell?"

"She's better."

That got me a scowl. "Men!" She stalked toward the number three room, knocked, and went in. "Bob-bee, poor dar-link. Me you tell all about eet." The door shut with a muffled *whump,* the closest she could get to a slam.

Recognizing defeat, I fled to the end, where Roland now waited alone. "Where's Charles?"

"Something came up to call him away. How did it go?"

Shrugged. "Women."

"Ah. Yes. Wonderful, aren't they? Still, I wouldn't have them any other way or they'd be like us, and that wouldn't work at all. And we certainly can't be like them."

"Oh, yeah?"

"Absolutely, sport. We'd look ridiculous in their little jimjams, now wouldn't we? And I got the story of just *how* Faustine helped you with that crazed drunk with the gun. Now if I'd been there instead and done what she'd done, he'd have probably shot me on purpose. *That's* why we can't be like them."

Sounded right to me.

"I do need to talk with you about that . . ."

"I'm sorry, but I can't just now. Business." Like four groggy bouncers on the men's room floor.

He swallowed back whatever annoyance was brewing. "Later, then, sport," he promised.

There was no way of going invisible with him watching, so I had to use the door in the ordinary way and walk through the main room. Poor Teddy was still winging it, filling in for Bobbi's interrupted set. Jewel Caine should have been up there instead, reclaiming her career and going on to better things, sober and free of dragging anvils like her ex-husband. By God, if Hoyle was the one behind her death . . .

"Hey, Jack!"

Regulars hailed me from their tables. I dredged up a smile, waved, and kept going. No one remarked about my miraculous appearance on the dance floor, but I got stares.

That's when I realized I was less than perfectly turned out. My clothes were messed around, suit scuffed and dirty from rolling on the floor, shirttails hanging, a bloody streak where I'd been grazed (now healed), tie crooked, buttons torn off. I continued on like the display was in their imagination.

The bouncers were gathered around the lobby bar, pale and holding ice-filled towels against their heads. Three had drinks, the fourth a Bromo-Seltzer, Wilton's brand of Red Cross aid. Escott was also looking after them, and had a special glare ready for me as I came in. Like any of this was my fault.

"They insist they will be all right," he said.

"But we're gonna kill Ruzzo," said Bromo-Seltzer. The others growled collective agreement.

"After you've seen a doctor," Escott added.

Less growling, more grumbling.

I got the story, and it was pretty much as I'd guessed. Ruzzo, both of them, had invaded, getting the drop on them all. Two men guarding the outside were marched in at gunpoint to join their pals, then the party was quietly moved to the men's room, where they were bashed from behind. It had been accomplished very slick and quiet since neither Wilton or the check girl had noticed anything. Hell, not even Myrna had flickered so much as a single bulb. Was everyone on sleeping pills?

"I'm not sure just when Mitchell made his entry," Escott concluded.

"And I donno if he's working with Hoyle and Ruzzo," I said. "It sure looked like it." I gave him details about the fight and the outcome, but nothing on the reason behind it.

"We'll keep in mind that an alliance has perhaps taken place between them, though God knows why or how, but it might well have been chance. Now I'm going to take these fine fellows off to make sure their brains are still in place. There's a doctor they know who—"

"Yeah, I think I know the one. Thanks."

"And about Bobbi . . ." He took me to one side, voice lowering.

"She's better," I said. "She tell you about Mitchell?"

"Not much. Too upset. I was the shoulder to cry on until you were free to take over. But I got that Mitchell was an extraordinarily bad memory from her past, and it was a terrible shock to see him again. Also, she was afraid it would in some way destroy your relationship."

"No! No, nothing like that. We're fine. I listened, she talked, it's fine, all fine now."

He seemed about to say something to the contrary.

"Faustine's with her, she'll be all right," I insisted.

"She can't be candid about everything. It's good she has another woman to confide to about you, but your condition is a significant influence on matters. Keeping *that* a secret rather precludes a full lifting of the burden."

"Oh." Not good. The way she looked when I walked out . . .

"But—" he continued. "You should know that she seems to think you're worth all the trouble and bother. There's no accounting for women and their taste in men."

Yeah, maybe. But Bobbi was miserable, and it really was all my fault.

Escott took the four guys away in his Nash, and a few law-abiding citizens of Chicago still ignorant of Lady Crymsyn's unplanned renovation into a shooting gallery came in to enjoy themselves. By then I'd tucked my clothes more or less back into order, hiding rips and bloodstains by buttoning the coat. I glad-handed a few people, told them they'd have a great time—leaving out the whammy—and was about to go back to see Bobbi when another guest walked in.

Whitey Kroun took one gander at me and frowned. I returned the favor.

"What the hell happened to you?" he demanded. Nothing like an experienced eye to recognize the aftereffects of mayhem.

"That idiot lieutenant of yours," I snapped.

"Oh, yeah? Explain."

I threw a look past him to make sure Mitchell wasn't in his wake along with Hoyle and Ruzzo. No one like that, just a lot of women (and men) picking up on Kroun's magnetism and like the check girl perhaps mistaking him for a movie star. "My office. This way."

We climbed the stairs, I ushered him in. The radio was on, but low. By now I couldn't remember if I'd left it that way or not. Kroun took his hat off, brushing his hand over the streak in his hair, and sat on the couch. He pitched the hat by its brim toward the desk, and it landed square on top of the papers. "So what gives with Mitchell?"

"He came by tonight and bothered my girlfriend."

Kroun waited for more. "That's it?" he finally asked.

"It was enough. He pulled his little reunion stunt smack in the middle of a show, threw her into hysterics . . . I had to drag him backstage." I told the rest, sparing no punches, ending it by putting Mitchell's gun on the desk next to the hat. "If he comes back for this, I'll ram it down his throat."

"You think he's working with Hoyle?"

"I donno, but it was pretty damned coincidental of them showing up at the same time. Hoyle tried to kill me—with Mitchell urging him on—got within a breath of shooting an innocent lady, and his pals Ruzzo lambasted four of

Gordy's best. If they are working together, then you should tell me why."

"You think I'd know that?"

"He's your boy. Where's he been all day?"

"Out." Kroun's eyes were hotting up.

"This isn't just me with a gripe. It's about Gordy, too, because of his men being here. If you know what Mitchell might be up to—"

"I don't know a damned thing!"

"Then you should find out. If he was doing a job for you or someone else or for himself, he's been made,"

"What kind of job? Killing you? Hoyle tried to do that the other night all on his own, he doesn't need Mitchell."

"Then take me out of the picture. What else would he need Mitchell for? What else would Mitchell need Hoyle and Ruzzo for? The four of them wouldn't be hopping into the same bed just to knock *me* off. Something's brewing."

"Until tonight Mitchell had no reason to kill you. Now he might go with Hoyle just to help out."

"Not going to happen. They've crawled out of whatever hole they've been hiding in, and someone's gonna spot 'em and pass the word to me. You better hope Mitchell isn't there when I go in."

Kroun leaned forward. "You listen to me, kid, you don't take any action about Mitchell. He's my department. You got away with bumping Bristow because of special circumstances, but do anything to Mitchell, and nothing will save you. You will disappear the same as Bristow: dismembered and in the lake."

Well, that would do the trick of killing me for good. Death, the ultimate solver for all my problems. "Okay, I got that. But you get this—your boy was warned off from seeing my girl and came in regardless. He got his ass kicked because he deserved it. So long as he stays away from her I won't have to repeat the performance. That's all I'm concerned with. If Hoyle's a separate thing, then I'll take care of it separately. But if Mitchell's cooking up something *with* him—"

"You bring him to me, and *I* will deal with it."

The silence stretched. For a long moment I was tempted again to influence Kroun over to my side, find out for sure if he was truly ignorant about Mitchell's actions. Again, just thinking about it made me ache. I knew I didn't want to risk that stab-in-the-eye agony; I might not be able to vanish fast enough.

"Well?" he asked.

"No problem. In the meantime you might want to locate your boy and find out where he's been keeping himself."

Another silence. Kroun almost seemed to be waiting for something. Finally, he nodded. "Fair enough. You just remember we each have our own corners."

"I'll remember. How long's Mitchell been with you?"

"Couple years."

"You friends?"

"What's it to you?"

"I have friends. I look out for them."

"Like Gordy."

"Yeah."

Kroun grunted. "I need to talk with him. Face-to-face. Derner doesn't know where he is, hasn't got a number. Said you'd know."

"He safe. Resting." And healing, I hoped.

"Take me to see him, then."

I was tired of getting the kid-brother treatment. "What's with Gordy that you can't settle it with me?"

"It's about you. You want more, you put me and Gordy in the same room."

That set up a whole new batch of speculations, most of which I was sure I wouldn't care to know anything about. I could guess it had to do with me taking over for Gordy permanently. Or not. "Not" was fine with me, so long as Gordy was the one back in charge.

I reached for the phone and dialed Coldfield's club office. It rang a lot, then someone picked up the receiver. "The boss there? It's Fleming."

Coldfield agreed to allow Kroun a visit, but not until tomorrow. Apparently Dr. Clarson put his foot down after seeing the condition of his overtired patient. He'd barred all visitors, and the phone was off the hook. I asked if Gordy was better, but Coldfield had no information, only that the patient was safe and quiet. I passed the meager news to Kroun. He nodded, but wasn't pleased by the delay.

"I'll be by tomorrow, then," he said.

"Come just after opening, and I'll get you there."

"Why not earlier?"

"Because it's what the doctor ordered." That lie came easy.

Kroun picked his hat up along with Mitchell's gun and walked out. It was only after he'd gone that I realized he'd made no comment at all about the Caine murders, and the papers were still on the desk, big as life with headlines and pictures. I thought Kroun had come over in the first place to talk about them. Mitchell's behavior could have knocked that out of his head, seeing's how it was closer to home. But Kroun might have turned up to see my reaction to Mitchell's threat and Hoyle's shooting.

Damn it all, I should have tried hypnosis no matter what it did to me. Too late now.

Lady Crymsyn's second show was nearly over by the time I worked up enough spirit to leave the office. I was drawn out by the sound of Bobbi's glad voice. She was back onstage, confidence firmly restored along with her smile as she belted her closing song. She was amazing. Not one sign of what she'd gone through showed. It was as though it had never happened, and that was unsettling.

I watched from the entry, just out of sight from the patrons in the main room, not wanting to distract her. The damage was covered up, I thought, and covered very well, but still there under the surface. Escott would say to be patient and let time do the healing, but I'd hurt her and would continue to hurt her. No way out of that.

Some small commotion in the lobby got my attention for a moment. By now the front entry was closed to new customers, but someone wanted in, banging on the door. I heard Escott's muffled voice and the doorman's response. I went back down the passage in time to see Escott hurry across the lobby toward the stairs, his arm around a huddled-over female in a too-large coat.

The female was Evie Montana.

12

EVEN after all this time, when I should have been used to it, Escott still had the ability to make my jaw drop. How he could have left with four of Gordy's goons and returned with Betty Boop I could not imagine.

He glanced over his shoulder as I dogged him to the office. "Oh, good," was all he said, and continued on. Evie wore her dancing shoes and spangled stockings from last night's show. Her long overcoat seemed several sizes too big until I realized it was a man's coat. Not only that, it was a tan-colored vicuna, and had belonged to Alan Caine.

Jeez, what now?

Escott guided her to the couch, made her sit, then went to the liquor cabinet, poured her something, and made her drink. I kicked the office door shut and stood in front of it.

"What gives?" I asked.

"She said she saw the murder."

"I didn't see! I *heard* it!" she choked out, then fell into tears.

I'd had enough of those for one night and left Escott to deal with the deluge. My only help was to go to the washroom across the hall and bring back a roll of toilet paper. She traded her drink for the roll and began pulling off yards at a time, blowing her nose between bouts of howling.

It took a while before she settled down enough to answer questions. Escott filled in things up to a point. Evie left the Nightcrawler Club in a hurry, rented a flop someplace, and hid there, trying to think what to do. Eventually she remembered Escott had been a nice man. She'd been hanging around outside Lady Crymsyn for hours hoping to spot him. When he'd returned from driving the muscle to the doctor's, she made her move.

"Poor child's half-frozen," he added. "I doubt she's had anything to eat, either."

"We'll get her an eight-course dinner with music if she'll just tell what happened."

Evie did more carrying on, but I figured out she was enjoying the attention and barked her name, loudly. That hauled her up short.

"What?" she asked, sounding hurt.

"You tell us. What did you see?"

"I didn't *see*. I *heard*."

"Okay, what did you hear?"

It came tumbling out almost too fast to follow. She'd gone with Alan Caine to his dressing room as she usually did between shows. They liked to spend time together . . . talking. They were shy about people knowing anything, though, so when someone knocked at the door, Caine bundled Evie into the closet. That always made her giggle, but she was real quiet when he called his visitor in. Caine pretended to be alone; it was their secret.

Caine said, "Hello, you. Come back for more? I think I can—"

Then he stopped talking and made a funny sound. Then there were some vague, thrashing noises. None went on for long, but they were odd. Evie couldn't see any of it since the closet was fast shut, and she knew how mad Caine would be if she left before he said so.

The dressing-room door opened and closed, so it was plain that the visitor was gone. Caine didn't call to her, though. Finally, after a long, long time, maybe a couple minutes, she ventured to peek out.

She didn't like what she saw. Nearly fainted from it. Survival instinct overcame her fond feelings for Caine, and she knew she'd have to leave and quick. Not knowing who had done the deed, she could trust no one. She didn't dare go back for her own coat, and lit out wearing Caine's instead, using the stage door and running as fast as she could in her dancing heels.

"Did you see anything in the alley?" I asked. "Anyone?"

"No."

"What about Jewel Caine?"

Evie seized on the name. "That *witch!* She did it. I know she did!"

"She didn't," I said.

"You don't *know* her! She *hates* him."

"She didn't do it."

"She *did!* I'll make her tell!"

"Fine, we'll go talk to her. Where does she live?"

"I don't know. You go do that, call the cops, I don't care, I just wanna get out of town and go home!"

Unless Evie was a remarkable natural actress, she truly was ignorant about Jewel. Escott signed to me to step into the hall for a conference.

"There's only one way to remove all doubt here," he said. "Will the drink she had unduly interfere with your work? I wasn't thinking when I gave that to her."

I quelled a sudden flare of nausea. "I . . . uh . . . I can't."

"What?"

"You heard. No hypnosis." Damnation. I'd hoped to somehow avoid having to say anything about this to him.

"Why ever not?"

I worked very hard not to yell. "Because I just can't. It hurts."

He paused, at a loss. "But . . . it's always hurt you to a greater or lesser degree."

"Not like this. Something's changed, gone wrong. I think if I tried again . . . it could kill me. The last time I tried, I thought my head would explode."

"You're serious." He seemed flabbergasted.

"Yeah, and it keeps getting *worse*. Maybe building up to—I don't know. But I don't dare try. It might even damage Evie." I was more worried about damaging myself, though. "I'm deadly serious, Charles. I can't help you."

"Well," he finally said. "That is a bundle of news. I'm sorry."

"Yeah, me, too." It got quiet, and I thought he might ask more questions than I wanted to hear, but he held off. I motioned toward the office. "What d'ya want to do with her?"

"Keep her out of sight, for one thing. Here should be safe enough until I can arrange for other digs. We can get her out before dawn."

"Why hide her if the killer doesn't know she was in the room?"

"Because you have half the city looking for whoever took that vicuna coat. The killer knows Evie's the only other person besides himself who had any close dealings with Caine. Even Ruzzo might work it out. She could be murdered for no more reason than that."

"Okay. But we get her safe, then what? I may personally think it was Hoyle, but there's no guarantee he's going to be found. And if I turn out to be wrong, then who knows if we'll ever find out who did it?"

"According to you all we need do is check the hands of anyone involved and look for scratches. Admittedly it's not too practical, and time will certainly heal the damage, but if—"

"I know. I've got Strome and Derner checking that angle. Everyone who went out the Nightcrawler's doors last night had to show their hands. They didn't know why, but it cleared them. I managed to keep from tipping Kroun off about that detail just in case his boy Mitchell was the one. He's missing, but he can be more missing if Kroun arranges it."

"Did he ever come in tonight?"

"Oh, yeah." I told about the deal I had with Kroun. "Damn, if I hadn't been wound so tight about what he did to Bobbi I could have had a look at Mitchell's hands then. Might have avoided some friction. Kroun's real touchy about his territory. If Mitchell pulled that hit on his own, I think Kroun might send him over, but I can't be sure. He could just as well send him back to New York."

"It would be a mistake on Kroun's part to keep a viper so close."

"People get stupid."

"Unfortunately, yes."

"I'm hungry!" Evie wailed.

"Oh, my God." He didn't quite roll his eyes. "There are

few things more inconvenient than a witness who's not seen anything."

Actually I could think of worse stuff, but volunteered to remedy the food situation if he'd baby-sit.

"Only if I may avail myself of your alcoholic stores."

"Avail away."

Downstairs I gave the doorman five bucks and asked him to run over to an all-night diner that everyone usually went to after work. I told him to bring back a half dozen sandwiches, a dozen donuts, some milk, and he could keep the change. His eyes popped at the windfall, and he hurried off.

Not inclined to hear more of Evie's tiny little voice, I filled in for him as customers finished their last drinks and sauntered out.

In the main room the band began "Goodnight, Sweetheart," and the trickle became an exodus. Too many of the regulars wanted to stop and chat with the friendly owner, and there wasn't anything to do but get through it until they said their piece and left. I used to enjoy that kind of stuff.

Going to the lighting panel, I switched off the outside sign and the canopy light. Lady Crymsyn was officially closed.

The main room was empty of customers, the band breaking up and packing away their instruments. The waiters were yanking tablecloths and flipping chairs onto the tables, in a hurry to leave. Stale cigarette smoke hung thick in the air along with the pungent cleaner stink. The bartender had already divided up the tips for them and handed me the till and clipboard. The liquor was locked away and the last glass wiped clean and stored. I wished a general good night to all.

Wilton was closed out; I collected his till and clipboard and carried them upstairs, putting them on the desk over the papers. Escott sat on the couch next to Evie, patting her hand in what I hoped was a big-brotherly way.

"I sent out for food. Should be here soon," I said.

"Excellent. Evie's remembered something more."

I waited. So did he. She looked bewildered.

"The smell?" he prompted.

"Oh!" She seemed surprised. "Cigarettes. He smoked. Alan doesn't smoke, says it's bad for his voice. Whoever was there, it was all over his clothes."

"It was a man? I thought you were after Jewel for this. She smokes."

"She coulda *made* a man do it for her. It was a man. There was sweat, too."

"Sweat?"

"I smelled sweat, and it was a man's sweat."

"Don't women sweat?"

"Not the same. The smell's different."

"Uh-huh."

Escott patted her hand again. "He's just getting used to the idea. Jack, I'm inclined to trust her senses on this one."

I read between the lines. Evie wasn't an intellectual giant, but knew how to survive and get on in the world. Her edge was more to do with intuition than anything else. Some part of that would be geared to knowing the difference between male and female sweat. "Okay."

"Am I gonna stay here?" she asked.

"For a few hours," Escott said. "You may nap right here on this nice comfy couch if you like. We'll watch over you." He sounded like he was addressing a ten-year-old, and Evie didn't seem to mind.

I was glad he limited it to a few hours. When it got past

dawn, I would be hard to explain. Sure I had a bolt-hole under the tiers of seating, lockable and light-proofed, but I liked the couch for myself, dammit.

The doorman brought his delivery upstairs. I had the till money counted, ledgers updated, and everything sealed in the safe, so the desk was cleared for a feast.

"I can't eat all that!" Evie declared, eyes big.

No, but she'd likely pack away at least half of it. I knew dancers. "Charles will help you, won't you, Charles?" It was a long-running battle for me to make sure he ate if not well, then at least at regular intervals. He said he would be delighted to join her for dinner. I told him I needed to take Bobbi home and could I borrow his car?

"Of course," he said, handing over the keys to his Nash.

"What about a hiding place for Evie?"

"You've a phone and a phone book. I'll get on very well indeed finding something."

She cocked her head. "You're English, aren't you, just like in England?"

I had a moment of déjà vu. She'd said exactly the same thing in the same way the other night. Escott obviously recalled it, too, and shot me a thin smile. It was going to be a long night for him.

Wilton and the hatcheck girl left together. Usually he or the doorman would walk her to the El. Coat and hat on, I made a sweep through the main room. All was quiet, the bartender and waiters having departed by the backstage exit. I yelled down into the basement, rousting out a lagging horn player before dousing the light and locking that door.

All the dressing rooms but number three were closed and dark. I hesitated before knocking, unsure of my reception. Until that night Bobbi and I had never had any real fight.

Not that that'd been a fight. It was more that I'd let her down in a big way and couldn't make it up to her.

But I still had to take her home. I tapped softly.

Bobbi welcomed me in, nearly finished with her change to ordinary clothes. She greeted me a little too brightly, acting as if that all was well again between us. It was, so far as the business with Mitchell was concerned, but not the business with me.

"Are my seams straight?" she asked. She twisted around, trying to check them in a long mirror, the skirt of her dress raised high.

"Uhh—they look Jim Dandy to me."

"Yes, but are they straight?"

"I could get a ruler to make sure."

"You men . . ."

"Oh? You ask other guys for help with your stockings?"

"All the time."

The banter was there, but with an artificial note to it. I thought I should talk to her about things, but this just wasn't the time. "We're closed up, but Charles is staying on for a while. We've got a case going. I'll take you home, then have to come back here."

"What case?"

"It's to do with the Caine murders."

"I saw the papers. Poor Jewel. Are the stories true?"

"They're totally wrong in a big way. It's murder-murder, not murder-suicide."

"Does it have to do with Gordy?"

"I don't think so, but with Alan Caine having been employed at the Nightcrawler, I have to be around to keep the boat from rocking. That's why I had to leave earlier and . . . and I'm sorry about that."

"Okay." She looked like she might have more to say, but

turned to straighten stuff on her dressing table. There seemed to be a lot of unsaids growing between us.

When we reached her hotel, Bobbi leaned across the seat and kissed me good night. It was a nice, safe kiss, very sisterly.

"You wondering why not more?" she asked. She could always read me.

I didn't know how to answer that.

"There will be when it's the right time. You'll know when."

After she left the big car and was in the lobby waiting for the elevator to take her up I gave in to a long shudder. No doubling over, no groans about remembered pain, no needing to vanish to head off the screaming. You could call it progress. But I hung on to the Nash's steering wheel so hard that it bent in my hands.

The fit gradually passed. I didn't hurt all over, just felt like I should.

Then I drove off quick. Headed for the Stockyards.

No hunger, yet I needed blood. Craved it. Had to have . . .

I'd stopped thinking and turned into an automaton.

When I came back to myself I was slumped against one of the high fences of a cattle pen, my arms looped over it, holding me up. Every part of my body was stretched and bloated. Even my eyelids felt swollen. It was hard work to blink.

I glanced at the pen's occupants, half-expecting to see a dead cow lying in the muck, but they were still on their feet.

Had I been careless coming in? This seemed to be the same spot from the night before. To cut down the odds of being seen I always went to different locations. This craziness was out of hand.

Despite the excess of blood—my face was smeared with it—I began shivering from cold.

It's fear, you idiot. This is fear. Get that through your thick skull.

"Okay, I get it," I said aloud to the head-demons. "Now lay off me."

The glut made it easy to vanish and soar above the crossword-puzzle pattern of fencing. I had to go high, partially materialize, and look around since I couldn't remember where I'd left the car.

Dimly I recalled trying to pull myself away from gorging, but at the time there didn't seem much point. I was well and truly started, why not keep going so long as I was there?

Winced at the memory.

God, yes, when I lost control like that I had every right to be scared. I had to keep myself away from Bobbi.

The Nash was parked close by under a streetlamp, something I'd never normally do. The keys were in the ignition. It was just my good luck no one else had been by to find such a choice offering. I got in and checked the wheel. The damage wasn't too bad, more of a bend like a warped phonograph record than anything else. It would need to be replaced, but was otherwise fine for driving.

Where to drive to . . . ?

Escott's office, to clean up. I'd not been careful during my binge.

It was only a few minutes away. This time I took the keys when I got out.

On the other side of his office door the place was much too quiet and dark. Though there was plenty of light filtering through the closed blinds—pitch-dark to anyone else—I wanted more and flipped switches on my way to the back.

Eerie feeling in the washroom as I bent over the sink and scrubbed my face with cold water. I'd come here after staggering away from the gory wreckage of Bristow's party. He'd been drunk, and his blood had turned me drunk and brainlessly foolish. That was the why behind my insanity then; what the hell was I doing to myself? That horror was *over.* If I kept up with this inner sickness, I'd only be finishing the job he'd started.

Sickness. I made myself use that word. It was the right one.

There wasn't a lot of difference between me and Alan Caine. For him it had been gambling. For me it was blood. And before that booze. Roland Lambert was the same. He'd traded his drinking for womanizing, which had hurt the one women he loved. If he went back to the bottle . . . a different kind of self-destruction.

But you could live without drinking, and if you absolutely had to, without women. There was no way I could live without blood.

Perhaps I could limit things and prevent myself from overdoing. I had lately begun siphoning it into bottles, keeping them in the icebox for emergencies. One a night was plenty. More than enough. I'd been able to dole things out like that before my change. A beer a day, then cut loose with a good rip on Saturday night, only I'd just not have any Saturday nights. I could do that.

Which still left the problem of Bobbi not being safe with me. In the throes of passion I could kill her.

And then Escott would have to kill me.

I'd make him promise to do it.

If not him, then Gordy. What are best friends for if not to trust them with the hardest favors for you?

Shaking cold water from my face, I dried off and told myself to shut the hell up before the dark possibilities chorusing through my head turned themselves into a grand opera.

I went back to the car, started it, and let it idle, not sure where to go. Escott liked driving his Nash around at night. For relaxation. Used to, anyway. His insomnia was pretty much gone now.

There were still some long, lonesome hours ahead, though. Before things had gone so far off course I'd either spend them with Bobbi or put in extra work at Crymsyn or pound on my typewriter or just read. Life had been so much simpler a week back. I'd had my share of horrors and grief, but could live with them. The good old days. Not nearly enough of those.

Kroun's advice to find a place in the middle of nowhere and do nothing but fish was very appealing. The wild temptation to take off this very moment was almost overwhelming. What tore it away were my countless obligations to everyone I knew. Between them and the drive to have my own business I'd cemented myself into the pavement in front of Lady Crymsyn and couldn't leave. It was better than swinging from a meat hook, but I was still stuck just as firmly in place.

I pulled into the alley behind the club rather than my special parking spot. If Escott wanted to get Evie away later without being seen, that was the place to do it. Ghosting out, I passed through the locked door and walked through the dark and silent club.

Very dark and silent. Myrna wasn't playing with the lights at all.

"Myrna? You there, baby?"

She must have tired herself out last night making that rose scent for me. It really had helped. For a time. I wanted to thank her, but how do you thank a ghost?

At least the lobby light was still on. She was very dependable about that one. Before going up to the office I got into the phone booth, dropped in a nickel, and dialed the Nightcrawler. Derner didn't answer, but someone got him for me.

"Yeah, Boss?"

"Have you heard about the trouble here tonight?"

"Yeah, the guys told me. They're mad as hell at Ruzzo—"

"That's great, but this snipe hunt for Ruzzo and Hoyle's been going on too damned long. Is *anyone* actually *looking?*"

He avoided sounding defensive. "They're doing what they can do. The boys are covering all the hotels, from flops to the fancy places, boardinghouses, bordellos, and rooms to let. There ain't a bed in this town they ain't looked into or under. If Ruzzo's in Chicago, we'll find 'em sooner or later. But if they've blown town or run off to the sticks . . . maybe not."

"I want them even if they are in the sticks. Where does Hoyle hang around?"

"Here, usually."

"Where else?"

"We looked in those places. He's letting himself be missing."

I gave out a disgusted sigh.

"We got the word out you only want to talk with him, but since he's trying to shoot you, I guess he misunderstood."

In some mobs "talk" meant beat a guy up, just not to the point of crippling him permanently. "Keep at it. Get me a location. We are not dealing with the Harvard debate team here."

"Who?"

"Never mind."

"Boss? That special guest we got was back here, looking hot under the collar. Anything I should know?" Derner was yet on guard against listening wires. Good man.

"He's lost his traveling friend."

"That's what he said in so many words. He's plenty bothered about something."

"Let him work it out. Help him however he wants, and tell me if anything screwy happens. I'll be at my club until morning."

"Got it. Any word on the other boss?" That would be Gordy.

"He's resting is all I know. They're taking care of him. Soft berth."

"That's good to know. Should I pass that on?"

"Yeah." It would be reassuring to a few that Gordy was still around. Certainly reassured me.

I rang off and was about to trudge up to the office when someone banged loud on Crymsyn's front door. What and who the hell now? Hoyle? But if it was a determined bad guy, he'd have shot the lock off, not knocked and given warning.

Standing to the side just in case, I yelled through the door, "We're closed!"

"Jack, it's me!"

Roland Lambert. He said he'd wanted to talk to me. Must be pretty damned important to get him back here at this hour in the cold. I unlocked and went outside rather than inviting him in. He didn't need to know Escott and I had company, and if we were both out in the wind, the business wouldn't take as long.

"What's the matter?" I asked. His green Hudson was parked right in front of the canopy. No passengers. "Is Faustine all right?"

"She's fine, probably asleep by now. I told her I'd forgotten something and had to come back. You often stay until very late, don't you?"

"Uhm . . ."

"Faustine's why I'm here, sport. It's about the shooting tonight."

"Roland, I'm sorry. That's never going to happen again, I promise. I'm getting special locks for the doors, and people are looking for that bum. He's not coming back."

"I'm delighted to hear it. Don't think I'm ungrateful the way you tackled him. It turned out well, and Faustine had a great time, but it was also terribly, terribly dangerous. She thinks it was a lark, something out of the movies."

"I got that from her."

"And we know better. Look, I've played my share of derring-do roles in films, and it is fun, but in real life, it's just *not* the done thing."

"You going to leave?" I didn't see how they could afford it. Faustine was not cheap to keep, and they were making steady money working for me.

"I'd really rather not. You're a grand fellow to work for, one of the best. It's just this is extremely disturbing to me."

"I don't blame you. If anything happened to Bobbi . . ." I didn't want to finish that thought.

"Then we understand one another."

"What do you want me to do?"

"Well, there's not much you *can* do beyond what you've already said. I'm reassured, bu—"

They were getting smarter, more crafty at it. Instead of a

car roaring up the street to give warning to anyone paying attention, they'd all but coasted in.

Hoyle hung halfway out an open window; one Ruzzo drove, the other was busy keeping Hoyle from falling out. They drove up, sedate as any honest citizen, but when they crested the front of the club Hoyle cut loose with his semi-auto.

I pushed Roland aside, but not quite in time. Bullets bit and banged around us. Roland caught one, yelped, and dropped like a stone.

13

A FEW seconds of mind-numbing panic, the taste of metal on my tongue, then I shoved the fear as far away as I could. As Ruzzo hit the gas to take them away I kicked open Crymsyn's door, grabbed Roland, and hauled him inside. His legs weren't working, and once on the black-and-white marble tiles he gasped out a sudden halt. Blood seemed to pour from him, the scent sharp and arresting.

Before I lost all sense I bellowed for Escott to get the hell down there and rushed to the bar for towels. I was in cold syrup; nothing I did seemed fast enough or smart enough or good enough. Escott was halfway down the stairs and stopped to gape for all of a second, then also rushed forward.

The lobby lights blazed on. I whirled; this was the perfect time for an ambush, but no one was there. Myrna, then. The lights went out, then on again. She'd done it for me once. Trying to help.

"Leave 'em on, goddammit!"

They stayed on.

"My God, how——?" Escott began.

"Hoyle. Trying for me again."

"Bloody bastard." He got Roland to lie flat while I ripped the man's trouser leg open to the knee and pressed a towel to the wound. The white cloth soon loaded up with blood despite the pressure I put on. God, if that was an artery . . .

"Hospital," I said. "Now."

"Is it safe outside?"

"Probably not." I turned pressure duty over to him and shot through the passage, the main room, the backstage, moving silent and fast. I'd traded solidity for speed and regained it in the alley after bulling right through the club's walls. The Nash was still warmed up and easily roared to life. I hurtled it around two corners and braked just short of ramming the parked Hudson. I'd have used Roland's car, but the Nash was bulletproofed.

The street was empty of Hoyle and his crew, and just as well for Roland, or I might have gone after them. I bailed out, leaving the motor running.

Evie was in the lobby by then, visibly upset, asking questions in her little voice and not being too damned helpful. She was still in the vicuna coat. I told her to go out and open the back door of the brown car outside. If I'd said Nash, she might not have been able to pick it out.

"The brown car?"

"*Go!*"

She made a single yipping noise like a small pooch and fled outside.

"Roland?"

"Right here, sport. Remember my talk about doing this in films? Well, a make-believe bullet is much better." He forced out a ghastly grin.

Escott had cut Roland's suspenders off with a folding knife and improvised a tourniquet, which seemed to help, but the stack of blood-soaked towels had grown. "Come on, let's get him to the car."

"Yes, please hurry. This hurts like a bad review!"

I hoped joking meant he was going to be all right. When I'd been in the War—and this suddenly and unpleasantly reminded me of it—I'd seen guys cracking wise to the very end.

Opening a door on a brown car was evidently not one of Evie's talents. She'd overdone it and opened them all. What the hell, we could manage. I had Roland's shoulders, Escott his feet, and we somehow got him into the back. Escott slammed the door on his side, urged Evie into the passenger's, and came around to close mine on his way to the wheel.

"What the devil . . . ?" He stared at the warpage.

"Later," I said. "Get this bucket moving."

He got us moving.

Roland held on through the drive to the hospital, which was hair-raising enough to distract me from the fresh blood-smell. I didn't think Escott planned it that way, he was just in an unholy hurry. He skidded to a halt, missed rear-ending an ambulance, and bolted inside the hospital. As a kid he'd worked at one or for a doctor, I couldn't recall which, and would be better at raising the troops. I told Evie twice to get out and open the door. She kept blinking and saying, "I don't like this, I don't *like* this."

Perhaps playing to the hilt the devil-may-care suave, Roland grinned, "That's all right, my dear, you're in the *best* of company on that opinion."

"Huh?" She saw his smile and responded with a little laugh, the kind people with no sense of humor give when they know you've made a joke, but they don't get it, they're just being polite.

"Open the damn door!" I snapped at her, in no mood to be a gentleman. A couple of orderlies with a stretcher were on their way over, double-quick. She barely made it in time. Thankfully, Escott took her arm and kept her clear while I helped ease Roland out. The men took over, loaded up, and swept him toward the hospital's receiving area.

"I don't *like* this!" she cried.

This was the time for the deep-night predators to venture forth, but they would be elsewhere in the city, creeping through the cheap, run-down jungles where the desperation was greater, the victims more plentiful. I was where the victims ended up if they were lucky enough to survive. The waiting room was crowded.

I'd phoned Derner first and told him what happened and to send someone to Bobbi's hotel, then I phoned Bobbi to tell her what had happened. She was stunned for only a few moments, though.

"You need me to help with Faustine?" she asked.

"I was hoping."

"Of course I will. I'll be dressed again when you get here."

"I've already sent a car to pick you up. The driver will take you anyplace you want."

"One of Gordy's?" She sounded weary.

" 'Fraid so. I have to be here. With a gunshot wound they bring the cops and . . . uhhh . . . I'm thinking you know all that."

"A lot too well. I'll get Faustine and be there as soon as we can."

"I'll see you then."

"Be safe, sweetheart."

None safer. From bullets. Insanity and rage and fear were other matters entirely.

About ten minutes later several large guys with big coats and mashed noses walked in and not for emergency treatment. They spotted me and came over. "Derner sent us," one of them told me.

"Thoughtful of him," murmured Escott. He sat with an arm around the supremely unhappy, but heavy-eyed Evie. She was tucked up on her chair, the tan coat covering her like a blanket with just part of her face showing. None of the mugs seemed to recognize her.

"Fine," I said. "Spread out, on your toes, and if you see Hoyle try to make it look like self-defense, there's cops here."

The man smiled. "Cops." Apparently he was unimpressed. Where had Derner found this bunch? They were tougher-looking than the bouncers had been, and came across as made men. No matter, so long as they were on my side.

"No shooting civilians," I added.

He grunted. Disappointed, maybe. He jerked his head at the other guys, and they trundled away. Everyone got out of their path except the nurses.

And a cop.

My favorite cop was Lieutenant Blair, but he must have had the night off. This new guy was Sergeant Something who flashed his badge too fast. Escott patted Evie's shoulder and spoke low to her. She didn't move. Asleep, I hoped.

The sergeant got a statement from me about the shooting. I used to be a lousy liar but had since improved my skills. I can lie to strangers better than to friends, and this guy heard one of my best efforts. He got the facts as I knew them, but I pretended ignorance of the identity of the shooters.

"You're pretty calm about it, Mr. Fleming," he noted.

"It's late, I'm tired, and I'm worried about my friend. Call it shell shock."

"Don't you want to get the guys that shot him? They could come after you next."

"I think they were after me in the first place, and Roland just happened to be in the way." There, an absolutely true statement.

"Why would anyone want to shoot you?"

"You know how this town is. I opened a great club, there's other guys jealous, they want to take me down a notch, even scare me out of business."

"Has it worked?"

"Hell, yes. I'm closing until further notice. Nobody else is gonna get hurt."

This last was caught by a guy whose job I recognized as easily as the mugs who'd walked in. I used to dress just like him. He scribbled in a notebook and threw a question at me, but the cop shooed him off like an out-of-season horsefly. I knew what that was like. No nostalgia stirred in me to go back to the simple life of being a reporter. You ask so many questions and then one day you get more answers than you really want.

The cop finished with me and skipped talking with Escott, who hadn't exactly put himself forward. I'd said Escott hadn't seen anything and had only helped with the wounded.

When the cop cleared off the reporter moved in.

"It's just a shooting," I said to him. "What's the big beef about it?"

"A shooting at Lady Crymsyn." He grinned. "You are headline material for me. After that 'Jane Poe' case—"

"That's yesterday's fish wrapper. This is nothing. I donno who did it. I just want my friend to be okay."

"Your friend being the famous Roland Lambert, star of stage and screen. Why's he tripping the floor in your place if he's such a big star?"

"He's just doing a favor for a pal. Thought it'd be a lark. He and his wife are cut-ups like that, always having fun." It was a better story than the truth about trying to make ends meet. I shoveled a lot of bull at the Fifth Estate and made Roland an altruistic hero who'd saved my life at the risk of his own. The reporter, apparently not good enough yet to have thought up the angle himself, went away happy. If he could write it fast enough, he might make the afternoon edition.

Bobbi and Faustine turned up next with their driver, who turned out to be Strome. He hung off to one side and smoked a cigar to fill the time while I did my best to calm Faustine down and give her the same story I'd passed to the cop.

I also advised her not to mention the shooting incident she'd been involved in earlier.

"Vhy ever nodt?" She was startled enough to stop demanding to see Roland.

"I'm shutting the club down for now, but if they catch wind of any more fishiness, they could keep it that way."

"Budt de show musst go on!"

"So we all keep quiet about it."

"About vhat, doll-ink? Poof! I forgedt whole tink. Now vhere iss my poor Roland? I musst see heem. I musst see dok-tor."

*   *   *

Eventually we all saw Roland, from a distance. His leg was bandaged and elevated in some kind of pulley contraption, and he was too groggy to say anything. Only Faustine was allowed in with him.

The doctor was optimistic. There was a lot of damage, and the bullet cracked, but hadn't broken, one of the leg bones, but if there was no infection, he would get well soon enough. I saw to it at least one of the mashed-nosed guys was to be within call at all times. Bobbi explained to Faustine that they were there to look after them and left it at that.

We were all told to go home, but Faustine refused to leave, and Bobbi said she'd stay to keep her company. I knew better than to talk her out of it.

She gave me a look, though. "Jack, I know this isn't your fault."

"Oh, yes it is."

"Shh! I just want to know when you get the guy who did it."

"So you can slug him, too?"

"So I know when it's safe to come back to the club."

"You'll be the first. I got eyes and ears out. We'll find him."

"*They'll* find him. You're not one of them, remember?"

"I'm trying, doll. I'm trying."

Escott announced he was taking Evie somewhere safe. He'd found a suitable hotel to go to ground.

"You got proof you're a Mr. and Mrs.?" I asked.

"I fear none is required for this establishment. I only hope Vivian never opens an inquiry into this."

"It's in a good cause. Call at the club if you need anything."

"You'll be asleep."

"I meant the Nightcrawler. Derner knows who you are."

"Oh, dear God."

"What?"

"Does this mean I'm your gangland lieutenant?" He said it with an "f" again. Someday I'd ask him if that's how it was spelled in England.

"Let's just keep it 'baby-sitter to dancers' and leave it at that."

"And what happened to my steering wheel?"

"I . . . had another . . . another damned fit."

"A fit." He went still, waiting for more.

But I shut down, shaking my head. "I'll get you a new one."

"You bloody well better," he finally said, then went to rouse Evie from her nap. She protested but went along with him. I had two of the mugs follow to see them off.

After a run by Crymsyn to check things (normal) and Escott's office (also normal) I had Strome drop me a block from Escott's house, telling him I'd walk from there, that I needed the fresh air to clear my head.

"Pick me up tomorrow around . . . oh, just come after dark." I couldn't remember the time for sunset. Dawn was my main concern. I kept track of that.

"It's freezing," he said. "You noticed? You shouldn't walk."

"Yeah, but I don't mind." The chill that had plagued me before was either gone or I'd just gotten used to it. Waiting until his taillights were a memory, I vanished, speeding along the sidewalk until I figured to be in sight of the house. I went solid and had a good look around the neighborhood, front and back.

Nothing. Dammit.

I'd been hoping, really, really *hoping* that since the club and the office came up empty, Hoyle would catch a case of the dumbs from Ruzzo and be lying in wait for me here.

Too bad. Pounding their heads together would have improved my mood a lot.

I ghosted inside the house, went through it for intruders (none), ran a bath, used it, shaved, put on fresh clothes for tomorrow, and dropped invisibly into my basement sanctuary.

The light was on, as I'd left it. The dim bulb didn't use much juice. It also didn't heat the place much, as in dry out the damp. Was I in for another broken pipe?

This spot used to be cozy and safe, and it was fireproof, but still . . . I wanted to *not* be home.

Maybe if I fixed up something better, larger, took over the whole basement.

Jonathan Barrett had a great place, lots of room, bookshelves, lots of lights, but then he was richer and had a rich girlfriend who didn't mind the improvements in the cellar of her Long Island palace.

Maybe I could get my own place.

Actually I already had one. Lady Crymsyn.

And I didn't feel safe there, either.

Strome was punctual. I was on the phone with Derner within minutes of rising to find out what had happened during the day when the doorbell rang. I let Strome in and went back to my call. Shouldn't have bothered. Nothing new on the hunt for Hoyle. He'd gone to ground again and had either found an exceptionally good place for it, or no one would admit to knowing where. With there still being a substantial number of men against my sitting in Gordy's chair, a stonewalling might be in progress. Paranoid of me, but I had a right to be so, and, without hypnosis to force things my way, I was stuck with the situation.

Speaking of stuck . . . "Is my car back yet?" I asked Derner.

"No, Boss. I got them to lay off and just do the tires, though."

Dammit. I could have gone to Detroit and back and had a whole new car made by now. I suppressed a growl, and asked, "Has Kroun been in?"

"Not today. If he was steamed last night, he's gonna be boiling tonight."

"Why?"

"The papers."

"What's in them?"

"They're screaming about a mob hit on Roland Lambert."

"*What?*"

"That's what they got. I didn't write it, that's what they got. Your club's all over it, your name, and they pulled out the Jane Poe case again."

Oh, hell. I shouldn't have talked to that reporter. I knew better. Give them one straw, and they'll spin a mountain of gold. I'd been known to do it myself. "Hoyle will know that he missed killing me again."

"Yeah, that's gonna piss him off."

"I'll send him flowers."

"Hey, Boss, it's the way it is."

"Yeah-yeah. Look, the guys who do know where he is ain't cooperating, that's plain enough. You put the word out that his location is worth two grand to them."

He nearly choked. "But that-that's—"

Two years' income to most, a tip to others. "Take it out of petty cash. These bozos are gonna cost us five times that if they're left running loose. I'll be at Crymsyn if anything new comes in."

I hung up before the sputtering started. The phone rang as I shrugged into my coat. My hat was gone. I suspected I'd lost it in the Stockyards during my binge.

Escott was on the other end of the line. His tone was tense. "Good, I wanted to catch you before—"

"What's wrong?"

"Bloody Evie Montana. The little—she slipped her leash."

"Ah, jeez. How?"

"Oldest trick in the book, through the bathroom window and out."

"When?"

"This afternoon. I should have anticipated. She'd been harping all day about wanting to go home. I think the girl is rather backward—"

"Can it, Charles, we both know she's the original Dumb Dora."

"Yet she managed to outfox me. I'd tried to explain the situation to her, but she seemed to think—oh, bloody hell, she doesn't think. That's the problem."

Hanging around smart women like Vivian and Bobbi had gotten him spoiled. "Well, meet me at the club, and we'll try to hash out a way of finding her again."

"Right." He sounded tired. Apparently a day with Evie had not been a picnic.

With a twinge of guilt I realized I should call the hospital and ask after Roland. It wasn't his fault the papers were in a lather about the shooting. I had the operator connect me, not wanting to bother searching the phone book. Eventually I got through to the nurses' station on Roland's floor and was informed he was doing well, whatever that meant. When I asked for more details I was told when evening visiting hours were, then the line went dead. Standard replies to the standard questions. If something was truly wrong, the answers would have been different. Maybe.

"Two grand for Hoyle?" asked Strome on the way to his car.

"Yeah. You know where he is?"

He shook his head. "But I might know some guys who might know some guys who might. And they don't need to hear about the two grand."

"No, they don't." If Strome had been holding out on me . . . but I decided I didn't care. Whatever it took to get Hoyle in a box.

Roland's Hudson was still parked in front of Lady Crymsyn, along with another car. A hopeful reporter. Strome drove around back. I let us in that way, we walked through, then I unlocked the lobby door and let him out again. Less than a minute later the hopeful drove off at a good clip. Strome came in, his face bland. I didn't ask questions and went up to the office.

Lights *and* radio off. Myrna was being different tonight. I turned both on and rummaged in the desk, finding a piece of cardboard in a box of typing paper. I lettered an optimistic CLOSED, BUT BACK SOON! on it in black ink, then went down to tack it on the entry door.

The lobby phone rang, startling me. I was the one who usually called in on it. Strome kept his hands in his pockets, so I answered.

"Jack?" Bobbi's voice.

"Yeah, honey? You okay?"

"I'm fine, we're all fine. It's been rough, but I got some sleep. I was hoping to catch you. I already tried at Charles's."

"Oh, yeah?"

"I thought you should know I called everyone not to come in tonight."

She just saved me a ton of effort. "You're an angel. How's Roland?"

"He's in better shape than me and Faustine put together. The papers have been all over him. He's enjoying every moment."

"Enjoying?"

"His name is in the news, people are wanting his autograph. This is the best thing that's happened to him in ages."

"Yeah, but will he dance again?" That was a huge nagging worry I'd tried not to think about.

"He seems to think so. I wouldn't put it past him to be up and rehearsing tomorrow. I told him you'd closed the club for the time being, though. He said to tell you not to do that. I couldn't really explain that there was more going on, mostly because I don't know anything."

"I'll tell you all about it whenever you want."

"When it's over, then."

Which could be never at this rate. "It's a deal." And I hoped she didn't pick up on the pain that lanced through me just then. The false front between us wasn't going to come down.

After last night's uncontrolled debauch I knew I'd have to get away, especially from Bobbi. The longer I stayed, the worse the hurt would be for us both. Club or no club, responsibilities aside, I had to get clear of this mess before I lost my head and killed her.

"Boss?" Strome called up.

Calling *up? What the . . . ?*

I looked around and had to steady myself. I was in my *office.* Didn't remember leaving the phone booth or climbing the stairs.

"Oh, God . . ." I sat on the couch, my knees gone weak.

No scent of roses for comfort. Just me alone and crazy in my own skull.

"Boss? Mr. Kroun's here."

I must be in hell, I thought. *Or a nearby neighborhood.*

"Be right down." My voice sounded frighteningly normal, like there were two of me. The man who worked the front and kept things moving and the guy in the back who was losing himself in wholesale lots to the darkness within.

Stood up, squared my shoulders, and started to shut down the radio before leaving, then changed my mind. Maybe Myrna would like to have a little music going.

"I'm off to see some bad guys, Myrna. Keep an eye on things, would you?"

I collected my coat, wrapping up and pulling on leather gloves.

That's when I noticed the gun on my desk.

For several mad seconds I froze completely. I could not think how it had gotten there. It was the same Colt Detective Special I'd acquired once upon a time. How in hell . . . ?

I picked it up, hefting the solid, otherwise reassuring weight and broke it open. Fully loaded, with the brand of bullets I favored, still smelling of its last cleaning, it was definitely the same gun. I went cold all over, put it down and backed away, the flesh on my nape going tight.

Had I somehow opened the safe, taken the gun out, placed it on the blotter, and totally forgotten? If that was true, then I really was crazy, and in a much more serious way than before.

A table lamp next to the couch went on and off suddenly. I twitched and whirled to face it.

Oh, jeez . . . what a time for . . .

"Myrna?" I whispered. "Was this your doing?"

No more light play, but I knew the answer, however impossible it seemed. She switched vodka and gin bottles around as a joke, and cut lemons up to help Wilton, but this was a first. A big first. Was she getting stronger? And how far was this kind of thing going to go?

"Thanks, honey," I said to the air.

I made myself relax and put the gun in my overcoat pocket. At least I'd not been the one who'd done it and forgotten, so I wasn't all that crazy. Just haunted.

"Look after the place, okay?"

No lights flickered in reply as I shut the door.

Kroun was in a shut-mouthed mood, which suited me just fine. He'd parked behind Strome's car, driver's side to the curb. When it was time to leave he slid across the seat. I didn't think he was tired of driving Gordy's car, but only I knew where we were going, and this way minimized conversation.

Strome said he was going to go someplace and see someone, and I hoped it meant turning up Hoyle.

I took a lot of unnecessary turns on the ride toward the Bronze Belt. Kroun would probably know where we were on arrival and could find his way back again, but this way I could tell Coldfield that I'd made an effort. I took one final corner onto a street lined with parked cars and spotted a single opening halfway down. It seemed suspiciously clear, and I expected to find a fireplug, but Isham, one of Coldfield's lieutenants, stepped from a little grocery store next to the space. I parked Gordy's tank and got out.

This was one of the border areas of the Bronze Belt, where the whites and coloreds had to intermingle as dictated by geography. Despite the presence of so many vehicles, it was a hard-knock area; the Caddy stood out.

Isham nodded at the car. "Shoe said there'd be you and Kroun. That him? Everything okay?"

"Pretty much."

"Where's your Klansman?"

He meant Strome, who did not behave well in mixed company. Isham had made a hobby of baiting him. "He wet the rug, so I tied him in the yard."

Isham chuckled, and I went back to the car. Kroun slid across the seat again to get out on the curb side. He tried his stare out on Isham. Isham looked past him in such a way that he had to eventually turn to see what was so interesting. There were suddenly a lot of guys visible that we hadn't noticed before. They were in doorways or coming out of other stores or the alleyways. They all had the look.

Kroun grunted, almost smiling. "Peachy."

We followed Isham into the store, which was a small-time husband-and-wife operation. The couple stood behind the counter, watching the parade with flinty faces. I'd been through there before on a case for Escott and politely saluted the lady since I was minus a hat. Neither of them reacted.

Isham took us out the back door, turning right down the rear alley, then went into another door, this one to an eatery. I got a partial whiff of grease and stale coffee, then made a determined effort not to inhale accidentally. Food smells made me nauseous, even the expensive stuff.

We didn't bother going to the front, but through an inside door to a small washroom. Isham opened a closet door, revealing a narrow space with a mop and bucket and shelves crowded with cleaning supplies and junk. He pulled on one of the shelves and the wall—rather a door fixed to look like a wall—swung out. A bare hall, badly lighted, lay within.

Kroun paused. "Jeez, what kinda place you got here?"

"The kind that's safe," said Isham. "Fleming knows the rest of the way."

"It's okay," I said, going in first. Kroun doubtfully followed. It was only twenty feet, not enough to make me nervous, and the opposite door also opened into a storage closet, this one full of bed linens and towels. I pulled on the light cord. The bare bulb above us went on, and I carefully shut up the passage behind. It clicked softly into place and once more resumed looking like a back wall supporting a couple coat hooks. A work apron dangled limp from one of them.

"Up and through," I said.

"Then what? Secret ladders?"

"Nah, just stairs."

Outside was a regular back hallway, no frills. Shiny linoleum, plain white walls, a hotel maids' cart shoved to one side. At the end were service stairs, and we went up two flights.

"Where the hell are we?" Kroun was puffing. You'd think a mobster would be in better shape.

"Somewhere in the next block from the car. You saw the neighborhood. It wouldn't do for a couple of white guys to be seen going in and out of a colored hotel."

"Why'd you bring Gordy here, then?"

"Is this where you'd ever look for him?"

"Huh. That's good. How'd you fix it?"

"Connections and a donation or two to a good cause."

Dr. Clarson and those of his colleagues who took care of Gordy were being well compensated, as was the owner of the hotel, but that we were here at all was Shoe Coldfield's doing. Without his blessing and help, Gordy might have been a sitting duck even in his own territory. Coldfield would have done it anyway as a favor to me and Escott, but he was also doing himself a favor. With someone like Gordy owing him in such a big way, a gang boss could get a lot of things done for his turf.

When we reached the right floor I knocked twice and pushed slowly on the service door. A guy a little shorter than Isham stood with a revolver in his fist. He knew me by sight but didn't put the gun away. I slowly emerged, my arms out a little. Kroun did the same.

One of Gordy's boys, Lowrey, came up and said we were okay. The other man nodded and retreated a few steps, watchful.

Lowrey and another trusted man had taken turns standing watch since all this began. Strome might have been here to help, but he wasn't much of a mixer with color. Lowrey didn't give a damn one way or another, it was just a job. Most of the real guardianship was done by Shoe Coldfield's people.

Lowrey took us along the length of the hotel hall and up another flight. This floor had rooms with open doors, plush carpeting, and people, but nothing noisy. It was almost like a library. So long as it didn't turn into a funeral parlor.

Adelle Taylor emerged from one of the rooms, apparently expecting us. She was soberly dressed, not in her usual film-actress style, but everything looked nice. She gave me a smile.

I bent a little and bussed her cheek, then gave her a good looking over. "Woman, you have him get on his feet pretty soon, or I'm gonna start asking you out."

She reacted well. "Is that a promise or a threat?"

"Both."

At the sight of her Kroun underwent an amazing transformation. He dropped the dour face and blazed out with his charm once more. "A pleasure again, Miss Taylor. You're looking very fine tonight."

"Thank you, Whitey. It's so much better here. Like a weight's been lifted."

"I'm glad to hear it. If you need anything, absolutely anything at all, I'll make sure you have it."

"You're very kind." She beamed, and I could tell that made Kroun's whole week.

I was on her side—whatever put him in a good humor was good in turn for her boyfriend.

"The doctor's with Gordy now," she said. "We can wait in the hall."

She led us a little farther, pausing just short of an open door halfway down. A table outside was stacked with medical-looking junk and a food tray. I ventured a whiff of air and got the unmistakable scent of chicken soup.

Within the room I heard Dr. Clarson asking a question, then responding to the murmured answer with a heavy sigh

"Well, Gordy," he said sadly, "you're going to die. Just not today."

Adelle shifted next to me, gaze raised toward the ceiling. She was not an aficionada of the doc's sense of humor.

"Fine by me," came Gordy's reply. There was a hint that his usual low rumble was returning.

"And you don't go waking me up for the rest of the night. I've had a tough day like you wouldn't believe and need my sleep."

"No problem."

Clarson emerged, wearing the white coat of his craft, the sterile white in sharp contrast to his dark skin. A similarly clad and dark-toned nurse came out, carrying a tray that she put on the table. Clarson looked us over.

"You may have two minutes," he said. "I'll be out here with my watch."

"That'll be fine, Doc," I answered for Kroun. I put my head around the door. "Hi, Gordy."

He was in bed, propped up on a lot of pillows, with the sheet and blankets pulled high, almost to his chin. One bare arm was out, the other tucked under the coverings. He was pale, but that awful hollowness looked more filled out than before. " 'Lo, Fleming."

"You better?"

"I'm better."

This time I believed him. "Mr. Kroun's here."

"Send 'm in."

Adelle moved off to another room, by now well schooled to be scarce when business was afoot. I would have liked to have heard what Kroun wanted to say to Gordy; but if it concerned me, I'd find out later, and if it didn't, then I didn't give a damn. Instead, I asked Clarson for a verdict on Gordy. He didn't want to get optimistic about his patient, having seen too many others carried off.

"He's much better, and that's as far as I'll say, 'cause I don't want to jinx him."

"If there's anything I can do . . ."

"Have that fine little lady of yours come up and visit Miss Taylor tomorrow. She'd do better for some company. Everyone else keep clear so Gordy can rest."

"I'll see to it."

"Then that's all right."

Something about the arrangement of the bed coverings nagged at me. A familiar outline . . .

"Doc? Is Gordy's sleeping with a .45 in his fist part of your remedy?"

He snorted. "Not really. He usually has it on the night-stand, but that company you brought in . . . he felt better having some heat close."

Hell of a world, I thought.

"Out the way we came in," I told Kroun when he emerged two minutes later.

He hesitated, looking past me toward Adelle's room.

"What, you want her autograph?"

He continued to hesitate. "We can come back later, right?"

This guy was a pip. "When she's not as distracted."

We retraced our steps without escort, but in the alley between the buildings Kroun paused. "You know what that was about?"

"You'll tell me if I need to."

Kroun snorted. "Smart boy. I can see why Gordy likes you. He looked like hell. I thought he'd be better than he was."

"He'll be fine," I said.

"If he isn't, there's gonna be changes. He asked you to step in for him as a temporary thing. You say you don't want the job, which means somebody else takes over."

"Derner."

"Uh-uh, Mitchell."

A flare of real anger rose in me. "Mitchell?"

"If the worst happens, Mitchell's taking over. He knows

the ropes. The boys won't object to him the way they've been doing with you."

"They won't, but I might. You pulling another Bristow here?"

For a second I thought he was going to slug me. His dark eyes blazed a moment. "Listen up, Fleming. You say you don't want to be boss, but you sure as hell don't mind throwing your weight around when it's convenient. You handled yourself okay dealing with that Alan Caine mess, and you got lucky surviving those hits from Hoyle; but when all that clears away and you're standing in the sweet spot, you still don't have what it takes to be a boss."

I kept my anger belted down tight. I had to hear him out. There had to be some way of getting Mitchell off the list of replacements. Gordy was improving, but next week he could be hit by a bus. "What am I missing?"

"The guts to kill and to order a killing. That's not in you. Mitchell can do a piece of work and not think twice about it—but you think too much. You're a stand-up guy, but not for this kind of job."

On one hand I agreed with him. I'd killed before, but I didn't like it. Some nights I carried those souls around on my shoulders like a flock of carrion crows. Kroun must have seen it. He was the kind to read people. "What about Derner? Why not him? He and Strome are both made."

"They follow. They don't lead. Not enough imagination."

"And Mitchell's got that?"

"You don't know him. If you're worried about him making trouble with your girl or you, I can get him to lay off, and that's a promise."

I didn't have much confidence that Mitchell would obey, though.

"He was supposed to have Chicago in the first place."

"That's what he told you when Morelli died?"

"Yeah. But Gordy moved in faster. He turned out to be good at the business, so we kept him."

"Mitchell didn't like that?"

"Nope."

"He got a grudge on?"

"Not that I've seen."

Hardly a reassuring answer. But I nodded like it meant something. "But all this is just so much eyewash. Gordy's better. You and Mitchell will eventually go home, and we all settle back to business as usual."

"Yeah. But if that changes . . ."

On our return the small grocer's was empty except for one very large man in a custom-tailored overcoat. He threw a dark, impersonal glance at me, then pretended to study a stack of canned goods. I walked outside with Kroun and Isham, getting partway to the car, then excusing myself.

"Just remembered I forgot something," I said, and motioned for Kroun to go on to the car. He shrugged and kept going, opening the front passenger door, but not getting in. He leaned against the body of the car and watched the guys in the street who were watching him.

I turned back to the shop, but Shoe Coldfield was already emerging, filling the doorway a moment. The building seemed smaller with him in front of it.

"So that's the man," he rumbled in his deep voice. "He ever on the stage?"

"Don't think so."

"It's a wonder he's doing what he does. It's too easy to pick someone like him from a lineup. Makes an impression."

"Unless you got a lot of intimidation going for you."

"That's true. I expect he's one of that type. Knew a few, but they were all onstage. Could play meek and mild, then open up and cut you in half with it. Good actors they were, the ones who knew how to control it."

"I don't think Kroun's in the meek-and-mild club."

"No he is not. I've done some checking around since getting his name, and he can be damn dangerous if you don't watch yourself."

"He's leashed." Sort of. I'd come to think the suggestion on friendship was wearing off faster than it should.

Coldfield approved. "You're just playing with him?"

"Not for long. I'm hoping he and his boy go back to New York tomorrow. Soon as I get them clear I've got other things to work on."

"Like that singer who got the noose?"

"Yeah."

"I'm sorry about that. I saw Caine perform once. Hell of a talent."

"It's less for him than for his ex-wife, Jewel. She's got the blame for his death, and she didn't do it. That's not right."

"Yeah, Charles filled me in today about all the trouble. Said you were looking dangerous."

"Only to the killer."

"That's what's bothering our mutual friend. You're planning to kill the killer."

"I haven't decided yet."

"Charles thinks you have. He's on your side for it."

"I thought he might be."

"Well, the fewer criminals walking around, the better is how he likes it. Of course, I'm the exception to the rule."

"I've wondered about that."

"So have I," he admitted.

"If Charles likes the idea, why's he bothered?"

"It's not over the killing, it's you. He's not been too happy about your state of mind. He's worried what it'll do to you. He doesn't say it like that. He dresses it up in a hell of a lot more words, but that's what it is boiled down."

Escott had a valid point. "I've been shoved against the wall on this kind of business before, and I've learned I can live with it."

"Uh-huh. But not too happily."

"Shoe, I know you want to help, but what's going to work best is for me to find the bastard who killed Jewel and make him pay for it. No, I won't be happy afterward, but it'll be better for me than if I did nothing at all."

"I know what that's like. On the other hand . . ."

"What?"

"Have I told you lately how I really *hate* scraping you off sidewalks?"

"I'm on the lookout. I know who I'm after, and so far they don't know I'm after them."

"Who would that be?"

"A troublemaker named Hoyle is the odds-on favorite, two idiots named Ruzzo—"

"Oh, God, *them?*"

"You've met 'em?"

"Yeah. Two brains and not a mind between them. They're stupid, but cunning and faster than rats when they need to be."

"I won't turn my back on any of them. Hoyle's the favorite for this job. I gotta find him, ask a few questions, then make a decision."

"As in just how to bump him?"

"You reading minds?"

He shrugged. "I've been doing this a while."

"With any luck I'll settle it tonight, then we can try

and"—I almost said "forget it" but that wasn't going to happen—"get back to what passes for normal around here."

"Yeah, my guys are getting their noses out of joint for all the extra marching around in the weather."

"Listen, I don't want you putting yourself out—"

"Forget it, it's good for them. Walk some of the fat off their shanks. They're keeping a sharp watch on Gordy. There's no white people come within a hundred yards of this neighborhood we don't know about. He'll stay safe."

"I appreciate it, Shoe."

"It's good for business to look out for him," he said.

I didn't gainsay. If that's what Coldfield had to put about to seem to have a tough, practical front for his troops, then I was all for it.

"That movie star mutt of yours looks like he's tugging at the leash."

Kroun had begun to pace up and down a few times, looking my way impatiently.

"If he's cold, why doesn't he get in the damn car?" Coldfield asked.

"Probably thinks I'll forget him if he's out of sight. I better go."

"All right, but watch yourself. I'm fresh out of brooms and scrapers."

I walked toward the car, the wind picking up and pushing at my back. Kroun saw my approach, putting on an "it's about damn time" face. He dropped into the front seat and hauled the passenger door smartly shut.

It made a hell of a lot louder noise than it should have. Rather than a metallic bang, there was a deafening *krump*, then it was like the sound itself slammed me in the chest. I was hurled backward, right off my feet, not understanding why. I glimpsed smoke suddenly blacking the windows of the Caddy on the *inside* before I hit the pavement. Some instinct told me to keep rolling. Each time I saw the car a different view presented itself.

Smoke flooding from under it, thick and black.

Another explosion, the boom too loud to hear, only feel.

The rear end suspended five feet in the air and nothing holding it up.

The heavy body abruptly crashing down on all fours, flames engulfing the back.

The tires ablaze, adding smoke and stink to the picture.

Pieces of metal shooting by like hot hail.

A tumbling wall of fire and blackness roaring toward me like a train—

14

INSISTENT, annoying things plucked at me, at my clothes. I waved them off, but they made a solid grab, pulled strong, and dragged me over a rough, hard surface. A man yelled in my ear, but it was muffled, as though I'd vanished. He might have been cursing.

Fire rained down. It was almost leisurely. Fat drops floated confetti-like or struck the cement, bouncing to scatter yellow-and-blue flames. A second look, and they proved to be attached to dark bits of burning things. It seemed a good idea to get out of their way, so I got my feet under me and working together. Hours later we reached the cover of a building and ducked in. Someone had broken the front window, and the lights were out. When I chanced to breathe, the air reeked of gasoline, burned rubber, and hot metal.

Doubled over, coughed it clear. Two other men were with me, Coldfield and Isham, also coughing.

Eyes stinging, I looked through the window—the shattered glass had blown inside—and saw the big Cadillac's shell engulfed in a fast and furious inferno. Smoke roiled from its stricken, blackened carcass in a wide, twisting cloud that was fortunately blowing away from us. Even at this distance the heat warmed my face, but I couldn't hear anything from what should have been a blast-furnace bellow. Touched one ear. Came away blood. A lot of it. My face, too. Damn. Without thinking, I vanished and returned. My hearing popped back to normal and other hurts that were starting to make themselves felt ceased altogether.

"Jack?"

Turned. Coldfield stared at me, concerned. So did Isham, but with a different expression. He rubbed his watering eyes, shook his head, looking puzzled.

"Jack? You hear me?" Coldfield again.

"Yeah." What the hell had happened?

"You okay?"

"Think so."

"That makes one of you. Your friend out there's gone."

I didn't get him. "What? Something happen to Gordy?"

"The guy you came with. Kroun."

"What? No . . ." Looked again at the wreck. Too much smoke to see inside the car, but that was just as well. For some things you don't want details.

"There was no way to help him."

"Oh, goddamn."

"Yeah. This puts everybody up shit creek. Gonna be hell to pay." He wiped his streaming eyes with a handkerchief.

Someone touched my shoulder. The woman who always stood behind the counter offered me a damp towel. "You're hurt, Mister. Your face."

I accepted the gift and used it. My ears no longer streamed blood, but the leftover gore must have been an alarming sight. "Thank you."

"Come in back, we'll get you cleaned up."

Back, meaning a bathroom or kitchen, meaning mirrors at some point. I pulled enough of my scrambled thoughts together to thank her again. "This is more than enough."

"We gotta get him out of here," Coldfield told her. "We gotta all get moving."

"The hotel," said Isham.

"Farther than that."

"The club." He'd mean Coldfield's place, the Shoebox. But we had to check another place first.

"Call Lady Crymsyn," I said. "Charles is there by now. If there's other bombs . . ." It finally got through that I'd seen one going off.

"Jeez." Coldfield, moving with astonishing speed for his size, threaded past dark aisle displays toward a door, where presumably he would find a phone. I hoped Escott would answer.

"The lobby number," I called after. "Try that one. Let it ring."

The fire rain of blown-up car pieces had stopped, but not the smoke. The wreckage lay all over the street, shattered windows gaped, their stares blank and cold. Most were ground floor, though a few second-story ones were gone. I hoped to God no one had been in front of any of them.

Isham left the grocers for a look-see, keeping a healthy distance from the car and moving fast. I went as well, standing just clear of the door. No other casualties were in view, but people were cautiously emerging, Coldfield's soldiers. Isham talked to some of them, and they began to melt away from the attraction. By the time I heard the first fire-engine siren, the street was empty except for civilian types. Other cars rolled up, full of vultures who'd come to view the burning body. The smoke forced most of them upwind. A white man came over and asked if I was all right.

I swabbed the towel around, hoping to get the telltale blood off my face and neck. "Yeah, I'm fine, got cut by flying glass. Did you see what happened?"

"Was gonna ask you. Looks like the gas tank blew. Must have been a humdinger. Anyone in it?"

"I donno. Hope not."

"Anyone else see?" He pulled out a notebook and a chewed pencil, and I recognized yet another of my own kind. What used to be, anyway.

"I don't think so."

"Hey, I know you, don't I?" He gave me a squint. "You got that fancy nightclub. The one what had the body in the basement—"

"I gotta go." I retreated into the grocery. People on the sidewalk parted for me, but closed up for him. He shrugged and looked for other witnesses.

It hadn't really sunk in yet about Kroun. Hard to think beyond the burning car. The flames were less now, running out of fuel.

Coldfield returned. "Charles is fine. He'll keep his eyes open and not be driving. You and me, this way." He headed to the back.

He was in a hurry, but I paused long enough to leave the stained towel on the counter and fish out my wallet. I pressed five twenties into the woman's hand.

She backed a step. "No, we couldn't . . ."

"For the window."

"It's too much!"

"I'm apologizing, as well, ma'am."

I rushed after Coldfield, who had cut left down the alley and was waiting impatiently by a row of trash cans. As he turned I only then noticed his coat was smeared with street dirt. Apparently the blast had knocked him down, too. I'd been much closer. There was a singed patch on my jacket and holes torn in my shirt. It was black so no staining showed, but I could smell my own blood on the fabric, along with the smoke.

With me half a step behind him, he led us down a much more narrow alley that opened to the next street. Just as we emerged Isham pulled up in Coldfield's Nash, barely braking, and we dove into the back.

This car was also armored, for all the good it would do.

I looked when we had enough distance and saw the smoke rising over the buildings, thundering fast and black against what for me was pale gray sky.

"No one's gonna follow," said Coldfield, misinterpreting.

"Where we going?"

"My club."

"Drop me at the Nightcrawler."

"You joking?"

"I got things to do or there really will be hell to pay. Kroun comes to Chicago, gets killed, and, if I don't get the blame, it will drop like a ton of bricks on Gordy. I gotta steer that away."

"Seems to me you should be keeping your head a lot lower. I give you a talking-to, then *bang-boom*, there you are on the damn sidewalk being another damn mess."

"Thanks for pulling me clear."

"Thought you were a goner when that hit. Isham, who the hell got close enough to the car to rig that thing?"

"No one, Shoe. We watched it good."

"It didn't happen here," I said. "Someone had to have done it earlier. The guys know Gordy's car and that Kroun and I have been using it. Anyone could have wired it up at any time."

"Why didn't it go off sooner, then?"

"The trigger might have been on the passenger door. Kroun didn't get in on that side when we left. It was pure chance. It was supposed to take me and Kroun out together." I'd survived a hell of a lot, but being blown to pieces might have done the trick for real.

"So who did it?"

"Mitchell. Kroun's lieutenant."

"You sure?"

I spread my hands. "If that was meant just for me, then I'd have other names to give you. But if Kroun was supposed to go, too . . . the passenger door trigger changes things. A lot of people might know I'd be driving him and that he'd probably sit in the front. Mitchell's the only one I can think of who'd stand to gain by Kroun's death. He might be set to take over Kroun's job if anything happens to his boss. With Kroun getting killed here, the Chicago outfit gets the blame, and Mitchell is clear to walk in. He wouldn't be the first mug in the world trying to improve himself by knocking off his boss."

"It worked great for Cassius. Didn't last. He bought it later."

"Hah?"

"In *Julius Caesar*? Cassius got a bunch of other guys to go in with him for the hit on Caesar. Dropping you at the Nightcrawler strikes me as being a really stupid thing to do. You don't know who could be on Mitchell's side."

"I got an edge."

"Yeah. Sure was helpful against that bomb."

Actually it had kept me alive and had certainly cured a couple of busted eardrums if not more, but Coldfield needed to grouse and grumble and get it out of his system. He was shaken by the business, and this was his way of handling it.

When he ran down, I said, "I still have to go there and deal with him. I can't let Gordy catch hell for something I didn't do."

Coldfield managed not to heave a huge sigh, just most of one. "All right. Isham, drive this guy to the lion's den."

"Thanks," I said.

"Uh-uh, I'm not taking the responsibility."

"No problem."

"You're certain Mitchell's the guy?"

"At this point he's the likeliest, but there might be stuff going on I've missed or never knew about. I wasn't exactly tailor-made for these kinds of fun and games."

"The hell you're not." He gave me a look that was meant to include my supernatural condition.

"Maybe now, yeah, but I never wanted this job. That's why I don't get all the stuff happening. Too damned trusting. Soon as Gordy's better I step clear."

"Amen, brother. This shit's bad for business."

"The cops are going to be all over that wreck once it's cooled down. They'll eventually trace it to Gordy and want to question him. You got the name of his lawyer so he can run interference?"

"Yeah, Adelle's had to deal with him. That's covered."

"You sure about this trip to the den?"

"I'll go very carefully." I checked my watch, but the crystal was cracked right across, the time stopped at the moment I'd been flung backward. It could probably be fixed, even the damaged innards, but I would replace it, buy something with a different face to it so it wouldn't be constantly reminding me. "You wanna do me a real favor, you and Isham run over to Crymsyn and help Charles stay out of trouble. They might target there next."

"I told him to get out, go to my club, and I'd put him up, but he said he was staying put."

"Playing lieutenant," I said, saying it with an "f."

Isham dropped me a block from the Nightcrawler and drove off. I ghosted the rest of the way in, brushing quick between pedestrians on the walks, giving them a brief, intense chill that had nothing to do with the weather. When I encountered the uncompromising solidity of a building, I rose high, found a window shape, and sieved in. Men were in the room and a radio was on, tuned to some fights, but they didn't pay much attention, talking over the commentator. I identified a couple of the voices as being regulars who worked the gaming tables below. They were expecting some local politicos tonight, and the pickings would be good except for one guy who was to "win" his weekly payoff. There was a discussion going on over the best way to make it seem like a genuine game.

Shifted from that room to the hall and floated along, counting doors until reaching Gordy's office. I eased through to the other side and listened, handicapped by this form's cottonlike muffling. No one seemed to be in. That wasn't too likely. I pushed on, finally going solid in the bathroom. I kept quiet and waited. Derner was on the phone, and he was pissed.

"Oh, yeah? Well, you get your ass moving and *find* him!

The boss is raising hell over this. If we don't find Hoyle tonight, tomorrow there's gonna be fresh food in the lake for the damn fish."

Since the phone was probably tapped I hoped he meant that threat for effect and wasn't planning to carry it through. On the other hand, the FBI would like nothing better than for the wiseguys to knock each other off. Less work for them.

Derner hung up. I peered around the door. He was consulting a book for the next number. He dialed, let it ring a long time, then hung up in disgust. Before he could find another to try the phone rang.

"Yeah?" He sounded impatient. There was a glass of water on the desk and a toppled-over bottle of aspirin. He'd been busy. And frustrated.

Silence as he listened. So did I. I could almost make out the speaker's words on the other end of the line.

"What? What'd you say?" His voice lost its decisive force, like the air had been sucked right from his lungs.

The caller repeated, his tones emphatic.

"Th-that's impossible. I was just on the phone with him tonight. You sure?" Now he sounded uneasy. I could guess what the bad news must be. "*Both* of 'em? Where? You *sure? Are you?* Okay. Stick around, keep an eye on what the cops do. Call me again. I know it's been busy, you just keep calling!" He slammed the receiver down, staring at the opposite wall with its pastoral painting and probably not seeing it.

After a moment, with elbows on the desk, he slumped until his head was between the heels of his hands. He let out a long low groan, gently rubbing his temples.

"Ahh, jeez. This is too much," he whispered, eyes shut.

I went semitransparent, floating noiselessly over the floor. Stood right in front of him, going solid. Waited.

He must have had a really bad headache; he didn't look up. He gave a sluggish jump when the phone rang and muttered a curse.

Then he straightened to answer, saw me, and froze.

After the first yelp, no cursing, no nothing, just pure shock on his face. Couldn't tell if it was from dismay or guilt, then it slipped suddenly into genuine relief.

"You-you're okay!"

I nodded, keeping a sober and somber mask on. "What did you hear?"

"One of the boys . . . said a bomb, the car blew up. Took you and Kroun . . ." He looked around. "Where is . . . ?"

The phone continued ringing. "Get that," I said. "I'm still dead. Understand?"

He answered. It was someone else relaying the same bad news. He said he'd heard already and told them to leave the area, then hung up. "Was that what you want?"

"That's fine. Take the phone off the hook."

He did so.

"Kroun's dead. I was there."

"How'd you get away?"

"I wasn't in the car when it happened."

"But you—" He just now noticed my appearance.

"Stuff hit me. I'm not hurt much. Listen, I think Mitchell might have arranged it."

Derner seemed to hold his breath. He let it out, picked up his water glass, and finished what was left, not looking well.

"Who in this town knows how to rig a bomb?"

The man visibly winced.

"Well?"

"You ain't gonna like it."

"Aw, don't you be telling me—"

" 'Fraid so, Boss. Hoyle."

I didn't quite hit the ceiling. "Oh, that's great! That's just *peachy!* I thought that son of a bitch was a boxer!"

"He was. But before that he did mining. Out West. He learned how to set charges as a kid. He learned boxing in the mining camp, and that was his ticket out."

"And in the good old days did he used to run around with Mitchell?"

He shrugged. "I donno. Could have."

"So how is it Mitchell's able to find Hoyle when no one else can?"

"Maybe Hoyle found him. It's no secret him and Kroun came to town. Coulda looked him up, they got to talkin' . . ."

"Yeah, then decide to kill two birds with one boom." Which didn't explain Alan Caine's death. Maybe he'd overheard something he shouldn't.

"He ain't getting out of Chicago alive." said Derner. "None of them."

"Make sure New York knows what really happened. I want them to hear it from you first, not Mitchell."

"Right." He reached for an index book with phone numbers, then slapped his hand on it. "Damn! I got some good news for you! Ruzzo—they been found. That two-grand reward tipped things. One of the guys phoned in with the name of a hotel and a room number. Not five minutes back. They probably been there under some other name this whole time. I can send some guys to get them now."

"No, I'll do it."

He looked me up and down. "But you need a doctor."

"The address."

He gave me what he'd scribbled on notepaper.

"I'm going now. You go on and do what you've been doing and play the angle that me and Kroun are *both* dead. You don't tell anyone different. Make sure New York understands they have to play along with the act, too, in case Mitchell calls them. If he comes in, pretend go along with whatever he says, find out all you can of what he's up to. Don't let him kill you, though."

"No, Boss."

"Protect yourself, but we need Mitchell alive to tell us what he's been doing." The last thing I wanted was Mitchell catching lead before I had the chance to take him apart myself.

"Right, Boss."

I hurried to a smaller room off that one. It had once been Bobbi's bedroom when she'd been with Slick. Completely redone, the stark white walls were partially hidden by gray metal file cabinets, a five-foot-tall map of Chicago, a large neon beer sign meant for outside display, and a desk too ugly for any place public. As depessing as an army barracks, no fond memory of our first encounter stirred in these surroundings.

It did have a fire escape, though. I opened the window and climbed out, thereby giving Derner a plausable explanation for how I'd gotten in in the first place.

Outside, I shut the window, vanished, and, holding close to the side of the building, slipped down to terra firma, then glided over the sidewalk until reasonably sure I was out of sight of the club.

The street where I materialized was busy with early-evening traffic. I walked quickly toward an intersection and waited, palming some dollar bills. I used those to hail a cab, figuring my now-scruffy clothes were not something to inspire trust in any driver. On the third try I got one to pull over and gave him the street for Ruzzo's hotel.

It was west of the Loop. A good place twenty years ago, less so now. They couldn't charge the pre-Crash fancy prices to travelers anymore, so they switched to bringing in long-term tenants who didn't mind that service wasn't what it used to be. I paid off the driver and sauntered in the opposite direction, circling the block to see what the back alley looked like.

Pretty much what I expected, but the loading-dock area was taking a laundry delivery and full of busy men in work clothes. I blended with them, waving a familiar and confident hello to complete strangers who nodded in return. You can get away with nearly everything doing that. Obligingly I shouldered two paper-wrapped bundles and took them in. I dropped them onto a flat trolley cart with other bundles and, without looking back, kept going down a short hall until I found the service elevator. There was no operator at the moment; he might have been on a coffee break or helping with the delivery. I stepped in and took myself up to the sixth floor.

The inside layout was in a squared off U-shape with the elevators in the middle. I went down the wrong branch, retraced, and found the right door. Ruzzo's room was at the very end, next to the window that opened to the metal framework of a fire escape. I wondered if they'd chosen it on purpose to have an extra exit or just naturally got lucky.

As I bent down for a look and listen at the keyhole the air in my dormant lungs shifted from the motion, and I got the first whiff of bloodsmell.

Quickly I backed from the door, hands out defensively.

As though the damn thing would break off from its hinges and jump me.

It didn't.

After a moment, I pulled together enough to think twice about entering. Both times the decision was to go; I just couldn't bring myself to move.

Never mind peering through the keyhole, just get it over with. Before I could think a third time, I vanished, streamed through the crack above the doorsill, and re-formed just inside, but taking it easy.

No lights on, but the blinds were up on the window across the room; plenty of glow came in for me to use.

Nothing fancy about this place. A bathroom opened on my immediate left, an alcove served for a closet on the right, then the entry widened to a larger area with a sofa along the right-hand wall. Two beds were at the far end on either side of the window, and a couple chairs and a table, as normal as could be except for the bodies.

The Ruzzo brothers were collapsed, loose-boned in the chairs, having fallen forward across the table. Their heads were wrong, strangely misshapen. One had his face toward me, and his eyeballs were half out of their sockets, his tongue protruding, like a cartoon mocking surprise. The realization finally came that their heads had been bashed to pulp, and exactly in the middle of the table between them was a bloodied baseball bat.

The light changed, went suddenly gray, and I thought Myrna must have been acting up, only she wouldn't be here, she was at Lady Crymsyn.

I blinked, looking around. I was in the hall again, my back to the Ruzzo door, with my guts about to turn inside out.

Oh, hell, not now . . .

Drew a steadying breath. Wrong thing to do with blood-smell filling every crevice of this place, and the scent of it and death hovering so close was too much, and it dropped fast and hard, and I doubled over, hitting the floor like I'd been shot.

My own blood seemed to hammer the top of my skull, and for a second it felt like I was once more swinging upside down in that meat locker, then I was creeping purposefully over the red-washed cement floor seeking life from another's death, and after all that I still thirsted for more human-red fire to pour down my throat . . .

The memory of pain and the nightmare of failure left me curled, stifling the urge to vomit, and clutching my sides where the cold, taut lines of the scars prickled along new-healed flesh. My eyes rolled up, and I shivered and held back the rising wail and hung on, hating, hating, *hating* this weakness and not wanting to give in to it. If I vanished, it would mean surrender. This stuff had power over me, and it had to stop. I had to *stop* it, I just didn't know how.

But gradually . . . gradually, the seizure passed.

Exhausted, I couldn't move for a while. No one came down the hall, and, even if someone had, I'd have not been able to do anything for myself. This was soul-weariness, and I couldn't control it.

When I thought I could start to trust my coordination, I pushed up, one stage at a time, eventually gaining my feet. The tension left over in my muscles was bad, but beginning to ease. I stretched cautiously, and you could have heard the pops and cracks at fifty feet.

I regarded the Ruzzo's door with bleak and chill thoughts. They were long dead, I was sure. Going in for a second look wouldn't change that or help me. I couldn't go in there. They were dead, and that's all there was to it, leave them and get out.

I was five steps toward the elevator, then turned around

and went back and went in, because that was what bosses had to do.

The second visit was less bad because I was careful to not breathe and not look at them, letting my gaze skip over the bits that threatened to add to my internal library of evil memories. With enough practice anyone can learn to create temporary blind spots in their sight.

The baseball bat placed so neatly in the center of the butcher's chaos could have been one from the party in the cornfield. I checked the alcove closet and found a cache of other bats standing in a corner, a bonanza for sandlot kids. Someone had reached in and lifted one away, then turned to where Ruzzo sat having a drink at the table—there were two unbroken glasses on it. He'd perhaps playfully hefted it, making a couple practice swings, having a laugh. Then the next two swings were utterly serious, and he'd kept on swinging, just to be sure.

No one would have heard any of it even through these walls. What were a couple of dull cracks, followed by meaty thumps to this place? Just another sound effect on a radio show and who wants to bother Ruzzo, anyway? Surly pair, just stay outta their way and hope they shut up. This wasn't the kind of place where people wanted to notice things, so I'd leave questioning the tenants and staff to others. As easily as I got in, the killer could have gotten out. Hell, he might have taken the fire escape stairs easy as pie or hijacked the freight elevator as I'd done.

Blood splatters generously freckled the walls and ceiling, long dried out. Several hours at least had passed since their creation. Ruzzo had been killed long before Kroun and I had driven away from the Nightcrawler.

Why, though?

If they were helping Mitchell, wouldn't he want to have them around? They might have been dumb, but extra muscle could be useful. Unless he couldn't trust them to keep their mouths shut. If they knew Hoyle had readied a bomb for Kroun, it wouldn't do having them running loose.

I went through the rest of the room, not touching anything, fists stuffed in my jacket pockets. Just looking was enough. They didn't have much: some clothes, a radio, old racing forms, a scatter of magazines you had to ask for special so the druggist would pull them from under the counter.

The two beds were unmade, and there was a tangle of blankets and a pillow discarded on the long sofa. I suspected that I'd at last found where Hoyle had been staying. Was he the killer here? With all three sharing a common hatred of me, they might have stuck together until Ruzzo became a liability.

If not himself the killer, Hoyle could well be a target, too. Only it didn't fit what I knew of the man.

A very quick sideways glance toward the table. It would take a hell of a lot of strength to do that kind of damage, and to be able to do it cold, without working yourself up into a muscle-charged rage. Hoyle was big enough for the work. The punches he'd landed on me in that snowy field were meant to disable and might have succeeded on anyone else. I'd felt killing force behind them, seen it in his face.

Last on my way out was the bathroom. Someone had rinsed off using the tub tap and slopped around, leaving diluted red stains all over. Those were also long dried. In the sink were two wallets, empty of cash. Well, the killer had been practical. When you're on the run you need money, and whatever had been there would serve to give the cops a motive, however flimsy, for the crime.

Nothing left to discover here, but I had more questions. I'd have to return to the Nightcrawler and wait for the answers to straggle in. Unless he was already on his way back to New York where I couldn't get to him right away, Mitchell would have to show himself sometime to put in his claim for the boss's chair. It would give him a chance to bitch at the locals for not having enough protection for Kroun. Of course, Mitchell could be blameless and been off having a fine time at another club while Kroun was blown to bits. The whole business with the passenger-door trigger could easily be a misinterpretation. Not my first one.

But first a stop at Lady Crymsyn. Escott should know this latest.

I ghosted through the door, materialized, and found myself staring Strome square in the face.

15

He was surprised enough for three, rocking back on his heels with a sharp yelp. I almost did the same, but the door was directly behind and wouldn't allow the movement. Instinct took over. I struck out fast, popped him one, and he dropped.

I stared down at him, considering my situation.

Two dead guys in the room and an unconscious one out here in the hall.

Who had seen me appear out of thin air.

A simple problem to solve—if I could still hypnotize without risk of killing myself. No. Couldn't chance it.

Damnation.

Well, first I had to get Strome out of here, then I'd deal with what he'd seen. I hauled him up on one shoulder and took the freight elevator. The area below was clear, though there were three flat trolleys piled high with paper-wrapped goods parked along the hall. People were talking around a corner, coming our way. I hurried toward the exit and pushed awkwardly through, Strome's weight throwing my balance off. The cold air didn't wake him.

We were in an unused part of a blind alley. Not much sun could get in between the buildings, so the last snowfall, glazed over by a layer of sleet, was still in thick drifts. I braced Strome against a wall, scooped up some mostly clean snow, and rubbed it in his face.

"Strome? Hey, c'mon!"

His eyes flickered, then he came shooting awake, staggering and staring around, his hand automatically going for the gun in his shoulder rig.

"What the . . . ?" he focused on me.

I glared right back. "Did you do it?"

Confusion. Just what I wanted. "Do what? Where am I?"

"Outside the Ruzzo's hotel. Did you kill them?"

"What? I—" He felt his jaw and froze. "Ruzzo's *dead?*"

"Since earlier today. Someone bashed their heads in Capone-style with a baseball bat. That's why I popped you one. Was it you?"

"No!" He was outraged and perhaps a little scared. I was scared myself.

I was used to his stone face as the norm, but this reaction rang true. Besides, it took his mind off other matters. A clout strong enough to send you unconscious was usually enough to scramble your memory. You could lose the last half hour or the last month, or even the whole works of a lifetime. All I wanted gone were the last ten minutes. So far he wasn't asking inconvenient questions. That was *my* job.

"Why were you at the hotel then?" I asked.

"Looking for Ruzzo. I got a line they were hiding there. Thought they might be hiding Hoyle, too."

"Sure you didn't kill them?"

"Never! I never went near 'em! No!"

I took him off my suspect list for the moment; even if he'd changed clothes and washed, I'd have picked up the bloodsmell on him. Plenty of other crimes to check out, though. "Did you put a bomb in Gordy's car?"

His reaction to that one was also convincing. "A bomb? What the hell you talking about?"

I told him, and he didn't believe it. I stood back so he could get a look at me. "Believe it," I said. "Kroun's dead. I think Hoyle teamed with Mitchell, and I need to know which side of the fence you're on."

"With you and Gordy!"

"What about Mitchell?"

"I hate that weasel-eyed son of a bitch. He ain't stand-up. Never was."

"Do you know where he is?"

"No."

"What about Hoyle? You know where Hoyle is now?"

"Yeah . . . I got a line. Maybe."

"Maybe?"

"If he wasn't with Ruzzo, I was gonna check on it. Word's out on that reward, but the guy I talked to don't have the stones to go after him. I promised him a hundred for the news, but only if it was solid."

Interesting. "Why didn't you tell me that before?"

Strome looked at me like I was being unfair. Which was true. He'd hardly had time to work up to it. "Listen, I was gonna call Derner, get some boys, and go in. Hoyle ain't the sort to come quiet."

"Where is he, then?"

"The garage where he keeps his car."

That made sense. Wish I'd thought of it.

"You wanna check out Hoyle's garage, Boss?" he asked.

"Lead the way."

Strome was plenty shaken to judge by the backward glances coming my way as I followed him from the alley. I must have been giving him the creeps. Not my problem. He took us to where he'd parked his car, and we got in. I thought about phoning Lady Crymsyn. Escott would be in by now, but there was no telling how long Hoyle might stay in this garage or if he was even still around. If he had brains, he'd be putting distance between himself and the murders.

If he *really* had brains, he'd have never crossed me from the start.

"Ruzzo's murder," I said. "If Hoyle didn't do it, who else would?"

"Anybody who met them."

"Seriously. What about Mitchell?"

"Yeah, he could do it. Donno why he would. You just covering the bases, Boss?"

Considering how the murders had been accomplished, his choice of phrase was unfortunate. "Yeah. Can you think of any reason why Mitchell would want to kill me?" So far as I knew, Strome was unaware of the run-in I'd had with Mitchell at Crymsyn.

"He'd only do it if Kroun told him to."

"That's what I thought. Kroun must have been the real target from the first, but they rigged things to take me, too. The trigger was on the passenger door. It was meant to go off when he had company. Derner said Hoyle knows explosives."

"Yeah, learned 'em in a mining camp out West. So Mitchell got him to make one? But why should Mitchell kill his boss?"

"With Kroun gone, Mitchell moves into his spot with New York, while Chicago gets the blame for the death. He's keeping his own backyard clean doing it here. Sound reasonable to you?"

"Yeah."

"Ruzzo becomes inconvenient to Hoyle for some reason, and they die. What you bet maybe Hoyle becomes inconvenient to Mitchell?"

"Because he don't want Hoyle to talk about the bomb?"

"All he has to do to get away with bumping Hoyle is say it was payback for Kroun's death."

"Smart stuff, Boss."

"Would it fool New York?"

He shrugged. "Depends whether they *want* to believe him or not. Could be Kroun's got pals back there who don't like him much, and they have Mitchell here to bump him. We get the blame. You will, anyway. Far as New York goes, they don't know you and don't want you."

"The feeling's mutual, I'm sure. We gotta find out one way or another from Hoyle."

"Not easy. I might have a chance to talk with him, but otherwise he'll start shooting. He's got a grudge on for you, and I never heard of him holding back ever on one of those."

"He'll just have to take his chances. I'm not feeling too damned kindhearted toward him, either."

The area Strome drove to was one of those little pockets of the city where the deep-night creeps could make themselves very much at home. During the day it was a place of cheap shops and small factories with obscure names turning out God-knows-what for who-knows-why. The grimy building fronts indicated business wasn't good, but struggling along. At noon the workers could descend upon the corner bar at the end of the street for a quick beer, sop up the sports scores, and lay bets down for the next event with their friendly local bookie. It was very likely part of Gordy's operation, and if I troubled to walk down there and give my name, I'd have his same level of respect.

Or be shot at. Territorial concerns were ongoing and strong in this town.

Strome parked the car and pointed. At the other end of the block from the bar was a low, one-storied structure. It looked like it had started out to be one thing, then changed to another halfway through, then no one finished the job. Brick and mortar with blackened windows, the roof was sheet tin that cracked and rattled as the wind passed over it. Part of one wall had been cut wide enough for cars to roll inside. There was no real driveway into it, someone had simply smashed the curb down and hauled off the rubble, so the change from street level was fairly abrupt. A faded sign next to it offered rates and a number to call.

We crossed the street, looking both ways a lot.

No watchman seemed to be on duty; the place was purely to park a car under shelter and good luck to you if it was still there in the morning. Actually, they just might be very safe there. Organized thieves would know better than to go after anything belonging to the mobs, and wiseguy stink was all over this block.

Nothing much to see, about twenty cars parked nose to the wall, ten to a side, all berths full. No lights. There was a string of bulbs hanging from a wire running down the middle length of the building, but a thrifty landlord had switched off the juice.

The racket from the stage-thunder tin roof was first nerve-racking, then annoying. The pops and bangs were irregular, and if anything else made a noise, I might not hear it.

The far end wall had been likewise cut open for a wide entry, but one of the berths was empty. I thought that might have been Hoyle's space and he'd long cleared out, but there was his car right next to it. I remembered the color from when he'd run the shooting gallery in front of my club. Good news at last. I hoped he'd be close to his transportation.

Right against the wall next to the entry were cement stairs leading down. The steel door at the bottom had a serious-looking bolt-type lock. Strome said Hoyle might be hiding out down there. I don't know how Strome thought he'd be able to talk his way in. When I gently tried the knob, it turned, but the door remained fast shut.

Strome produced a skeleton key and got the lock open, then shot me a sideways look. "Better let me go in first."

"I'm boss. It's my job. You watch my back and come if I yell. Get up top and keep your eyes open, he might not be in, and I don't want him surprising me."

He didn't much like that, but went up the stairs. As soon as he was out of sight, so was I. The gap at the bottom of the door was more than wide enough, sparing me from having to sieve through the bricks. I hated that.

I very slowly re-formed on the other side.

The pessimist in me expected to find pitch-darkness, but light there was, electric, its source at the other end of a cellar that was as wide and long as the building above. It strongly reminded me of Lady Crymsyn's basement before we changed everything. This one didn't look like any amount of new paint and lights would ever chase away the shadows.

The rough ceiling was low and, from where I stood, only a bare inch above my head. A long passage flanked by walls and support columns led the way to what might be a partitioned-off room; there was a blanket hanging across the opening. I breathed to get a scent of the place; the thin vapor hung miserably in the air. Cozy. The smell was of damp cement, oil, gasoline, with a strong hint of urine and sewer stink.

No bloodsmell. Encouraging. Quite a huge relief, too. I'd been mentally sweating about what might be down there.

Breathe in, sort out the flavors . . .

And there . . . very faint . . . human sweat.

It acquires a truly distinctive tang after reaching a certain age. This sample wasn't quite to the level of workhouse bum, that would take another couple weeks; so someone else was using the place for shelter. A dump like this was for emergencies only. Hoyle's circumstances must have qualified.

I also picked up cigarette smoke and . . . perfume?

The crazy thought that Hoyle had gotten lonely and hired some company to help pass the time danced through my head. Then a far more insane idea cropped up: Evie Montana.

If he'd killed Alan Caine, too . . . oh, hell. Had to get down to the end, see if she was still alive.

I'd been right about the noisy tin ceiling; it almost covered a humming sound coming from the direction of the light. Partially transparent, I moved cautiously forward for several yards, floating silent over the uneven floor. Coming to rest just short of the source of the light, I went solid, hugging the wall, and listened.

And son of a bitch, he was *behind* me.

Began to turn, began going transparent again.

"Hold it!" Hoyle's voice boomed in the confined space.

I halted the turn and the change. If he shot me, it wouldn't kill, but it'd hurt like hell. Hoyle thought he was in charge, but that could be a valuable advantage.

Half-turned, I glimpsed his revolver aimed square on me, and the muzzle was for at least a .32. Of course, from my angle it gave the illusion of being much larger. He was ten or twelve feet away. He could hit me if he wanted to, and he was right on the edge for it.

"Hands up! Stay right like that."

No problem. I raised my arms up and out, mostly out.

"How the hell did you get in?" he asked.

I thought his first question would be how the hell had I made myself float around half-invisible. The light was pretty bad in the alcove, though. He'd seen me come in, but perhaps only as a shape in the darkness, and could have missed the real fun. He might not even know it was me. One way to find out.

"I bought tickets. There's a bunch more of us on the way to take in the show."

"Fleming?"

"Yeah." I went semi again, expecting him to shoot. Counted to five. Nothing. Wanted to see his face. Solidified, I turned a little more.

"I said hold still!"

I cooperated.

"Out there. March."

I assumed he meant go to the end of the line where the light was and ducked under the hanging blanket. Since he didn't fire when I did that, I must have called it right.

He had more space than my walled-up sanctuary, but that was all the nice you could say about it. A mechanic's light hung from a nail, casting harsh shadows. There were bits of debris on the floor, empty tin cans, a lot of beer bottles. In one far area were some relatively clean boxes with warning and danger signs painted all over them. Next to those, spools of wire and less identifiable things, and tools. I knew just enough about bomb-making to be uneasy.

More prosaically, a pile of blankets lay on an aged army cot, and close to it stood an electric heater, the source of the humming sound. Home sweet hideout. Evie Montana, still wearing Alan Caine's tan coat, was tied up on the cot, a rag stuffed in her mouth, a blindfold on. Her body was tensed head to toe, listening.

I paused in the middle, feeling the ceiling pressing hard, and started to face him.

"No, you stay just like that." Hoyle was close behind, but not too close. I could still spin and take the gun away much faster than he could react, but he'd talk more if he thought he was the boss.

"Okay, you got me. Gonna bash my brains in like you did for Ruzzo?" That was one danger that was real for me, I was exceptionally vulnerable to any weapon made from wood. So long as he had only a gun, I was fairly safe.

"What do you know about it?" he snarled.

"I found what you left of them not long back. Then I talked with some guys, and they said where you kept your heap. Just call me Sherlock Junior. Why'd you do it?"

"Maybe they had it coming."

"That's all?"

"An' they knew some things they shouldn't."

"Like about the bomb Mitchell had you put on Gordy's car?"

"Who told you that?"

"I figured it out. You're going to have to buy Gordy a new car, you know."

"Stupid punk. Think you're so damned funny, think the sun rises and sets on your ass?"

"Not quite." No point sharing the irony of that with him.

"Well, there's some of us who know how things really work around here, and punks like you don't know squat."

"Why don't you tell me, then?"

He fired the gun. The bang was deafening.

I flinched, but was unharmed. The bullet bit a hole in the wall in front of me, above and to the right. I'd fired three into the ground next to his head, this was just returning the favor. We were lucky the mortar was soft and the bricks crumbly. A ricochet would have made this room a hell of a lot smaller, fast.

"How do *you* like it?" he asked.

"I'm gonna faint in a few days if there's much more excitement."

Another shot. I'd expected it, so I didn't flinch as much. My ears rang. I swallowed, trying to clear them.

"And that?"

"Hoyle, this wall's getting pretty boring. Even looking at your mug would make a change." I started to turn, but he told me to stay put again, his voice going up. Bad sign. He was the boss of the room, but he was nervous. "What's the matter? You think I can still follow through on what I said about killing you the other night? *You've* got the gun."

"I know how you work. I heard the boys talk. They say you can just look at someone and get them to do what you want."

"That's right. That's how I grew up to be president of these United States. I talked everyone into voting for me."

"Shuddup!"

Quiet now. Creepy to hear his breathing so near. Surprising it was that I could hear anything after the gunfire boom. I waited until he seemed more settled. "You got me. Now what?"

"I kill you."

"Not a good idea. Gordy's on the mend—"

"Gordy's on the outs! You can't hide behind him no more."

"I never did. I was only saying that you bumping Ruzzo is one thing, but bumping me . . . very bad idea. Too many people will go after you for that one."

"Yeah, and if I don't take you out, you'll still be after me."

"Not necessarily. Depends on what information you can give about Mitchell's plans."

"I don't know nothing."

"He told you plenty. That's how he was able to talk you into the bomb. He wanted Kroun removed and thought you'd be the best bet. Am I right? Then he sees to it you're protected from payback . . ." A new thought popped into my head. "Of course this place ain't his idea—it's yours. You're hiding from him."

No response.

"An' the only reason you'd wanna hide from him is if *he'd* killed Ruzzo. It's a double cross. Am I right?"

"Maybe."

"Come on, help me out here and help yourself. What happened with Ruzzo?"

"I went there and found 'em like that. It wasn't me."

"But you emptied their wallets, didn't you?"

"What if I did? They weren't needin' it."

"You were hiding with them?"

"At first. Then Mitch came over, an' we got to talkin'. He knew me from when he worked for Morelli. I tol' him how you was screwing things up, so we went off private for a drink and made some plans."

The plans being to send Kroun and me in pieces to kingdom come. "You make your bomb here?"

"In his hotel room; I was hiding with him for a day. I'd moved outta Ruzzo's place, but left some things, an' when I went back . . ."

"Must have been a shock." From which he quickly recovered and was able to coolly pick their pockets for spare cash. Nice guy. "Where's Mitchell?"

Silence.

"Why have you got the girl here?"

"Why do you think?"

He was just egging me. There were still bullets left. I make a move and boom. He'd want that. "You got the girl because Mitchell wanted her. Now why in the middle of all this malarkey does he want a date?"

"You tell me."

I couldn't see Hoyle's hands, couldn't see if they were scratched up or not, but the fact that he'd not killed Evie sparked a new line of thought about Caine's and Jewel's murders. "Because she knows something she shouldn't. Because he's afraid of her."

"Mitchell afraid of a twist." Contempt in his tone.

"Because he thinks she saw him kill Alan Caine."

More silence.

"But you worked that out already, didn't you? So why did Mitchell kill Alan Caine?"

"Damn you . . ."

"Come on, Hoyle. Bump me, and Gordy feeds you to the fish. You can definitely count on Mitchell disappearing you—you know too much. But ease off, and you get out alive."

"Mitch won't kill me."

"The hell he won't. He has to give New York a corpse for killing Kroun, and you're it. But I've got people waiting to grab him. If we walk into Gordy's office and say the same thing, he's toast. You can say he asked you to make a bomb, only he didn't say for what. I *can* get you clear."

"Why should you?"

"Because I'm just really tired of people getting killed. Kroun took me down a notch tonight because of that. Almost the last thing he said was I didn't have it in me to order people killed, and he was right. I'll look after myself and my own, but I don't mark through names on a page."

"No guts."

"That's right. But I can get you clear. Evie can back us up, too."

"You kiddin'? She's an idiot. That's how I got her so easy. She was dumb enough to go back home to pick up an extra pair of socks, then take a ride from a stranger. But what a mouth for saying a whole lot of nothing."

I could imagine that's why he'd gagged her, so he wouldn't have to listen to her talk. He'd likely questioned her, though, and figured out why Mitchell wanted her. "You wanna get out of this breathing? What d'ya say?"

He didn't say anything while I stared at the wall.

"C'mon, Hoyle." I must have cut close to the bone, given him too much to think about. Counted a slow ten, then said, "If we don't do what Mitchell expects, don't kill each other . . . then we can both go after him. We win, he loses."

A very long silence. Cautiously, I tried turning again. He let me get all the way around.

He looked bad. Unsteady on his feet, having to brace with one hand on the ceiling, unshaved, and eyelids twitching. He was scared. Of me. I understood now. My threat to kill him, with or without eye whammy, was something he'd taken to heart.

"Where's Mitchell?" I gently asked.

"I donno. If I did, he'd be dead."

"We need him alive to take the whole blame."

"None of that matters," he said.

I recognized the finality of his tone. Scared or not, he'd

made up his mind. "I get ya. It's how it's supposed to be. You can come clean with me, I won't be walking out with anything you say. Why did he kill Caine?"

Hoyle made a slow smile. On his broken, rawboned face it was a very unpleasant sight. "You'll never guess." He centered the aim of the gun. "And you'll never know . . ."

Even as I rushed forward and grabbed—

—another gun went off and Hoyle's right eye exploded in a puff of red that splattered hot on my face. Bone and brain hit a fraction behind that, and Hoyle dropped heavily on me.

I reeled under his sudden weight, dizzy from the abrupt change, struck the wall, and felt my legs go. Couldn't do anything but fall over with his body on me, my wet face against the freezing concrete floor, arms loose, hands spasming. Too much like that other place where Bristow had . . .

No . . . please, God, no not again . . .

The stuff within unsympathetically took over, set me to groaning and shivering as though from malaria. I was cold inside and out and empty and lost in the dark forever; it would never let go its grip. I might as well declare a surrender and vanish.

But I couldn't. A dim part of me was aware I had a witness who'd already seen too much.

"Boss? Hey, Boss? Fleming? What is it?" Strome's voice cut into my fog. There was a concern in his tone that told all I needed to know about what he saw at the freak show.

The weight lifted as he dragged Hoyle's body off me.

"You're okay," Strome insisted. "I got him. It's over! Hey! It's over!"

Oh, God . . .

I pulled my arms in tight, tried to suppress the shaking. Locked my jaw, refused to let any more sound escape.

Nothing to do but wait for it to fade. I hated him seeing me like this. God, I felt sick.

The humiliation finally played itself out.

Strome knelt on one knee next to me, gun in hand, his stone face showing worry. "Jeez, I dint know you were so bad off. Thought for a second he shot you. You okay, now? You need a doctor or somethin'?"

"I told you to stay put," I rasped. A change of topic. Anything so long as it wasn't about me.

"Seemed like I waited there long enough. Thought I should check on you. Good thing you left that key in the lock on the outside. Heard you guys, saw he had the drop on you. Jeez, you ain't mad 'cause I killed him, are ya?"

Shook my head. I felt a lot of things, but mad wasn't one of them. I was too tired and ashamed of my weakness to feel anything else.

"I'll back up whatever you wanna say about this," Strome added.

"I don't wanna say squat. Ever. If we work this right, Mitchell gets the heat for it."

"Sounds good. You need help?"

I was making ready to stand, and let him take some of my weight as I struggled up.

"You find out where Mitchell is?" he asked.

"No." I paced a little to make sure my legs weren't just fooling, making a point not to look at Hoyle's long form huddled on the floor. My face was still wet with his blood. I went to the hanging blanket and tried to wipe away the evidence. It'd take an all-day dip in that damned lake to clean this kind of stuff from my soul.

"Who's the twist?" He noticed Evie Montana. She lay so still I thought she'd been shot, too, but it was an animal's defense. Stillness meant you could be overlooked.

I went to Evie and told her who I was and to relax, she was going home. I said this before removing her gag and blindfold. Her eyes were crazy; I thought she might be in shock. She wasn't talking any. I found my folding knife and cut off the bonds, massaging her wrists, told her everything was going to be all right.

She must have been chilled through, but her flesh felt very warm to me, very soft and warm. I liked the feel of it too much. She looked up into my eyes, blanched, and launched clumsily off the cot toward Strome. She fit right under one of his arms. He looked surprised that anyone would come to him for protection.

"Take her up to the car, drive her where she wants," I said.

"What about you?"

Ignored him. "Tell Derner everything. Mitchell killed Alan Caine and Jewel Caine, God knows why. He's running loose, I want him landed. I'll look through this mess in case there's a lead to him. Now get out."

He got out, taking the strangely silent Evie with him.

I waited until they were quite gone, until the only sounds were caused by the heater and the wind playing on the tin roof. I waited, and if my heart had been working, it would have been going faster than any drum.

My brain was frozen, but the rest of me moved just fine.

My hands shook as I turned Hoyle so he was faceup. I pulled on his coat and shirt, opening them, freeing his neck.

Hovered over him, wavering, feeling the press of appetite. A part of me that stood outside myself looked down on at the dangerous, crazy man crouched on the floor next to a body so freshly dead it was still twitching. Hoyle was gone—there was nothing left in his eyes—but that shot in the brain hadn't stopped everything yet. I heard that after death the brain could still send out messages, and the flesh, not knowing the futility of it, would try to respond.

My corner teeth were out.

And here was my food.

I dug into his exposed neck with the same force I used on the Stockyards cattle, ripping the skin to open the big vein. When I was with Bobbi I never went so deep. The smaller veins close to the surface were sufficient. If I went in like this, tearing into her carotid, she would die, bleeding to death in seconds.

Didn't have to worry about that with Hoyle.

I fastened my mouth on the flesh and drew on the blood. Even without a heart to pump there was plenty for me. Death was in that first taste, not life. Dark, heavy, fascinating, and final.

For everyone else.

The realization flared through me like a storm.

It was my nature to feed from this kind of destruction. I was immune, so my craving for death was a safe, fundamental thing, inherent to what I'd become. Really. It had been like that with Bristow as he hung upended like a slaughtered animal, his blood flooding me, bringing me back from the edge. I'd thought the shadow taint was from his booze, but now I knew it had been his dying.

Another long draft, then I made myself lift away, sat up, and let it work in me. The cattle blood was pure and filling sustenance, but human blood satisfied another kind of hunger.

Or rather appetite.

They're different.

The awful and eager thing within urged me to go back for more, to empty him, take everything he had to try to fill my own void.

He won't need it, and didn't the taste feel so good?

This was why I so freely drained it from the cattle, trying to capture the too-swift thrill of red life that can only come from humans. Living, dying, or already dead, it didn't matter.

Yes, it was good. Much too good. I liked this far too much.

That was ugly to know.

But I continued to drink from this broken vessel, not caring, not caring as my soul slipped away.

The next time I noticed anything besides blood, I was on the street, walking hunched over, hands in my pockets. My face was very cold at first, especially around my mouth. That was where Hoyle's blood had smeared.

I found a drift of snow and scooped some to clean up a little. Left behind a lot of fresh red on the pavement. Kept walking. I wasn't sure where I was and didn't have the energy to worry about it. My mind was fogged in. I wanted to sleep, but that wasn't going to happen. It was almost like being drunk, except with the opposite effect on my senses. I heard and saw everything, only none of it was worth my attention.

So I walked and walked and hated what was in my head, hated what I had become. Now *I* was one of those deep-night predators. Always had been. It had just taken me longer to figure it out.

With a kind of internal "Huh, how about that?" I realized I'd walked all the way to Lady Crymsyn. The look of the street seemed changed, but that was my doing. I was changed, and my perceptions made the world different.

I had company. Coldfield's car was in Crymsyn's lot next

to Escott's. I tried the front door. It was locked, but, no problem, just vanish.

Listened when I went solid again.

Radio music upstairs, low conversation from the main room. Light on behind the bar as usual.

I whispered. "Hi, Myrna, I'm back. How was your evening?"

Nothing blinked in response. Maybe she was enjoying the radio in my office.

Wandered into the main room. Escott, Coldfield, and Isham had taken over a large round table closest to the curving passage. Before them was a litter of glasses, full ashtrays, and cartons gutted of their Chinese food. The boys were playing cards and hailed me as I came in. I stood in the shadows of the curved entry.

"Something wrong?" asked Coldfield.

I shook my head.

"Jack!" said Escott. "Derner called to say that Evie Montana is alive and well and that the other problems have been solved, but he refused to go into detail on the phone."

I stepped clear of the shadows.

"My God, is that blood on you?"

I looked at their alarmed and questioning faces and realized this long night was about to drag on even longer.

God, I wanted a drink. The old-fashioned, alcoholic kind. It was safer than the other stuff.

Talking about it made it real all over again. That's why I'd sent Strome to deal with Derner. I didn't like the remembering or the taste of the words. The bloodsmell clung to me; I seemed to notice it more here. I skipped the ugly business with Hoyle. Even I didn't want to know that part, but was stuck with it. When I finished, the atmosphere had turned irredeemably gloomy, and no one seemed to want to speak first.

"Everything was quiet here?" I asked after a moment.

Escott stirred slowly, as though reluctant to move.

He shot a look at Coldfield, who asked, "What about this Mitchell bird? Your guys covering places like the train station and the buses?"

I almost winced at his calling them "your guys." They weren't mine, just borrowed. "Mitchell probably won't leave until he's killed Hoyle. He doesn't know he's dead yet." The leftover smears of Hoyle's blood seemed to pull at my skin. I wanted to wash them off. "Mitchell's our proof. If we can bring him in alive and send him back to New York in one piece, that'll clear up the whole mess and keep Gordy from getting blamed for Kroun."

"But Kroun's death happened while you were on watch. Won't they be blaming you?"

"It'll still come back on Gordy because he put me in charge. My reputation's not hot with the big boys, but I can live with that."

"You sure?"

"I'm sure. No problem."

Coldfield, Isham, and Escott went off their separate ways. I told them I was tired and wanted to clean up. Escott gave me an odd look, but didn't say anything. I felt sorry for him.

Once I'd locked up I went to the basement, turning on all the lights. We had a small workshop there with tools and other equipment. I found what I needed and made what I wanted. It took about an hour to make and get the fit perfect. I'd only need one.

Then I went upstairs and showered. Emptied the hot-water tank again. No matter. It still didn't warm me. I was past shivering, though, cold and numb inside and out.

Up to my office. Bathed, shaved, fresh clothes. They used to improve my frame of mind. Not tonight. Fortunately, there wasn't much night left.

I found box of stationery and used a few pages. In the end none of the pathetic scribbles seemed right, so I tossed them in the trash.

Dawn was a minute away when I stretched on the couch. I would fight off the temporary death to the last second so it would seize me faster, preventing the awful paralysis from taking over a slow inch at a time.

Only a few seconds to go, my body beginning to stiffen up, I lay flat and shut my eyes. I sensed the sun's approach and fought it, fought its weight on my bones, its freezing of my joints.

When I was utterly anchored in place, so solid that it would be impossible to vanish and heal, I knew it was time—and that I could do it.

Absolutely my last conscious act was to put my revolver's muzzle to my right temple and pull the trigger.

16

I HURTLED awake shrieking, then vanished almost in the same instant. The agony abruptly ceased, and, floating in the grayness, my dazed mind slowly grasped the appalling truth that I'd failed.

Solid again. Lying as before on the office couch. Blood-smell on my left. A spray of long-dried rust brown blood on the lighter brown leather by my head. Hole in the leather from my carefully crafted wooden bullet. It'd passed right through my skull.

I still lived. Would continue to live.

God *damn* it.

Then I noticed Escott standing over me.

I'd never seen such a look on his face. Infinite rage. Infinite pain. It was raw as an open wound and still bled, the pain carving deep lines into his gray flesh.

"You bastard," he whispered.

I made no response.

His eyes blazed, hot enough to scorch what was left of my soul. Why couldn't I have just stayed dead?

"You bastard. You idiotic, selfish *bastard*." There was enough venom in his voice to kill an elephant.

I stopped meeting his gaze. Maybe he would get fed up and leave, then I'd find some other place to be at dawn and try again. Next time, a shotgun. Wood pellets in the cartridges. Ugly. I'd have to blow my whole head off. So be it . . .

Anger like a living force rolled from Escott to smash against my body. For a second I thought he had hit me. His fists shook at his sides. He trembled all over. "You bloody *coward!* Did you even *think* how it would be for her walking upstairs, opening the door, and *finding* you?"

Bobbi. He was talking about Bobbi.

"How could you *do* that to her?"

I'd done it *for* her. He just didn't understand. "She saw?"

"No, thank God. Instead *I* came in first and found you."

I shrugged. Better him than Bobbi, I guess.

"I've waited all day to see if you'd bloody wake up. *All bloody day,* DAMN *you!*"

"And I woke up," I murmured to myself.

His lips twisted. Teeth showed. "How could you *do* this to—"

"Because I *hurt,* dammit!"

"And how do you think *she'd* have felt?"

"She'd get over it. She's better off without me. Everyone is."

I saw it coming and didn't duck. He hauled back and landed one square and hard, one of his best. It knocked me clean from the couch. He'd know I wouldn't feel much; this clobbering was about expressing anger, not to cause pain. I had plenty of that already.

"Get your head out of your backside and think of some-body else for a change—"

"*I was!* Don't you *see?* I'm no good to her or anyone like this. And I *hurt!*"

"We *all* hurt! But you *don't* inflict your pain on others by doing this!"

I dragged off the floor onto the couch again. "Yeah-yeah, well, too bad, I thought it over, and it's better for everyone if I'm gone."

He called me a bloody coward again and knocked me over again. Much harder. The second time made bruises.

Dammit. Why couldn't he just leave me alone? I started to get up . . .

He got a good one square on my nose. I heard and felt it break. While he rubbed his battered knuckles and glow-ered, I sat ass flat on the floor with blood slobbering down my chin.

"What the hell's with you?" I snarled, snuffling messily at the flow. "You *know* what I went through!"

"That's no excuse!"

"It *is.* I'm never gonna get better from it—"

"Not by killing yourself you won't!"

"*I can't live like this!* Every night it gets worse—"

"So you have a few bad memories, poor, poor fellow. It gave you a reaction you don't like. Very scary, I'm sure. You're going to let *that* destroy you? Destroy Bobbi—"

"It's not your business, Charles. This is *my* choice, only I know what it's like in my head, not you!"

"I know what it's doing to the people who care about you. Don't you give a tinker's damn what you're doing to Bobbi?"

"Since when do you have to butt in about her? I never asked."

"But *she* did! We're here to help, but you shut us out—especially Bobbi. You're ripping her apart."

"That's what I'm trying *not* to do! This is to save her, dammit!"

"How?" he demanded.

The words stuck in my throat.

"How?" he roared. He rose, loomed over me.

"Because . . ."

"What? Come on, tell me! Save her from what?"

I couldn't. It was too much. "Go to hell. Just goddamn get out and go to hell!"

"Tell me!"

I got up, grappled him, pulled him toward the door to throw him out before I lost myself. Bloodsmell clogged my nose, in another minute I'd fall into another damned fit. He could sell tickets to the freak show.

Then he got his arms up and twisted and somehow slipped my grip and threw another punch, this time driving deep into my gut. There was surprising force behind it, powered by adrenaline and sheer fury; I doubled over and dropped.

His face was so distorted I didn't know him. "Tell me! You don't *know*, do you?"

I spat blood. "Get out! It's none of your damn—"

Then he really started in. Brakes off. Down the mountain. Full tilt.

Escott was *always* in control of himself. That iron reserve had only ever slipped once. He'd been blind drunk, then. Now he'd gone lunatic. He got me up only to knock me over, and when I was down he slammed my head against the wood floor again and again, cursing me over and over under his ragged breath.

Wood damaged, could kill me—and he knew it.

I didn't fight, wanting him to cut loose. If he pounded me unconscious, that'd be one less night I'd have to suffer through. He pummeled until his sweat ran and his face went bloated and scarlet from the effort, until his breath sawed and he finally lost his balance and fell against the desk and ended on the floor, too, glaring at me. That look said I'd made the right choice about killing myself.

He hated me, they all did for what I was doing to them. I had to get myself away from it, spare them from the wreckage Bristow's torture had left. No one needed to see me like this. *I* didn't want to see me like this.

Neither of us moved for a time. I lay in the pain and stared at the ceiling and ignored Escott. My head thundered, and when I blinked the ceiling dipped and pulled a sick-making half spin. Shut my eyes, kept still. With no need to breathe it was as close to being dead as I could get at night. Not close enough, though.

I felt it come. The churning within, bursting outward from my battered guts, settling cold into my bones, hearing that pathetic whimper leaking between my clenched teeth as the shakes took me.

Escott suddenly within view, staring down. Yeah, look, get a good look at the crazy man.

"Jack . . . ?"

Tried to vanish. Nothing doing. No escape. Was stuck solid because of the wood. *Damn you, Charles . . .*

"Jack, stop it!"

"I . . . c-can't!"

"Oh, yes, you bloody *can.*"

He hit me again, an open-handed crack across the mouth.

It didn't work, either. Another strike. Another.

I was kitten weak, limps thrashing, no control, and he kept *hitting me*.

Damn you . . .

"Come *out* of it, damn your eyes!"

Crack.

"You're better than this!"

Tried to push him off. Swatted hard with one arm, caught him firm in the rib cage.

He grunted, but kept hitting, harder, more frenzied. His eyes . . . he was right-out-of-his-mind berserk.

Using me for a punching bag. Wouldn't let up. All that rage . . .

"Dammit, Charles!"

". . . bastard . . ." Hitting. *Hitting.*

I hit back. Full force.

Wasn't sure when I woke out of it. Gradual return of awareness, of senses.

Of pain. A lot of that. Body pain for a change, not soul pain. That was there someplace, though. Had to be.

Pain followed by perception, then growing horror.

Escott's body lay across the office on the floor under the windows. He faced away from me and was very, very still.

Could not move myself. Only stare.

Oh, God . . . no.

"Ch-charles?"

No response. Stillness.

"Charles!"

Nothing.

I crawled over to him, afraid to touch him, but I had to see.

A heartbeat in the silence.

His.

Damn near fainted from the relief. There was life in him, but . . . turned him, very carefully. He was a bloody mess in the literal sense. I checked his eyes, rolled up in their sockets. He was definitely out for the count.

Crawled to the desk, dragged down the phone, and called for an ambulance. I could barely see to do it, barely speak to the operator.

He groaned as I hung up. Went back to him.

"Charles?"

He took his time answering, seemed to have trouble breathing. I went to the liquor cabinet and got the brandy. Wet his split lips.

"You bastard," he finally said.

"I'm sorry, Charles. I'm so sorry."

"Good."

"Help's on the way, you just hang on."

"Oh, I'm not dying yet. I won't give you the satisfaction, you sorry bastard."

"Just don't move. Is your breathing okay? Your ribs? I could have broken some."

"Shut up, Jack. Check me, see for yourself."

I didn't understand him, but he clawed for one of my hands and pulled it onto his chest. Something hard beneath his coat.

"Think I'm a total idiot? That I'd pick a fight with you without preparation?"

He had on his bulletproof vest. There was steel plating under my hand.

"I will have some hellish bruises, but nothing permanent."

"Oh, God. I thought I'd killed you. I thought you were dead."

"And how did it feel?"

"How do you *think?*"

"I already know, you fool." He sounded tired, tired to death. "I went through it for most of the day looking at your corpse, wondering if you'd wake at sundown. Not knowing, not daring to hope. Hours of it. The whole time wondering what I'd done, what I'd not done, how I'd failed you. Reading over and over the unfinished notes you wrote. Wondering how I could ever break the news to Bobbi."

Stunned, I watched tears stream from his eyes. He seemed unaware of them.

"And I *hated* you, Jack. I hated you for giving up. For not talking to us, to anyone. You gave up. I can't forgive you for that."

I lurched away, tottering blindly to the washroom, made it to the basin just in time.

It was all red. What was left of Hoyle's blood flooded out of me in a vast body-shaking spasm. I came close to screaming again. Or weeping. I hurt too much to know the difference.

When the bout passed, I crept back to the office and sat on the floor. I didn't trust myself not to fall out of a chair. Escott had propped himself up a little against the wall. His puffed and bruised eyes were hot with fresh anger.

"How long did Bristow torture you?" he asked.
What?

"How long did it go on? Tell me."

"Too long."

"How long? An hour, two?"

"An hour, I guess." I wouldn't have had enough blood in me to last beyond that. "So what?"

"An hour. Think of it. One hour."

I didn't want to think of it. "What are you getting at?'

"One. Hour. Out of the *whole* of your life."

What the . . .

"How many hours have you lived, Jack?"

"How the hell should I know?"

"How many hours are ahead of you?"

"Charles—"

"An unlimited span if you're careful. Are you going to let all that's come before and all that can follow be utterly destroyed by *one* tiny increment stacked against the broader span of time? It's one hour of your life, Jack. Only one."

"The worst I ever had."

"There's worse to come if you don't do something about yourself. And I don't mean eating a bullet. You've been letting that single hour control you. Hog Bristow is still torturing you so long as *you* allow it."

"*Allow?* You think I *want* this?"

"You're stuck in that damned meat locker until you make up your mind to leave."

"You don't understand. I've done things."

"Then *cease* doing them, you fool!"

"I can't help it."

"Of course you *can*! You're the strongest man I know! It's sickening to hear you bleat on like that. While you're buried in your hole for the day, Bobbi and I have to wonder what it's going to be like when you wake up. We're walking on eggs the whole night catering to you, trying not to add to your pain. Do you think we can't *see* you *bleeding* inside?"

"She hates me."

"You wallowing idiot! She loves you! You're so turned in on yourself you can't see that. You'd rather sit there and whine than accept such a precious gift."

"I could hurt her, the way I hurt you. Worse."

"Bollocks! Ultimately, *you* are in control, you are responsible. You can cower and let your fear run rampant like an ill-mannered child, or *you* can be in charge. Don't tell me you can't. If I can do it, you can, too."

"What do you mean?"

His look was steady and burning. "After what happened to my friends in Canada, those murders . . . they were my whole *family* for God's sake! Dead in one night. I couldn't sleep for months. Kept waking up screaming. Drank myself unconscious, and I still kept waking up. Nothing I ever faced in the War was that awful. It was Shoe who finally helped me realize I had to get control of myself or . . ."

"What?"

"Or he'd beat the hell out of me again." He paused, his gaze inward for a moment. Then, "*I* had to climb out of that pit. You're stronger now than I ever was then. And you're not alone. You are still *needed* here. This isn't your time."

I wanted to believe him.

"And however you think you could hurt Bobbi, it couldn't possibly be worse than taking yourself away. Don't put her through that, Jack. You're her rock. Don't crumble under her."

"She's strong."

"Because *you're* here! Stay! Stay for her sake. Or I swear I *will* beat the hell out of you again."

The white-jackets came with a stretcher and for a couple of guys who had to have seen everything, they gave us a double take.

"You can't ride in with us," one of them told me. I figured he wasn't chancing my taking another shot at Escott.

"I'll follow then."

He didn't seem to like that idea. They carted Escott downstairs and were gone in a minute. I looked for my coat, couldn't find it, and borrowed Escott's instead. A very neat and organized man, he'd left it lying on the floor like old laundry. Must have had it draped over one arm when he'd walked in and seen the inert, bloodied mess on the couch. He'd have stood frozen in the doorway a moment, the coat slipping away . . .

The office phone rang, jolting me.

It was Bobbi.

This wasn't a good time to talk, but Escott would kill me if I brushed her off. "Hello, sweetheart. How are you?" I hoped nothing to tip her off was in my voice.

"Just *fine*," she said, sounding very cheerful and awake. Quite a change from the last call. Certainly she was unaware of what I'd tried to do. "When you coming over, Sweetie?"

Huh? "I can't right away, I've got to—"

"Oh, *Jacky*, you've been busy *every* night this week." Her voice went sharp, shrewish, petulant.

What the hell . . . ? I went cold. Deathly cold. "Well, Roberta, I got things to do."

She was pouty now, and completely ignored my use of her given name. "Oh, come on. I'll make it worth your while. Come on, you can spare a girl ten lousy minutes. Just come over and *do* it."

Sickness bloomed in my gut. "Well, maybe I could . . ."

"When you see what I'm *not* wearing, you'll wanna stay longer." She giggled seductively.

"Okay, but I gotta to do something first. I'll call again in an hour and let you know if I can get away. You'll have to hold your horses until then."

"You'll call in an hour?"

"And you better answer, sweetheart, or just forget about having any fun tonight."

"I'll be here. Make it a *fast* hour." She hung up.

Before I was aware of having moved I was down the stairs, heart in my throat.

But an apparition stood square in the middle of the lobby, blocking my way. I was in such a panic that the out-of-place presence didn't register. I nearly collided, then halted at the last second, backing in confusion from a snub-nosed revolver shoved hard into my belly.

Looked down at the gun, bewildered, backed another step, then truly *focused* on the man holding it: *Whitey Kroun.*

He was worse for wear, eyebrows gone and some hair singed off. There were cuts on his burn-reddened face, and his left hand was crudely bandaged. His torn and bloodied clothes stank of smoke and sweat, but he was standing, solid, and very much alive.

"Surprised?" he asked, his voice whisper-hoarse.

My lack of reply was answer enough.

"Thought you'd be." His dark eyes blazed. "All right, you son-of-a-bitch punk, you tell me why you tried to kill me."

"*What?*" I didn't have time for this.

"You set me up, but for the life of me I can't think why you would. What's your game, Fleming?"

"No game. It wasn't me."

"I had the car, so I had to be the target. Was it some kind of deal with Gordy?"

"Kroun, listen to me—"

"*Why?*" His arm straightened to fire. He would shoot to wound. Killing would come later.

"It was *Mitchell*, dammit! I got half of Chicago looking for him!"

Kroun hesitated. "Mitchell. No . . . I don't think so."

"Why the hell not?"

He made no reply.

"Listen, dammit—he got with one of his old pals from

here and *they* cooked up the bomb. I donno if he wants to take over your spot in New York or Gordy's spot here like he wanted before, but you gotta believe me, *he's* the one who did it! Now put that damn thing away—I know where he's hiding!"

"Uh-huh. The hell you do." He swung the muzzle up toward my chest.

I moved faster than he could fire. Snagged the gun from his hand and gave him a push. He spun around, but without his heater he was in no shape to take me. On second look he was banged up pretty bad. I couldn't see how he was able to walk. He should have been in the ambulance with Escott.

I started for the door, then thought better of it. "You're comin' with me," I told him.

"Where?"

"Mitchell's got my girlfriend. You want proof? Come on." I hauled him out the door, pulling it closed behind, and going left. "Into that Nash."

Kroun was limping, his left trouser leg was crusted brown from dried blood. He wheezed badly. I gunned the motor, shifted, and shot us away.

"What's with you?" I asked.

"Got some smoke. Coughed most of it out by now, but jeez."

"What else?"

"Some burns, the concussion from the boom was the worst. Like someone hit me all over with a building."

"How the hell did you survive?"

"Gordy's car."

"What about it?"

"The damned thing's built like a safe. There's so much metal in it I'm guessing most of the blast went down and sideways, not up and out. The bomb was bad, but not enough to get around all that armor. It bought me a few seconds. I didn't know what I was doing, only that I was doing it. The whole thing was smoke inside, and I couldn't see, but I found the door handle and rolled clear and kept rolling. My eyes were watering, but there was another boom, and I just kept going. There were some trash cans on the street, and I hid behind them. They were full and didn't go flying like everything else, so I stayed there."

"And you didn't show yourself thinking I'd done that?"

"I was too damned hurt to think much of anything. The whole street was fulla stinkin' smoke, so I just got out of there before something else dropped on me."

"Where did you go?"

"Found an empty building. Picked the lock, went in, and coughed my guts out for a few hours."

"You couldn't call anyone? Even New York?"

"I was thinking again by then, and it didn't seem like such a good idea. With my looks I'd be too easy to spot walking around, and I don't know who's who in this town, so I sat tight and rested up. I thought I'd give it a day, then go after you for answers, but your goddamned club was closed."

"Yet you came in."

"I saw you and the guys with the ambulance. What the hell was that?"

"Me being stupid. Forget about it."

"How do you know Mitch is with your girl?"

"I think he made her phone me to get me to her place."

"She that singer, the blond?"

"Yeah. She tipped me off something was wrong, but I gotta get there fast in case she didn't get away with it."

"God, I hate this business," said Kroun, between clenched teeth.

*   *   *

I parked on the side of the hotel opposite Bobbi's flat. Mitchell could be watching from her windows and even from that high up might recognize me walking in. If he saw Kroun, it would be a disaster.

We went in through a smaller entry that led to the lobby and the elevators. There was still an operator on duty; I gave him the floor just above Bobbi's. He stared at Kroun, got a red-eyed stare in return then focused on his job. When he opened the doors again I waited until he descended before heading for the stairs at the end of the hall.

"What's this?" Kroun asked. He was gray of face as we hurried along.

"I don't want Mitchell hearing the elevator stop on her floor." At the service door, I listened, then cautiously opened it. The hall, identical to the one we'd left, was empty. "Okay, here's the deal: There's a servants entrance to her flat, and I've got the key. I can sneak in that way, but I need you to knock on the front door to get his attention."

"Then what?"

"Just knock. He might think it's me, so do it from the side in case he shoots through the door."

"Yeah, okay. Hand me back my piece."

"You won't need it."

"I sure as hell will. Don't worry, I'll only shoot him, not your girl."

I didn't want to trust him on that.

"I get my gun or you get no help. Come on."

Dammit. I gave it over. "But no shooting. You won't need to, anyway. I just need you to distract his attention. Stay here, count to a hundred, then knock loud."

He went into "one, two, three, four," and I counted along

with him to match his pace. Kept counting softly as I slipped out, vanished, and sped forward, going solid just long enough to find Bobbi's door. Gone again, I sieved under it and listened as best I could in the grayness.

No one talking. Damn.

Nineteen, twenty . . .

Made a sweep of the front room and didn't encounter anyone. Tried the small kitchen. No one here, either. Decided to risk going solid.

Lights out, except for some spill from the living room. More than enough to see by. Listened. Would have held my breath if I'd had any.

Twenty-nine, thirty . . .

It took a few seconds to get it, like tuning in to a hard-to-find radio station. Vague movements, a heartbeat. More than one . . .

Invisible again, I floated toward her bedroom. Very much on purpose I wasn't thinking about certain things. If he'd touched her I would rip him apart. Literally.

No sound in this room. My muffled hearing worked against me. Swept through, located one person sitting on the bed, the second in a chair next to the telephone table. Another extravagant convenience of her very modern apartment was having two phones, one in the living room, the other just steps away, next to the bed. She usually kept that one in the bath so she could talk while soaking in the tub. Were they waiting for my call? And who was who? I could tell general shapes in this form, but nothing more specific. If one of them would just make a noise, I'd know who to tackle.

I drifted close to the one on the bed, brushing as light as I dared.

Unbelievable relief when Bobbi shivered and went *brrrrr.*

"What's the matter?" Mitchell asked from his seat by the phone.

"I'm cold. Can't I turn up the heat?"

"No. Pull on a blanket. Why is it you dames are always so damn cold all the time?"

Apparently recognizing a rhetorical question, she didn't reply.

Where the hell was Kroun? He should be knocking by now. Had he mistakenly gone to the other end of the hall? I could go solid and jump Mitchell, but I wanted Bobbi in the clear. He'd be armed and too many things could go wrong. I wanted them both—especially her—alive and safe.

"I know a way to warm you up," he said. "We got time."

Of course, *he* didn't absolutely have to be undamaged.

"Oh, *puh-lease.*" A tone of voice like that always went with a rolling of the eyes.

"You turned into a real snot, didn't you? Slick had the right idea keeping you on a leash. You weren't too good for me then. You were plenty hot for me. I remember."

"I'd have been hot for a baboon if he coulda gotten me out of there."

"Well, you got a close second with Fleming. When the hell did he get to be such a big noise?"

"Just happened."

"I'll bet. You smelled the money and—What's that clicking?" he snapped.

Clicking? Then I remembered Kroun was an expert with picklocks. He wasn't going to wait or follow instructions . . .

Mitchell left the room. I went solid.

Bobbi suppressed her gasp of surprise, but it was enough to alert the nervous Mitchell. He stood in the living room facing the front door, but swung his gun at me.

"Fleming?" He was flat-footed for only an instant, then

squared up the gun. Bobbi came forward; I shoved her back hard so she fell across the bed, then I started toward him. "Freeze!" he yelled.

I froze in the bedroom doorway, arms out. The .45 he carried would put holes through walls, and Bobbi was very much still in range. No shooting. Please.

The front door swung open. Kroun didn't show himself.

"Who is it?" Mitchell asked me.

I was within tackling distance, but wanted him distracted from me. "Your boss. It's payback time."

"What d'ya mean?"

"You missed with the bomb. Kroun's alive."

Mitchell laughed once. "No way. He's dead meat. Hoyle said—"

"Yeah, he did. He's dead, too, by the way."

"You're lying."

"Thought you'd be happy about it. You bumped Ruzzo, so of course you had to bump Hoyle. Can't leave witnesses to screw up you taking over Kroun's spot. That's what you're after, right? With Gordy still alive, you might never get a chance at this town, but there's no reason why you can't take Kroun's job if he's gone only he ain't."

"Kroun's dead."

"Not so much," said Kroun. He eased around the front doorway, gun in hand, aimed at Mitchell. "So what's the story, Mitch? Anything to it?"

Mitchell didn't know how to handle failure and just stood there blank-faced a moment. Then he slowly went a deep, ugly red. I didn't read that as shame for what he'd done; this was sheer humiliation for having gotten caught. "How could you have . . . Hoyle said he'd—"

"Said what? Is that how it ran? You boys bump me to move up?"

"No! Hoyle was on his own. I didn't have nothing to do with—" Mitchell choked. It had to be impossible for him to think straight with a dead man asking such questions.

"C'mon, Mitch. You can tell me." Kroun's eyes seemed darker than ever, bottomless and hell-black.

Mitchell shook his head, abruptly recovering his internal balance. He wouldn't have time to aim the gun at Kroun, so he held fast on me. "Stand still, or I kill him," he said.

Kroun shrugged. "Go ahead. He's just another mug."

"I thought he was your new best pal."

"You would."

Mitchell went dead white, then red again. "Shaddup."

"With this in the picture some other stuff's making sense."

"What stuff?" I asked, drawing attention back to me. If we could keep him distracted enough . . .

"Alan Caine's murder," said Kroun. "Check Mitch's hands."

I'd seen. Gouges and scratching from Caine's nails as he tried, in a very few seconds, to fight his killer off. "Heh. Guess you could call that 'the mark of Caine.'"

Kroun wheezed a short, unpleasant laugh. "Ya think?"

Mitchell told us to shut up, face getting redder.

I didn't listen. "So why did you do it? Did Caine overhear you and Hoyle? Did Jewel Caine see you running away?"

Sweat, lots of sweat pouring from him. The stink of cigarettes.

"I'll tell you why," Bobbi called. She'd rolled off the other side of the bed and was on the floor in the far corner against the wall. There was a full bookcase between her and harm. Sensible girl. "He had to shut Jewel up, too. Jewel would have guessed."

"Guessed what?" Kroun asked, his thick voice still fighting against the smoke damage.

"What Mitchell—"

"Shaddup!" Mitchell practically screamed it. "Shaddup or your boyfriend gets it!"

But Bobbi could count on me being mostly bulletproof. "Mitch and Alan Caine got drunk one night. *Real* drunk. I heard it from Jewel. Alan bragged about it to her to hurt her, the bastard."

"Shaddup, you lying bitch!"

"Alan liked women *and* men! Mitch was so drunk that—"

Mitchell fired through the wall, too high. I was on him, a full body tackle. He kept shooting.

Grabbed his gun hand and yanked at a bad angle for him. He yelped and bucked, trying to twist around, but kept a solid grip. He was mad out of his mind and stronger than he looked. I used my other hand to slam his head sharp against the floor and still he fought.

I tried to take the gun. Another shot. The bullet went through my palm, but I was too pissed to feel it. Gut-punched him, blood flying. He didn't notice. Had gone crazy. We rolled and kicked and hit, and he fired again. How many goddamn bullets were in this thing?

His hand over my face, fingers digging in my eyes, I turned away . . .

And glimpsed Kroun, his arm out, his own gun ready, coldly and carefully choosing his moment. His face was blank, eyes gone black with that hell-pit look; he seemed a different man altogether. Fast as things were moving, I still felt a swift, icy jolt of panic. When a man's soul isn't there, you know, you just *know* it, and you don't want to be anywhere near what it's left behind.

Mitchell saw it, too, his own damnation staring down. He wrenched his gun around and up with that strange, desperate strength.

Two shots. Close. Deafening.

And it was over. Mitchell went inert, his body collapsing on top of me in a horrible reprise of Hoyle's death. Blood-smell, blood pouring onto me, warm and still vital . . .

I threw him violently off, scrabbled over the floor to get clear of the thing he'd become, terrified that another seizure would rip away what sanity remained in me.

Then Bobbi was there. I caught her up, maybe too hard, but she kept telling me everything would be all right, it was okay . . . *Jack, it's okay* . . .

I waited, fighting it, waited, forcing down the shudder that tried to rise.

Fighting.

Her voice helped. A soft, melodious, songlike droning as she held me, reassured me.

I allowed myself a single, choking sob. There was more in me, eager for its turn to emerge from the darkness. I couldn't think about it, about what it might do if it got out, what it might be. Another siezure, or would the mindless craving take me over? If that happened and I hurt Bobbi . . .

I made myself focus on her sweet voice, the feel of her arms around me. I held on to that distraction from the internal demons. She was real, but they were so . . .

You are in control, you are responsible. You're stronger now than I ever was then.

Hard to believe. But Escott had never lied to me. He was right. I had a choice about being in charge or not. Of giving up and—

And however you think you could hurt Bobbi, it couldn't possi-

bly be worse than taking yourself away. Don't put her through that, Jack. You're her rock. Don't crumble under her.

No. I wouldn't do that to her. She deserved better. I had to *try,* to believe that I could beat this.

Don't tell me you can't. If I can do it, you can, too.

Hell of a tough act to follow.

Stay for her sake. Or I swear I will beat the hell out of you again.

Damn you, Escott . . .

Something brittle and sharp inside seemed to break up and fall away, suddenly allowing my soul to breathe again.

There were no words for what it was, I just understood that something had shifted and *it* was gone.

Over.

Past.

Done.

It had been heavy. So damned heavy. Only when the weight was no longer there did I understand how heavy it had been.

Then it was my turn to collapse. I sank to my knees, and Bobbi came with me, letting me lean on her. God, but I needed her.

And Escott said that I was *her* rock.

"Jack?"

After a moment, I dredged a smile for her. "Hey, baby. You okay?"

"How 'bout yourself?"

"Just peachy." It felt so good, her holding me, but the hurt on my hand . . . it was knitting up, but damn, that burned. " 'Scuse me a sec."

I vanished, came back. Much better now. Much . . .

Kroun—he'd have seen—

Turned to look. He hadn't seen anything. He'd caught a bullet.

He sprawled flat, a hole in his chest that bubbled air every time he moved. The pain had him helpless and gasping, and blood ran from his mouth. I knew the signs, he didn't have a minute left.

I went to him. Knelt close.

"Fleming." My name made more blood come out of him. He coughed and tried to suck air past the stuff clogging his throat. The smell filled the room, but now I was able to ignore it.

"I'm here, what can I do?" Hell, what *can* you do for a dying man? He looked like himself again, though. Whatever he had for a soul was back again, struggling hard to stay, but losing as his body failed.

"Mitch. Dead?"

Had to look. "He's dead."

" 'Fraid I'd missed. Your girl?"

"She's fine. You hold on, I'll get a doctor."

"Past that." Coughed. "Damn stuff. First I burn my lungs, now this. Life ain't fair."

"No, it ain't."

"Promise . . ."

"Anything."

"No fish food."

What?

"No lake. No chopping. No oil drums. You bury me proper. No cremat . . ."

"I promise. Kroun? I promise. You hear?"

Then the rattle. His last breath going out. The slack stillness that went on forever.

Oh, damn. Damn it all. He couldn't have known about my nature. If he'd just held off I could have . . .

Feeling very old, I stood. Went to Bobbi. Had to hold her again, hold her and get and give comfort, quick before dread practicalities rose up.

"Your neighbors . . . the shots . . ." I finally said.

"We'll bluff them out. I'll say I was rehearsing a radio skit, a-a-and the fake gun was louder than it should be. I'll make 'em believe it."

"Just don't let anyone in. You're not staying here tonight, either."

"Damn right I'm not."

"I'll get you over with Gordy and Adelle. Shoe can look out for you all until this is cleared."

"God, Jack, what will you do?" She looked at the bodies. Any other girl might have fainted. Instead, she held on to me.

"I gotta call Derner, get some boys over here to clean up."

"But how will you explain?"

"I'm not. I won't have to with them, but no cops. We can't. I'm not putting you through that kind of hell. Mitchell can be disappeared."

She went pale, knowing what that meant. "And the other man? Kroun?"

"I made him a promise. You make a promise, you gotta be stand-up about it. Derner and I will figure something out, do the right thing."

Bobbi nodded, held me again, then suddenly went rigid and shrieked.

With a groan, Kroun rolled on his side. There was pain all over his face, but he used one arm to push and was slowly sitting up.

I gasped. Had an insane thought that he'd worn a vest like Escott's, but the blood was real, his absolute stillness, the wound . . .

Was closing.

He pressed his fist against it, wincing. "Ah, *son of a bitch.* That *hurts!*"

I gaped and couldn't seem to come out of it.

He grunted, groaned, and snarled. Then glared at me. "What? You think you're the *only* one?"

"Oh, my God, he's like *you,*" Bobbi whispered.

Kroun's mouth twisted with disgust. "Ain't that the pip? And now you two know *everything.* I tried to not move, but *damn* . . ." He failed to suppress a cough.

I stared and recalled and wondered and realized. "You never told me," I said, voice faint.

"Why the hell should I? I didn't know you. You run with an outfit like Gordy's and think that's a good character reference?"

"But I hypnotized you."

"You *thought* you did. I was wondering, 'What the hell?' and then played along to see what you'd do. Ahh! *Damn!*"

He pulled himself toward Bobbi's couch and eased down with his back against it, long legs sprawled on the floor, arms tight around his chest, pressing hard, visibly hurting. Why was he putting himself through that? Why not vanish?

Bobbi broke away from me and into the kitchen, ran water, and returned with wet dish towels. She knelt and Kroun let her try to clean him up. He gave her a bemused look as she swabbed blood from his face.

"You're all right, kid," he concluded.

"Are *you?*" She made him move his arms and opened his shirt. "The hole's gone, but . . ."

"Just on the outside, cutie. Inside stuff . . . it takes longer. I need to rest a little. I'll get better." He winked the way you do to reassure someone, then made null of it when he began to cough. He grabbed one of the towels, hacking blood into it. The bullet must have gone through a lung.

She glanced at me, clearly thinking the same question. *Why wasn't he vanishing?*

When the fit eased, Kroun said, "You surprised me, Fleming. During the hypnosis when you were trying to get me to change things . . . I expected a left, and you went right."

"What did you do?" Bobbi asked. "Jack?"

I shook my head. "I just wanted him to keep Gordy in charge. That's all."

"It was enough," he said. "What you wanted told me a lot about you. You didn't order me around, you didn't do a lot of stuff that others might. Didn't ask for anything for yourself. All you did was look out for a friend."

"But you weren't under."

"I *played* along. You *get* that, yet? I faked being under to learn more. Then you went funny, had—whatever that was—some kind of fit, I don't know, you were bad off, then you just weren't there. And that clinched it for me on what you are, what I was dealing with. But just *try* to pretend to still be out of things when someone pulls that on you. I damn near lost it there."

"Well, you fooled me."

"You had other problems than just worrying about my taking you on a ride to the boneyard. I wanted to know about 'em. I figured it was to do with Bristow's work. What he did messed you up. With hypnotizing. That right?"

"I think so." I flinched inside. "Yes."

Bobbi looked at me. "What's he mean?"

She had to find out sometime. "I . . . I can't do that any-more. Whammying people. It's . . . like my head's exploding. I don't dare try it again. Maybe not ever. Bristow messed me up, all right."

Kroun snorted. "Face it, kid, what Bristow did left you crippled, the same as if he chopped off one of your legs. You'll just have to live without. The way you looked, it could kill you if nothing else can." He winced again, coughing more blood into the towel. "Damn, this hurts."

"Vanish, then. Heal up."

He gave a short laugh. Coughing. "Believe me, I'd like to."

"Why don't you?"

"You know why I was talking with Gordy so much? To hear about you. He's always a gold mine of news about all kinds of stuff, but this was the mother lode. He knew everything, including why you were hanging in the meat locker instead of kicking Bristow's ass. You had a piece of ice pick stuck in your back. The metal kept you solid."

"What? So you've got the same thing? Shrapnel or something?"

"Or something. Remember I told Adelle Taylor about a guy getting cute and grazing my skull?" Kroun brushed at the white streak on the side of his head. "It wasn't a graze. That was how I *died.*"

"Oh, God," Bobbi's jaw dropped. She started to sway. Kroun shot a hand out and steadied her a moment.

"Sorry, cutie. You okay? Good girl. The bullet that killed me is still inside. I'm as crippled as you are, Fleming. Between us we make a whole vampire—ya think?"

"But your looks," said Bobbi. "When the change happens . . . you—you get younger. Don't you?"

He shrugged. "Far as I know I look the same as the day it happened. Maybe the bullet screws that up, too. I can't exactly go to a doctor and find out, can I?"

It made for a hell of a good cover. Now and then I'd look twice at some young mug in his twenties, thinking he might be a vampire. I hadn't once considered Kroun to be a member of the club. "Guess not," I said. "But what now?"

He waved a bloody hand. "Damned if I know. I can't kill you—not the state I'm in, anyway—and I can't make *you* forget, but I don't want anyone else knowing about me."

"We can keep shut. You got my word. Both of us." Bobbi nodded.

Kroun gave us each a long look with those dark, remarkable eyes. I wondered if mine had that kind of power behind them. "I think I can believe you. There's just one thing . . . I really don't want to go back."

"Back to . . . ?"

"Back to the business. It stinks. You know how it stinks. I'm tired of it. Mitch trying to blow me up . . . that could be my ticket out. A blessing in disguise. A real, real *good* disguise."

"But there's no body in the car. The cops'll know that by now. That'll get public."

He pointed a finger toward his eyes. "There are ways around cop records. Maybe you can show me where to find them, then I do a little talking to the people who matter. Whitey Kroun can die in Chicago and stay here. Fake burial, the works. Shouldn't be too hard to fix." He cocked his head. "Do me a favor?"

"No problem. And then what?"

"And then . . . maybe . . . maybe I go fishing."

I called Derner, told him how things had fallen out with Mitchell and what had to be done. I said I'd get Bobbi someplace else, and he was to send a cleaning crew over, not just to disappear the body but to scrub the place better than any hospital.

That took a while to arrange. He wasn't a happy man.

I had spare clothes in her closet and put on fresh ones. Blood was on my overcoat, but the coat was dark, so nothing incriminating was visible. Bobbi also changed and packed some things together. There wasn't much we could do to clean up Kroun. When he was able to stand, he washed in the kitchen, coughing over the sink to get his lungs cleared of blood. That done, he went down to wait in the Nash, out of sight.

When Derner's crew arrived, Bobbi left with one of them, bound for Shoe Coldfield's special hotel in the Bronze Belt. The way things were going, Escott could wind up recouperating there as well.

If he was going to be all right. He'd been sitting up and talking, but I knew how that could turn around in an instant. Before the night was gone, I'd have to see him, make sure he was all right, try again to apologize for what I'd put him through.

I'd tell Bobbi later why he was in the hospital; I hadn't quite figured out just how much to say about what prompted two grown men to beat the hell out of each other. She really didn't need to know about me trying to kill myself.

As for Kroun . . . I got the impression that he'd been alone and on his own with this for a long time. It must have been a hell of a novelty to meet people who could deal with his big secret, though I was still digesting what to think about him.

We're a rare breed. Hard to make. He'd not said anything about his initiation and who was responsible, what had led up to his death, how he'd dealt with his first waking. We would have to talk. Hell, maybe I could go fishing with him.

Derner's people came, and I handed over the key to Bobbi's place and left.

Kroun was in the backseat of the Nash, still hurting from the gunshot.

"Is *that* bullet still in you?" I asked, getting behind the wheel.

"Nah. They tend to go right through."

"You've been shot other times?"

"Let's talk about something else, okay?"

"Like why you didn't just continue playing possum on the rug?"

"I couldn't help the coughing. Even without it you'd have tumbled soon enough. Besides, you told me what I needed to know. You made a promise about burying me and were going to keep it."

"That's it?"

"Hey, come on. It's easy to make a promise to a dying man. Just as easy to break. You're crazy, but you're a stand-up guy."

I grunted. "Not an easy job."

"Yeah. But you do okay."

"And that's it?" I repeated.

"There's one other thing . . ."

"Yeah?"

"Well, any guy who's that good of friends with Adelle Taylor can't be *all* bad."